D0349145

The
CONQUEROR'S
QUEEN

Also by Joanna Courtney

The Chosen Queen
The Constant Queen

Ebook novella
The Christmas Court

The
CONQUEROR'S
QUEEN

JOANNA
COURTNEY

MACMILLAN

First published 2017 by Macmillan
an imprint of Pan Macmillan
20 New Wharf Road, London N1 9RR
Associated companies throughout the world
www.panmacmillan.com

ISBN 978-1-4472-8203-7

Typeset by Palimpsest Book Production Ltd, Falkirk, Stirlingshire
Printed and bound by CPI Group (UK) Ltd, Croydon, CR0 4YY

For my mum and my dad who,
despite being chemists, have always been so
supportive of my mad desire to be a writer.

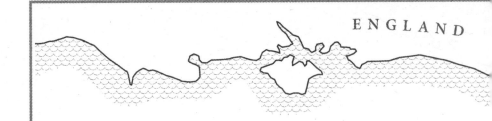

ENGLAND

THE NARROW SEA

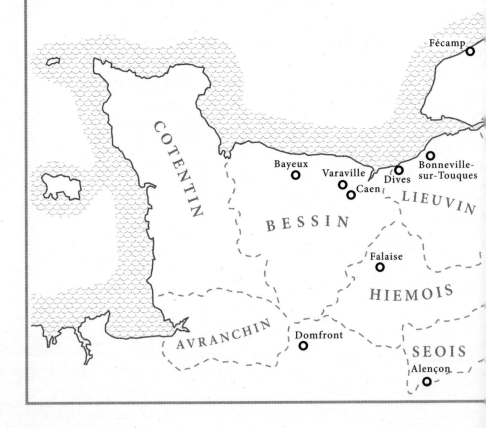

Fécamp

COTENTIN

Bayeux   Varaville   Dives   Bonneville-
Caen   sur-Touques

BESSIN   LIEUVIN

Falaise

HIEMOIS

AVRANCHIN   Domfront   SEOIS

Alençon

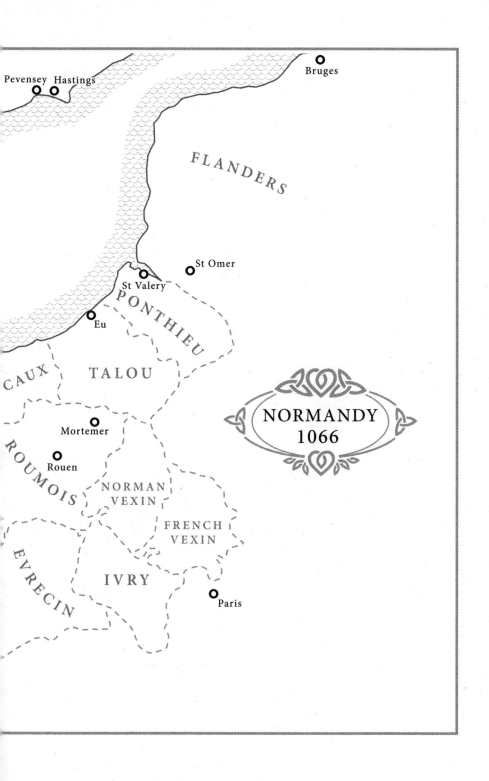

Pevensey Hastings

Bruges

FLANDERS

St Omer

St Valery

Eu

PONTHIEU

CAUX

TALOU

ROUMOIS

Mortemer

Rouen

NORMAN
VEXIN

FRENCH
VEXIN

EVRECIN

IVRY

Paris

NORMANDY
1066

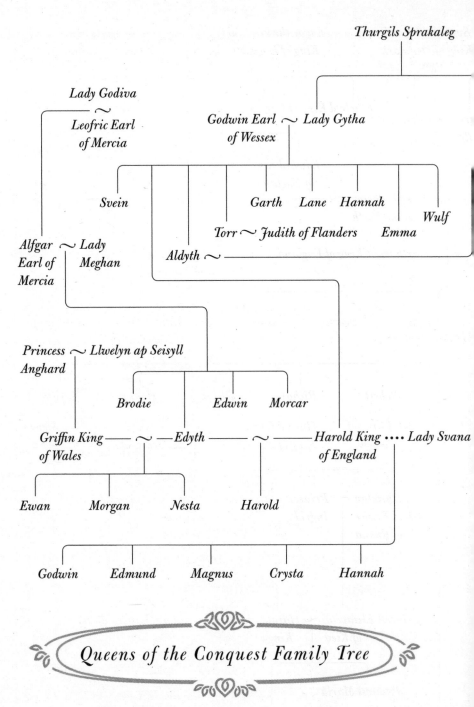

Thurgils Sprakaleg

Lady Godiva
~
Leofric Earl
of Mercia

Godwin Earl ~ Lady Gytha
of Wessex

Svein

Garth   Lane   Hannah

Torr ~ Judith of Flanders   Emma

Wulf

Alfgar ~ Lady
Earl of   Meghan
Mercia

Aldyth ~

Princess ~ Llwelyn ap Seisyll
Anghard

Brodie

Edwin   Morcar

Griffin King —— ~ —— Edyth ——— ~ ——— Harold King ···· Lady Svana
of Wales   of England

Ewan   Morgan   Nesta

Harold

Godwin   Edmund   Magnus   Crysta   Hannah

Queens of the Conquest Family Tree

Note: A dotted line undicates a handfast marriage

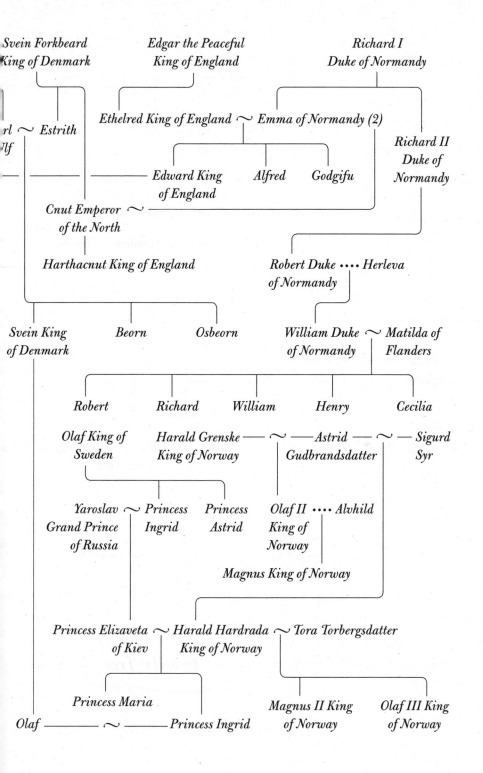

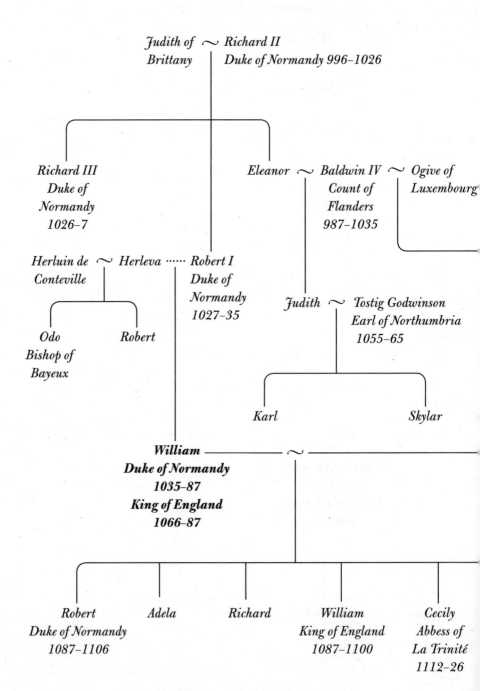

Judith of ∼ Richard II
Brittany   Duke of Normandy 996–1026

Richard III   Eleanor ∼ Baldwin IV ∼ Ogive of
Duke of   Count of   Luxembourg
Normandy   Flanders
1026–7   987–1035

Herluin de ∼ Herleva ······ Robert I
Conteville   Duke of
                            Normandy   Judith ∼ Tostig Godwinson
                            1027–35   Earl of Northumbria
                                                            1055–65
Odo   Robert
Bishop of
Bayeux

                                          Karl   Skylar

                    William ————— ∼ —————
                    Duke of Normandy
                    1035–87
                    King of England
                    1066–87

Robert   Adela   Richard   William   Cecily
Duke of Normandy   King of England   Abbess of
1087–1106   1087–1100   La Trinité
                                                                     1112–26

Note: A dotted line indicates a handfast marriage

William and Mathilda's Family Tree

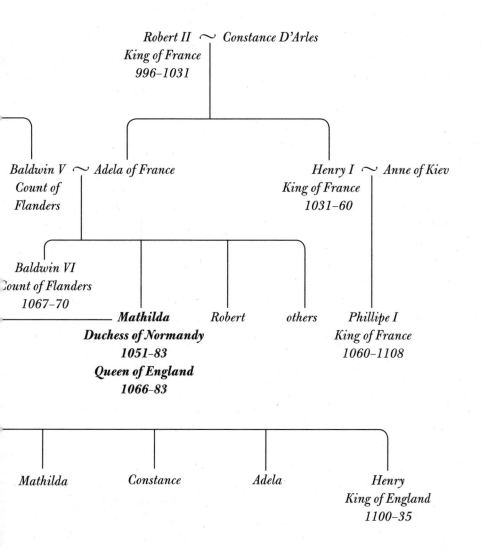

Robert II ∼ Constance D'Arles
King of France
996–1031

Baldwin V ∼ Adela of France
Count of
Flanders

Henry I ∼ Anne of Kiev
King of France
1031–60

Baldwin VI
Count of Flanders
1067–70

Mathilda
Duchess of Normandy
1051–83
Queen of England
1066–83

Robert

others

Phillipe I
King of France
1060–1108

Mathilda

Constance

Adela

Henry
King of England
1100–35

The
CONQUEROR'S
QUEEN

PROLOGUE

*Sometimes, when she closes her eyes, Mathilda can feel it still –
the driving pulse of the whirling, beating dance that first taught
her the power of a man. She'd thought dancing so fine until then,
so elegant, so magical, but that night she discovered its darker side
– and she liked it. She thrilled to the insistent thud of heart against
heart, the light turn of the reel lifting her high onto her richly
slippered toes, the sweeping assurance of strong arms.*

'You are too good for me, my lady.'

*His words had whispered across her cheek like butterflies, trail-
ing blushes.*

'I am,' she'd agreed, because it was true.

*He was Lord Brihtric, Saxon ambassador to the court of Bruges;
she was Lady Mathilda, eldest daughter of the great Count Baldwin. He was a quiet landholder in some green corner of southern
England; she was the niece of King Henri of France. He should
marry minor gentry; she was destined for a great match linking
Flanders with an advantageous land. And yet he carried himself
like a powerful man and, more than that, when she was in his arms
he made her a powerful woman.*

'No one, surely,' she said, 'is too good to dance?'

*He smiled at that and lifted her closer to his broad chest and
then, with a low laugh that laced deliciously through the feast-
smoked air, he spun her until her royal blood pulsed against her*

skin as if trying to escape and laughter burst from her lips in heady joy.

The rush of the reel was a potion stronger than any wine and the music seemed alive around her – the merry melody of the fiddle the trill of a tiny flute and the pulse of the drum beneath. The air was ripe with the exotic perfume of the ladies – cinnamon and allspice, bought in the vivid markets of Bruges and now mixing with the meaty smoke of the fire and the warm musk of men. And his eyes were Saxon blue, like summertime skies as they bore into her own, all laughter gone and in its place a rich, deep intent.

Had it been a kiss? Not truly. Not in the way kisses were giggled over in the bower, all frenzy and moisture. No, it had been more as if his words had run along the curve of her mouth and disappeared again into the press of other dancers jostling and turning and chattering as if this were just another night at court.

'You are too good for me, my lady.'

Words or a kiss? Still she cannot tell, cannot separate the two, for they were lost almost before they began and then, in a crash of cymbals, her father ordered the dance ended and Brihtric was gone and trouble came tumbling down upon her poor romantic head.

PART ONE

CHAPTER ONE

Bruges, June 1049

'I will not marry that man.'

Mathilda put her hands on her hips. Her whole body was quivering with anger but she forced herself to stay calm for she knew from long experience that her father did not take kindly to rages. Already the skin was tightening around Count Baldwin's usually genial lips and his fingers were clenching on his wide leather belt. Mathilda took a hasty step forward, being sure to keep her copper-haired head demurely low.

'That's to say . . .' She fought for words. 'I thought that you were looking for a "great match" for me, your eldest daughter?'

Baldwin's eyes narrowed.

'This *is* a great match, Mathilda.'

Her head snapped up, stunned.

'But Father, how can it be? He's a bastard.'

Mathilda felt the warm air of the family bower settle uneasily around her father's silence. She looked to the arched window opening, longing to escape into the pretty city of Bruges just beyond the palace yard, but the glass her mother had had fitted last year made the roofs and spires warp and mist. She forced her eyes back to Count Baldwin.

'It's true, Father, is it not? Surely we can talk about this reasonably? Is that not what you have brought us up to do? Question everything, you've always told me.'

'Everything but *me*,' Baldwin snapped back. 'I must see you wed, Daughter, before you recklessly try and do so yourself – *again*. Duke William is as good a prospect as any, bastard or no. Perhaps he will be able to tame you as I clearly have not.'

Mathilda felt treacherous tears spring to her eyes and fought frantically to keep them inside.

'This, then, is because of . . . of Lord Brihtric?'

'Not *because* of him, Mathilda, no. This match is a carefully considered one, of great political and personal advantage to Flanders and to you. The timing, however, is good, as your unseemly outburst has proven. You are grown too wild and I cannot have you making fools of us all again.'

'I did not . . .'

'Silence!'

Mathilda ground at the rushes on the oak floor, furiously crushing a sprig of rosemary beneath her toe. She had not 'grown wild'. It had just been a letter, just a suggestion that if Lord Brihtric were to pay another visit to Flanders she would be pleased to welcome him. She hadn't actually said that she'd marry him; her father's thick-headed spies had misinterpreted the language, that was all. She still didn't know whether to be angrier with them or with Brihtric for letting them see the damned letter. And now it seemed that his weakness would have her shackled to some rough-edged upstart of a Norman duke. She crushed another sprig of rosemary then forced herself to look up again.

'I do not question you, Father, merely ask for a little more detail. You have always told me that I have royal blood and must not let it be joined to a man with any less and yet . . .'

'And yet, Mathilda, royalty can be won as well as inherited.'

'No, it cannot,' Mathilda countered. 'A crown can be won, perhaps, but blood cannot be changed.'

Count Baldwin looked to the elegantly painted rafters and sighed.

'Whose idea was it to educate these girls?' he demanded, his sharp eyes suddenly fixing on his wife, Adela, who had been watching the exchange with the same quiet, dignified interest with which she approached everything.

'It was mine, Husband,' she said, unflinching, 'as I was educated before them in the French royal court. Education gives women finesse and makes them useful helpmeets to their husbands.'

'And defiant daughters to their fathers,' Baldwin countered. 'I've never heard the like of it – refusing a husband who has been carefully and lovingly chosen. Speak to her, Adela.'

Mathilda turned deliberately to her mother. This would be interesting for Adela was fiercely proud of her French royal blood and had brought her girls up to believe in breeding and lineage.

'You would see me, Mother, wed to a bastard duke of a province barely one hundred years old?'

'Mathilda,' Baldwin growled but Mathilda kept her eyes fixed on Adela who had turned an entertaining shade of plum.

'Duke William,' she said carefully, 'cannot help on which side of the sheets he was born.'

'Ha!' Baldwin crowed delightedly, eliciting a nervous squeak from the third woman in the room.

Mathilda looked scornfully back at the young woman she called her cousin, huddled against the stone wall as if she might gladly blend into the rich tapestry hanging upon it. Judith was two years younger than eighteen-year-old Mathilda, but sometimes seemed half her age. She was intent on art and liked nothing better than to bury her nose in fusty manuscripts

9

or spend hours in heavily painted churches, both of which bored Mathilda no end.

Judith was actually her aunt – born to Count Baldwin's father by his second wife – but after the elder Baldwin had died her mother, Eleanor of Normandy, had gone scuttling home to a nunnery without her. And now, it seemed, Mathilda was destined to follow her over the wretched border. Unless . . .

'Why not Judith?' she suggested eagerly. 'She's half-Norman already. *She* can marry Duke William.'

'I don't think that's what Duke William wants,' Judith said primly.

Mathilda tutted.

'Normandy would suit you, Judi. And you could see your mother again.'

Judith's blue eyes clouded.

'My mother made it perfectly clear she had no interest in seeing me when she took the veil, Mathilda – why should that change now?'

Mathilda heard the hurt in her cousin's voice and felt bad but it didn't mean the idea was wrong.

'Even so, there are many churches in Normandy with lots of pretty paintings. You'd like that and . . .'

'No.' Baldwin cut through her, his voice like ice. Mathilda swallowed and looked slowly back at him. 'There will be no marriage for Judith, not in Normandy at least, for she is Duke William's cousin and too closely related to marry him.'

'And I am not?'

Baldwin shifted and she felt a flare of hope.

'You *are* related, but only distantly. It would take a petty churchman indeed to consider it an impediment. It is a good match, Mathilda.' His voice brooked no further argument.

'What manner of man, then, is this William?' she asked nervously.

'Manner of man?' Baldwin spluttered. 'He is a duke, Maud.'

'But what is he like?'

Baldwin wrinkled his nose.

'I don't know. He's tall, I suppose, and dark. His hair is cut very short – I did notice that – and he has no beard. A bare chin. Totally bare. He must be at it with a knife every damned morning. He has a clipped, efficient way of speaking. I like that – no frilly chit-chat. He doesn't waste time, Duke William, and he's strong. They say he can bend a bow further than any other man.'

'Bend a bow? What use is that to a duke?'

Baldwin shrugged.

'I'm not sure but I hear tell that William is innovative. He fights with cunning.'

'But how does he dance, Father?'

She asked the question lightly but Baldwin tensed.

'I know not, Mathilda, and I hope very much that he dances not at all. Dancing is trouble, especially . . .' he jabbed a finger in her face, making her flinch back ' . . . where you are concerned.'

'But . . .'

'Cease, Mathilda. Drop these foolish notions. I will not have this nonsense all over again, do you hear me?'

Mathilda's skin needled and she had to put out a hand to the wall to stay upright. Rogue tears pricked again at the bittersweet recollection of those magical dances with Brihtric. She'd thought herself so happy but it had all been an illusion.

'Would you not like to be a duchess, Mathilda?'

The quiet question came from Adela. Mathilda's eyes locked with her mother's and she tried to give it proper consideration. Adela had always taught her to think things through. 'Men are stronger in arm but women can hone themselves the stronger mind,' she'd always said, adding, 'believe me, a sharp wit cuts deeper than the finest sword.' Mathilda had to think now – and fast.

'Duchess is an honour, Mother,' she agreed carefully, 'but you raised me to be a queen.'

Adela's sharp intake of breath rattled around the rich bower but she recovered swiftly.

'As your father said, Mathilda, crowns can be won.'

Mathilda laughed bitterly.

'Oh, and where is Duke William going to win a crown? France? Is that the plan? Because I think your royal brother King Henri might not be best pleased, Mother. Or the empire perhaps? Will Duke William give you swords to fight Emperor Heinrich for Germany, Father?'

'Mathilda, you are going too far.'

'But if my intended husband is to win a crown, surely I deserve to know which one?'

'Hush, Mathilda,' Judith protested from behind her. 'This is treasonous talk. It is . . .'

'England.'

Baldwin spoke the word so low that Mathilda thought she'd dreamed it. She framed her lips to repeat it but dared not. England was an ancient land, rich in both treasure and tradition, and coveted throughout Europe. Lord Brihtric had owned vast lands there; that had been part of his attraction. She blinked furiously and when her vision cleared again Baldwin was upon her, his big frame looming over her tiny one.

'I did not say that,' he told her urgently.

'But . . .'

'There is talk, that is all. They are saying that King Edward is favouring the advisors he took with him from Normandy when he claimed the Saxon throne and that he might be persuaded to nominate his cousin, William, in the absence of another heir. But it is mere rumour, Mathilda, and you are being crass to push these matters. We are talking of the future – of dreams, possibilities, intangibles. These are things to keep in the richer wells of your mind but it is the present that counts and for you that present will be Normandy.'

'And a bastard as a husband?'

Baldwin's smile vanished again and Mathilda felt his angry shadow engulf her.

'This defiance, Daughter, does not suit you, any more than your foolhardiness suited you last year. You have had your dalliance, Maud. You have had your taste of "romance" but it is an empty dish. Love is not something that can simply be allowed to sweep over you. Love must be earned – earned with years of partnership, with mutual goals and considered plans.

'Did I love your mother when I married her? Did I hell!' Adela shifted awkwardly and Judith gave a stifled sob but Baldwin did not even notice. 'Politic, that's what she was. We have built our "love", if we must use such a word, as I have built Bruges, and it is the better for it, is it not, Adela?'

Adela nodded mutely but Baldwin's eyes were still on Mathilda.

'Duke William is a fine man, Daughter. He is a great warrior and an astute and ambitious ruler. He may dance, I know not, but I doubt it and I like him the more for it. You have danced enough, my girl – it is time for the music to stop. Duke William will arrive at my court next week and you will welcome him. Is that clear?'

'Very clear, Father.'

'You will welcome him?'

'With all politeness.'

'With an open heart?'

Mathilda bit her lip.

'With an open mind.'

Baldwin nodded curtly.

'That will do.'

He patted her awkwardly on the head and strode away, leaving her feeling as bruised inside as if he had rained her with punches. So this was to be her fate – her punishment. One moment of foolishness, one little dance, would saddle her to a bastard duke for life.

'A sharp wit cuts deeper than the finest sword,' she reminded herself and, pushing Judith's proffered kerchief away, she left the bower in her father's wake, running from the yard to find time and space to think. The bastard Duke William was coming in a week and she must be ready.

CHAPTER TWO

Bruges, July 1049

'I've said I won't marry him,' Mathilda said, pulling away from her ladies' ministrations, 'so what's the point in all this fuss?'

Emeline tutted and held tight to Mathilda's copper hair so that it pinched her scalp. Mathilda winced. She was in a bad mood already and this wasn't helping. Duke William was due at any moment and Adela had ordered her to be 'beautified', a task that her ladies were taking very seriously. She felt as if she'd been trapped in her chamber for hours.

'Why bother trying to attract the bastard duke if I'm going to reject him?' she demanded but Emeline just laughed.

'Ah, *ma cherie*, it is when you are going to reject them that you must look at your most attractive.'

She leaned over to wink at her mistress and, despite her black mood, Mathilda had to smile. Emeline was the daughter of a French nobleman who had died young, leaving his widow to enjoy many and varied bedmates, a habit her daughter had learned well. Dark-haired with a comely figure and inviting eyes, Emeline was never short of admirers and made shameless use of them. She had come into Adela's service when her mother had finally succumbed to a second marriage but had proved far too high-spirited for the countess, who had gladly handed her to her daughter. They had been firm friends ever since.

'So who are you rejecting this time, then, Em?' Mathilda asked, taking in her artfully tight dress, carefully arranged hair and lightly rouged lips and cheeks.

Emeline pursed her lips in teasing silence and it was left to Cecelia, Mathilda's other attendant and as like to Emeline as warp to weft, to reply.

'It is poor Bruno.'

'Bruno?' Mathilda looked at Emeline in astonishment. 'My father's chamberlain? But Em, he's old.'

'Forty-three. It's not so old. And besides I wanted to see what it would be like.'

'And?'

Mathilda knew she should not ask. 'Ladies of royal blood should not gossip,' Adela always insisted, though, Lord knows, she was often enough forehead to forehead with her own friends. Mathilda had challenged her on that once and Adela had insisted haughtily that they weren't gossiping but 'sharing information'. It had been one of the more useful lessons of Mathilda's whole education and now she looked expectantly up at Emeline.

'It was good at first,' she admitted with a coy smile that fooled no one. 'He was very attentive and very . . . grateful.'

'At first?'

Emeline sighed dramatically.

'He lacked . . .'

'Energy?' Cecelia suggested.

Born of a solid Flanders family, Cecelia had already been in Mathilda's service when Emeline came along and had at first resented her. As square as Emeline was curvy and as quiet as she was loquacious, she had struggled to understand the

French girl but Emeline had persisted in drawing her into her confidence and Cecelia had swiftly grown fond of her. These days she, like Mathilda, lived vicariously on Emeline's adventures.

'No, not that – stamina!' Emeline giggled. 'I need a younger man again. But perhaps this duke will bring some nice Normans with him.'

Mathilda grunted, her bad mood instantly recalled.

'Normans are not "nice", Emeline. You, of all people, should know that.'

Emeline's mother's eventual second husband had been a Norman count and it was because Emeline had hated Normandy so much that her mother had offered her to Adela. Now, though, she just shrugged.

'I don't want them *nice* any more.'

Mathilda groaned and looked to Cecelia.

'You'll be on the pallet bed again tonight, I fear.'

Cecelia nodded, unperturbed. Mathilda's two ladies were meant to sleep in a small chamber adjoining Mathilda's but frequently Emeline had someone more entertaining with her and Cecelia retreated to the pallet at the end of Mathilda's big bed. If Adela ever came in they had to claim Mathilda had been restless in the night and Mathilda feared her mother had very misplaced concerns for her sleep.

'At least marriage will tire you out,' she had pronounced the other day, making Mathilda curl away in embarrassment.

It was all very well discussing the bedroom with Emeline, who treated such matters as lightly as if they were hunting or dancing, but not with her mother.

'What if I don't like him?' she'd snapped, to which Adela had offered a wry smile that hadn't suited her.

'You will learn to put up with it. You must produce heirs after all.'

'Yes, but . . .'

Adela's eyebrows had risen painfully and Mathilda had gratefully abandoned the conversation.

'Are you done yet?' she asked now, putting a hand up to her hair.

'Nearly,' Emeline said, slapping it gently away. 'You will look beautiful, Mathilda. See how the bronzes in your hair glow like ancient mysteries. See how the dress trim brings out the blues and greens in your sea-eyes?'

'Sea-eyes, Emeline!' Mathilda scoffed but Emeline just gave a pretty shrug and held out the little hand mirror.

'Just so, *ma cherie*. The duke will be dazzled by you.'

'Oh, good,' Mathilda said dully, though glancing in the glass she had to admit that her two ladies had done a fine job.

Her long plaits were strung through with threads of gold and tiny rosebud jewels and shimmered in the sunlight spilling in through the window opening, drawing out the bronze and copper shades in her hair.

'This will be a fine rejection,' she said bravely but as she rose she felt her wretched knees quake and had to put out a hand to her carved oak dressing table to steady herself.

The truth was that though she had striven to hone her wit in these last days, Mathilda could find no clever way to talk her father out of this match and could only pray negotiations would go poorly. Every time she thought of being sent out of Bruges, with its elegant buildings, exotic markets and vibrant court, and into Normandy where, from all she'd heard, everyone hid in gloomy, high-walled castles and considered killing each other prime entertainment, she felt her very heart hesitate to beat.

She couldn't understand it. All her life her father had shown her such favour. He'd lavished money on her gowns and horses, funded her extensive education and encouraged her to come into society from an early age, so why would he now shut her away in Normandy with a duke who'd inherited his title aged seven and had apparently been fighting off rebellions ever since? There must be a high chance her new groom would be killed before the marriage was weeks old.

A little cheered at the prospect of a swift widowhood, she smoothed down her wine-red dress just as the door flew open and Judith tumbled inside.

'He's here.'

All Mathilda's new courage seemed to run down her limbs and away in an instant and she moved nervously to the window, cursing her lack of height for it was hard to see those immediately below. Even so, she could tell that the whole court was gathered outside, stood in desultory groups, chatting in low voices and fanning themselves in their finery as the sun burned mercilessly down. The gates on the far side of the large yard stood welcomingly open, guards alert on either side, but no one yet approached over the myriad bridges that led travellers over Bruges' many canals to the comital palace at the heart of the city.

'There's no one here, Judi.'

'Not *here* here,' Judith corrected herself, 'but at the outskirts of the city. A rider just came in. The count says you are to go down immediately. We must all be before the palace to welcome the duke.'

'I see.'

Mathilda peered at the carved oak fencing surrounding the elegant palace yard. Whenever Adela gave birth to another ducal child Baldwin would order a panel replaced with one bearing the name of the new prince or princess. Mathilda loved them and if she was ever feeling lost or unsure of herself she would stroll out to look at her elegant oaken name marking her place in the busy Flanders court. She searched for it now but it was obscured by crowds.

Judith tugged on her arm.

'Now, Maud, please, or the count will be angry.'

'And the duke?' Mathilda asked, resisting stubbornly. 'Will the duke be angry?'

'I imagine so. They say he is very fierce. Oh. That is . . . I'm sure he won't be with you, Mathilda.'

'You're sure of nothing, Judi, none of us is. If he is angry, though, he may not wish to marry me. Tell Father I am not ready yet.'

'Mathilda, no!' Beyond the palace came a faint sound of cheering. 'You *must* come.'

Judith tugged again but, despite her cousin being almost a head taller than petite Mathilda, and stronger with it, Mathilda resisted still. Finally, Emeline placed a hand in the small of her back and gave her a firm push.

'You cannot reject him from up here, my lady,' she whispered.

Mathilda forced herself to smile. Fleetingly – and not for the first time – she wished she might be Emeline, free to do as she chose, but instantly she remonstrated with herself. She was a lady of Flanders; it was a privilege and a joy, even now.

'Come then,' she said crisply and, with Judith panting gratefully in her wake, she strode from her chamber to greet the man she would do her utmost not to marry.

Mathilda took her place at her father's side on the marble platform before the palace as the rising cheers in the streets beyond heralded Duke William's imminent arrival. Baldwin had had this magnificent block of stone imported from Byzantium several years ago for just such parades and occasions. It stood in front of the palace, elegant in its stark white simplicity, and set them half a man's height above the rest of the crowds. In honour of today's proceedings Mathilda had been granted precedence over her smug older brother Baldwin and she could not resist a teasing smile at him as she took her place. He was not, however, easily cowed.

'Make the most of it, Sister – you'll soon be under the bastard duke after all.'

Mathilda itched to push him away but an unseemly family tumble would not please the count so she contented herself with words: 'At least someone wants to marry me, Baldwin. You're too ugly for a bride.'

Baldwin grinned easily.

'But I'm heir to Flanders, Maud dear. I could be ugly as sin – which I'm not – and *still* take my pick of the ladies.'

Mathilda ground her teeth at the truth of it and glanced over at her other siblings, gathered around their mother and chattering away as if this were just a normal state occasion. She patted self-consciously at her gold-studded hair and steadied her stance on the raised wooden heels designed to give her just a little more height. She was used to joining her father on display but never before had she felt so exposed. Everyone knew why Duke William was here. Every finely clad member of the court, every servant scuttling to prepare the feast and every dark-skinned market trader knew and she felt all eyes looking at her as if assessing her worth for this honour.

'He's just a bastard duke,' she wanted to tell them, but whatever had previously been whispered about William, the occasion was now gathering its own momentum and the crowds were in a mood as festive as if King Henri of France himself were riding in.

'He's here!'

It was Judith again, squeaking excitedly from her lowly position at the rear of the family pedestal. Mathilda felt her heart quicken and forced her weight down into the smooth marble to keep her legs steady as the Norman delegation turned in through the gates. Duke William had asked for her, she reminded herself. She did not have to impress him in any way, save to make him sorry for what he would miss out on. Glancing to the window of her chamber high above, she saw Emeline and Cecelia leaning eagerly out and wished they were at her shoulder but the guests were approaching and she must stand tall and do this alone.

The crowds were thick and the new arrivals, mounted on huge horses, were moving carefully round the edge of the yard, giving Mathilda time to take them in. They were a sombre group, dressed in mail as if afraid of being set upon by Flemish peasants. The only colour was in their cloaks, which were all a uniform red, the same red, she was horrified to note, as her dress.

'You will fit right in, Maud,' her brother whispered in her ear.

She did not flinch but stepped carefully back, grinding the raised heel of her shoe into his toe. Hearing him muffle a cry of pain she felt better – though not much. How on earth was she meant to know which of these matching men was the duke? They all looked the same, their dark hair close-cropped beneath stern helmets, their chins as bare as boys'. They had told her this duke was a soldier first and foremost but she had thought he would at least stand out as a leader. And then, as they turned the bend of the pathway round the yard and drew towards the comital family, the front riders parted and she saw him – unmistakeably him.

Duke William was riding on a jet-black stallion several hands higher than his fellows'. The beast's saddle was scarlet and it wore a ceremonial hood of the same that drew your eyes into its dark gaze, though only for a moment for the rider was even more mesmerising than the horse. Duke William wore armour like his men but his was silver and gleamed as if he were the sun. His cloak was scarlet too but embroidered all over with golden crosses and around his helmet was a simple but shining diadem studded with rubies. He sat rigid in the saddle as he reined in his magnificent horse several paces back from the marble block, his eyes sweeping over the family and settling with fierce certainty upon Mathilda.

'Greetings, Duke William,' Count Baldwin called, raising his arms wide. 'You are most welcome to my humble palace.'

'It is magnificent, Count, and does you great credit – as does your daughter.'

Mathilda jumped. Already he spoke of her. Had he no manners?

'I thank you,' Baldwin said easily.

'I look forward to a fruitful alliance between us,' Duke William went on loudly.

The noble ladies of Flanders giggled as if they were closeted in the bower and Mathilda glanced to Adela who looked, she was pleased to see, as uncomfortable as Mathilda felt. Count Baldwin, however, was taking it all very genially.

'May I, Lord Duke, present the Lady Mathilda.' He took Mathilda's arm and pulled her to the front of the platform like some slave girl on sale. Mathilda resisted furiously and felt her father's hand tighten. 'My daughter,' he said quickly to the duke who was watching without a word, 'is a little nervous.'

Nervous! Mathilda opened her mouth to protest but before she could even draw breath, Duke William had spurred his great stallion forward. It pounded across the short space towards her, its nostrils flaring and its dark eyes intent beneath its dark red hood. Mathilda felt locked into the advance, like a mouse beneath a falcon's dive. She heard the gasps of the crowd, felt her father fall back, half-saw her mother gather the younger ones against her skirts, and then a mailed hand shot out and clasped her waist, catching clumsily at the fabric of her dress to yank her like a poppet onto the horse.

It was still moving at pace and for a moment she dangled, her little body bumping against the stallion's powerful flank, her legs dangerously close to its flying hooves, before William hefted her, like so much straw, into an ungainly embrace before him. Her golden diadem flew off and bounced across the cobbles in a spin of light, and her plaits caught in his silver mail, bringing tears of pain to her eyes.

'What on earth!' she finally gasped out as they gained the far side of the yard.

She could feel all eyes upon them as people dived out of their way and she scrabbled to sit more decently for her ankles were showing and there was a tear in the waist of her beautiful dress. She twisted in the saddle to glare at her captor.

'How dare you?'

He looked taken aback. He was handsome, close up. Unnervingly so. His shaven face was lean, the strong line of jaw starkly evident with no beard to hide it, and his surprisingly full lips prominent. His eyes were as dark as his horse's but they were flecked with a silver that, this close, brought them to life. She forced herself to keep glaring. She ached from his unceremonious grab and one of her plaits was still caught in the rings of his mail so she dared not try to jump free, even had the horse not been so very tall or the arm at her waist so very determined.

'I am a lady of Flanders,' she spluttered, 'not some common wench to seize at will.'

He frowned.

'I'm sorry you see it that way.'

Mathilda blinked.

'What other way is there?'

He shrugged and suddenly seemed, for all his imposing looks, very young.

'I meant,' he told her, his voice low, 'to impress you with my strength. I take it I did not achieve my aim?'

'I feel more bruised than impressed,' she admitted.

'I'm sorry. My mother told me to sweep you off your feet.'

Mathilda tensed at the mention of Herleva, the beautiful concubine who had captivated Duke Robert and given him the bastard who now held her against him in front of the whole of her father's glamorous court.

'You certainly did that,' she said and to her surprise he smiled.

'I will endeavour to do better next time. I want you as my wife, Mathilda of Flanders.'

'Why?'

'I have scoured the noble houses of Europe for someone strong enough to match me. I am told you are the one and from what I see now I believe that to be correct. We will work well together, Mathilda.'

Mathilda blinked. What he said was almost ridiculously blunt but she could not deny a strange flattery within it. William was not what she had expected at all but it was clear he was a man of purpose and determination and that she had to admire.

'My father says the church may forbid our match,' she said cautiously.

'Not with good reason. My best men have studied every chart and see no just cause for prohibition.'

'Nor unjust one neither?'

He smiled grimly.

'I cannot speak for that but we must trust to God to see that the truth prevails. And to our own ability to ensure that men see it also.' He looked intently into her eyes, fixing her in his dark stare. 'So now you know what I look for, Lady Mathilda, I must beg the same question of you – what do *you* wish for in the man you will spend your life with?'

It was a good question – too good. She looked down.

'Right now, my lord, to free my hair from his mail.'

'*His* mail? You will marry me then?'

Mathilda glanced up at him. They were coming back round to the platform so she had but a moment before they were engulfed in ceremony. She owed him an answer – she owed *herself* an answer. She looked straight into his dark eyes. She had always thought that what she wanted in a husband was charm, impetuousness, joy – romance. That is what she had known with Brihtric, but she had been young then and foolish. She was not just any girl, free to dally with whoever had the prettiest words, but a princess with a duty to rule. And this man, she felt sure, would rule well.

'Yes, Duke William of Normandy,' she agreed. 'I will marry you.'

CHAPTER THREE

Bruges, November 1050

Judith glanced anxiously to the window opening and, seeing the first tell-tale scraps of pink in the sky, groaned quietly to herself. Already the sun had sunk to the level of the Bruges townhouses and its light seemed to run as if molten along the elegant lines of the slated roofs, pouring off in golden streaks and streaming along the criss-cross canals in between. It was a glorious sight but an infuriating one too. She'd only had the chance to sit down a little time ago and already the wretched light was fading.

All day she'd been longing to get to her art and all day – as most days – she'd been prevented. She daren't work on her illumination when Baldwin was in the palace for he didn't approve of her doing 'monk's labour' so she had to snatch time where she could. She looked longingly at her half-formed picture of the Virgin and wished she were brave enough to paint it in public, but she wasn't made to cut a new path and it was easier just to keep it to herself. With a resigned sigh she rolled it up, stored it away in her oak casket, and headed to choose a dress for dinner.

She made for the guardrobe on the other side of the central antechamber. Adela had commissioned this several years back, complaining to Baldwin that her gowns were getting crushed in their tight chests. Baldwin, intrigued, had allowed the innovation and now he proudly showed it to all his finest guests. It was a simple room, hung on all four sides with rails as tall as a man, studded with hooks from which gowns could be hung to keep as loose as if they were being worn. Adela's gowns ran along the longest wall, Mathilda's down one side, the younger girls' down the other and Judith's tucked behind the door.

She moved inside but seeing Mathilda she hesitated, for her cousin had been in a hideous temper ever since Count Baldwin had returned from the Council of Rheims a month back, choked with rage.

'Prohibited,' he'd spat at Mathilda, almost as if it were her fault. 'The damned match is "prohibited".'

'But why, Father?' Mathilda had demanded, clearly dismayed.

'They're insisting on consanguinity. The Pope has some up-his-own-arse churchman with a fancy chart that "proves" – his word, not mine – that you and Duke William are too closely related to wed. All it proves, I can tell you, is that the Pope is as bitter and politically twisted as the rest of us. It's a den of iniquity, Rome. His "Holiness" is doing this entirely because Emperor Heinrich secured him his office and Heinrich hates me and fears Normandy. Consanguinity be damned, it's a finger up at me and at William, that's what it is.'

Judith's heart had quailed at such blasphemous talk but Mathilda's response had been more practical.

'So what now, Father?'

'I don't know, Maud. We must bide our time. Popes die regularly so let's hope this one does so soon.'

'Father!'

'What? He's no more God's representative on this earth than I am. He's just a prince protecting his lands and I'd respect him for it if he did it with sword in hand like a decent man, but this underhand manufacture of false prohibitions curdles my blood. Ah well, William has sent a delegation to appeal, so we'll just have to hope it is persuasive. And it's not as if you liked him that much anyway, did you, Maud?'

But the prohibition had, to everyone's surprise, sharpened Mathilda's appetite for a Norman husband far more than any blessing might have done. She had been stomping around with more curses than her father for weeks and it was therefore with some trepidation that Judith slid in next to her now.

'Trouble choosing?' she said lightly.

'I just don't see the point of going to any effort,' came the grumbled reply.

Judith hid a smile.

'But Maud, you have such beautiful gowns. What about this one – the lilac is so pretty. Or this – the yellow. You look stunning in the yellow.'

'I look like a flower in the yellow.'

'A beautiful rose, perhaps?'

Mathilda rolled her eyes.

'Fine, I'll wear the yellow but if there are bees all over me I'll blame you.'

'Perhaps the honey will sweeten you up,' Judith retorted and Mathilda, after a shocked glare, gave a rough laugh.

'Perhaps it will, Judi. Something has to.'

Judith laid a hand on her arm.

'Duke William has a great reputation for achieving his goals, Maud.'

'He does,' Mathilda agreed stiffly, but then, to Judith's astonishment, her composed little cousin seemed almost to crumple against her. 'But how?'

Judith pulled her close.

'With diplomacy, I suppose.'

'Diplomacy has failed.'

'With might then.'

'We can hardly take up swords against the Pope, Judi.'

'Cunning?'

'Cunning?' Mathilda cocked her head. 'Perhaps. I suppose I must trust William's delegation will be successful, yes?'

'Yes.' Judith squeezed Mathilda tight, feeling her small and unusually frail in her arms. 'You must trust to that and keep content so that you stay beautiful for him.'

'How, if he is not here to see it?'

'Word carries.' Judith struck a pose and adopted a rough attempt at a man's voice: 'Oh, my lord duke, I was at the court of Flanders the other day and the Lady Mathilda shone in her yellow gown. I swear she is the prettiest flower in all the rose gardens of Europe.'

Mathilda let out a laugh, a reluctant one perhaps, but a laugh all the same.

'Nay, Judi, you jest.'

'A little,' Judith allowed, 'but there is truth in it too. You are William's prize, Mathilda, and must remain so for him. You are a lady of Flanders after all.'

'As are you. What will *you* wear, sweet one?'

Judith looked at her own more limited choice of gowns.

'The blue perhaps.'

'Good idea. It matches your eyes.'

Judith blinked at this unexpected compliment.

'Will I be a flower too, then?' she asked.

'Of course – a beautiful cornflower.'

Judith smiled ruefully. That would be right – she was a cornflower to Mathilda's rose. She was pretty enough, she knew, but with her sky-blue eyes, pale blonde hair and soft, peachy cheeks, she was so obviously so as to be almost unremarkable. Not like Mathilda. Mathilda's hair was shot through with shades of copper and bronze that made it glow mysteriously in even the lowest light. Her eyes were part blue, part green, like a shifting sea, and despite being nearly a hand's breadth shorter than Judith she walked into any room as if she were the tallest one there. No wonder all eyes followed her; no wonder Duke William wanted to fight for her.

'The blue one,' Judith agreed determinedly but a cough in the doorway stopped her and she spun round to see her brother's chamberlain shuffling in the antechamber. She looked the balding little man up and down, trying to imagine him with Emeline and gratefully failing, before remembering her manners. 'Lord Bruno, can we help you?'

'Beg pardon, my lady, but the Count asks you to attend him in his chamber before dinner.'

'Me?' Judith looked at him, astonished. 'Not Mathilda?'

Mathilda looked surprised too but Bruno nodded firmly.

'He asked specifically for his sister, the Lady Judith.'

His sister! Baldwin rarely called her that, despite the truth of it, for she had always been brought up more as a daughter, or, at least, a sort of favoured niece. She sat awkwardly with him, she knew, just as she sat awkwardly with Mathilda – half aunt, half sister.

'But Mathilda must come too?'

'If she wishes, I suppose.'

'She wishes,' Mathilda said firmly, curiosity burning in her green eyes.

'Then you should hurry. The count seemed very keen to see you.'

He was looking pointedly at Judith again and she blushed under this unusual attention.

'Oh! Oh, yes, of course. Thank you.'

*

In as short a time as possible, they were at Count Baldwin's door. Judith was glad of Mathilda's company for she had never been entirely at ease with her half-brother, but as she entered the chamber she was surprised by the count leaping from his elegant chair and rushing towards her.

'Judith, come in, come in.' Judith let him lead her forward, looking warily to Adela, sat on her own chair with her hands primly in her lap. 'Take a seat, my dear. Drink?'

Baldwin clicked for his servant who rushed forward with a jug of wine. Judith accepted but did not take a sip for fear that her throat might close up. She was aware of Mathilda behind her but for once Baldwin gave his favourite daughter little more than a cursory glance.

'Is all well, my lord?' she asked nervously.

'Well? Oh, yes, indeed, all is very well, Judith.'

'Has Duke William succeeded in securing the Pope's blessing?' she hazarded, looking again for Mathilda.

'Duke William? Oh, him! No, no, nothing like that. This is about *you*, Judith.'

'Me?'

Judith decided maybe she would take a little of her wine after all. The count was looking at her very intently. Oh please, God, don't say he was going to take her illumination away from her. Was he cross? He didn't seem cross.

'You, my dear sister, have received a proposal.'

Judith nearly fell off her stool. Wine sloshed onto her dress and she put the cup down abruptly on the side table. Baldwin chuckled.

'Don't be so surprised. It is well deserved.'

Judith still couldn't find her voice but Mathilda had no such trouble.

'A proposal for Judi? From whom?'

Baldwin steepled his fingers together and looked to Adela

who sat up a little straighter. Judith drew in several deep breaths and tried to compose herself as her brother rose and spoke straight to her.

'From England, Judith.'

Judith heard Mathilda gasp and, remembering her cousin's heartbreak over the Lord Brihtric's departure, prayed her brother was not cruel enough to have come to an arrangement with her lost love.

'With whom?' she squeaked, feeling Mathilda leaning over her shoulder like a dark angel.

'Lord Tostig Godwinson,' Baldwin announced delightedly, not even noticing both girls shaking in relief. 'His father, Earl Godwin, has sent envoys asking for you.'

'For me?'

Baldwin shifted.

'He may,' he allowed, with only the slightest of backward glances, 'have spoken of Mathilda at first but I told him she is betrothed already and he is content to take you in her stead.'

Judith's heart sank a little; who would be content to take her instead of Mathilda?

'Mathilda is not truly betrothed though. The Pope . . .'

'The Pope will come round. William is most certain his delegation will arrange matters, is he not, Mathilda?'

'Well yes,' she heard her cousin stutter. 'That is . . .'

But Baldwin was not to be put off.

'I know he is. This is an excellent match for you, Judith. Lord Tostig is a fine man, very handsome they say. That will be nice for you, will it not?'

'Er, yes, Brother. Thank you. But you have truly asked him if he is happy to have *me*?'

'Of course. You are a lady of Flanders, are you not?

'I am and Flanders is of course worth much, Brother, but you said King Edward has Norman advisors. What if they are set against the Godwinsons? What if Mathilda and I find ourselves with husbands who are opposed to each other?'

'Why, then,' Baldwin shot straight back, unblinking, 'it will pay to have one of you on each side.'

'But would that not mean Mathilda and I would have to stand against each other?'

'That would be up to you. Come now, women are more subtle than men so you two can surely manage any minor conflicts?'

Judith looked at Mathilda as Baldwin began nudging them towards the door. They had had their little disagreements over the years – mainly when Judith dared to challenge Mathilda – but they had always sorted it out. They had not before, however, had whole nations at their backs.

'Come, Judi,' Mathilda said with a laugh, taking her arm. 'What dispute can Normandy and England possibly have with each other? They are divided by a whole sea.'

'A *narrow* sea,' Judith pointed out but no one seemed to be listening.

CHAPTER FOUR

'It's not that I begrudge Judith her happiness,' Mathilda said, stepping thankfully out of her gown and diving for her bed at the end of an excruciating night of drinking her cousin's health.

'Of course not,' Emeline agreed archly, shaking the creases from the gown and examining it for marks.

'I don't. I love Judi. She's all but my sister and I want to see her happy.'

'Of course you do.'

'I *do*. Why must you question me so?'

Emeline handed the gown to Cecelia.

'I do not question you, my lady. I think, perhaps, it is more that you question yourself.'

Mathilda sighed and pulled the covers up to her chin.

'Maybe you're right, Em. I admit, I am a little jealous. *I* should be marrying, not Judith.'

Cecelia busied herself with hanging the gown but Emeline sat down on the end of the bed.

'You will, my lady.'

'When?'

'When God wills it.'

'And the Pope – what is his will? Because that's what this is all about.'

'Perhaps,' Cecelia suggested from across the little chamber, 'he fears an alliance between Flanders and Normandy, especially with Judith marrying into England. If you went to Normandy your father might have control of the Narrow Sea.'

Mathilda looked over at her.

'So Judith's marriage is costing me mine?'

'No, Mathilda!' Emeline chided. 'Don't be churlish.'

Mathilda bit her lip. She longed to remonstrate with her attendant, but Emeline was right – she *was* being churlish. It was just so frustrating. It was over a year since William had ridden into Flanders and convinced her to become his duchess and yet here she still was, stuck in Bruges, unwed and unable, it seemed, to do anything about it.

Everyone was busy but her. Even Baldwin had new plans for the future. There had been German architects at court tonight and they had demonstrated how some neat little baked-clay blocks they called bricks could be made into a wall in no time at all – had built it right there between the dining tables. Baldwin had been nearly as full of it as he had of Judith's damned engagement and was already ordering huge supplies. Everyone was moving forward – everyone except her. She flung back the covers and leaped out of bed again, sending Emeline sprawling on the floor.

'I'm going to write to William,' she said, pacing to the window as Cecelia rushed to help Emeline up. 'I'm going to say that we are fools to bow to a council who plot against us. If politics are our only obstacle, we should proceed anyway and trust in God's mercy to ratify our marriage once peace is established.' Her ladies gaped at her. 'What? Can you fault my logic?'

'Not your logic,' Cecelia said, 'but perhaps your wisdom. Marrying in direct defiance of a papal edict could mean excommunication from the whole church.'

'He wouldn't dare.'

'He dared pass the edict in the first place.'

Mathilda tossed her head angrily.

'Tell her, Em,' Cecelia urged. 'Tell her it's madness to suggest such a thing.'

Emeline considered.

'It is madness,' she agreed. 'But not because of the Pope for he is just a man, and a fallible one too if Count Baldwin is to be believed. No, the madness is in writing such a forward letter after what happened with Lord Brihtric.'

Mathilda flinched.

'Brihtric was a fool. He preferred to court my father rather than me. Duke William is not such a man; he agrees with what I say.'

'Then why has he not come to claim you already?'

Mathilda's heart bumped. She had wondered that herself, many a time. Had he maybe found a better bride? There was only one way to find out.

'I will send to him,' she said again, more firmly. 'Emeline – you are still courting your Norman beau, are you not?'

Emeline had, true to form, found herself a new lover from amongst William's entourage and the man was forever riding into Flanders to see her. All too often it had made Mathilda guiltily bitter to see her attendant with a Norman at her beck and call when her own suitor was kept from her, but at last it might be useful.

'Lord Everard remains attentive,' Emeline agreed coyly.

'Good. Then you can write to him and I can conceal my letter within yours.'

'Write?' Emeline said, horrified. 'I cannot write and anyway, what on earth would I say?'

'I don't know. Whatever you say to the man when you are together.'

Emeline laughed dirtily.

'I can just picture the poor scribe who had to write *that* down.'

'We don't need a scribe,' Mathilda pointed out, determined now. She was sick of waiting, sick of being stuck in limbo before a misty altar. 'Cecelia can write.'

Emeline looked over at her friend.

'So she can. Well, that will spare the scribe's blushes.'

'I don't want to transcribe her filthy thoughts, my lady,' Cecelia protested. 'They're not worth wasting ink on.'

'Oh, come on, Cee,' Emeline said. 'I'll make it sweet, I promise. And I'm not filthy, men are just my weakness. It could be worse – I might have fallen for pastries instead and then I'd be all fat and wobbly and you'd have precious little room in our bed.'

'I'm hardly ever in "our" bed,' Cecelia grumbled but now Emeline was leaping forward again.

'All is well, my lady. I've just remembered that Cecelia need not write down my "filthy thoughts", for Everard said he would be visiting soon. He can take William's letter to him in person.'

'Perfect!' Mathilda said. 'Is that not perfect, Cee? We will write my letter and Everard will carry it.'

'And William will show it to your father and we will all be confined to the bower for months like last time.'

'No,' Mathilda said. 'This is not like last time. Brihtric was weak.'

Her heart prickled with the treachery of criticising her Saxon love but it was true. He had written her beautiful poetry but what use was being the 'only star in his velvet night' if he ran away at the first hint of trouble?

'Brihtric saw sense,' Cecelia corrected briskly. 'Your father would never have sanctioned such a match. You were bred to be a queen, Mathilda.'

'And now I am struggling to even secure a duchy. We must do something, whatever the risk. Cecelia, fetch a quill. Emeline, sharpen your wit. This must be good.'

It took long into the night to compose the letter and by the end, Mathilda was still unsure. She'd considered every possible approach – arcane allusion, courtly flattery, hidden meaning – and, in the end, remembering William's own direct style, settled on three short sentences:

I, Lady Mathilda of Flanders, greet you, Duke William of Normandy, and assure you of my continued commitment to our betrothal. I see no valid opposition to our marriage and wish you to know that if you see fit to proceed to the altar, I will gladly meet you there. I believe my father agrees.

She signed it with the Jerusalem cross that she had practised under Judith's keen guidance as an original mark. The signature looked fine but the letter felt stilted and formal and frighteningly to the point. There was no doubting its intentions and she could only pray it was well received.

For days she paced. Everard arrived, spent three days in Bruges with Emeline and left looking a little dazed but carrying the precious message. Almost the moment he had carried it away and its path was set, Mathilda regretted it. She went over and over the blank words, hearing them as forward and shameless. She paced again, Judith following anxiously after her, muttering of physicians.

'I'm not ill, Judith,' Mathilda assured her, 'just impatient to hear from Duke William.'

'Lovesick,' Judith pronounced wryly. 'Ah, poor Maud.'

Mathilda laughed. This was not love. She'd only met William once and was sure already that he was too hard a man for anything as frivolous as love, but she did want to marry him. And now he knew that. She paced again.

'Perhaps he's off at war,' Emeline suggested.

'Or at the far side of his duchy,' Cecelia said.

'Or,' Mathilda snapped, 'disgusted at my forwardness and even now sending an envoy to my father to call off our betrothal.'

Why had she written the dammed letter? Why was she so wretchedly impatient? William would tell Count Baldwin and he'd hit the roof and she'd be married off to some obscure lord from Hungary or Poland and sent into the darkness. And it would serve her right.

And then, days later, Mathilda returned to the palace from market to see a magnificent black stallion tethered in the yard. She clutched dizzily at Emeline's arm, the sweet chestnuts she'd bought churning wickedly in her stomach.

'He's here, Em.'

'As you wanted.'

'I don't want it now. To the bower, quick.'

But it was too late, for one of her father's guards was rushing towards them.

'Lady Mathilda, your father wishes to see you in his chambers.'

'No,' Mathilda gasped. 'I can't. I'm ill.'

'You are not,' Emeline said. 'You must go, my lady.'

She was right, of course, but still Mathilda's heart quailed. What if William was angry?

'You knew this would happen when you wrote the letter,' Cecelia pointed out reasonably but Mathilda did not feel reasonable.

She ground her teeth and looked over to the stallion, standing tall and proud, its dark eyes seeming to bore straight into her. Suddenly it stamped one black hoof down on the cobbles. The sound echoed round the palace yard like a command and Mathilda thrust her head up and made for her father's rooms before her legs gave way.

Count Baldwin was sat in his great chair, Adela on one side and on the other, Duke William. It was the first time Mathilda had seen him in over a year and she had forgotten quite how handsome he was – and how imposing. The Norman was perched on the edge of his seat and as soon as he saw Mathilda he leaped up and bowed low before her. She offered her hand and as he took it he glanced up, his dark eyes gleaming. Her nerves steadied a little.

'What a pleasant surprise, my lord,' she said politely.

Again the look and now he straightened, close enough to touch had she so dared, but he did not speak and it was left to Baldwin to break the silence: 'The duke is impatient to marry you, Mathilda.'

'He is?'

She looked questioningly at William.

'I am, for I see no valid opposition to our marriage, my lady.' She gasped at the sound of her own words and he smiled. 'None, that is, save the earthly machinations of a misguided prince.'

'Several misguided princes,' Baldwin put in heartily. 'They are conspiring against us, Maud, and we must cement this alliance between Flanders and Normandy. Northern France is a cockpit. William feels we will stand stronger within it if we stand together, and I must say, I agree. It is time, my dear, to act.'

'Act?' Mathilda asked, as lightly as she could.

William took her hand.

'If, my lady,' he said, still looking straight at her, 'you could see fit to proceed to the altar, I would gladly meet you there.'

Her own words again; he was taking them as his and she had to admit that it sent her pulse, if not her heart, racing. 'Your father, I believe,' he went on, word-perfect, 'agrees.'

'But the Council of Rheims,' she protested softly.

'The Council of Rheims was so far up its pompous arse it couldn't see anything clearly,' Baldwin snapped. 'Emperor Heinrich controls the Pope like a poppet and things are very unsettled in Rome. Nothing for you to worry about, my dear, save that neither William nor I believe a dispensation will be forthcoming for some time.'

'You are suggesting, Father, that we risk being cut off from the whole church and marry without it?'

'*Before* it, Daughter, that is all, is it not, William?'

'Correct,' William confirmed crisply. 'The church will soon see the sense of it if we lead the way. So – dare you do it, Mathilda? Dare you marry me?'

His eyes were flashing secret signals to her. He knew she dared, knew, indeed, that she had instigated this, and he liked it. The risk had paid off. She lowered her eyes.

'If you think that is best, my lord, then of course I will do as you and my father wish.'

Count Baldwin laughed out loud.

'Do not be deceived, William, she is not, I'm afraid, as biddable as she sounds.'

'Oh, I am not deceived,' William said. 'I know exactly what manner of wife I will marry.'

'Good, good. Come then, let us drink.'

Baldwin turned to summon wine and William stepped a little closer to Mathilda, standing nearly a head taller than her and excitingly broad with it.

'I know exactly what manner of wife I will marry,' he repeated, pressing something into her hand, 'and I welcome it.' Mathilda looked down to see her letter. 'I will let you burn it,

Mathilda, but know this – we will do great things together, you and I, for you are a woman in my own mould.'

Then he was turning, accepting wine and pouring her a cup, and she could only stuff the letter into the dainty leather pocket at her belt and join the good cheer. She tried to concentrate as her parents talked dates and plans and the need for secrecy but William's words ran round and round in her head. A woman in his own mould? She pictured him as she'd first seen him, a stiff-backed warrior in silver armour upon a dark-eyed stallion. Was this her mould? Of course not, but if it suited William to believe so, so be it. Her wedding date was set, with or without the Pope's blessing. She had achieved her goal and there was no time left for misgivings.

CHAPTER FIVE

Eu, March 1051

Mathilda stared up at the great castle and her hands twitched nervously on the reins, sending her horse skittering and the escort behind into total confusion. The procession came to a chaotic halt, hooves clattering on the rough road and horses whinnying indignantly, but Mathilda was fixed on the fortress before her. So this was Normandy. All she had heard, then, was true. Duke William's handsome bearing, clipped courtesy and bold defiance of the church had convinced her that his duchy could not be as austere as was whispered but she'd been wrong. All day they had ridden along flat, low roads until at last a valley had dipped below them and the castle had appeared like a wart above.

'My lady, is all well?'

'Look at it, Em – look at the castle.'

'It is a little forbidding.'

'A little?!'

Mathilda's eyes roamed over the harsh grey walls of the Castle of Eu, sitting atop the hill like a brutal extension of the scattered rocks. It cut off the horizon in a precise, stark line interrupted only by square turrets on which she could see guards pointing at her and calling down. She'd been seen; there was no escape.

'It's so dark,' she murmured.

'It is a border fortress, my lady, designed for defence not comfort.'

She was right. Mathilda drew in a deep breath and forced herself to sit taller in the saddle. Eu was an outpost, a martial station. And yet . . .

'People do live here,' she said. 'Not just soldiers, Emeline, but a noble family. The Count of Eu is William's cousin and an honoured member of his council. This castle is clearly considered a worthy dwelling so they must all be this way.'

She looked hopefully at Emeline, willing her to deny it. As she had been in Normandy for some time before she'd begged Adela to rescue her she was, in the absence of any other, Mathilda's expert on the duchy.

'Not in Rouen,' was all Emeline could offer. 'It's very lively in Rouen and doubtless elsewhere too. It's been years since I was here, remember?'

'Years in which everyone has done little but fight each other and raise their walls higher as a result.' Mathilda was struck by a sudden thought. 'Is your mother still here, Emeline? We might find a friend to . . .'

'She is not here, my lady. She went running back to France the moment she wore her poor husband into his grave.'

'Oh. You did not wish to go with her?'

Emeline shrugged.

'I could hardly leave you with just Cee, could I?' She grinned as her friend yelped in protest, then added, 'Besides, I liked it in Flanders. If I'd known where we were heading, however . . .'

She looked sardonically up to the stark walls and Cecelia nudged crossly at her.

'Don't be mean, Emeline. I am sure it is very comfortable within.'

'Well, we're about to find out,' Mathilda said. 'The gates are opening.'

Count Baldwin had noticed this too and rode forward, Adela in his wake.

'Come, Mathilda, let us go to meet your betrothed.'

Mathilda nodded and took the reins firmly in her hands. She thought of her beautiful wedding gown, carefully packed in layers of linen. It was a glorious midnight blue, embroidered all over with silver stars, and when she had tried it on back in Bruges she had felt like a duchess indeed. Now it was time to prove she deserved that role and she would not show nerves, not even if the castle walls seemed to hang over her and the thick-set guards forming a sombre welcome either side of the road looked like angels of death.

'Stop imagining things,' she told herself sternly and moved forward to Eu as, with a fanfare, Duke William rode out of the gates. He looked magnificent. He was in his silver armour again, this time topped with a gold-trimmed cloak. He wore a helmet, making Mathilda wonder if they were like to be attacked, but a closer look revealed that it, too, was silver and was worked with intricate patterns that caught the weak sun in shimmers of light. He was clearly keen to impress again and this time it worked.

Mathilda's breath caught and she put up a hand to smooth her hair, wishing that she'd thought to pause in the trees to arrange herself. She was in her finest travelling cloak of dark green wool but it was spattered with mud. What if her face was too? She looked around for Emeline but Count Baldwin had guided her forward and it was too late to do anything but smile and hope.

'Welcome, my lady, to Normandy. My duchy has keenly awaited your arrival and is eager to embrace you as her duchess.'

His words, so loud that Mathilda had to force herself not to cover her ears, carried around the plain before the castle and bounced off the walls above: 'duchess, duchess, duchess'. Mathilda felt the title shiver deliciously through her.

'I thank you, my lord. I am delighted to be here and hope I will make Normandy proud.'

Their eyes met and Mathilda saw, to her relief, approval, even pleasure in his. Maybe she wasn't muddy after all.

'You will. Do come within. My family are gathered to greet you, my nobles also. You are not too tired?'

It was framed as a question but sounded more like an order.

'No, my lord,' Mathilda agreed, despite having been half the day in the saddle.

She let herself be led up between the dark walls, across a rough earth yard, and into an imposing stone hall. This, thankfully, was as opulent as its exterior was stark. Rich tapestries hung on every wall, dancing in the lively flames of big rush lights on the wide columns supporting the high wooden roof. More light came from a hundred candles burning in elegant holders on two tables draped in cloth and laid all along with silver plates and goblets that winked and glittered as if hiding glorious secrets.

Some twenty or thirty people were gathered between them, chattering intently, though they stopped as she entered. For a moment the world was suspended, then from the richly dressed crowd a woman came forward, slim and elegant with skin as smooth as marble and startling blue eyes bright against her mahogany hair. She carried her beauty with ease and grace and her smile, as she moved to Mathilda and extended her hand, was sweet and open. This must be the infamous Herleva.

'Lady Mathilda, welcome. It's so very lovely to meet you at last. William has talked of little else for many months.'

'This match is of great import for both our provinces,' William said stiffly but Herleva just laughed.

'Of course it is, William, and the beauty of your future duchess is vital for this, is it?'

'It is, Mother. Normandy deserves a jewel.' His tone was flat but he was almost smiling and Mathilda saw his eyes shine as he looked at his mother.

'My son,' Herleva told Mathilda, 'is trained in keeping his finer emotions hidden, but it does not mean they are not there.'

It was spoken lightly but Herleva's blue eyes burned with sudden fierce intent.

'Dukes must stay ever on guard, I am sure.'

'But not with their duchesses.'

She smiled at Mathilda who felt a sharp urge to live up to this welcoming woman's quiet appeal. She would be William's helpmeet in the rule of this stark duchy. It would not be love but it would be so much more. She watched as he moved aside with Count Baldwin, men following eagerly after, and felt a thrill at the thought of what that future might hold for them, but now her mother was coughing pointedly at her side and she turned reluctantly back.

'Lady Herleva, this is my own mother, Countess Adela.'

She ushered Adela forward, noting her stiff bearing as she approached the lady who had once been northern France's most renowned mistress.

'It is a pleasure to meet you,' Adela managed with studied politeness.

'And you, my lady,' Herleva agreed with quiet grace. 'We are honoured by your presence in our humble duchy. I wish we could have received you at Rouen for it is so much more elegant than Eu but William thought a little privacy would be best at this stage.'

'Very wise,' Adela agreed, still stiff. 'We do not want unwelcome intrusions at our celebrations.'

Mathilda shifted uneasily at this reference to the continued lack of papal dispensation. They were to marry in the castle chapel she'd been told and now she could see why – Eu's high walls would keep them safe from the public eye until the marriage was completed and, indeed, consummated. She swallowed and Herleva took her arm.

'There will be no such problem, my dear,' she said softly. 'These objections are just a part of men's endless petty war games and we need not let them trouble us, especially not today. Come, let me introduce my other son, Odo, Bishop of Bayeux.'

Odo came forward – slim and sharply made with an intensity in his narrow eyes.

'Welcome to the family, my lady,' he said, bowing low. 'You make a most beautiful addition.'

'Odo,' Herleva warned in a low voice, adding dryly to Mathilda, 'my second son is yet to embrace the sterner strictures of his office.'

'Your second son,' Odo said easily, 'does not see that they are necessary. Celibacy helps no man.' A laugh burst unexpectedly out of Mathilda and she clapped a hand to her mouth. Odo grinned wolfishly at her. 'I'm glad the new duchess agrees.'

'I . . .' Mathilda started but thankfully Herleva was turning to Judith now and she was spared finding a response.

'Lady Judith, welcome. We invited your mother to join our celebrations but I'm afraid she is frail these days and sent word that God wished her to stay in the cloister.'

'No doubt,' Judith said tightly.

'But William is keen to meet his cousin and over there is your shared uncle, Mauger, Archbishop of Rouen, who will marry William and Mathilda tomorrow.'

Mathilda jumped.

'Tomorrow?' she burst out.

'Does that not suit?'

'Oh. Oh, yes. Yes, it suits very well. I'd just . . .' She glanced nervously to Judith but then caught herself. She was here to be Duchess of Normandy, so why wait? 'It suits very well,' she said more firmly as William rejoined them.

'Cousin,' he said, taking Judith's hand and kissing it. 'Welcome. It is good to have another of the family here in Normandy and, of course, tomorrow Mathilda will join us.'

Judith looked a little stunned to be an 'us'.

'That will be lovely,' she stuttered out. William smiled.

'It will. Family is very important to me. My kin have been my rock when all else has, at times, felt like quicksand.'

Mathilda looked up at him and saw the silver in his eyes flicker as if a ghost had passed behind them but before she could ask more he was taking her arm and turning her to face the room.

'And now,' he called out sharply, 'my nobles!'

He gave a nod to the guards either side of a large internal door and they leaped to open them, revealing a multi-coloured crowd who crushed into the hall like animals released from a pen. They surged forward, pouring around the stone pillars like springwater, every one of them looking huge as they tumbled in on Mathilda's little form so that it was all she could do to stand her ground. Foremost amongst them was a bright-faced man who thankfully skidded to a stop just before reaching Mathilda with a triumphant, 'I won!'

'William FitzOsbern,' William told Mathilda. 'Known to all as Fitz.'

'Because Duke William is William,' Fitz supplied cheerily.

Close up she could see that he wasn't the tallest man in the boisterous crowd but he had broad shoulders and naturally springy limbs and held the rest back with assurance.

'Exactly,' William agreed easily. 'It would be too confusing otherwise. Fitz and I were raised together. His father, Lord Osbern, was one of my guardians until . . .'

The ghost flitted behind William's eyes again but Fitz leaped in: 'And now *I* take care of him.'

'Does he need taking care of?' Mathilda asked, as lightly as she could.

'Oh, yes,' Fitz agreed, his eyes suddenly solemn. 'I'm afraid, my lady, our duke ever puts himself in the path of harm.'

'And yet never,' William countered, 'does harm find me.'

'That much is true. He has the devil's own share of luck but he needs us all the same.' Briefly Fitz looked sad then he visibly shook himself, his messy blonde hair flying out around his open face, and produced a broad smile. 'Now, let me present this fine troop to you, my lady. Firstly – Fulk de Montgomery.'

A huge man with shoulders as wide as hawk-perches pushed easily through the crowd and bowed before her.

'You are welcome to Normandy, Lady Mathilda.'

'I thank you. I . . .'

But already Fitz was pulling forward someone new – a wiry man with a kind face and intelligent eyes.

'Hugh de Grandmesnil,' he introduced him. 'And his cousin, Arnold de Giroie, though you need not worry about him for he is off to Italy any day, following many of Normandy's sons to glory in that land.'

Cousin Arnold bowed.

'I delayed to be here for your wedding, my lady,' he said with a grating obsequiousness.

'You're too kind. Italy?'

'That's right. I have family already established in Calabria and they write that there is much land ripe for the taking. Rich land, sewn with corn and vines.'

'You wish to farm vines?'

A roar of laughter from Fitz made her jump.

'Farm! Brilliant. You have hit it exactly, my lady. His family would have you believe they are brave adventurers, conquerors even, but the brave ones were in Italy ten years ago and have made it safe for all. Farm! Oh, yes. You must remember your plough when you leave, Arnold!'

He laughed again, the others joining in. Arnold looked furious and Mathilda rushed to appease him.

'The land must be won, though. That cannot be easy.'

'Exactly,' Arnold agreed bullishly. 'A man needs a strong sword-arm to thrive in Italy. Look at the Guiscard.'

William sucked in a sharp breath and Mathilda looked anxiously at him but to her surprise he was smiling widely.

'Robert Guiscard was my hero when I was a lad,' he told her.

'Guiscard?' she questioned, the Norman word unfamiliar to her.

'It means cunning, my lady – a fine trait. The Guiscard made his fortune as a robber baron in the hills.'

'A robber baron?'

'Turned great prince, yes. He has taken half of Italy – proof that a man can rise as far as his desire will take him.'

The silver in William's eyes was steel now, sharp as a blade. *A crown can be won*, Baldwin had told Mathilda when she'd first objected to this marriage. She had thought it idle talk, persuasion tactics, but maybe it was more. Did William have his eye on southerly lands?

'You would like to go to Italy, my lord?'

'Me?' William laughed indulgently. 'I would have done,

perhaps, if my fate had taken a different path. I even, perhaps, *should* have done.'

'In what way?' Mathilda asked, intrigued, but Fitz leaped in again.

'But praise God your path has brought you to marriage instead, William.'

'Praise God indeed,' William agreed easily. 'We must get you all wives – it might calm you down.'

Fitz put up both hands.

'I am ready to be "calmed", my duke, if that's what it takes but Fulk here is first in line, are you not, friend?'

'No.'

'He is,' Fitz told Mathilda firmly, as if the big man were a child, 'save that his intended is not so well disposed towards him as he to her.'

'And save,' added Hugh de Grandmesnil quietly, 'that his intended is a venomous snake. Beg pardon, my lady, but Fulk is fool enough to have his eye on Mabel of Belleme.'

'And why not?' Fulk demanded. 'She is heiress to the largest of Duke William's estates.'

'Largest and most rebellious,' Hugh agreed, his voice harsh. 'Besides which she has also inherited her family's talent for treachery and villainy. No one brews poisons like Mabel de Belleme.'

'That's a little harsh, Hugh,' Fulk protested, though not, Mathilda noted, with any great conviction. 'Mabel is just high-spirited.'

'Is she here?' Mathilda asked, looking around and noticing for the first time that the milling crowd in the rich hall was made up almost entirely of men.

'Sadly not,' Fulk said.

Fitz laughed.

'There's nothing sad about it. She's holed up in the south, Mathilda, concocting poisons.'

Mathilda felt her eyes widen foolishly and was glad when William stepped in with a low, 'Easy, Fitz.' He put up a hand to separate him from Fulk whose ham-hock fists had clenched. 'Lady Mabel could not make it, Mathilda, but she sends her regards and fine gifts.'

'Pray they're not edible.'

'Fitz!'

'Sorry.'

Fitz looked anything but sorry. Mathilda scanned the jostling group of young men and felt like a little queen bee in the hive as they buzzed around her, their energy palpable. She wasn't sure she wanted to meet Mabel of Belleme but *some* female company would be nice.

'Are there no women in Normandy?' she asked Herleva quietly, glancing to Adela and Judith, huddled nervously behind her.

Herleva grimaced.

'Very few. The court has, for too long, been a martial one. I pray that may change now.' She looked around. 'Ah, but here is Della!'

She waved and Mathilda saw a large hand wave back. The next moment the group of men was parting and a woman – if woman it was – strode into the gap. She wore a pretty gown of deep pink trimmed with delicate silver leaves, but she was as broad as a man with a face over-filled with features.

'This is Della,' Herleva told Mathilda. 'That is – Lady Adela de Beaumont.'

Mathilda heard her mother splutter behind her at this unlikely namesake and smothered a smile.

'It's a pleasure to meet you, Della – may I call you Della?'

'Lord, yes. Everyone does. Delighted you're here, my lady,

truly. This place needs a feminine touch. The damned duchy is full of savages.'

'And you the most savage of us all, Della,' Fitz countered.

'Nonsense. All you men do is hunt and drink and play tafel.'

'Tafel?'

Mathilda knew the game vaguely. Lord Bruno had a board and was always trying to find opponents but most people avoided it like the pox.

'They are very keen on it here,' Della said wearily.

'It is a game of great tactical skill, Della,' William told her.

'Too great for ladies, clearly,' Fitz teased and Della stiffened.

'I'm sure I could master it if I chose to waste my time that way but I very much hope that Duchess Mathilda will refine the court with more gentle amusements.'

'With sewing perhaps?' Fulk suggested.

'Well . . .'

'And music maybe, or dancing?'

'Dancing?' Mathilda seized on this eagerly. 'Do you like dancing, Della?'

Della shuffled her wide feet.

'It is not perhaps one of my finest talents.' Uproarious laughter. 'But I see the joy of having it. All civilised courts have dancing.'

'Exactly,' Mathilda agreed. 'Will there be dancing tomorrow, William?'

William looked as perplexed as if she had asked for a dragon.

'I had not considered it. Would you like to dance?'

'Oh yes, I'd love to. So would Judith.'

She seized her cousin's arm, forcing her forward. William looked from one to the other.

'I see. Well, then, we will have dancing. Fitz – sort it out.'

'Dancing? For tomorrow?'

'Exactly. Come, man – how hard can it be?'

Now it was Fitz who looked perplexed.

'It matters not,' Mathilda said hastily. 'Truly, my lord, I do not wish to put anyone to any trouble.'

'It is no trouble, is it, Fitz?'

Fitz shook his head mutely.

'But if there is no music . . .' Mathilda said unhappily, noticing for the first time the lack of any minstrels in the hall.

'There *will* be music,' said a new voice from behind her. 'I shall see to it personally.'

She turned to see a dapper man with a warm smile. He looked older than the rest, only by a few years but it showed in the soft lines in his face and the poise in his bearing, despite a very slight limp. His hair was light and unlike all the rest of William's men he wore a beard cut in an impeccable egg-shape on his chin, topped with a matching moustache curled at the edges with oil so that he seemed to perpetually smile.

'Roger de Beaumont,' he introduced himself. 'I believe you've met my lovely wife Della and somewhere amongst the rushes are our two sons, Robbie and Henry.'

Mathilda looked instinctively to her feet as Della hit at her husband, a fond blow but one delivered nonetheless with considerable force.

'Nonsense, Husband. The nurserymaids have them quite safe – look.'

She gestured to a pair of chubby-faced lads fighting to escape the arms of their slender nurses.

'Oh, they're lovely,' Judith said.

'Are they?' Della squinted at her babies. 'They're healthy,' she allowed, 'and I daresay they'll get more interesting as they grow.'

Mathilda exchanged a look with Judith, and Herleva, seeing it, took her arm.

'We have a fine nursery in Rouen,' she told her, 'though of course you may wish to make alterations before . . .'

Her eyes drifted to Mathilda's belly and Mathilda clutched at it nervously, feeling it taut and slender and struggling to imagine it swelling with a babe.

'Time enough, Mathilda,' William whispered into her ear. 'We have not, after all, even begun yet.'

Mathilda's belly spiralled and the room seemed to spin a little. It was all very well thinking of William as a partner in rule but they must share a bed as well as a throne and the boundaries must, surely, blur between the sheets. She blinked furiously. So many people, such a swirl of conversations. All she could see were faces leering in at her as the castle's grim walls had done earlier. She swayed and held tighter to William, willing herself not to faint. Not here, not now. He would think she was weak. She staggered.

'Give her space!' Della commanded, harsh and loud but oh so welcome. 'Poor girl, she doesn't need you lot crowding her and surely to God it must be time to eat?'

Herleva took the cue and signalled to the doors and to Mathilda's great relief a low gong sounded around the hall, shivering through the beautiful tapestries and shaking the rushes at their feet.

'Shall we dine, my lady?' William asked and gratefully Mathilda let him lead her through the crowd of men parting before them as if William were Moses himself.

At the top, beside a large chair that was clearly William's, was a smaller one, still grand and carved with intertwined leaves and flowers. Mathilda reached out a hand to trace the lovely patterns.

'It was my grandmother's,' William told her. 'Lady Gunnora, the last duchess of Normandy.'

'She is dead?'

'Has been some twenty years.'

'But . . .'

'There has been no duchess since, Mathilda, and as you can see we are ready for one. You are still glad you came?'

Mathilda saw anxiety in William's eyes and it melted away all the heat and confusion and tiredness. There was much to learn of this man and his boisterous male court but there would be time enough to do so in the years ahead.

'I am very glad,' she confirmed as she lowered herself onto the padded cushion. She placed her hands along the broad arms of the Duchess of Normandy's chair, trying to ignore the fact that her feet, even in their raised shoes, did not quite reach the ground. 'Very glad indeed.'

CHAPTER SIX

'*P*hew!'
Emeline sank onto the wide wooden bed and stretched herself out across the feather mattress.

'Emeline!' Cecelia admonished. 'That's not your bed.'

Emeline leaped up.

'Sorry. Sorry, my lady. I forgot myself.'

Mathilda was too weary to even answer. She waved her attendant's apologies away and lay down in Emeline's place, gesturing to the others to join her. Cecelia perched her substantial frame on one side but Emeline flung herself down again, curling naturally in towards Mathilda.

'What do you make of all these men then, Em?' Mathilda asked.

'Rich pickings! That Fulk is impressive – have you ever seen so much muscle? He's like a Grecian statue.'

'He's taken,' Cecelia warned.

'By some witch in the south – hardly much of a rival.'

'Hardly worth making an enemy of,' Cecelia corrected sternly. 'Besides, he's *too* big. What about Hugh de Grand-mesnil – he's much lither than Fulk. Quieter too.'

'*Too* quiet,' Emeline retorted. 'And he smells of horses – though I'll warrant he'd ride well.'

She giggled dirtily and Cecelia's eyes narrowed.

'Fitz seems fun,' Mathilda said quickly.

'Fitz *is* fun,' Cecelia agreed, 'though I'm sure he could be as fierce as any, especially if his duke was threatened. His eyes follow him all the time.'

'Like a hound at heel.'

Mathilda shushed Emeline, though she had to admit that there was something of a bouncy, big-eyed dog about William's liveliest companion.

'We all need faithful servants,' she said lightly, squeezing the hands of her own long-time companions.

Cecelia smiled at her.

'You should get to bed now, my lady. It will be an important day tomorrow and you need rest.'

'Can I not just sleep like this?'

'No. You'll crumple your lovely gown and you will need it again. It sounds as if William has many celebrations planned. We go to Rouen next week.'

'Rouen?' Emeline leaped up. 'Oh, that is good news. You will like Rouen, Mathilda. It is a lively place, far more like Bruges than this stark fortress. Come on – up you get and we'll have you tucked in as quickly as we can.'

Mathilda let them heave her to her feet and loosen her laces then stepped out of her gown, glancing as she did so to her wedding dress. Someone, Cecelia no doubt, had taken it from the casket and hung it from a wooden ceiling beam to let the creases drop out. She moved over and put out a hand to the full skirts, watching as the blue of the fabric shifted hue with the light and the miniature stars winked knowingly.

Her eyes moved to the real stars through the slit of a window opening. Her room was in one of Eu's four turrets and she could see the opposite one standing squat against the misty light of a low half-moon as if tensed to pounce. She shivered. All was quiet in the castle save for a murmur of male chatter from the hall. Fitz and his fellows had been drawing stools to the fire as she'd retired and clearly they were not yet abed. William had not, though, been amongst them.

'You will not drink with your friends?' she'd dared to ask as he'd come to the hall door with her.

'No, my lady. I see little merit in late-night ale.' There *was* little merit in late-night ale, though that rarely seemed to stop most men. But then William was not, she was swiftly discovering, most men. 'Besides,' he'd added, taking her hand and kissing it, 'I wish to be rested for tomorrow. It will be a big day for us – a big night too.'

Mathilda had been unable to find any response to this statement, spoken not as flirtation but fact, and had been hugely grateful when he'd released her hand and she'd finally escaped. Now she leaned her head against the stone wall, seeking comfort in its coolness. She could feel rogue tears gathering in the back of her eyes and, on an impulse, threw her arms around Cecelia, surprising her so much that she staggered and Emeline had to catch them. All three stood there for a moment, wrapped together.

'I'm so glad you're staying here with me,' she told them, looking from one dear face to the other.

'Of course we're staying with you,' Cecelia said. 'We'll never leave, will we, Em?'

'Never,' the other girl agreed solemnly. 'Never, never, never.'

She held Mathilda so tight it squeezed a smile, at last, onto her lips.

'Thank you,' she said quietly and made for her bed but she was stopped again by a sharp rap at the door.

She stared at it in fright as Emeline went cautiously to answer.

'Gift for the Lady Mathilda,' came a gruff voice from outside and they all watched, stunned, as Emeline pulled back the door and two guards entered carrying, most incongruously, a gown.

They set it down and it seemed to stand there all by itself as if waiting to be introduced. Mathilda took an uneasy step back.

'"Tis on some sort of stand, my lady,' Cecelia whispered.

'I knew that.'

Feeling foolish, Mathilda approached again. The dress was cream, though not the unbleached colour of a linen undershift but a richer, deeper hue like milk fresh from the cow. Even in the flourishing textile markets of Flanders, Mathilda had rarely seen its like and she put out a hand to touch it. It was wool but wool so fine it felt almost like silk and it was studded all over with pearls and jewels, sewn in with golden thread that laced across the surface like a delicate spider's web.

'It's beautiful.'

'Good,' one guard said.

'Wear it tomorrow,' the other instructed and then, with a curt bow, they were gone.

Mathilda watched the dark space they'd left behind then her eyes went back to the gown and from there to her original dress, hanging almost apologetically behind the creation in the centre of the room.

'I will not even have my own dress,' she said forlornly.

Emeline put an arm around her shoulders.

'You will have it still, just not tomorrow. But look, Mathilda, have you ever seen such beauty? Or such expense? William must treasure you indeed.'

'But a dress? From a man? Who, here in this court without even a musician, could arrange such a dress? And why did William not warn me?'

'Maybe he wanted to surprise you.'

'Well, he did that.' Mathilda turned and clambered into bed. 'Remember when Brihtric crept into my chamber and sprinkled rose petals between my sheets so that I would dream of him. That was a good surprise.'

Cecelia pursed her lips.

'That was a foolish surprise and a reckless one besides. You would both have been in trouble if your father had found out. William's gesture is far more appropriate to a lady of your stature.'

She was right, Mathilda supposed. She looked for Emeline who would always, she was sure, prefer the petals but for once the wilder of her ladies was avoiding her gaze. Sighing, she burrowed down into the soft covers but she could still see the dress, hovering like a spectre at her feet. So this was the wife she was to be – this was the queen bee's costume. It was beautiful, yes, but with all those jewels it looked heavy and that first night in Normandy she slept uneasily in its shining shadow.

CHAPTER SEVEN

$\mathcal{M}$athilda stepped out onto the top of the wooden staircase leading down the side of the hall from the upper chambers and gasped to see the myriad people gathered below her. Word of her nuptials had clearly gone out to the folk of Eu yesterday and it seemed that every local family was here to sneak a privileged first peek at the new duchess. They filled the big yard within the castle's high walls, save where William's crimson-cloaked guards were holding them back to create a pathway to the small stone church on the far side.

Mathilda blinked, feeling even smaller than usual before this vast crowd, and strove to gather herself. The morning had been lost in frantic preparations, for the new gown had been a little wide and only Cecelia's lightning needle had ensured she was not stood here looking like a costly sack of flour. She was glad of it now though, for as she stepped down the exposed stairs the radiant garment drew all eyes away from her face and was as much armour as ornamentation.

Her father was waiting at the bottom to lead her through the crowds. Taking his arm, she fought to keep her head high and tried to smile on those clamouring for a sight of her. But the myriad hands reaching out between the burly guards caught at her nerves, and she was grateful when she finally saw William waiting on the rough-hewn steps up to the chapel door.

Her groom matched her in almost every detail. His tunic was of identical fabric to her gown and was worn over light hose and beautiful leather boots polished so highly they shone almost as much as the golden threads. He was, again, wearing the glittering helmet he had greeted her in yesterday, its heavy shine shading his eyes, but as she approached he swept it from his head and fixed her in an appraising stare. Almost she stumbled and her father had to tighten his hold on her arm.

'You are doing well, Mathilda,' he whispered and when she looked up she could see his eyes shining with a pride that buoyed her confidence.

Holding the hem of her gown very carefully, she joined William on the church steps and his uncle Mauger came forward in his rich archbishop's robes. This was it then. This was her wedding. She should try and take it all in to remember later at some future point of calm but it was happening so fast for already the archbishop, with Norman efficiency, was moving straight to the exchange of vows.

Mathilda gave her answers as prompted and suddenly Mauger was placing her hand in William's and lifting them for all to see. Mathilda could feel the sword-calluses of William's huge hand against her fingers, the archbishop's sweaty grasp as he forced their hands up so high she was raised onto tiptoe, and the warm gold of the ring William had placed on her finger digging in as he gripped her tight.

'I now pronounce you husband and wife in the Lord's sight. May God bless you and shine His light upon you.'

Obligingly a low cloud completed its journey across the sun and they were flooded in light. Mathilda tipped her face towards it, feeling the warmth like a blessing.

'It seems God is not displeased with this union,' William said, the first words he had spoken directly to her.

'Would it have stopped you if He was?'

'Would it you?'

'No, my lord.'

'Nor I neither. I will continue to fight for the papal blessing, Mathilda, and I *will* secure it but I believe we can proceed firm in the belief that this is meant to be. We were designed for each other by the Lord himself.'

Mathilda thoughts leaped instantly to Lord Brihtric. She had believed God had intended him for her husband for it had felt so very perfect between them, but she had been wrong. She could only hope that this time she had judged correctly. She prayed that her father had burned the letter she had sent to the Saxon suggesting she would welcome his advances, for William, miraculously, seemed to have no knowledge of the incident and she intended to keep it that way.

'We will do much together, Mathilda,' William was saying. 'We must go within to pray in a moment but first . . .'

He looked almost shyly at the crowd, all eyes turned expectantly their way, and suddenly Mathilda realised what was coming. Her heart raced and she planted her feet firmly on the stone step to steady herself as she tipped her face up to her new husband. Their eyes locked in sharp understanding that this, their first kiss, was for show, but even so, when William put a gentle hand on her waist and bent low to press his lips to hers, she felt the touch jolt between them and gave way gratefully to his confidence.

She was pleased to see a few more women when finally they made it to the great hall for the feast. They were mainly the sisters of William's core men and they fell over themselves to tell Mathilda how pleased they were to have a duchess in Normandy. There was, Mathilda learned, no formal ladies' bower in any of William's key fortresses save at Herleva's Falaise and in Rouen, and she made many a promise to help ensure one was set up in various castles whose names she knew she would not afterwards remember.

'We should write all this down,' she found time to say to Cecelia.

'I shall secure some parchment tomorrow, my lady.'

'Good. There is much, it seems, to be done here.'

But before that, she must greet all the wedding guests, first amongst them a dark, elegant man.

'Raoul d'Amiens, my lady,' he introduced himself with a graceful bow. 'I come from the French court to bring you the good wishes of King Henri, Duke William's overlord and your own dear uncle. And with them this gift.'

He clicked his fingers and two servants rushed forward carrying a beautiful casket of dark wood, carved all over with leaves and flowers and woodland creatures. The lid was inlaid with pearl and bore, in gold lettering, the words: *Mathilda of Normandy*. Mathilda heard Adela exclaim in pleasure at this costly gesture from her royal brother, but she was fixed on her new title.

'It looks well, does it not?' William said at her side then, louder, 'King Henri does us much honour. He is a gracious and generous overlord and I am honoured to become his nephew.'

He took Mathilda's hand, rubbing his thumb proprietarily across the jewelled wedding band.

'Thank you, Lord Raoul,' Mathilda said and the man smiled at her, his dark eyes twinkling before moving aside to bow to a flushed Adela.

Mathilda watched him go. He was lithe and graceful and something about him drew you. It certainly, Mathilda noted with some amusement, drew Emeline. Her attendant was watching him intently as he conversed with Adela, her head tilted slightly to one side in a way Mathilda knew from long experience meant trouble for the subject of her attentions.

'What about Lord Everard, Em?' she whispered to her.

'Lord Everard is busy,' Emeline said, not taking her eyes off Raoul for a moment.

'Doing what?'

'Guarding.'

'Funny,' Mathilda said mildly, 'that never stopped him before.'

Emeline frowned.

'Yes, well, I'm attendant to a duchess now; I should set my sights higher.'

Cecelia groaned.

'Raoul d'Amiens is married, Emeline.'

'But for too long and not happily, I hear.' Clearly Emeline had been busy with her enquiries. 'The lady is not even here.'

'That does not mean he is free,' Cecelia said primly but Emeline waved this lightly away.

'Apparently he plans to marry his daughter to Lord Evelin of Mortemer, so perhaps he will be visiting Normandy more in the future. Don't worry, Cee. Marriages are just for political advantage – most people look elsewhere for fun.' Mathilda raised her eyebrow at her and had the pleasure of seeing Emeline for once flush in confusion. '*Some* marriages,' she corrected herself quickly. 'I'm sure yours, my lady, will be both.'

Mathilda looked to William, talking earnestly with slender Hugh de Grandmesnil, and wasn't sure that 'fun' was quite the right word but what did that matter? She was a duchess, not a loose-living attendant. Just then William turned as if he had caught her thoughts and in three long strides he was at her side.

'Shall we take our seats, my lady?' he asked, proffering his arm and adding, in case she was under any illusion that she had a choice, 'Come.'

She laid her hand on his and together they moved up to the wooden dais at the top end of the hall. Spotting the move, the court swiftly scrabbled to take their own seats, scrapping for precedence along the side benches.

'Like cats in a barn,' William moaned, glaring round. 'Why do they not know their place?'

'This is not battle, my lord. The ladies, in particular, have no clear rank.'

'The ladies!' William echoed almost wearily and Mathilda felt suddenly nervous that her new husband was not as keen on a civilised court as he'd made out.

'Perhaps we could arrange for placecards,' she suggested, 'to tell people where to sit.'

William looked at her admiringly.

'Excellent idea,' he said. 'Do so.' Mathilda glanced to Cecelia who nodded discreetly; placecards would be first on Mathilda's list once parchment was found. William took her hand. 'I am very pleased with you so far, Mathilda,' he said earnestly.

Mathilda spluttered her thanks and cast around for something to say in her turn.

'I must thank you, William, for my gift. The dress is truly beautiful.'

'Good. I'm so pleased that it fits.'

Mathilda resisted looking at Cecelia.

'Perfectly. How did your tailor know my size?'

William shrugged.

'I told him you were as high as my heart and as wide as my shield.'

'That's beautiful, William.'

'Is it? Oh. Good. It's certainly true.'

'And now *I* can shield you.'

He looked puzzled.

'I had thought of it more the other way round – that I must shield you.'

'That too,' Mathilda agreed. 'It should work both ways, should it not? We are to be a partnership after all.'

'We are,' he said thoughtfully, then more definitely, 'we are.'

'What, then, can l shield you from?'

He thought again and eventually said, 'Perhaps, Mathilda, you will shield me from myself. I am a rough-edged warrior. If my father had not died I might have had chance to become more . . . polished. But then I might *not* have had chance to be duke. My father would have married, had other sons. I would have been pushed down the ranks.'

'Left to adventure in Italy?' Mathilda suggested, suddenly understanding his words yesterday.

'Like the Guiscard, exactly.'

'You would have liked that?'

'Maybe. But we must take the path God chooses for us and this is mine. Being a warrior has kept me in Normandy but it does not, perhaps, enable me to govern her in a civilised way. You will help me do that, Mathilda, won't you?'

'Of course, my lord, in whatever humble fashion I can.'

William laughed and leaned closer.

'Come, Mathilda, this is you and I now. We are a – what did you say? – a partnership. We need not be falsely modest with each other. I do not think you are any more humble than I am and I like you for it.'

Mathilda was lost for words. Such frankness was disarming. William was right of course. 'Humble' was not a word she could in all honesty associate with herself but to have that spoken aloud was disturbing.

'I shock you, Mathilda?'

'Not shock. I am just not used to people so openly saying what they mean.'

'Surely all else is a waste of time?'

'You are right,' Mathilda agreed. 'The truth should be enough but maybe it is just that, at times, a little honey coating is nice.'

William laughed and Fitz looked over.

'Your wife entertains you, my duke?'

'She would have me coated in honey, Fitz.'

'A glorious idea, Duchess, but would we not, then, stick to him?'

'Do you not already?'

There was a moment's pause in which Mathilda feared she had overstepped the decidedly faint mark of manners in this strange Norman court but thankfully Fitz was not one to offend easily and he just laughed again. And now, at last, people were settling, some more contently than others, and the meal could begin.

It seemed to last forever as course after course was brought out – light fish in buttery sauces, rich rolls of pork stuffed with wild mushrooms, soft-fleshed peacock with sweet onion – until even Count Baldwin, a man who loved his food, pronounced himself 'as stuffed as a boar at Christ's mass'. William smiled in satisfaction and waved in one final course – a giant pastry braid, studded with nuts and dripping with honey and elegantly twisted into the joined initials: WM.

'Look,' William said happily, 'we are each other's inverse.'

The proud chef demonstrated this for all by turning his great confection both ways to show it still read the same.

'That's so clever,' Mathilda said, delighted. 'My compliments,

Chef.' He bowed low as everyone clapped and Mathilda turned to William. 'And see, my lord, we are honey-coated.'

William laughed.

'So we are, Mathilda, so we are. Is it time, do you think, for your dancing?'

He pronounced the word as if it were somehow foreign but already Roger de Beaumont was hurrying lopsidedly to the far end of the hall to usher in a troop of three minstrels he had conjured up from somewhere.

'See,' Fitz said, 'La Barbe has it all sorted.'

'La Barbe?' Mathilda queried but then, looking at Roger pulling at the ends of his fine moustache as he marshalled the musicians, she saw the reasoning for herself. La Barbe – the Beard. It suited him.

La Barbe glanced awkwardly around, then Mathilda saw Raoul d'Amiens move to join him and understood – the minstrels were French. Perhaps Raoul travelled with them as a matter of course; he seemed the sort of man who might. The Norman court were looking at each other, William's men with uncertainty, their sisters with delight though, too late, Mathilda realised that without partners versed in the basic steps there might be little to enjoy in the dances.

'You will lead them out, my lord?' she asked William.

'I will not. I cannot dance.'

'It's not hard. I could . . .'

He put up a hand and she bit her lip to silence herself.

'I cannot dance. I have always been a man for the tafel board after dinner, so I have no skill. I *will* dance, if you wish it, but only once I am competently trained. Let Raoul do it – he's French. Raoul!'

The Frenchman turned, bowed and approached. He looked at Mathilda, clearly unsure what William intended, but she shook her head firmly and his eye was thankfully caught by Emeline, bobbing eagerly up and down along the table.

'Would you do me the honour, my lady?'

She was up like a frog in springtime, taking one of Raoul's hands with a pretty blush as he waved for more dancers with his other. Adela rose and Count Baldwin, rolling his eyes to William, let himself be led into the space between the tables by his wife. Herleva was next on her feet, led by kind-faced Lord Herluin, the noble husband William's father had found for her before he went away on his fatal pilgrimage. Roger de Beaumont dragged a protesting Della into the line on Adela's other side and Odo, in full bishop's dress, pulled a startled but delighted Judith into place beyond them to complete the scrappy set. Then, with a flourish from Raoul, the dance – if dance it was – began.

Raoul and Emeline were naturally graceful, Baldwin and Adela more formally so. Mathilda was delighted to see Herleva and Herluin matching them easily but the rest were less smooth. Roger and Della threw themselves into the moves with enthusiasm if not with much style, Roger's limp giving them a certain sideways skew. Odo had some natural ability and, had he let Judith guide him, would have danced well, but instead he took the lead with a certainty that was admirable if misplaced. The overall effect was chaotic.

'So this is dancing?' William said curiously to Mathilda.

'This is a *form* of dancing,' she corrected him. 'Try and imagine it with all dancers mirroring each other.'

'Like a tafel board?'

Mathilda glanced to the symmetrical pieces on the neglected boards at the side of the hall.

'I suppose so.'

'It would certainly be more orderly that way,' William said dryly, watching Della trip over Roger's feet and turn a fall expertly into a wild spin. 'They look a little foolish, do they not?'

'But content,' Mathilda dared to suggest as Herluin and Herleva floated past, holding each other tight.

For a moment William watched his mother then suddenly he said, 'We should retire.'

Panic shot through Mathilda. Other couples were rising to join the dances and she had thought the evening only just begun.

'Now, my lord?'

'Why not? This dancing seems to have everyone amused so they need us no longer.'

His logic could not be faulted.

'But if we leave,' Mathilda said, 'they will have to stop.'

'You wish to be formally escorted to your bedchamber?'

'No!' Mathilda looked at William and saw a wicked little smile on his lips. 'You would sneak away, my lord?'

'I will willingly sneak, Mathilda, if you will sneak with me?'

Mathilda glanced around the hall and saw all faces turned to the ever-growing number of dancers. Even sturdy Cecelia had been lured onto the floor by a laughing Fitz and for the first time all day no one was watching their duke and duchess.

'I will sneak,' she agreed and before she could change her mind she boldly put her hand into William's and let him lead her quietly through a little door behind them and out into the night.

CHAPTER EIGHT

*W*illiam put a hand to the heavy latch of his private chamber and looked to Mathilda.

'Ready?'

She wasn't, of course, but she would never be so she just nodded.

'Good.'

He lifted the latch. A clatter from within told of servants scrambling to compose themselves and William, to Mathilda's surprise, paused a moment to give them time before striding inside. Two young guards stood to attention either side of a roaring brazier but William dismissed them to the other side of the door with strict instructions to let no one come in and within moments they were alone.

'What now, William?'

He smiled at her.

'We should probably undress.'

'Yes.'

She looked around.

'Is that a problem?'

'I have no attendants and my dress is laced at the back.'

'Ah. Well, I can do that.'

He moved behind her and reached for the ribbons. Mathilda stood very still, conscious of his fingers against her back and his breath on her neck. Soon she would know what all the fuss was about – or she might, if William's warrior fingers could manage her laces.

'The knot is very tight,' he said gruffly, fumbling.

Mathilda caught the impatience in his voice and feared angering him.

'Shall I . . . ?' she suggested, trying to lift her hands over her shoulders but just then, with a little cry of triumph, he untied the knot and pulled the ribbon all the way out of the loops in a long fluid motion.

For a moment the gown clung to her shoulders and then the heavy fabric collapsed and slid to her wrists. Mathilda shrugged it away and the gown flopped to the floor as if exhausted. She looked down at the jewels now drowning in the folds of cream material but already William was taking her hand and helping her to step out of it and towards the bed.

'Sit down, Mathilda.'

She sank onto the edge of William's big bed, feeling the softness of the furs through her flimsy undershift as he knelt before her and reached for her foot.

'Heavens,' he objected, regarding her neat boots, 'these fastenings are tight too.'

'I have very small feet, my lord.'

'Call me William. Ah, there we are.'

He released her foot from the first boot and, untying the ribbon binding it below her knee, rolled away her hose. His fingers on the skin of her ankle made her shudder with anticipation and he stroked it thoughtfully.

'Do you like that?'

'It feels nice,' she agreed, 'but I am nervous.'

'Nervous? Please don't be. I won't hurt you, Mathilda.'

'I know. I know that, my lord . . . William. But I want to please you.'

'Oh, you please me, don't worry about that. What matters, Wife, is if I please you.'

'It is?'

'Yes. My mother was most definite about that.'

'Your mother?'

'She told me very firmly that I must remember that the act is not just for men but for women too and I should be sure to ask you what you liked.'

'But I don't know what I like.'

'So we will find out.'

He sounded so certain.

'This is not your first time?' she dared to ask.

He rose and began calmly removing his tunic.

'No. I lay with several women a few weeks ago in preparation.'

Mathilda blinked.

'A few women? All at once?'

He laughed heartily.

'No! Over several nights.'

'Oh. I see.'

'I don't think you do. I paid them, Mathilda.'

'Paid them? They were concubines? But you're a duke, William. You could . . .'

'Have anyone I choose? I know, Mathilda, believe me I know – my father spent half his life having anyone he could choose – but I wanted professionals.'

'Why?'

William was removing his tunic now, exposing a lean, muscular chest sprinkled, to Mathilda's surprise, with soft, dark hair. She reached up a hand to touch it and William moved closer and pulled her to standing. The hairs were feather-soft against her fingertips and the muscle rock hard beneath and she felt a shudder of something she hoped might be desire.

'I wanted professionals, Mathilda, to show me what to do – how to please you.'

'Oh. And, er, did they?'

'They showed me only that every woman is different. You will need to teach me about yourself.'

'But I do not . . .'

'We will learn together. May I remove your shift?'

Mathilda swallowed and nodded. She raised her arms and he bunched the skirts up in his big hands and lifted the garment cleanly away leaving her naked.

'Ah, Mathilda,' he said, 'I thought you were beautiful in that dress but you are much, much more so without it. No, please, do not cover yourself – why hide such glory?' He threw the shift to the floor and reached out towards her breast. 'May I?' he asked again.

'Of course you may.'

He stopped, his hand still hovering, so close she could feel the heat of its intent.

'I know I *may*, Mathilda. I know I am permitted. I have wed you. Under Norman law I can do more or less whatever I wish with you, but I wish to do what *you* wish.'

He was looking at her so intently she longed to turn away, to hide her nakedness under the covers and have him get on with it and leave her be. She felt exposed and awkward but she could hardly complain at his kindness.

'You may touch me,' she forced herself to say and then she dared to lean forward so that her breast brushed his finger. His grip tightened and she winced. 'Not so hard.'

She regretted the instruction immediately but William simply loosened his grip, running his fingers over her nipple instead so it rose to welcome him. Little shoots of something that might become pleasure rippled out from his touch.

'Good?'

'Yes.'

His other hand moved to her other breast. They both looked down at it, as if there might be some outward sign of her enjoyment but there was none, save the rounding of her nipples. He was right – the only way he would know if she liked what he was doing would be if she told him, but in all her extensive education no one had given her the vocabulary to express this. She would have to work it out for herself, as Emeline had presumably done.

She let her hands run round from William's chest to his back. The muscles flexed and she heard his breath catch and felt his excitement ignite her own. Dropping her hands to the waistline of his trews, she felt for the ties that held them.

'May I?' she asked.

'Please do.' But then he stepped back and put a hand over her own to stop her. 'I am aroused, Mathilda.'

'Good. That's good, isn't it?'

'Oh, yes, but I may not be as . . . controlled as I should.' Mathilda looked blankly at him. 'My mother says women need time and I may not, erm, last that long, not at first. It's just that you are so beautiful and you are my wife and . . .'

'And we have all night, William. Nay, all our lives.'

'Yes. Yes, you are right, Mathilda. How wonderful. It's just that my father, so I'm told, was a very great lover.'

'Your mother told you that?'

Mathilda thought of Adela's scathing comments about 'making heirs' and couldn't imagine ever having such a conversation with her.

'She did and half the court besides. He was known for it.'

'Is it any wonder,' Mathilda suggested, 'if he had as much practice as you say. Your mother was not his only mistress?'

'Lord, no. She was his favourite, I think, but Duke Robert was a man of . . . appetites.'

'And you wish to be like him?'

Mathilda heard her voice wobble and hated herself for it. All great men had mistresses, everyone knew that. She just hadn't expected to have to confront that on her wedding night. But now William grabbed her and clamped her close.

'No, Mathilda,' he said, so loud it echoed off the walls. 'I do not wish to be like him in that respect. We will share a chamber from now on, my wife, so I will be always at your side. I lay with concubines solely to learn how to do well for you.'

'Like military training?'

'Exactly like. How is a man to excel at something without experience?'

'You like to excel, William?'

'I do. I must if I am to hold my dukedom – and my duchess.'

'You are holding me already,' she pointed out, looking up at him through her lashes as she had oftimes seen Emeline do. She felt his response against her hips and, liking it, put her hands again to the ties of his trews.

'So I am,' he said, 'and you must know, Mathilda, that I will never hold another woman from this day forward. Though I may, my beautiful wife, wish to hold *you* quite often.' With a sudden, surprising grin, he lifted her into his arms and laid her on the bed. Winding his trews free, he knelt up over her, his arousal now clear. Mathilda tried not to look. 'I am going to touch you and you are going to say if it is nice. Yes?'

Mathilda nodded. This was nothing like she'd imagined. Nothing, she suspected, like the average bride's experience, but William was not the average bridegroom. He was looking at her with admiration, tenderness even, but also with fierce concentration as if she were a battle he would win. That made her feel both excited and terrified but it was a combination she was getting used to with her new husband and she understood there was little to do but submit.

'Are you going to kiss me, William?' she asked.

'Would you like me to?'

'Yes.'

'Then I will. And after that we will find your joy.' It was, as usual with William, a statement of intent. 'You are ready?' he asked again.

Mathilda looked at her body, naked before his, and reached an arm up around his neck.

'I am ready.'

William was true to his word and tireless in his diligence. At some point the court, alerted to their duke's escape, came to the door calling indignantly raucous jokes, but the guards stood firm and eventually they stomped away. William barely even glanced up, so intent was he upon his bride.

'That's good,' Mathilda told him so many times she lost count but he was not satisfied. 'There is better,' he insisted and then suddenly, somewhere in the darkest part of the night, there was better. Much better.

'You were right,' Mathilda panted into his chest afterwards, burrowing herself against him, ashamed of her own involuntary cries.

'I am always right,' he said easily. 'Do not be embarrassed, Mathilda. Pleasure is the goal in the marriage bed so to achieve it is a success.'

It sounded so calculated that way but also strangely comforting. Clearly love was not needed for effective union. Mathilda looked up at him and he kissed her.

'Can I sleep now?'

He kissed her again.

'Of course you can, my Mathilda, my Maud, my Mora.'

'Mora?'

'My *amor* – my love. Is that not right? I have little Latin.'

'Mora?' She tried the strange name. 'It is right enough.'

'You do not like it?'

'No, I do. I like it very much.'

'Then I shall call you it, just between us, as an indicator of my love.'

'Love?' she echoed squeakily. She was touched if a little thrown by his choice of word and hastily added, 'I am truly your duchess now.'

'You are. Are you pleased with your choice of husband?'

On that, at least, she was sure.

'Very pleased.' She could feel sleep tugging at her but fought it. 'I am delighted, William, truly.'

'Good.' He kissed her yet again and pulled the covers up around them, tucking them in. Her eyes closed blissfully. 'But do not,' she half-heard him say, 'be too content with duchess.'

'Why, William?'

'Because I swear, my Mora, that as I have brought you joy on this, our first night together, I will one day bring you a crown. It may take time and patience and we may have to try different means to achieve it, but I will bring you a crown.'

That woke her up.

'Which crown, William?'

He curled closer to her and dropped his own voice as close to a whisper as she suspected it could get.

'England, Mathilda.' She gasped and he kissed her quiet. 'I know people in King Edward's court. Influential people. The new Archbishop of Canterbury was previously Abbot of Jumièges and my confessor as a youth. He is kind enough to promote my interests to my cousin – my *childless* cousin.'

Mathilda felt a thrill shoot down to her core, chasing the sensations William's fingers had roused in her just a little time before, but did not dare surrender to it.

'Surely the Saxons will not want a Norman on their throne, William?'

'Why not? Cnut was a Dane and he ruled for years. And I am related to the crown. Edward's mother is my great-aunt and I knew him as a boy.'

'Edward?' Mathilda sat up, fascinated. She'd known King Edward had been an exile in Normandy for years but had stupidly not thought of William spending time with him. 'What is he like?'

'I don't know about now, but back then I remember him as mainly angry. The first year I was duke we gave him and his brother Alfred ships to try and claim the English throne after Cnut's death. I was only eight, Mathilda, but I was caught up in the excitement of it – for a while at least.'

'What happened?'

'It did not go well. Alfred landed and marched on London but was arrested. Edward decided to return to Normandy without ever even leaving the harbour at Sandwich, which was probably a wise decision but I remember being very disappointed. Plus, Edward was even more angry after that.'

'With you?'

'No, with Earl Godwin – for he was the one who arrested his brother and then had his eyes put out so hideously that he died of the bleeding.'

Mathilda grimaced.

'No wonder he does not like him.' Her thoughts flew to Judith. 'My cousin is to marry Tostig Godwinson, you know.'

'I'd heard, yes. I fear it is not a wise choice for her. That family's star is waning as Edward's rises.'

'And yours with it, William?'

'Perhaps. I was only thirteen when Edward left Normandy but I had been duke for six years and had done my best to support him. I believe I have his gratitude and he might, per-haps, see that I have the makings of a good king.'

'Of an *excellent* king, William.'

'Thank you.' He pulled her into his arms. 'And you an even more excellent queen. You have royal blood, so deserve a throne, my beautiful Mathilda.'

Again she felt the thrill and again she resisted. The thought of being a queen was exciting, of course, and the very possibil-ity of it felt like a vindication of her choice of husband, a reward even. But she did not want to inspire war.

'You need not win this for me, William, truly. Duchess is a good title.'

'It is, Mathilda, it is, but there is better. There is definitely better and I will find it for you.'

She did not doubt it and as sleep tugged at her again her thoughts drifted to England. It seemed she might truly be heading there after all and not through cowardly Brihtric but through Duke William. Forget love, she had made the right choice of husband and could face the future with pride.

CHAPTER NINE

Bruges, July 1051

'Tostig Godwinson,' Judith breathed, unable to believe he was really here.

He was a beautiful man, fine-boned and fluid, with a natural grace and a contained confidence that made Judith burst with pride.

'He's here for me,' she whispered to herself and was instantly overcome with a fear of disappointing him.

Her ladies, appointed once the Godwinson family's visit had been confirmed, had spent most of the day readying her. She could have painted all of the Virgin's veil in the time it had taken to wash and comb her hair through and wind it into a great coil of braids. She even had eastern rouge on her lips and kohl around her eyes, as if she were a painting herself, and the thought of that false beauty buoyed her a little as her intended husband approached.

'Lady Judith.' His voice was warm and lingered over her name, making it sound as exotic as her cosmetics made her feel. 'Are you truly to be my wife?'

'I believe so, my lord,' Judith stuttered, 'if you are willing?'

'Oh, I am willing, Judith. You look delectable.'

'Delectable?'

They were talking in the Saxon tongue, one, amongst others, she had learned to speak in Adela's schoolroom, but this word eluded her. Torr stepped closer.

'Good enough to eat,' he elucidated, his voice low.

Judith flushed.

'You are hungry, my lord?'

His eyes, the green of Italian olives, sparkled.

'Always, Judith, but please, you must call me by my name if we are to be . . . intimate.'

'Tostig,' she tried, the Saxon vowels unfamiliar on her lips.

'Exactly. Or better still, Torr.'

'Why?'

'It means "Tower". Many call me it – you will find out why soon enough.'

Judith flushed so deeply she could feel the heat running all the way to her stomach. She wasn't entirely sure what this handsome man meant but the tone was one she had heard from Emeline too many times to mistake. For once she felt no yearning to escape the hall and hide in her inks; tonight *she* was the colour.

'Where will we live,' she dared to ask, 'once we are wed?'

His face darkened a little.

'I have estates near Hereford, in the west. It is a beautiful area – rich and fertile. You will like it, Judith.'

'You are lord there?'

His face darkened further and he ran an agitated hand through his rich hazel hair.

'Lord of those lands, yes, though it is not my own earldom.'

The last words were ground out on a harsh rasp and she rushed to soothe him.

'Mayhap it will one day be yours?'

'Mayhap, for all the use that is. Wessex is the land to have, Judith, but my brother Harold will get that, for he gets everything. Be under no illusion, I am but a younger son and not like to get anything much.'

The colours of Judith's evening swum slightly but she had been bred at court and was not easily thrown.

'At least you *are* a son. I am Count Baldwin's sister. With our father dead and my mother gone into a nunnery I am last in the family line – a misfit.'

He looked at her curiously then suddenly snatched her hand.

'Then you are even more perfect for me than I knew, Judith of Flanders. We can be misfits together. Do you dance?'

'Oh, yes.'

'Good. I love to dance.'

Judith thought of Mathilda in Eu, frozen on a high-backed chair in her jewel-stiff gown, her husband staring at the haphazard Norman dancers as if they were mythical beasts to puzzle over, and felt a rush of pleasure. Relieved that his dark mood seemed to have lifted, she let Tostig – Torr? – lead her out onto the floor and, to her amazement, saw other couples scramble to take a place at their side as if she were suddenly someone worth following. The thought gave her another shiver of confidence and she lifted her ribcage.

'Heavens,' Torr said, his eyes fixed on her breasts where they swelled beneath the fine fabric of her gown, 'I think the sooner we are wed the better – do you not, Father?'

Judith turned, startled, to see Earl Godwin himself on her other side. She blinked, for the great Englishman dazzled. His bulky warrior's body was adorned with more gold than Judith had seen in her life, even on the precious days she'd been allowed to explore Adela's jewellery casket. He had huge twisted coils of it wrapped around his arms from wrist to elbow and more around the bulge of his muscles. His thick fingers were ringed with it and the double cloak-clasps he wore on either hulking shoulder glinted like boats sailing into a blazing sunset.

'Delighted to meet you,' he boomed, clasping her hand in both of his and shaking it earnestly.

'And I you, my lord. I have heard much of your great deeds.'

'Great deeds? Great treasures more like, yes? It's all men say of me.' He did not look as if this concerned him one jot. 'You will be a most welcome addition to the family, Judith. May I call you Judith? Excellent, excellent. Such a forward-thinking county, Flanders, so active, so connected.'

'Yes,' Judith said, wishing she could think of something more intelligent but Godwin did not seem to care.

'I have long looked for an alliance with your family.'

This did not quite ring true and Judith looked around awkwardly as the earl blustered on and the last couples slotted into the set. Torr was running his fingers over hers in a most distracting way and Godwin sparkled so much it was hard to concentrate but she remembered talk of the Norman advisors and had to be sure all was well.

'You sail with King Edward's blessing?' she dared to ask.

Godwin put up a meaty hand.

'Something like that,' he agreed, adding in a sudden, dizzying surge of confidence, 'Kings are contrary beasts, Judith. They ask to be advised then complain at that advice. They demand loyalty but don't always return it. They . . .'

'Hush, Godwin,' his wife Gytha said, grabbing at his hand, 'the dance is starting and poor Judith doesn't want to hear your old man's grumblings.'

'Oh, no,' Judith assured her, 'I'm very interested.'

But the minstrels were striking up a tune and Torr was pulling her close and his free hand was sneaking around her waist to guide her away from talk of kings and she gave in easily. She felt as if she were gliding, so sure was Torr's hold, so commanding his steps, and sensing other girls watching jealously, she moved a little closer. Torr responded immediately, his hand dropping down to brush the curve of her bottom with such a light touch it might almost not have been there at all save her blood singing in awareness of him.

'Steady there,' Count Baldwin said, moving past with Adela, 'she's not yours yet, young man.'

Judith was mortified but Torr did not for one moment loosen his hold.

'Oh, I think she is,' he said so low only Judith could hear, 'are you not, my Judith?'

And God help her, she was.

The days passed, each one giddier than the next. The wedding was set for seven days' time and every day Torr sought her out, riding at her side if they went around Bruges, hastening to bring her his game from the hunt, and moving to join her the moment she entered the hall. One day she even found him outside her room. She'd sent one of her ladies, a giddy girl called Aileen, to fetch her gown from the guardrobe and the fool had been so long she went after her. She found Aileen in the central antechamber, Judith's gown crumpled in her arms and her hair askew. And there, just behind her, was Lord Tostig.

'What are you doing?' she asked, surprised into bluntness.

'I came to find you, Judith.'

'I do not generally linger in antechambers,' she said, looking suspiciously from Torr to Aileen.

'As you should not. I intended to knock at your door but I found this young lady in some distress in the guardrobe.'

Aileen bobbed a sideways curtsey, catching her foot in the gown so that Judith had to put out a hand to steady her and save it ripping.

'I, I caught my hair,' Aileen stuttered.

'On one of the gown hooks,' Torr supplied. 'I think she must have tried to free herself but only got in a worse tangle. I heard her whimpering from the stairs.'

'I'm sorry, my lady,' Aileen said shakily. 'I didn't want to put your gown down because Countess Adela especially said to be careful with it, so I only had one hand and I can be a little clumsy, I'm afraid, as you know and . . .'

Judith shushed her. The girl was useless; she would not be taking her to England with her.

'But why did you want to see me, Torr?' she demanded.

'Why? Oh. I, I have a present for you.'

'You do?' He scuffed his feet, apparently shy, as Aileen took her chance to escape past them into Judith's chamber. 'What is it?'

'I'm regretting it now. It's a foolish idea. You are too delicate, too fine. Let me get you something else, Judith.'

'Don't be silly. What is it?'

He prised a ring, golden with a swirled inlay of silver, from his littlest finger and proffered it.

'A token of our commitment. I thought it would be fitting to give you something of my own but I fear I was mistaken. It is too coarse a bauble for your beauty.'

'It is not.' Judith held out her hand and Torr guided the ring onto her largest finger. He was not a thick-set man and it fitted well enough. She would have to be careful not to let it slip off but she loved it. It shone against her skin like gilt edging on a manuscript. 'It's perfect,' she said.

'It is?'

'Yes. Thank you, Torr. I shall treasure it.'

'As I shall treasure you.' He moved closer, claiming her as if they might dance and gently pulling her against him so that it seemed as if almost every part of her body was touching his.

'My lord,' she protested, 'should we?'

'Oh yes, Judith,' he said, 'we should,' and he was so sure that she protested no more but let his lips claim hers, so lightly and so softly but with such promise that she clung to him when finally he moved back.

'Should we?' he teased huskily.

'We should,' she told him firmly and reached for him.

'Oh, Judith,' he said. 'We are going to have such fun, you and I – once we are wed.'

And with that he pulled away and, kissing his ring onto her finger, was gone, leaving her quaking with a mix of fury and desire. Was this courtesy or the opposite? She knew not; knew only that she wanted more.

She wore the ring to dinner where Torr was all attentiveness once more.

'I am sorry I had to leave,' he told her when they had a moment alone. 'I was . . . overcome. I do not wish to dishonour you but, oh, Judith, our wedding cannot come soon enough for me.'

Warmth suffused her; it *had* been courtesy.

'It is but two more days,' she whispered.

'They will seem like an eternity and believe me, Judith, once you know what you are missing two days will seem an eternity to you too.'

'You know then?'

He frowned, bowed low.

'I confess I do. I am not so pure as you, my love – or rather, I have not been before. I was young, a little wild perhaps, and, of course, free.'

'You will not mind losing that freedom?'

'For you – never. You are enough woman for even a man of my appetites.'

Fleetingly Judith wondered if the pleasures of the bed-chamber were all her future husband talked of. He wished to flatter her, no doubt, to reassure her, but it grew a little wearisome.

'Tell me of England,' she suggested.

'England? 'Tis a fine place. You will like it. We will have a great hall.'

'Where?'

'Wherever you want. You can buy drapes and, and ornaments if you wish. Do you wish? My mother is always buying drapes. And we can, maybe, have a new bed – one with sturdy posts. You will like that, Judi.' And he was off on his favourite subject again, though his lips whispered across her earlobe so deliciously she lost track of the words.

'Judith!' She leaped away from Torr as Count Baldwin approached. 'Is he at you again, girl? Goodness! Can I tear you away a moment or two? Your sister is here.'

'Sister?' Judith looked at him, confused.

'Oh, you know what I mean – Mathilda.'

'Mathilda! Mathilda is here? Now?'

'She is. She has ridden from Normandy specially to honour us, is that not kind?'

Judith looked round. Her cousin must be surely there by the door where a chattering mob had gathered excitedly.

'And William?' she asked nervously.

'Surely Mathilda is enough?'

Baldwin took her arm to lead her away from Torr, parting the crowds with a gruff command, and there indeed was Mathilda. It was a few months since Judith had last seen her and she marvelled that she'd forgotten that peculiar radiance her cousin had. Mathilda shone as brightly as Earl Godwin but with not an ounce of gold about her slender person and Judith instantly felt clumsier and uglier and somehow larger beside her. But then Mathilda caught sight of her and her fine-boned face lit up girlishly and Judith felt ashamed of herself.

'Maud,' she said, rushing to her.

'Judi. It's so lovely to see you and you look so well. I swear you are twice as pretty as you were when I left and that was already prettier than most.'

Judith flushed.

'How is life in Normandy, Duchess?'

Mathilda smiled at the title.

'It is good, thank you. The people of Rouen have welcomed me as if I am some sort of treasure but then, do you know, they haven't had a duchess since William's grandmother and she died in '31.' She leaned in closer. 'As you saw at the wedding, it has been a duchy of little more than men posturing and cutting each other down, Judi, but I am working hard to change that. I am meeting more and more noble ladies and trying to bring some polite society to the different areas of Normandy. It isn't easy but I will do it, I swear.'

'I'm sure you will, Mathilda. And William is well?'

'Oh, yes! He has had some good news. That is why I am here.'

She looked shifty suddenly and Judith grabbed at her arms.

'You are with child, Maud?'

'Not that, no, though I suppose I could be. William tries hard enough. We share a chamber every night and I swear I get less and less rest.'

She chuckled, a low, throaty sound that Judith recognised from Emeline's earthy jokes and tales. Would she, too, laugh this way soon? She glanced over to Torr but he had been cornered by two ladies and did not see her.

'Have you seen my bridegroom, Maud?' she asked, proudly pointing him out. 'Is he not a fine man?'

'He looks very well,' Mathilda agreed. 'And is that his father, Earl Godwin?'

'It is. See all his gold, Maud. I swear he is almost made of it. Torr says it is the old way – a good Saxon keeps his wealth upon him to display it to all.'

'And so he has it with him if he needs to flee.'

Mathilda's voice was suddenly hard and she looked shifty again.

'Maud, what is it?' Judith demanded. 'What's happened? You're frightening me.'

Mathilda grabbed her hands, her grip so tight it hurt.

'I have to talk to you, Judi, and to Father too.'

'Why? When?'

'Now. I have to talk to you now.'

'But dinner is almost ready. We have guests. You haven't met Torr yet and it would be very rude to . . .'

'Now, Judith! Come.' She all but dragged her across to Count Baldwin, chatting easily to Lady Gytha, and Judith saw Mathilda gather herself in that almost regal way she had, so that as they approached she looked twice her small height. 'I am so sorry, Father, but could I beg a minute of your time on a matter from Normandy?'

Count Baldwin looked at her and Judith saw his eyes change as he, like Mathilda, shifted mode.

'Of course. Have you met Lady Gytha?'

'A pleasure,' Mathilda said, taking Torr's mother's hand. 'I look forward to talking more with you shortly but my husband, Duke William, begged me to bring a message to my father and I must do so before I go and forget it!' She gave a tinkling laugh that set Judith's teeth on edge and then took her arm with an easy, 'Will you come, Judi? I have missed you so.' And just like that they were easing out of the crowd.

'What is it?' Baldwin demanded as soon as they were alone in his antechamber. 'What's wrong?'

Mathilda pulled them both close to her.

'It is the Godwinsons, Father. Their power is waning.'

'Nonsense, child. Have you seen them?'

'Yes, I've seen them. They're very keen, aren't they, for this alliance?'

'As they should be. Judith is a fine match for the lad.'

'Of course she is, but why now?'

'Why not now? Judith is eighteen, the young man is twenty-four – now is as good a time as any. What's wrong, Mathilda?'

Judith looked nervously from her brother to her cousin and back. Beyond the door she could hear the hum of the court enjoying itself – of Torr, her betrothed, enjoying himself. She did not want to be shut in here with these bristling rulers. She did not want to play Mathilda's games. Not any more.

'I am going back,' she said.

'No, Judith.' Mathilda seized her arm. 'Listen. William and I had a visit from Archbishop Champart of Canterbury.'

'So?'

'He was an abbot in Normandy before he travelled to England with King Edward. He knows William well and has been . . . promoting his interests.'

Baldwin sucked in an awed breath which only irritated Judith further. Who cared about some ambitious cleric?

'So?' she demanded again.

'So, he says King Edward wishes to rid himself of the Godwinsons. He says their time is running out.'

'Why believe him?'

'He says Edward will invite William to his court.'

'Very neighbourly of him.'

'And that he will make William his heir.'

Baldwin stepped keenly forward.

'His heir, Mathilda? William will be . . .' his voice dropped '. . . King of England?'

'So the archbishop says.'

'Then you will be . . .'

'Queen.'

They looked at each other and Judith felt as excluded as if she were on the other side of the door. Baldwin clasped Mathilda's shoulders.

'I said England, did I not, Daughter? I said it.'

'You did, Father.'

'And now . . . Have you received the official invitation to court?'

'Not yet but we will, I am sure of it. The archbishop is not the sort to make empty promises.'

'I see, I see. Queen of England, Maud? Did I not tell you William was a good match? Did I not tell you crowns could be won? And if ever there was a man to win . . .'

Judith had had enough.

'Excuse me, Brother.' He blinked at her as if he'd forgotten she was there. He *had* forgotten she was there. 'Before you lose yourself in glee over this misty promise, you should remember that the Godwinsons will never allow a foreigner on the throne.'

'That's true, but . . .'

'But nothing, Brother. Earl Godwin has been the senior earl in England since King Cnut's day, you told me that yourself. He *is* the court of England.'

'Yet here he is scrabbling for a match with Count Baldwin's sister,' Mathilda said.

'Oh, and that is so poor a deal, is it? Am I so paltry a prize compared to you, Mathilda, that it must mean he is desperate?'

'No. Oh, Judith, no.'

Mathilda tried to take her arm but Judith yanked away with more strength than she'd known she had.

'I am honoured, Duchess, by your presence here for my nuptials to Torr Godwinson but if you wish to stay for the ceremony please do so to support me, not to oppose me.'

'Oh, Judith, I do not oppose you. I just seek the best for you.'

'And Torr Godwinson is it. How can we judge English politics on the say-so of some archbishop we have never met before? It's ridiculous, Mathilda. You are just bored or lonely, or, or jealous that I am marrying into England, not you.'

Mathilda gasped and Judith saw tears spring to her eyes and felt a sharp stab of guilt but Mathilda couldn't do this to her. She'd had such a lovely few days. She'd felt so happy, so wanted. They couldn't take that away on some whim.

'Please, Brother,' she said to Baldwin, 'don't stop the wedding.'

Count Baldwin gave a deep sigh.

'She speaks some sense,' he said to Mathilda.

Mathilda put up her hands.

'She does. And I'm sorry, Judi, but tell me something – why are all the Godwinsons not here? Why is Earl Harold not with his brother for this happy occasion? And why not their sister, Queen Aldyth, or indeed her husband, the king?'

'They are busy people.'

'Too busy to spare a week for the first earl of England's son? Too busy for a visit that could heal the diplomatic breaches between our countries in one go – if that is what they want?'

'Why does it have to be about what they want? What about why I want, Maud?'

'It is, in a way. You know I only seek . . .'

'The best for me? Yes, I know, so come out of this dark room and into my wedding celebrations.'

And with that, Judith turned on her heel and made for the door before they could drag her down further. To her gratification Torr came rushing over.

'Judith, there you are. I missed you.'

'You did? Well, in two days' time you need never miss me again. Tell me more of this bed we will order.'

He was all too happy to do so, and as Godwin and Gytha and the younger of their children crowded round as well, Judith basked in their attention. If there was even a grain of truth in these ravings from the archbishop then this family, her new family, would sort it out. Mathilda was just jealous because she, Judith, was on her way to England. Well, tough. Mathilda had chosen Normandy and now she would just have to put up with it.

CHAPTER TEN

Rouen, September 1051

Mathilda paced the great hall of the pretty Tour de Rouen, half-chasing a stray leaf across the floorboards as a group of petitioners were ushered out of the morning's hearing. She was weary and out of sorts and even the golden pastries being laid out on the side table for her midday meal could not cheer her up. She had come home from Bruges to find William about to ride out to put down a rebellion in the south and had found herself left behind in the care of La Barbe.

'Why can he not be in *my* care?' she'd demanded, but William had just laughed and said Normandy would not tolerate a female regent. He was sure she could keep the chamberlain in line, he'd said, riled, she had determined to assert herself in ruling but it had not proved as satisfying as she had hoped.

The rebels were being led by the Bellemes, primary amongst them Fulk's precious poisoner Mabel, and William was apparently laying siege to her border towns of Alençon and Domfront. William had put Fulk in charge at Alençon and for a while Mathilda and Emeline had been diverted by the idea of wooing by the sword, but the fun of it had soon paled. A siege, it seemed, took forever and the summer had been lonely and arduous – a bitter contrast to her first weeks in Normandy.

When she had ridden into Rouen a week after her wedding it had been to cheers and joy and a palace filling up with nobles keen to join the reinvigorated court. Women, in particular, had seemed to be coming out of holes in Normandy's fertile ground, blinking in the light of day and giddy with the novelty of life in the open. Fitz had keenly introduced her to a dark-skinned girl with huge brown eyes called Adelisa de Tosny and she had hoped to plan her first Norman wedding, but once the rebels had struck all such activities had ceased as if fun, too, were under siege.

It was all so wearisome and for the first time in her life, Mathilda was struggling to sleep. To her surprise she missed William's attentions in their bed at night and his warm form against her own in the mornings. Despite being bone-tired, she could not make it through a night without waking at least twice and she had lost her appetite for all but the strangest foods. All the signs suggested that she was with child but she did not know if it was that making her feel so poor, or the grind of life in an empty court.

'You should send word to the duke of his impending heir,' Cecelia told Mathilda every day but Mathilda didn't want to 'send word' to William, she wanted to tell him herself. She wanted to see his eyes light up at the news and fill with pride in her, and she wanted to hear him tell her, in that funny, stiff way of his, that he was 'pleased with her'. She put off sending messengers in the hope the siege would be won and William would return but every day the horizon remained as resolutely empty as the last.

The leaf caught a breeze coming in through the high window opening and whirled itself to safety behind a side table.

Obscurely frustrated, Mathilda paced back to La Barbe, organising witness statements on the dais.

'Did you want to go to war, Roger?' she demanded.

'Me?' La Barbe stroked at the upturned ends of his moustache. 'Not really. My leg hampers me.'

'A battle wound?'

'Nothing so glamorous. I was simply born with one shorter than the other. Some default in my hip. It aches at times but it would not stop me fighting if I wished. The truth is, Mathilda, that I am quite happy here. I can hold my own on a battlefield but I'm not a natural killer. I haven't the stomach for it, have I, Della?'

His bumptious wife, helping stack the stiff parchments, shook her head fondly.

'Useless with blood he is. He had to carry little Robbie all the way back from the woods with his eyes closed when the poor lad cut open his thigh on a snare once.'

'That was different,' Roger protested. 'Robbie is my son so his wounds are like my own. I can cope with enemy blood.'

'But what about the time . . .'

'Well, I'm glad you're here,' Mathilda leaped in, before the argument could progress. 'Now, come, what news from camp today?'

She didn't really want to know, for it seemed as if all news from the southern front was bad. Roger kept insisting that the troops had 'settled into' the sieges, William at Domfront and Fulk in Alençon, but it sounded horribly unsettled to Mathilda with regular reports of raids and sorties and ambushes. This morning's messenger had brought an almost gleeful tale of how William himself had been trapped with no more than twenty men and had only escaped by means of a daring ride down a steep bank.

'It could have killed him!' Mathilda exclaimed, horrified.

'But it didn't,' Roger said. 'William is lucky.'

'William is *skilful*,' Mathilda corrected loyally, adding, 'Has he always been this way?'

'I don't know about that. It depends if you think inheriting a dukedom at seven is lucky.'

'It must have been very hard for him.'

'It was very hard for everyone. He lost three guardians in the first year.'

'Lost?'

'They were killed, my lady.'

'Fitz's father amongst them?'

'No, he was later. Much later.' La Barbe's brow darkened and suddenly he said, 'William has not spoken to you of this?'

'There has not been time.'

'Maybe not, but there will be. You should ask him about Lord Osbern, my lady.'

'He is not here *to* ask!' she cried in frustration, whirling away again but not before she'd spotted the look that passed between husband and wife – the sort of look she used to see her parents exchange when she was being difficult as a child. She sighed.

'You should go to the Lady Herleva at Falaise,' Roger said kindly. 'It is much closer to both Domfront and Alençon and the duke may well go there once victory is secured.'

Mathilda considered. There was sense in the idea and, besides, she liked Herleva and imagined her home as a place of peace and contentment – both things she sorely needed at present.

'Very well.'

'Good. I will accompany you myself.'

Mathilda looked closely at him.

'You're bored too!'

He laughed.

'A little restless maybe and we all want news. Once I see you safe with the lovely Herleva I might take a ride over to Domfront to see how the siege progresses.'

'You might?' Mathilda's mind started racing. 'Is it far, Roger?'

'A day's ride.'

'I see. Is it dangerous?'

His eyes narrowed.

'Oh no, Mathilda. Oh no, no, no – you are not coming.'

'It's a siege, yes, so the enemy are shut inside their castle?'

'Well, yes, but . . .'

'And our men are camped outside?'

'It's not quite like that, Mathilda.'

'I think it's exactly like that. My father talked of warfare to me, Roger; I am no innocent. William will be as bored there as we are here. He would welcome a visit from his duchess, especially if she brings news.'

She placed a hand on her belly and Della rushed to her.

'It's true then? I was sure I'd seen the signs. I said to Roger just last week, did I not, Roger?'

Roger rose too, smiling.

'You did, you did. This is joyous news indeed, Duchess.'

'And how much more so for the duke?'

'Indeed. I will tell him myself.'

'No, Roger, *I* will tell him *my*self.'

Now though, La Barbe put his foot down.

'No, Mathilda. I'm sorry but I cannot permit you to ride into danger in your condition.'

Mathilda howled in frustration.

'But there's no danger!'

'That's not true. You've heard the tales of ambushes and warrior bands on the loose. I cannot let you ride out into such territory – you must see that.'

Mathilda ground her teeth. She did see, but it was so infuriating.

'Maybe,' she said eventually, 'by the time we get into the south William will have won anyway.'

'Maybe,' Roger allowed but neither of them really believed it for this siege seemed interminable.

Just two days later, however, as their party made camp on the road from Rouen to Falaise, they were met by messengers.

'Great news, my lord. William routed the last of the rebel bands on the loose so 'tis only the Bellemes lasting out now.'

'Which they won't do for long,' Roger laughed. 'They are probably already killing each other holed up in Domfront for so long.'

'So it's over,' Mathilda said, joining him as the astonished messengers sank to their knees before her.

'Not over,' Roger said.

'But safe.'

'No, Mathilda.'

'You said I couldn't ride to Domfront because of the threat of rebel bands and now that threat is gone.'

'True, but . . .'

Mathilda saw Roger look desperately around for help and felt a little sorry for him – but only a little.

'God saw us coming,' she told him confidently. 'He wishes me to have free passage to William so I can bear him my news and lift him to finish off the rebellion.'

'You think so?'

'I know so. Which way is Domfront?'

She squinted up the road. Just ahead was a crossroads. The nearest path led west to Falaise but the others must go south – to William.

'That way,' Roger said wearily, indicating the right one of the two lower roads, but Mathilda caught the messengers exchanging looks and ordered them to rise.

'Is William still there?'

'Begging your pardon, my lady, but he may not be. Domfront is a formidable fortress and there is little action before its walls. The duke was talking, now that the countryside is clearer, of a strike on the more vulnerable Alençon.'

'Alençon? That is further within the duchy, is it not?'

'Yes, my lady.'

'So safer for me then?'

The messengers looked helplessly to Roger, who shrugged.

'The lady is determined to see her husband.'

'I am,' Mathilda agreed.

'Then you should take the road to Alençon.'

'That one?' Mathilda pointed down the left-hand path.

'That one, my lady.'

'Good.' Mathilda clapped her hands together, relieved at last to be doing something purposeful. 'We ride at dawn.'

The sun rose clear and bright over their party as they headed south the next day, casting a cheerful light over the ripe corn in the fields, and Mathilda felt a warm pleasure in her new duchy as she rode through it. Her sickness was gone and her belly was swelling. It was just a little so far but she could feel it and she knew that when William put his strong hands around her waist he would feel it too. He would be so delighted. She urged her horse forward, willing the others to lift their pace to match.

There were many folk in the fields taking advantage of the sunshine to bring in the harvest. At first, hearing the horses, they would hide, but once word was whispered around that this was not a war band but their very own duchess, they came rushing to the roadside, calling out blessings. Mathilda begged pennies from Roger and distributed them where she could. In return the peasants pressed bread and butter and soft, rich cheeses upon them and they feasted on this simple fare beneath the trees as the sun curved low across the blue sky.

'How far now?' Mathilda asked Roger, who was pacing the road as they ate.

'Not far. I have sent scouts. We will await their report.'

'Wait? But I want . . .'

'Wait, my lady, please.'

He looked nervous and Mathilda tried to understand. This was rebellious territory and however pleased the peasants were to see her, a Belleme band would not be so welcoming.

'We're so close,' she moaned to Emeline and Cecelia.

'And so hot,' Emeline moaned back. 'I hear Herleva's residence at Falaise is beautiful. There is a river running right through the estate with willows dipping into the water and marble seating within their shade.'

Both her ladies sighed and Mathilda shushed them crossly.

'Time enough to cool ourselves once we have seen William and his men.'

Emeline perked up visibly at the mention of men. She'd been moping around empty Rouen every bit as miserably as Mathilda, for Raoul d'Amiens had dared to resist her advances. He had successfully married his daughter to Lord Evelin of Mortemer, in northern Normandy, but then fled back to France. He was, it seemed, so in love with someone at the French court (not, to Cecelia's disappointment, his wife) that he could not bring himself to even dally with any other.

'Not so much as a kiss,' Emeline had wailed. 'Am I getting old, Cee, is that it? Am I losing my charms?'

'Let's hope so,' Cecelia had said and then relented, throwing her arms around her friend and covering her pretty face in kisses. 'Is it not admirable of him, though, Em, to save himself for this lady if he truly cares so much for her?'

'Amazingly admirable,' Emeline had agreed faintly. 'He is quite the most gorgeous man I have ever met.'

She'd been sighing after him ever since but now, at the whiff of soldiers, she seemed at least a little revived.

'I bet they've all been horribly lonely stuck out here with only each other for company. Will we stay the night, do you think?'

'I imagine so,' Mathilda said. 'We can hardly ride back in the dark, can we?'

'No,' Emeline agreed gleefully. 'And the longer we wait here, the more likely that is. I might just have a little sleep to refresh myself.'

She drew her cloak around her and settled back but barely a soft snore later the scouts returned. The way was clear, they reported, and William was just riding into camp.

'Did you tell him we were coming?' Mathilda asked anxiously.

'No, my lady. Sorry, my lady.'

'Don't be. I wish to surprise him. Roger, shall we go?'

'We shall,' he agreed, though he still looked nervous.

'Fret not,' Mathilda said, patting his arm. 'William will reward you well for this happy day.'

'I pray so, my lady, but we must still be cautious.'

And they were. Scouts rode ahead all the time and they stopped endlessly to await their return. The journey took twice as long as it should have and Mathilda's hands twitched on her horse's reins, so desperate was she to kick him into a gallop. But at last they came out of a shady route through a low forest and saw Alençon before them. The town sat on a slight rise on the far side of a gentle river which was diverted around it to create a substantial moat. On the near side of the water a huge gate guarded the single bridge, sending long shadows towards them in the dipping light. The Norman camp was strung out across the plain a mere thirty paces from Mathilda's little group in the edge of the trees.

'Where's William?' she asked, eagerly scanning the men.

Her husband was easy to find, not because he was taller or grander than anyone else but because the whole camp seemed to revolve around its newly arrived leader. He looked well, his face weather-tanned and his hair a little longer than at their wedding, and Mathilda felt a stirring of desire. Her powerful husband might not write her poetry but he did, at least, make her pulse race. She clicked her horse forward but Roger grabbed her bridle.

'Stay back!'

'Why?'

'We do not want the Bellemes to know you are here, do we? I know you wish to see William but a crazy dash across an enemy plain is not the way. He would be furious at the unnecessary risk.'

'What then?' Mathilda demanded.

'You stay here. I will ride to William and ask him to come up to talk privately with me. You will get your surprise, I promise, but without inviting trouble.'

Mathilda smiled at him then stood on tiptoe to reach up and kiss his cheek, making him blush.

'You are right, Roger,' she said, 'and I bow to your judgement.'

'You do?'

He looked so surprised she felt ashamed. She had grown fond of La Barbe and come to look on him as a friendly uncle but out here he had a serious job to do and she had to respect that.

'Of course I do – but Roger, hurry!'

Now he smiled back and, with a little bow, tweaked at the edges of his moustache and leaped into the saddle. After another endless look around, he moved out of the trees and Mathilda pressed her little body into a trunk to watch. Roger edged forward, glancing back to check she was not following and she gave him an encouraging wave before she realised something was happening up on the walls of the town. Men were appearing along the top, though the dropping sun behind meant she could not make out their faces. Neither, at first, could she see what they were doing. They appeared to be throwing something over the walls, banners perhaps, or flags, though they did not move in the breeze.

'What are they?' she asked.

Cecelia moved up to her side.

'I think, my lady, that they are hides. I believe they make the walls smoother so siege ladders cannot grip.'

Mathilda looked to William's camp.

'But no one has a siege ladder.'

'No.'

Cecelia's face was grim. Mathilda looked back to the town and saw that now the men were bashing the hides with sticks and swords and even long-handled spoons. They were shouting too, their accent a rough, southern Norman but their words enunciated for all to hear: 'Alençon will not be defeated by a tanner's bastard.' They repeated the last words, harsh and hard: 'Tanner's bastard, tanner's bastard, tanner's bastard.' The jeer echoed off the wall and rippled over the moat, tangling in the trees where Mathilda and her 'surprise' huddled, horrified.

She looked again for William. He was rigid with anger, his face as pale as the heart of a flame and his hand clenched on his sword hilt. As she watched, he drew the long blade from the scabbard and ran a testing finger along the edge. Even from here she saw his blood run. He put the scored finger to his mouth and sucked slowly upon it. She shivered and pressed against the tree as Roger edged his horse back towards them, his eyes fixed on the field.

'You must get back, my lady,' he hissed, but Mathilda was not leaving, not now.

Odo, William's half-brother, had stepped quietly up at William's side the moment he'd heard the taunts about their mother, and now they called the other men to them. Mathilda saw William's key guard crowd round – Fitz, bounding to his lord's side; Fulk squaring his huge shoulders as if looking to hide the duke beneath their shadow; and Hugh de Grand-mesnil already calling over the cavalry horses.

There was urgency in the sprung coils of their young bodies and Mathilda dug her hand deeper into the whorls of the bark. Roger was pleading with her to leave, Emeline and Cecelia too, but she shut her ears to them. She had wanted to know what manner of man she had married and now she would.

'Hush,' was all she said and silently they complied, moving to their own trees as if they might make themselves part of the watching wood.

Below them the camp was moving, arranging itself purposefully into tight squares. Mathilda thought fleetingly of William's disparaging comments about the rabble of the court and understood his irritation. His soldiers moved with a precision that was almost beautiful and a purpose that seemed to hum through the warm ground and up into her body.

She saw the men on the walls of Alençon hesitate and their cries of derision waver but then one man shouted anew and, as if ashamed, they backed him. William put a foot in his stallion's stirrup and flung himself effortlessly onto its back, guiding it to the front of the near-perfect lines of men formed along the path to the great gates guarding the bridge. From somewhere his troops had found a huge trunk which they now ran at the gates, led by Fulk, so tall and broad he could almost hook the tree under one arm. The sharp crack of wood on wood tore the air, cutting off the jeers for a moment, but the gates held.

The guards in the towers either side fired arrows and stones but William's own archers retaliated with deadly accuracy, killing all resistance. Again William's Normans rammed, again the gate resisted, and again, and again, but the men, urged on by Fulk's roars, never gave up and at last the wood seemed to cry out and the gates caved in. A thousand soldiers were through them instantly, streaming onto the bridge towards Alençon as if the townsfolk's bitter taunts were a siren's call straight to their sword-arms.

'My lady, please,' Cecelia begged, 'it is not safe here.'

'Not for them,' Mathilda agreed, indicating the town as men snatched back the hides and scrambled for a safety they were unlikely to find.

Roger nodded stony agreement but made no further suggestion to leave and Mathilda had a clear view when, some time later, her husband re-emerged from Alençon with a long line of men tied behind him on a rope, guarded by burly warriors.

'Prisoners?' she asked Roger but he gave no answer.

William led them slowly over the bridge and out into the centre of his camp where they dropped to their knees like living tafel pieces, casting dark, spiky shadows across the cold ground. They were but thirty paces from Mathilda, hidden in the trees, and she could clearly see their terrified faces. All men in their prime, they were followed by a gaggle of women, children and frailer men, held back like animals by a fence of soldiers so they could offer no comfort to their loved ones. It was orderly terror and Mathilda could not for a moment look away.

William dropped the end of the rope and the guards moved closer, though not one prisoner did anything more than whimper or throw bound hands pleadingly towards William.

'You ask mercy now?' he boomed, his voice cutting through the cacophony of pleas and tears from the townsfolk. 'You plead with me for justice and fairness? Where was your justice when you threw those slurs into the air? Where was your fairness when you abused a ruler who has only tried to do what is best for you and for this, your duchy?'

'My lord duke,' one cried, 'we were wrong. We were stupid. We were disloyal.'

'And now you are changed?' William leaped from his horse and stalked over to the man. 'Now you are suddenly loyal? It does not work that way, not with me. Loyalty is steadfast. It chooses its allegiance and holds to it. It does not sway on the lightest of breezes.'

'But you are the victor, Lord Duke, and we submit to that absolutely.'

William's laugh rattled over the water and off the now-bare walls of the town.

'Of course you do, you have no choice. That is not loyalty but weakness.' He paced the line of captives. 'You picked the wrong side,' he told them fiercely. 'Do you know why it was the wrong side? Because it was not *my* side. I wished only the best for you and you defied me and now you regret it, yes? Yes?!'

He seized the chin of the nearest man who quaked in his hold.

'Yes, Lord Duke, we regret it. We were wrong. We did not know your strength.'

'And now you do.' William's voice was as still as an icebound river.

'Now we do, Lord Duke, and we swear to you.'

'No!' William paced the line again. 'It is not enough. I am tired of rebellion, tired of every last carpenter and market-holder and, yes, tanner, thinking he is better than me. It. Must. Stop.'

He turned and put up a hand. Two men lifted a steel bucket from a nearby fire and moved carefully over with it. Thick, dark fumes rose into the chill air and William took a rough club from one of them and dipped it in, lifting it high so they all saw the tar, black and cloying as a moonless night as it oozed down the length of the club and slopped back into the mixture with a sickening suck. Mathilda caught the acrid smell on the air and cowered back, though she refused to loosen her hold on the tree.

'Loyalty,' William cried, approaching the first man again with the shining black club still in his hand, 'is all I ask of my people – *all*. But I ask it to be given freely and to be cleaved to without doubt. You, men of Alençon, denied me your loyalty and then you tried to steal my honour. You are thieves, all of you, and must be punished as thieves.'

He nodded to the guards who flung the first man to the ground, one holding him spread-eagled whilst the other in four swift, brutal swipes of his sword, severed first his hands and then his feet from the helpless limbs. Blood ran out and was lapped up by the hard ground as William himself held the boiling tar to each stump, waiting patiently for the flesh to sizzle and seal before moving to the next, seemingly oblivious to the man's screams of agony. Finally he stood back and flipped his victim over to stare into his pain-clouded eyes.

'Like thieves,' he repeated and moved on.

'No more,' Mathilda gasped. 'Surely no more.'

But William did not stop, not once. He did not look down the line to the desperate men fighting their guards, squirming uselessly away from the cries of pain and the stench of their neighbours' searing flesh. He did not look to the women, weeping and pleading for mercy, nor back to the ranks of his soldiery, stood in line with their heads down. He did not look anywhere but into the defeated eyes of his victims as they sprawled in the dust at his feet, cauterised at every extremity, until at last, thirty-two men later, it was done. With a curt nod William ordered his guards to step back and the people of Alençon ran to what was left of their men.

'Will they live?' Mathilda whispered.

'Most of them,' Roger said. 'They will serve as a reminder of where their loyalty should lie. Where it *will* lie.'

'Freely given?'

He looked at her.

'Not freely enough, but what can he do? He spoke true, Mathilda – he only wants the best for them, yet ever they defy him.'

Mathilda put a shaking hand to her belly. The man who had sealed miserable life into those empty victims had also put this child inside her – and she had enjoyed it. The hand that had held the tar to their bleeding flesh had run tenderly over her naked skin and set her pulse racing at the power of her partner. And she had come here, like an innocent fool, to tell him of their babe as if this were a May Day celebration and not a war. Well, she was innocent no more and would not be a fool again.

'We must go,' she said, finally uncurling her fingers from the tree.

'At last.'

Roger was all too eager to hustle her away. Emeline and Cecelia followed but did not speak and they moved slowly, carefully, as if some part of their own selves had been cut away with the townsmen's hands. Their guards clutched their swords and looked anxiously about. One man even ruffled the grass behind them as they moved away, removing all trace of their presence. Mathilda's eyes locked with Roger's.

'We were never here.'

'Never, my lady.'

If only it were true. If only the imprint of this terrible day was as easily removed from their hearts as from the ground, but Mathilda knew William's axe had cut too deep for that. She had wanted to know what manner of man William was and now she did and she must face the fact that she had chosen him. She had turned her back on the likes of Brihtric with their poetry and their flowers and their dancing and picked a man who could offer her a grand future. She must accept all that went with that but seeing it so starkly before her pierced her very soul and it was a long, dark road away from Alençon that bitter night.

CHAPTER ELEVEN

Falaise, October 1051

'My sweetheart, my duchess.' William clasped her shoulders before the excitedly gathered crowd outside Herleva's lovely home at Falaise. 'My Mora,' he added, his voice low. 'Oh, truly I am glad to see you.'

'And I you,' Mathilda replied, trying to sound natural though her heart was pounding at having him so close.

For nigh on a month she had waited here in Falaise whilst William secured Domfront's capitulation – not hard once news of Alençon had reached the remaining rebels. She had been very well looked after by Herleva and Herluin who lived not in the stern ducal castle on the hill above Falaise, but in a simple timber-framed building set in soft meadowlands by the pretty river. Yet, torn by images of her new husband at Alençon, she had found little peace. And now William was stood here looking down at her so confusingly sweetly.

'I have dreamed of you,' he said. 'I have dreamed of holding you, of lying with you.' His arm slid to her waist and stopped. 'Mathilda?'

There was no hiding it now; her precious 'surprise' was clear for all to see.

'I am with child, William.'

'You are?' He spun to the crowd, lifting her hand as if she had just won a bout. 'My wife carries Normandy's next duke. God be praised! He favours us. Already, He favours us.'

The crowd cheered wildly.

'When is it due?' William asked, as if they were alone in the bedchamber and not standing in front of several hundred soldiers.

'Next spring.'

'The best time. I was born as the days grew shorter not longer. My first months were spent in the dark and cold but this little one will be luckier.'

'I pray so.'

'And you are well with it, Mathilda? You seem a little anxious.'

'Only to keep it safe, my lord.'

'William, please. Have you forgotten me already?'

Mathilda tried to smile a denial but it was true that she had forgotten this courtly William. He had been obliterated by another tarred one and yet here he was, openly attentive in front of the very men who had helped him cut the hands and feet off lowly townsfolk.

'Is the war over?'

'It is over, my sweet one. The Bellemes are subdued and the south is ours once more. We have brought many of them with us as honourable prisoners, including a noble girl who might, one day, make a good wife for this little prince.'

He patted her belly and Mathilda blinked. It made her head spin to think of the child inside her being one day ready to marry.

'You have only just this moment found out of our baby's existence, William, and already you plan his future?'

'Why not?'

Mathilda looked more closely at her husband but he would not meet her eye.

'You knew, William.'

'Knew what?'

'You knew of the babe. Someone told you. Who told you?'

'Does it matter?'

'It does to me. I wanted to surprise you.'

He bent down and kissed her.

'And I love you for it, truly, but I am not, my duchess, a good man for surprises. I prefer to know.'

'So who told you? Was it Roger?'

'La Barbe? No! No one so grand.'

That at least was a relief; she needed Roger to keep a bigger secret than the babe.

'Then who?'

'It matters not, Mathilda. I have people everywhere. I like to be kept informed.'

'You have spies on me?'

She shivered. Had one of William's spies been in their little party at Alençon? Did he know about that too? If he did, he showed no sign of it.

'You make it sound so sinister. It is simply, Mathilda, that I prefer to hear about things as soon as possible. Truly, it matters not. I made this child with you and that is what counts. Come, do not be cross. I have had enough harshness at war and would like to shake it off in the company of my wife.'

A picture of him, tar in hand, whipped across the front of Mathilda's mind as if some devil had painted it there. She blinked and staggered and William caught her.

'Mathilda, you are not well?'

'I am perfectly well, William. It is just hard to, to stand for too long.'

'Of course, of course, and here I am keeping you out in front of all these crowds. Come within. Let us find you a seat. Stand back for the duchess!' The crowd fell away instantly and William personally led Mathilda across the yard, into the pretty wooden hall and up to her seat at the head of the room, now fitted with a footstool for her little legs. 'Do you need anything? A cushion? A blanket? It is quite chill, is it not?' He clicked his fingers. 'A glass of warmed wine for my wife!'

Wife! The word jarred. She reminded herself that their marriage was not yet sanctioned by the Pope and could, were the church so inclined, be dissolved, but then swiftly dismissed the thought as weak. She could not wish such an outcome, for it would make her baby a bastard and she lived daily with the knowledge of what that could do to a child.

Mathilda took her drink from William, marvelling as he saw her served and personally tucked a soft cover over her legs like the best husband alive. And indeed he *was* the best husband, so what did the rest matter? War was a man's affair. No doubt her father had inflicted cruelties on his enemies and come home to throw her and her siblings around the nursery. No doubt Lord Brihtric had slain many a Welshman in anger and she must quash the niggle in her heart that said he had not. War was a game to men, a tafel board of life. The blood did not stain their skin so maybe it did not stain their souls either. It was her weakness that had let it colour hers.

'The sieges were lifted?' she dared to ask William.

'They were. You have heard tell of it?'

'No.'

That much was true. No one had spoken of Alençon since the dark night they'd crept away.

'It was a nasty affair. Men died – though less than might have done. And now the south is subdued. The Bellemes too.' He grinned suddenly. 'Have you the strength, my sweet, to meet Fulk's new wife?'

'Wife?'

'Odo married them at Domfront the very night it surrendered. Spitting fury, she was, but Odo covered it up with some fancy sermonising and Fulk did not seem to mind.'

'Mabel de Belleme is here?'

'Fulk will not let her out of his sight and quite right too. If he can tame her, Mathilda, he will do me a great service.'

'Must a man tame his wife?'

'This one must. Fulk! Bring your lovely bride to meet mine, will you?'

Mathilda glanced behind her and was glad to see Emeline and Cecelia at her shoulders as Fulk pushed through the crowd, cheerfully dragging a battling woman as if she were no more than a poppet.

'Let me go,' she spat, tugging furiously on her new husband's huge arms but Fulk did not even flinch as he bowed to Mathilda.

'My duchess, may I present to you my lady wife, Mabel of Belleme.'

Mabel stopped pulling and drew herself up tall – very tall. Mathilda was glad she was seated for the woman would dwarf her. And she was stunning. Mathilda could see now exactly what held Fulk de Montgomery in her spell. Her hair was dark, her cheekbones high, her eyes oak-brown and narrow as a cat's. She wore an elegant dark green gown, cut impossibly tight around her slender frame and her fingers, caught in Fulk's, glittered in the candlelight. Mathilda leaned forward and saw that each nail was set with a diamond, embedded deep into the flesh. Goodness, that must have hurt!

'Duchess,' Mabel said coldly, inclining her head the smallest possible amount.

Mathilda felt the insult prickle in her blood and dragged her eyes from the newcomer's diamond-studded nails.

'Welcome, Lady Mabel,' she said, every bit as coldly. 'You must be glad to be free.'

'Free?' Mabel cast a scornful look at Fulk, still clasping her hand.

'Why, yes. The shackles of marriage are surely lighter than those most rebels must bear?'

Mabel gasped but then gathered herself.

'I am no rebel, my lady. I am but a woman who must do as she is bid.'

'Come now. I'm sure you have ways of persuading your new husband?' Just behind Mabel, Fitz laughed. Mabel jumped and looked around, confused. 'If you are unsure,' Mathilda went on, 'we can perhaps talk further in the bower.'

She laid a hand lightly on her belly to more laughter. Mabel looked furious.

'Well done, my lady,' Emeline whispered in Mathilda's ear and Mathilda gave a small smile.

Some part of her was still trembling in the trees at Alençon but she was a ruler now and she could not allow that part of her to win. Let William battle as he saw fit on the field; she would do so at court. She threw the rug off her knees and rose.

'Fitz, you look well. Not too fat.'

He chuckled and bowed low.

'Swollen only with pride in our victory. Not so goodly a bulge as your own, my lady. You look more radiant than ever though no doubt you have been bored without us?'

Mathilda's eyes slid to Roger de Beaumont.

'Very bored,' she agreed. 'Thank heavens you are returned. You have, I trust, been practising your dancing?'

'Of course. It is all we have done around the campfires.'

He snatched at Hugh's hand and together they did a funny little jig, Fitz playing the lady to the slimmer Hugh's lead, flicking his wild hair as if it were three times the length and kicking up his feet with mock delicacy. This time Mathilda's smile was genuine. It was not just William who had punished the rebels but all these hard-working Normans. Even ever-smiling Fitz and quiet, gentle Hugh had been a part of it. They did what they had to do and then they got on with life, as must she.

'You lie, Fitz,' she said.

'Dissemble only. Come, you can teach us now.'

But William put up a hand.

'In a moment. First I need you. Fitz, Fulk, Hugh, Roger – here, please.'

They edged forward, confused.

'For years,' William said, his voice rising so that all turned to look, 'I have been told to rely on my elders for guidance and, recognising the value of experience, I have tried to do so. But this rebellion has taught me that experience is not necessarily a substitute for courage and it is certainly no match for loyalty.' Mathilda shivered but William was looking at his men with such pleasure that warmth stole back through her. 'These young men have proved in this campaign that they are the best advisors, supporters and fighters I could possibly have and I wish to honour them with titles that befit their service to me.'

Mathilda saw the men look to each other, embarrassed but pleased, and had to admire William. He was so stridently earnest but so very strong in his belief of what was right.

'William FitzOsbern, I wish you to take on the office once filled by your dear father – I name you my steward.'

Fitz's eyes widened even more than usual and he dropped into a stumbling bow, glancing delightedly over to little Adelisa de Tosny who looked suitably impressed. Mathilda remembered William's tight mention of Fitz's father that first night in Normandy and her own sense that Fitz had battled to fill his shoes ever since and was glad he now had recognition of that.

She determined that the next big occasion would be his wedding.

'Hugh de Grandmesnil, you are my finest and most diligent horseman and so I wish you to be my cavalry captain.'

Slender Hugh flushed scarlet and beamed around as if he might see his precious warhorses at the back of the crowd, clapping their hooves in approval.

'Fulk de Montgomery, you have proved yourself brave indeed in subduing the south . . .' The crowd allowed themselves a small titter as Mabel growled audibly at Fulk's side ' . . . so you will be my high commander.'

'My lord duke, you are too good . . .'

'I am not. I reward as befits service. You are all of great value to me and should know it. And lastly, Roger de Beaumont. You have kept my government safe and my wife besides.' Roger and Mathilda exchanged another nervous glance. 'I wish you to be my chamberlain.'

'I, I thank you,' Roger stuttered, stroking furiously at the ends of his moustache as he blinked back an emotion that would not be approved of in this fiercely martial court.

'And I you. I will see the appointments ratified in the morning and my dear brother Odo can, I'm sure, devise a suitably grand service to see you all blessed, but for now – let us celebrate!'

The men needed no second urging and the evening passed in banter and teasing and laughter, a blanket of civility to keep the chill of war at bay. Fitz whirled Adelisa de Tosny non-stop around the dance floor and quiet Hugh, flushed with his new title, let a laughing Emeline draw him out alongside them. Even big Fulk seemed boisterously happy, despite Mabel's scathing repulsion of his attentions and everyone else's merry teasing. Mathilda, stuck in her seat at William's side, watched the queen of the rebels uneasily and when Emeline finally paused for a rest, she sought her out.

'See anyone who catches your eye in this fair company?'

'I've scarce had chance,' Emeline grumbled. 'I made the mistake of asking Hugh de Grandmesnil what is better, a mare or a gelding, and he hasn't shut up since. He is very passionate about his subject. It's sweet but, heavens, he does go on, even when dancing! Did you know it was the Romans who first crossed our native ponies with larger mares to make these fine creatures we ride now?'

'No.'

'Me neither. Am I the richer for that knowledge? No. Have I lost half the night to it? Yes!'

'Well praise be, then, that there is still the other half left. Do you see that man there – is he not handsome?'

Mathilda pointed to a long-limbed young man who she'd seen following Mabel around as if chained to her.

'He is handsome enough,' Emeline allowed. 'Why him?'

Mathilda smiled at her.

'I thought you were lonely, Em, now that Raoul D'Amiens has resisted you?'

'I am often lonely, my lady, but you have never before seen fit to solve the problem for me.'

'He seems athletic, does he not?'

'Perhaps. Who is he?'

'Bertrand de Belleme.'

'Oh. Oh, I see. You think he has secrets in his bed?'

'It would not hurt to find out . . .'

Emeline licked her lips.

'It would, I think, annoy your new friend Mabel.'

'Shame.'

Emeline grinned and with a swish of her hair, moved purposefully into the crowd. Poor Bertrand would not know what had hit him and Mathilda watched, intrigued, as Emeline sidled round behind the young Belleme lord and then, with a little gasp, seemed to catch her toe in a floorboard and fall. Bertrand's arms shot out and he caught her and, just like that, she'd caught *him*.

'Your attendant is incorrigible.'

'William! You made me jump.'

'I'm sorry but really, Mathilda, is it seemly for her to parade herself that way?'

Mathilda swallowed.

'She's French.'

'But she's part of your household so it reflects poorly on you, does it not?'

'I'm sorry, my lord.'

'William. I am not a tyrant, Mathilda.'

'Of course not. I did not think it.' The room felt crowded suddenly, though not too crowded to miss Emeline fluttering her eyelashes up at a helpless Bertrand. 'It's my fault. I just thought . . .'

'Thought what, Mathilda? You can tell me. You can tell me anything.'

Mathilda hung her head.

'I thought it might be helpful to have someone who is close to me, close to *them*.'

William bent down slowly, so slowly, until his face was level with hers. He looked deep into her eyes and she forced herself to hold his gaze, though her knees quivered with the effort. She saw the silver in his pupils glow like moonlight and then, without warning, he kissed her hard on her lips right there, in front of everyone.

'We are so alike, you and I,' he said huskily as he drew back. 'So very alike.'

'We are?'

Mathilda's mind raced; he was wrong, she knew he was. How could she be anything like this tar-black husband of hers? But then, she told herself sternly, she need not be like him for this marriage to work. She need only be his inverse, like the pastry letters of their wedding feast. And she need not love him either, only accept him for what he was – a ruler who would make Normandy great. And maybe England besides. She could only pray William was right about King Edward's favour, for if the people of Normandy knew their duke would one day be a king they would stand behind him with all the loyalty he so craved and there would be no further horror.

'Shall we to bed, William?' she murmured.

She was rewarded by a broad smile and a hand that clasped her with utmost certainty. Enough certainty, surely, for them both. Alençon was behind them and they must shake off its bitter clutches and move forward together.

CHAPTER TWELVE

The North Sea, October 1051

'Oh, sit down, Wife, and stop snivelling. At least now you get to see your precious father again.'

'Brother.'

'Sorry?'

Judith glared at Torr.

'Count Baldwin is my brother.'

'Oh yes, of course. You're the misfit. Well, we're all misfits now, my sweet – all caught on the wrong tide. Now do sit down.'

Judith retreated to the far side of the boat, staggering as the waves tossed her sideways and catching her already bruised legs on the sodden rower's benches. This had looked a beautiful ship on land but out here on the open waves its luxurious trims and fancy figureheads were little use. The skies over the North Sea were black and the mood in the boat even blacker.

Torr's mother, Gytha, sat in the stern, her arms around her pretty daughters whilst his brother, Garth, restless at twenty-one, was taking a turn on the oars as the men battled to steady the craft against the vicious waves. Torr himself stood at the prow bickering with his older brother Harold, the grim mist clinging to their hair, Harold's the blonde of corn, Torr's the warmer colour of ripe hazelnuts, but both now dark with the pervading damp. Earl Godwin himself stood dead centre, arm around the mast, face frozen, and all his glittering gold hidden beneath a plain, dark cloak.

Why had Mathilda said he wore all that gold? 'So he has it with him if he needs to flee.' That had been back at Judith's nuptials just a few short months ago when all had seemed golden and she'd thought her cousin was making trouble to spoil her big day for no other reason than because she could. Judith had compared Mathilda's dour Norman husband to her own sparkling English one and believed she might be jealous but, oh no, Mathilda had just been right. Mathilda was always right.

Even before Judith had sailed into Dover with her new family, the Norman faction at court had successfully fed the king's antipathy to his longest-serving earl to such an extent they had landed to riots. The Godwinsons had fought back, rallying support all over the south but finally, under threat of civil war, the people had crumbled and allowed the family to be exiled. All Judith had seen of England had been the inside of the fortified hall at Dover before, with the first winds of autumn, she'd found herself forced to leave a country into which she had not travelled more than a hundred steps.

Now the chalk cliffs of Dover were fading into a low mist and they were adrift on a growling sea, returning to Count Baldwin with the bitter aftertaste of failure cutting through the sweetness of her marriage. It had all gone so wrong. Even her wedding night, despite all Torr's extravagant promises, had been a disappointment – a perfunctory, fumbling affair whose only real virtue had been its speed.

Torr, to be fair, had apologised in the morning pleading too much mead and excitement, and had tried again but that time too Judith had been left with a depressing sense of let-down.

From all those years of Emeline's breathless tales and insinuations she'd expected more. Maybe she was doing something wrong; or maybe Torr was? Not that she'd ever dare suggest as much. Torr's sexual prowess seemed to be, as well as his main topic of conversation, his primary source of personal pride and she could not take that from him.

He had been kind enough at first. On the boat towards England – an altogether different journey from this one, sunny and full of song and laughter – he had repeatedly told her he wanted her to be happy. The king regarded him very highly, he'd insisted, and the queen, his sister, would be certain to see him promoted. She would have halls, he'd promised, and bowers and chambers. She would have a kitchen full of all the best equipment and the finest chefs and a stable packed with beautiful horses. She would have looms and embroideries and music.

'Will I be able to paint?' she'd asked.

'Paint?' He'd squinted at her. 'Like the monks do? Don't see why not, if that's what you'd like. Paint? Really?'

He'd still looked puzzled but he hadn't objected and to Judith that was all that mattered. She'd so looked forward to having her own household and being free to do as she wished once they reached England but now it seemed she was heading back into Baldwin's choking control.

'Is it a good idea to return to Flanders?' she dared to ask. 'Perhaps . . .'

Torr's hand caught her chin, so hard her words felt as if they were being forced back down her throat.

'Of course it's a good idea – why do you think I married you?' She gasped and he sent his olive eyes skyward before, with exaggerated patience, releasing her chin and kissing her. 'Just sit down and stop snivelling. Set your back to England, sweet one, for she has set her back to us.'

Judith twisted away and hunkered miserably down into her sealskin sleeping sack, looking neither back to England's lost cliffs, nor forward to her childhood shores. No doubt even now Mathilda was nursing an invitation to the English court. It would be Mathilda, not Judith, who rode into Westminster; Mathilda who was fed at King Edward's table and taken out around precious Wessex; Mathilda who was introduced to all the fine ladies; and Mathilda who would be promised a future in England. Normal order, it seemed, was restored and Judith felt a fool for ever believing it could be otherwise.

CHAPTER THIRTEEN

Westminster, Christ's Mass 1051

ondon glowed beneath the low midwinter sun and Mathilda drew rein to take it all in as the guards approached the huge bridge over the great Thames River. She could hardly believe they were actually here. The long-awaited letter had arrived just a few weeks after the terrible news of Judith's exile, offering King Edward's warmest greetings and a cordial invitation to spend Yule in England with 'your cousin who has ever esteemed you greatly'. William had gone into a flurry of preparations and Mathilda, thankful for the distraction after the still-lingering horrors of Alençon, had followed his lead. The sail across the Narrow Sea, William's first time in a boat, had been a nervous one, but the grey waters had been thankfully calm and now here they were, approaching Edward's palace at last.

The city of London was vast – at least three times the size of Rouen. The soft wooden houses seemed to sprawl in every direction, some even being built on the marshier south side of the river as people clamoured to be a part of the capital. Boats of all sizes moved up and down the Thames, loading and unloading goods from all the markets of the world, and the cries of sellers and crews filled the frost-bright air. Mathilda had heard much of England's riches but to see them before her was something else.

And you might be her queen.

She bundled the thought nervously aside and glanced at William. He, like her, was stiff with anticipation. They had dressed for the occasion in their costly wedding clothes for William had been determined they should look 'throne-worthy'. Even their precious horses were apparelled in state, William's stallion, Caesar, in scarlet and gold, and her own, Mercure, a beautiful bay gelding Hugh de Grandmesnil had chosen for her, elegant in silver. They had paused at a place called Southwark to don their finery and one of William's men had produced a pot of molten silver and painted it on Mercure's dainty hooves so that Mathilda almost felt as if she were riding a unicorn.

'Beautiful,' William had pronounced. 'Definitely fit for a . . .'

But she'd shushed him even as he'd silenced himself and they'd exchanged a look full of excitement and awe and fear – fear that this would come to naught, that they might be making fools of themselves by daring to believe it at all. Preparations for this great visit had brought them closer and they had lain in their bed together in the cold weeks leading up to Yule, huddled beneath furs whispering the words 'king' and 'queen' on candlelit breath until they almost hung there in a little cloud above them. It had not been the giddy connection of love but had felt every bit as potent and Mathilda was unendingly glad to be here at his side now.

'Shall we go?' William said, sitting high in his saddle.

Mathilda nodded and lifted her chin to raise her little form as tall as it might go as William's select band of men, led by Fulk, Hugh and Fitz, fell into step behind them. Fitz had married his Adelisa just a few weeks earlier and insisted on bringing her and she was alongside Mathilda now, eyes wide as she took in the great crowds lining the packed-earth streets. Mathilda knew how she felt and had to stop herself gawping too as they crossed the huge bridge and turned east along the far bank towards the West Minster.

The church stood tall and grand on the horizon, though to Mathilda's great surprise it was made of wood and as they grew closer she could see that both the church and the royal palace, sat at its side on a pretty island carved out by two tributaries of the Thames, looked worn, almost splintered. Both were shabby in comparison to the dainty elegance of Bruges or the soaring splendour of Rouen but they stood proudly all the same. Perhaps it was because they had been there so long in comparison to the buildings in the far younger Normandy or Flanders. The Saxon kings could trace their line back to Roman times, even beyond. These people's roots were so far into the ground that no one, surely, could dig them away. And Mathilda might be a part of that.

Might, she reminded herself sternly – the next few days would tell.

The crowds thickened as they approached Thorney Island and they had to slow to a walk to cross a much smaller bridge into the royal compound. There was a flurry of fanfares and Mathilda kept her horse tight at William's side. She tried to keep her eyes forward but then noticed that the nobles were gathered in front of the hall and decided sideways was better, just in case Lord Brihtric were here. She prayed desperately that he had made his excuses, for seeing her onetime beau would be agony now.

'Where's Edward?' William whispered out of the corner of his mouth.

Mathilda cast around but could not see the king anywhere and then suddenly, to her left, there was a commotion. A serving boy darted from a building and all but ran under one of the

Norman horses ahead of William and Mathilda. It reared and a woman screamed. Mathilda felt a bolt of panic as Mercure shied back but the next moment one of William's guards had somehow reached down and scooped the helpless woman onto his own horse out of danger.

'Did you see that?' William asked. 'That guard – Heriot d'Argences I think it is – did you see how effortlessly he lifted that girl? That's how I wanted it to be with you in Bruges, Mathilda.'

She reached out a hand to touch his leg.

'It was something like.'

'It was *nothing* like. He was so smooth, so elegant, and look how the girl is staring up at him as if he were a god. I should have done that.'

His brow creased and his eyes grew grey and Mathilda squeezed his leg tighter, forcing him to look at her.

'He was not seizing a count's daughter, William. All eyes were not upon him as they were on you.'

'All the more reason why I should have got it right.'

'But you did, truly. It convinced me to marry you, did it not?'

'You were unsure before?'

She drew in a breath.

'I was not entirely sure about marrying a duke, William, no, but our time on your horse, short as it was, showed me the man and *him* I was sure of. I still am.'

He put his hand over hers.

'Thank you, my Mora. And I might not, you know, remain a mere duke.'

His eyes lit up a little, the grey turning back to the silver of Mercure's hooves as the commotion settled.

'We cannot live as normal men, William,' Mathilda said to

him. 'We must lead our lives as much for others as for our-selves.'

He looked around the excited crowd and nodded.

'That is true, Wife, and it is why I am grateful to have found you. With each other, at least, there need be no performance, no secrets. That is of great value to me.'

'And me,' Mathilda agreed faintly, trying not to look into the group of Saxon nobles ahead of them.

Please God Brihtric had had the sense to stay away. She dared a quick look, just to prepare herself, but the crowds were too thick to see anyone clearly and at last, in another run of trumpet notes, a man was stepping out of the great hall and all eyes were turning his way. It had to be King Edward for he wore a rich crown and all men dipped to their knees at his arrival. Yet, but for that, Mathilda would not have known him for a monarch.

He was thin with wispy grey-white hair and a lined, almost drooping face. He wore a sombre robe of coarse wool almost as long as a monk's and, even with frost thick on the ground, simple sandals. Yet, like the minster behind him, he stood proudly and his hand, when he raised it for silence, was assured and certain of obedience.

'Welcome William, Duke of the Normans – Cousin. You honour my court with your presence.'

'And you mine with your kind invitation, Sire.'

William dropped from his horse and knelt before Edward, who raised him instantly and clapped him on the back with surprising strength.

'Good to see you again, William. It has been too long. And with such a lovely wife too! Duchess Mathilda, welcome.'

Mathilda put her hand in Fitz's as he rushed to lift her down, though she would willingly have stayed in the saddle. On Mercure she felt tall and commanding, but on foot she was all too aware of her lack of height. She was used to William standing head and shoulders over her but King Edward, though slim, was taller yet and his narrow eyes were fixed upon her as she curtseyed. Her gown was cut to disguise her thickening waist and her bump was neat yet but she could swear he saw it immediately. Well, let him, she thought defiantly. Edward wanted an heir and in William he would find two – one for now and one to follow, and all thanks to her.

'I thank you, Sire, for your gracious invitation.'

'And I you, Duchess, for accepting it. We will get on very well I am sure.'

Mathilda prayed that was true. He did not, at least, seem angry. Perhaps his years on the throne had dulled his pain – though not, she hoped, his memory of the young duke who had sent him to claim it. They had five days in England, five days to make her their own. They could not fail in this, not now they were so close, and Mathilda went into Westminster's hall with her heart feeling as frail as the palace's proudly rotting walls.

Two days later and she was no more confident. Edward was all courtesy. He fed them the finest dishes, housed them in the most luxurious rooms, and was an attentive host. He spoke at length of his time in Normandy, of his plans for a stone church based on the beautiful one at Jumièges, and of his desire to set up 'neighbourly relations', but he did not speak of the throne. Instead, they all trod on the thin ice of pretence and Christ's mass was rung in on creaky but glorious bells with William and Mathilda still unsure of their place in England's lively celebrations.

It was a wonderful day all the same. Snow had fallen at first light, coating all the buildings in the royal compound and covering their rotting edges in soft, crystalline white. They'd gone out to the Yule market where children had been playing in the snow and adults picking their way happily through it seeking gifts for their loved ones. William had bought Mathilda a beautiful pendant in an intricate Celtic design with a ruby at its centre and she wore it proudly to church that night. The psalms, sung by a myriad plain-clad monks, were beautiful and although the church was old, the shining altar treasures and the array of bishops in ceremonial robes gave it an aura of grandeur. Flanders had only three bishops, Normandy six, but the Saxons had fifteen and they looked like a painting of heaven itself grouped around the altar.

'Judith would have loved this,' Mathilda thought sadly as the communion was prepared.

Her thoughts had flown often to her cousin, whose poor feet, it seemed, had barely touched Saxon soil before being kicked off it again. Deep in her heart, Mathilda wasn't certain that she and William deserved to stand in Judith's place but, then, however unchristian it might sound, what people 'deserved' was rarely of much consequence. You had to go out and take what God was offering and that was exactly what she and William were doing.

She closed her eyes as the 'Te Deum' soared up to the creaking rafters of the old minster. Lord Brihtric *was* here. He had not, thank the Lord, asked to be introduced but kept in the rear of the turning court, yet she was as aware of him as if he were right at her side. Someone, surely, in this gossipy gathering would tell William of her entanglement with this handsome lord? Or at least tell someone who would tell William. His network was too efficient to miss it and what then? She heard his voice bouncing off the walls of Alençon and into her heart: 'Loyalty is steadfast. It chooses its allegiance and holds to it and does not sway on the lightest of breezes.'

She reminded herself that she had not known William when

she danced with Brihtric but it was small comfort. He wanted them to have no secrets. She'd said she wanted that too but it wasn't true and Brihtric's presence at this Yule court felt almost like a treason to her husband. Luckily, though, William had only thrones on his mind.

'The king is teasing us,' he grumbled to Mathilda when dinner was finally concluded and a huge group of minstrels struck up a lively tune. 'There will be no parley tonight. Look – he is half-asleep.'

It was true. Edward was dozing on his throne. At forty-six, he wasn't an old man but he looked weary, certainly too weary to make an heir of his own even if he'd had his Godwinson queen in his bed. An inheritance might not be that many years coming – if it were offered.

William leaped up impatiently, making Edward jerk awake, wiping a line of drool from his thin mouth.

'I'm for bed,' William said.

'But my lord duke, the evening is just beginning.'

The king gestured vaguely down the hall where trestle tables were being cleared away to open up a dance floor all the way to the great doors. William did not even look.

'Not for me. Mathilda!'

He held out his arm with such determination that she had no choice but to rise and take it. She cast a longing look around the hall as the dance began. Fitz had his new wife tight in his arms and the guard, Heriot, was dancing with the girl he had rescued on their arrival. Even Hugh had taken to the floor, partnering Cecelia, though his eyes, she noted, were all for Emeline, sparkling in the arms of a lively looking young Saxon.

'My wife is tired,' William was telling Edward. 'She is, as you know, with child and I must care for her and my future heir.'

It was a heavy-handed hint but Edward just smiled and nodded absent agreement.

'Quite right, quite right. I shall retire myself soon – leave the revelry to the youngsters, hey?'

Mathilda bristled. She was twenty, William only twenty-three. She looked to her husband but if he was riled by this too, he gave no sign.

'I hope, Sire, that we can talk again tomorrow.'

'I hope so too, William, though tomorrow we hunt.'

'Hunt?' Despite himself William's eyes lit up.

'Of course. We always hunt the day after Christ's mass – clears heads and replenishes store cupboards. You will join us?'

'I will.'

'Good, good, and after that we can talk. Sharpen your spear, Duke, and you should bag a goodly prize. Good night.'

William and Mathilda left the hall as they were becoming accustomed, by sneaking out of the side door. It had started snowing again and the earlier scuffle of courtly footprints was covered so that their own treads were the only ones in evidence as they picked their way towards the cluster of wooden sleeping huts on the far side. They had been honoured with separate bowers as a mark of their status but, as was their custom, had spent every night so far together in Mathilda's. She headed that way now.

'A goodly prize,' William kept repeating. 'Did you hear that, Mathilda? A goodly prize. What does he mean by that, do you think?'

'I think,' Mathilda said carefully, 'that this king does not like to truly mean anything. He much prefers obscurities.'

'He does, he bloody does. Do we even want his promise if it is so begrudged?'

He looked at her, serious for a second, and then they both burst out laughing, a pure, blissful release. Mathilda clung to William and together they shook with mirth at the peculiar, almost ridiculous nature of their situation. William sobered first.

'I think, my Mora, that I will be of no use to you tonight. I will not sleep with all of this in my head and I will only disturb your rest.'

'I mind not.'

'That's kind but your health is precious, you know, especially with the babe, and besides I would like a little time to consider where I have come from.'

Mathilda looked at him, surprised. It was a curiously thoughtful suggestion for a man usually so eager to avoid introspection.

'You could tell me,' she suggested. 'I would like you to, William. I would like to know of your past and I could, could . . .'

'Could what, Mathilda?' he demanded, though gently. 'Could you change it?'

She blew out her breath in an icy cloud.

'Not change what happened, but perhaps alter the way you view it.' He tipped his head curiously on one side and, encouraged, she moved closer. 'Tell me of Lord Osbern, Husband.'

But at that he reared back as if she had stabbed him, leaving her flailing to keep her footing in the snow. He took several strides away and looked to the sky for an agonisingly long time before finally turning back to her. His eyes were black as charred wood but his voice, thank the Lord, remained calm.

'One day, sweet one. One day I will. The words are hard to find.'

'I could help you.'

'Oh, but you do, my Mora, more than you can know. Tonight, though, I will sleep in my own chamber.'

His voice had hardened all too familiarly and she wanted suddenly, desperately, to get away. Standing on tiptoe she placed a swift kiss on his lips then turned and ran, burning with a mixture of fury and tenderness. This was an important time for William and she respected that but she wished he would talk to her, would share his past with her. Then again, she had not shared hers.

At her chamber, she glanced back. William was standing by the door of his own, watching her, but now he gave an apologetic wave and went inside. She leaned back against the wooden wall to look gratefully up through the kiss-light snowflakes to the stars above. They were the same stars that she could look upon in Flanders or in Normandy for all were beneath God's skies. What difference really, if she were a duchess or a queen? But she wasn't naive enough to believe that one. She'd been raised in Flanders, the marketplace of Northern Europe, so she knew that everything had its value and titles more than most.

'Mathilda.'

The man was upon her before she could catch breath to cry out, clasping a hand over her mouth and pulling her into the dark alley beside the bower. 'Ssh. Do not scream. I won't hurt you. I want to talk, nothing more.'

'Brihtric,' she whispered between his fingers. 'What are you doing?'

Slowly he unpeeled his hand.

'I had no choice,' he said. 'The letter, I mean. Someone else saw it. They would have told and I thought it better from me.'

'How did someone else see it?' she hissed, pulling him further back into the shadows though the snow was high and wet between the walls.

Brihtric swallowed audibly.

'I, I showed it to them. I'm sorry. I was proud, Mathilda – too proud. You were so beautiful, so clever, so important. I couldn't believe you might want me.'

'I didn't,' Mathilda snapped nervously. 'You read it wrong, my lord. It was but courtly pleasantries.' There was a pause.

He would be looking sceptically at her, she knew, but it was thankfully too dark to see more than a hint of Saxon blonde in the ghostly starlight thrown up by the snow. 'You must go,' she said. 'This is madness. William has spies everywhere.'

'He spies on his wife?'

'Maybe – and maybe with good cause.'

'You feel it too then?'

His hands suddenly reached out, fumbling for her in the darkness, and she jerked back, banging against the wall of the bower.

'No! Go, Brihtric.'

She pushed blindly against him and stumbled out of the gap. No one, as far as she could see, was there and she leaped for the door, scrabbling at the latch, desperate to get inside before Brihtric tried anything else stupid. She all but fell onto the young server, Marcus, who leaped up in a panic.

'My lady. Come in, come in, you're covered in snow.'

Mathilda looked down and saw her beautiful gown was, indeed, thick with cloying clumps of white.

'I paused to look at the stars,' she said. It sounded foolish but the lad did not seem to notice.

'Wine, my lady? Come, seat yourself by the fire to warm up.'

His voice seemed loud and harsh, as William's had been, and suddenly Mathilda had had enough of such strident sounds.

'No need to shout,' she said, taking the drink gratefully and sinking onto the chair. She was weary, lonely, confused. 'I am tired. Fetch Emeline and Cecelia please.'

'Of course, my lady. I will go now.'

He went with a dramatic slam of the door and it was quiet at last. Mathilda tried to drink her wine and saw she was shaking all over. It was too much – Queen of England, it was a ridiculous idea. However throneworthy William might be, she couldn't match up. Had that crazy encounter with Brihtric not just proved it? And the higher she climbed, the higher there would be to fall.

Should she just tell William about her brief entanglement, she wondered? The letter surely did not exist any more. It would be easy to say that Baldwin had misinterpreted it, or that Brihtric had got ideas above himself, but imagine William's wrath? Best to stay quiet and pray for this all to be over tomorrow. She sunk to her knees, oblivious to the sounds of merriment drifting across the compound from the hall and the giggles of lovers seeking privacy in the snowflakes. Looking to God, she spoke the familiar, comforting words of the paternoster. Twice she spoke it, but it did not feel enough.

'God grant me the strength to be a good wife,' she said, her own audacity at so addressing the Almighty surprising her, but she needed help so badly. 'Grant me the wisdom to understand my husband's requirements and the grace to, to care for him as he sorely needs.'

Nearly she had asked to 'love' him but the word had stuck in her throat. She had loved Brihtric. Despite her fear, his touch had set a fire in her belly but now it did not so much inflame as scorch. Love was for fools, not for rulers. William would be a good king to England, she knew he would. He would labour night and day to serve his subjects as he did in Normandy – if he got the chance. Tomorrow was to be their last day in England, the last day for Edward to make his promise. She must forget Brihtric with his angel-curls and his summertime eyes and steel herself to her true purpose here as William's wife and, pray God, future queen.

The hunt was done and William was in a fine mood after bagging a deer in the morning and a large hare in the fading light of the afternoon.

'He has such energy, your husband,' Edward enthused to Mathilda as he and William bounded into her chamber at dusk. 'I remember him vividly as a child. I spent some time in the garrison at Falaise. Training, you know, to reclaim my damned father's throne.' For a moment Mathilda saw a flash of the angry exile William had described but swiftly Edward buried him back beneath the benign mask of kingship. 'I swear he's just the same as he was, your husband – always on the go and into everything. Drove his poor mother wild, he did. And oh, bedtimes! You could hear his protests from the hall even through the stone walls.' Edward chuckled and looked around. 'The Saxons don't have stone walls, not really. I am going to build a new church though, you know, one just like Jumièges. Did I tell you?'

He had but neither William nor Mathilda said so for now the stiff Saxon king had pulled a stool up to the brazier and suddenly it felt more like a time for discussing the future than the past. William hastily swept his tafel board from the little side table and Mathilda replaced it with a goblet of wine for their impromptu guest.

'I want a stone palace too,' Edward went on, drinking. 'Like in Rouen – a residence fit for a king.'

'Fit for you, Sire.'

'And for my successor.' Edward suddenly fixed William in his sights and Mathilda saw that, when he wished, this ageing king could be as sharp as any. 'You know why you are here, do you not?'

'I would presume to nothing.'

'Really?'

'Though I might, perhaps, aspire.'

'Aspire? Very good, William. You always were a cunning lad, like that Guiscard of yours, running around claiming half of Italy.'

William shifted, half smiled.

'A man should always look to better himself.'

'Indeed, indeed.' Edward stared into the fire then suddenly said, 'The throne is not, you know, mine to bestow.' Mathilda saw William freeze and edged closer to take his hand. He did not look her way but his fingers closed tightly around hers. 'The witan – our council – must approve the choice. They have the final say but a man's worthiness counts for much and a dying king's wishes for even more.' William opened his mouth but no sound came out. Edward smiled up at him. 'It is not easy, you know, being King of England. I found her confusing when I arrived back from Normandy and I'm of English blood. She is an ancient land, William, riddled with strange customs and practices, especially in the north. Northumbria is a law unto itself. The east too. A man can lose himself if he is not careful.'

'I would not lose myself, Sire.'

'No? No, I think not. But be warned, Cousin – crowns sparkle far more from a distance. Gold is a cold metal, whatever they might say of it. But there now, you will not take my word for that. I was the same, so desperate to claim the throne my father lost. But beware what it might cost you.'

Mathilda held her breath. She leaned forward and felt William do the same. Edward looked solemnly at them both.

'What is said here is between us, for now at least. The court is unsettled. The Godwinsons prowl our shores and cannot be dismissed. But we must look to the future all the same.' William's fingers, still in Mathilda's, closed so tightly she had to dig her toes into her boots to stop herself crying out. And suddenly here it was, the promise: 'It is my intention, Duke William of Normandy, in recognition of our family connections, and your strong reputation as a leader, and your kindness to me as a youth, to nominate you as my heir should I die without issue.'

'I am honoured, Sire.'

'You are, William, but I think you are worthy of that honour.'

'You are too kind.'

Edward smiled complacently and patted William's shoulder. Already though, he was turning away, reaching for wine.

'Will you announce this?' Mathilda asked and Edward looked back, frowned a little.

'No, Duchess Mathilda, I will not. We Saxons do not declare an heir until death is close and I pray it is not.'

Mathilda flushed.

'Of course. I pray not also.'

'I doubt that, but thank you all the same. Let us look upon this as a statement of intent. We can maintain relations and work together to a greater closeness as the years unfold.'

'Of course,' William said.

'You will, then, write it down?' Mathilda pushed but Edward just laughed as if she had suggested they might embroider it into a tapestry.

'No need, Duchess. You have my word; it is enough.'

His voice hardened, signalling the end of the conversation, but it seemed to Mathilda that this was a promise weighted with too much secrecy and concern. Surely an oath, at least, was needed. But now William's hand was slipping from hers to clasp his royal cousin's as they clunked their cups together.

'I have wine,' William said eagerly to Edward. 'Two barrels of the finest claret from Bordeaux, gifted to me by my overlord King Henri.'

'He will not be your overlord for England,' Edward shot back, his quiet voice suddenly sharp enough to slice under Mathilda's skin.

She had not thought before how her French uncle would

view this rise in William's status and she looked nervously to her husband but he was too taken with King Edward to have noticed.

'Of course he will not. We will be equals.' He was all but singing. 'This claret is a glorious vintage for a glorious night. We must share it with your court, Sire.'

'We must,' Edward agreed and Mathilda could swear she heard relief in the king's voice.

He took William's arm and led him out into the cold, the snowflakes losing themselves in his white hair even as they stuck to William's darker locks. Mathilda had no choice but to follow them across the white yard and into the great hall. Once safely within, she did not, as she had every time these last few days, check for Brihtric in the crowd for he was in her past now and must stay there. Instead, she looked up to the two thrones, set on the dais at the top end of the hall, and to her future.

One day it would be William and her sitting up there. One day the very same chairs, carved in wood and gilded with beautiful patterns, would sit empty, waiting for them to take their place. Those English thrones were now set upon the horizon of their lives and all they must do was keep on the path towards them so that, when the time came, they were ready.

PART TWO

CHAPTER FOURTEEN

The Thames, September 1052

'England – see how she rejoices to welcome us home!'

Earl Godwin flung his golden arms wide to the Thames spray. The motion threw water into Judith's face but she welcomed it for this time the ship was heading back towards England and not even the blackest of storms could have dampened the Godwinson spirits. All week Torr had been leaping around like a hare in spring as they sailed along the south coast to cheers in every port. Earl Godwin had stood at the prow, arms aloft to his people, gold bands glowing as if he were the figurehead himself. And, indeed, so he was proving to be, for the men of Wessex were flocking to him.

If Judith looked back now she could see a ragged but deter-mined flotilla following in their wake – fishing boats, trading vessels, small raiders, and every one filled with cheering Saxons willing their favourite earl back into power. There seemed to be no resistance – no ships in the mouth of the great Thames, no soldiers along its bank, no arrows or stones to challenge the Godwinsons' readied shields. It was as if the Saxons sat passively awaiting restoration of the natural order. Judith placed a hand on her belly, looking for signs of the new life she was certain was forming inside her, and thanked God that this child would be born where he was meant to be – in England.

'I see Thorney Island,' someone called from the prow. 'We are close.'

Everyone on the boat stiffened and Judith felt a momentary fear pulse through the family she was still learning to call her own.

'London Bridge,' Queen Aldyth breathed at her side.

The banished queen had joined the rest of her family at a place called Portland, riding there in secret with Harold's handfast wife, Lady Svana. Svana was a beautiful willowy lady who had arrived with two little lads and a tiny babe in arms, and had fallen upon Harold who had welcomed her with such love in his eyes Judith had had to put up a hand to shield herself from it. Torr would never look at her that way. Starting their marriage under the strain of exile had taught her that all too fast. He saw her with lust, maybe even with a little pride, but never with the soft, helpless devotion Harold clearly had for Svana. But it mattered not. Judith was here with Torr, with all the Godwinsons, and already they could hear cheers from the bridge.

'Are those for us?'

'I believe so,' Aldyth said. 'The Saxons love my father. They have missed him.'

'And he them,' Judith suggested as she saw the elderly earl look about him, tears openly shining in his clouding eyes.

'Oh, yes. He would do anything for these people and this land. And he certainly doesn't want to see it seized by creeping Normans.'

'Why do they not fight us?'

'Maybe Edward realises it is hopeless. A good king must

listen to his people and Edward's people are telling him they want my father back.'

'And you?'

'Perhaps. I hope so, though Edward may not agree. His Norman advisors have long worked to poison him against me.'

'Why?'

'Why do you think? If we have no heir the way is clear for another.'

'Duke William?'

Judith thought of Mathilda coming to warn them the Godwinsons' power was on the wane. She'd been so sure her husband would be offered the throne and, indeed, they had been in England at Christmas. Baldwin's spies had brought news of a very 'convivial' few days but not, crucially, of any announcement. Word had it that King Henri of France was enraged by the rumours and doing his best to track down any evidence of an arrangement but so far none had been found. And now Edward was, if not welcoming the Godwinsons back, then certainly not resisting them, and Godwin would never allow a Norman to take the throne. Judith hoped Mathilda would not be too disappointed.

Earl Godwin called the vast flotilla to a halt before London Bridge and Judith looked up at it with awe. The city was spread before her, an exciting sprawl of houses and churches, lacking order but rippling with as much energy as the Godwinson men in the boat. She moved forward to stand with Torr as a small rowing boat was sent out to the guards with a leather sack.

'What's in that?' she asked nervously but Torr just laughed.

'Money, Judith. Simple but effective.'

And indeed already the men were taking the sack and, with a crank that rent the afternoon air and sent the cheers to a new volume, the central portion of the structure before them began to slowly rise and separate to create a welcoming gap for the ships to sail through. Judith cowered, expecting an ambush, but none came. It was almost a disappointment. Even Earl Godwin looked slightly deflated but he soon gathered himself as the rowers heaved back on their oars and the great flagship moved in state through the bridge and approached Westminster. Judith's heart fluttered as she saw the ships of the royal navy along the far bank but they were tethered and empty.

'The king,' Gytha called suddenly. 'There's King Edward.'

She pointed to a slim figure in such a long gown that Judith mistook him for a priest until she saw the crown on his pale head. Aldyth wrapped her arms protectively around herself, her eyes fixed upon her husband but his, Judith noticed, were also upon her. Maybe an heir would yet be made on Saxon shores.

She touched a hand to her own stomach as Godwin manoeuvred cautiously before Westminster. She had not felt the sickness so many complained of, not even on the ship, but she was always hungry and her breasts seemed to have swelled. Torr had even commented on it, rubbing them boisterously as if their growth was some sort of response to his crude attentions. Judith hadn't disillusioned him. She'd wanted the secret for herself until she knew she was safe but maybe now that was close.

She looked longingly to her wooden chest, sealed up with wax against the damaging seawater. Inside were her inks and parchment, buried beneath her gowns in their own little casket. She'd had little chance to paint back in Baldwin's disapproving care, but perhaps very soon she would have a home of her own and blessed privacy in which to do as she wished.

She had been talking with the monks at St Donatian's church in Bruges and conceived of an ambitious plan to create a set of four gospel books. So far it had proved impossible but maybe at last God was rewarding her patience. For Earl Godwin was ashore now and bowing before his king who was raising him and kissing him on both rough cheeks as if he were his own son. And then, suddenly, a roar rose amongst the men on the banks: 'The Normans! The Normans have fled. The Normans are gone!'

The news was confirmed within moments. The Norman archbishop and his fellows had ridden out of the city, taking the back gate to the east at a panicked gallop. No man went after them, for all, it seemed, were glad to see them gone. Judith looked around the assembled court, flustered that their own arrival meant another's exile, but then Torr took her hand and squeezed it and the panic stilled.

'Welcome, at last, Wife, to England.'

Judith determined to tell him her news that evening, as the Godwinsons were feasted with raucous, near-hysterical cheer in the rather shabby great hall of what was apparently the royal palace. Torr had told her the Saxons favoured wood, not stone, for their buildings but she had not realised he meant their royal residences as well. Count Baldwin would have scoffed at a ruler who was happy to entertain in a 'hut', more like the Viking halls than the castles of continental Europe, but Judith thought it pretty. She loved the elegant painted carvings on the timber uprights and cared little that they were rotting in places, so long as they kept the roof up. She felt she could easily get used to English life, save that Torr was restless and fidgety, bored of all the overly polite chatter and staring intently at a group of young men and women trying to drag the minstrels to their instruments.

'Torr,' she said then, when he did not respond to her, 'Torr!'

'What?' he snapped and she flinched back. He softened immediately. 'Can I help you, Wife?'

'Maybe you already have?' She raised an eyebrow archly but he was clearly in no mood for such teasing. 'I believe, Husband, that I am carrying your child.'

That broke his strange mood and at last he angled his lean body fully towards her.

'You are? You are! Of course, your breasts. I should have realised.'

'How could you? It is as new to you as to me.'

His green eyes slid away.

'Yes. Yes, exactly. How could I?' He grabbed his ale cup, drank deep, and then suddenly leaped to his feet. 'My wife is with child,' he called wildly along the table. 'I will have a son!'

'Or daughter,' Judith said but her voice was lost in obliging cheers and suddenly Torr was kissing her and toasting her health and his joy seemed to make the evening spin delightfully.

'You must rest,' he insisted when he finally sat again. 'You must take care of yourself.'

'It will be nice to be settled.'

'Settled. Ah yes, settled. A home, drapes, all that.'

She smiled.

'Not drapes, Torr – I like the light. But a home, yes.'

'Yes,' he agreed keenly. 'That will be best. Settled, yes. You need not always be travelling about with me.'

'Nor, surely, will you need to travel once you are on your own lands?'

King Edward had already promised the whole family restitution. Godwin would regain Wessex and Harold East Anglia, much to the disgruntlement of Alfgar, Earl Leofric of Mercia's son, who had been holding it in his absence. Torr was to regain his lands in Hereford which he had assured Judith over and over were 'beautiful' but now he seemed less certain.

'Me?' He looked around the hall, everywhere but at her. 'Oh, I have to keep pace with the court. The king needs me.'

'What for?'

'Oh, you know, lordly duties. He will not, will he, make me an earl if he forgets I am even there?'

'I suppose not,' Judith agreed reluctantly. 'And you want to be an earl?' He gave her a scathing look. 'Of course you do. Sorry. So you will not stay with me in Herefordshire?'

'Sometimes. As much as I can, obviously, but the court moves and I must move with it if I am to, to . . .'

'Keep pace?'

'Exactly. Fret not, Judith, I will see you well cared for, the little one too. And you will prefer it, will you not, in our own home?'

He was half on his feet now. The dancing was starting and his body was twitching as if the minstrels were pulling their bow directly across it.

'I might be lonely,' Judith objected, trying to imagine it.

She had always been surrounded by people; indeed, she had complained bitterly about it on many an occasion. Briefly she saw a blissful glimpse of long days, just her and her inks, and was tempted by it but something felt wrong.

'Nonsense,' Torr said. 'You will have our son.'

'Or daughter.' He waved this away. 'You, then,' she asserted, 'will you not be lonely?'

'Me?' He laughed and then cut himself dead. 'I will cope,' he said gravely. 'Now, shall we dance? Oh no, you should not.'

'It's fine. I am perfectly well, Torr.'

'No, no, no. We cannot risk it. You are too precious, Judi.'

She looked longingly at the gathering dancers.

'But I would not want you to miss out.'

'No? Very well. I will not be long.'

And with that, to her great surprise, he was gone, leaping the benches and scooping up the nearest girl as if she'd been placed there just for him. Judith rose to object but saw the restored Queen Aldyth's eyes upon her and did not wish to make a fuss. Torr was probably right. She probably shouldn't risk it and, besides, it was only a dance.

It was later, on her way to the latrines behind the hall, that Judith saw exactly how hard her husband liked to dance and what a risk that might be. It was the girl she saw first, up against the wall, head flung back and face caught in a grimace of ecstasy, her breath escaping in short, thrilled gasps. The man was nothing more than a shape in the darkness, hands buried in bunched-up skirts. Judith ducked away – such encounters were not unusual later at night and were best ignored – but as she scuttled round the pair she heard the girl call out, 'Oh Torr, yes!' and turning, she saw her husband burying himself in her with a cry of joy. He looked over as if sensing a watcher, but it must have been too dark for him to see more than the outline of her skirts for he gave a low chuckle and beckoned.

'Room for one more, little one, if you like what you see.'

She should have said something, should have made some cold, dignified remark. That was what Mathilda would have done, but she was not Mathilda and she'd had nothing in her save a strangled cry.

'Uh oh,' she'd heard her husband say but she was gone, running for her funny wooden guesthouse, the rickety palace of Westminster swirling around her like a bad dream.

Torr caught up with her at the door, worming his lithe body into the frame before she could force the latch down.

'This then,' she threw at him, still striving to push him out, 'is why you want me more "settled"? This is why you want me shut away in the countryside whilst you gad about court bury-ing your sordid self in other women?'

He flinched.

'It was a moment of madness, Judi. I . . .'

'It was not.'

She saw it all so, so clearly now. It had been there through-out their awkward stay in Bruges – Torr in too-tight dance-holds, lurking in strange places, coming to bed late and smelling of sweat. Lord, she'd even caught him with that giddy Aileen before their wedding and had not recognised his excuses for what they were – lies. She'd taken his hastily proffered ring like a naive, blind fool but her eyes were open now.

'I thought it was I who was "appetising" to you, Husband, but I see that it is all women.'

'You're just such beautiful creatures. And you *are* appetis-ing, Judi. I just, just . . .'

'Want more?'

'I'm sorry. I'll try to . . .'

'No you won't, Torr. Or, at least, if you do you won't suc-ceed. You will not – cannot – be faithful to me.'

She spoke it calmly for the clear truth it was and he looked intently at her.

'And you . . . you are content with that?'

'Content?' She rolled the word around her tongue. 'Not content, Torr.' His face fell but her mind was working fast now. 'But I could, possibly, find consolation elsewhere.'

'Elsewhere?' His eyes widened. 'Now Judith . . .'

'Oh, not with other men,' she said impatiently and stood back to let him into their guesthouse at last. He sidled nerv-ously past and faced her across the clutch of seating that formed the receiving area below their bedchamber. 'I wish to commission a set of gospel books, Torr.'

'How many is a set?' he asked cautiously.

'Four.'

'Four?! Could we not start with one?'

She tipped her head to one side, pretending to consider.

'One for this transgression, Torr? That seems fit, yes.' He smiled but she wasn't finished with him. 'And then, of course, another for every future . . .'

'Four is a good number.'

'I think so.'

'It will be expensive, Judi.'

'I carry your child, Torr.'

'Which is obviously priceless to me. But there will be parchments, inks, an artist . . .'

'No artist.'

'But . . .'

'*That* will be my consolation, Torr. I wish to illuminate these books myself.'

'You? But you're . . .'

'Moderately skilled with a quill. We all, Husband, have our favourite pastimes . . .'

She looked pointedly at him and he shuffled his feet.

'And if you pursued yours . . .'

'Then it would be only fair for you to pursue yours, yes – discreetly.'

'Of course.' His eyes had lit up almost boyishly and he seized her, pulling her up against him. 'I can see you will make an even more excellent wife than I first thought, Judith of Flanders.'

Judith smiled tightly. This was not exactly what she might have hoped for but the moment her mother had chosen God over herself, she had learned to be realistic about her chances in life. She had made her way as a half-daughter up until now, so a half-wife should be easy. It had been a hard year since

Mathilda had tried to cut off her wedding to Torr with news of the Godwinsons' imminent fall but miraculously it was all turning around. Mathilda was back in Normandy and it was she, Judith, who was in England at last with the Godwinson fortunes on the rise. She would be a fool not to enjoy that as best she could.

CHAPTER FIFTEEN

Rouen, October 1052

'Bloody Godwinsons,' William roared, striding into the ladies' bower and sending the weaving frame rattling. 'God damn them all.'

'William!' Mathilda admonished him as Cecelia dropped her shuttle and the carefully worked pattern collapsed.

William had the grace to look ashamed but did not retract his curse. Mathilda went towards him, taking her son from the wet-nurse as she did so in the hope of calming his father. Baby Robert had been born in the spring and was now a bouncing child, crawling everywhere with an energy that gave William great pride. His young heir usually made him smile on even the toughest of days in the bickering ducal court but today he barely even glanced at him.

'What's happened?' Mathilda asked, jigging Robert on her hip for fear of him crying and riling his father further – if such a thing were possible.

William was almost visibly crackling with rage as he paced the length of the long bower above the Tour de Rouen's great hall. It was a sunny day and light flashed across him with every window opening he passed. Robert, thankfully, seemed fascinated but Mathilda watched nervously.

'The bloody Godwinsons have sailed back to England,' William told her. 'The onetime Archbishop of Canterbury had to flee for his life like a common criminal, not God's own anointed. He has been to see me to beg to return to Jumièges. He is a broken man. Years of service to King Edward and he is stabbed in the back the minute Earl bloody Godwin marches back in.'

Mathilda flinched. It was clear from the tight line of William's jaw that he felt the wound in his own spine and, indeed, it felt like a terrible betrayal of their close conversation in Westminster just last year.

'But how did the earl manage it?' she asked.

'How? With ships, Mathilda. They're mad on their ships, the English, Lord knows why. Nasty, unstable, unpredictable things. Useless for horses – not that such refinements bother the fool Saxons.'

A sudden memory swiped, unwelcomed, through William's complaints. Had Brihtric not ordered a boat made so that he could take her out on the river? She flinched at the recollection. No wonder her father had been furious, for she had been running around like a hoyden with that man and all in the name of love. Thank heavens she had grown up. She stroked Robert's rapidly growing hair fiercely, pushing away the past and focused again on William.

'The wretched earl took some sort of motley fleet round the south coast where he was hailed by his damned Wessex subjects who all scrambled to join him. Then they sailed right up the Thames and King Edward simply lifted London Bridge and let them back in, as if he had not proclaimed them traitors, as if he had not told the whole world that Earl Godwin murdered his brother, as if *they* were his friends and not the Normans who harboured him when none else would. They are reinstated in their earldoms, all of them, and the damned queen is back in Edward's bed.'

Mathilda swallowed. She was painfully aware of Della and Emeline squabbling over the tangled weft behind her and drew William to the far end of the bower.

'Edward did not seem a man fit to make heirs,' she told him in a low voice. 'The crown could yet come to you.'

'It could,' William allowed, 'but those Godwinsons will do everything they can to be sure it does not.'

She knew he was right for she had seen at Judith's wedding how the whole family sparkled with intent.

'Is Judith with them?' she asked.

'Judith? Your sister?'

'Cousin.'

'Oh. I suppose she must be, for Lord Tostig most certainly is.'

'That is good then.'

She said it without thinking but he was upon her in an instant.

'In what possible way is it good, Mathilda? Why would you say that? Whose side are you backing?'

'Yours, of course. William, please . . .'

'Do you know where they sailed from, these fancy ships?' Mathilda shook her head wildly, though she feared she did. 'Flanders,' William spat. 'Your father has been harbouring our enemies. What make you of that?'

'I am not my father, William.'

'And yet who went back to Flanders when first we had news of Edward's favour? You did.' He stuck a sharp finger in her face and Robert reared away with a terrified wail that, thankfully, made William step back a little. He collected himself with an effort. 'We are struggling, Wife. It is not just the ex-archbishop who is in trouble. All the Normans who crossed to

England with the king ten years ago have fled, some home to us here and some north to Scotland. They know England is not safe, for Edward has forgotten his past and caved before these impudent Godwinsons and they will rule him now. It is wrong. Wrong for England and wrong for God's blessed office of kingship and wrong for *us*.'

His voice had risen again. It rattled in her ears and his anger hit her and the now-weeping Robert in a burst of furious spittle.

'I'm sorry, William. I rode to Bruges to warn Judith, that is all.'

He stared down at her for so long that she felt like a mouse caught in a hawk's fierce intent but then Robert reached out a beseeching hand and, with a heavy sigh, William took it in his own and lifted the child into his arms. Robert quieted instantly.

'You are right. For Judith it is indeed good, but as she rises so we fall.' He took deep breaths, sucking in calm. 'It is kind of you, my Mora, to think of your cousin in that way, but I'm afraid we cannot afford kindness in this matter.'

He took Robert to the nearest window, looking intently down at him in the light spilling in from the high arch. Mathilda saw hurt silver-bright in his eyes and felt foolish for being afraid of him. This was her husband, the father of the child he now held and, if she was not much mistaken, of another already in her belly. This threat to him was a threat to her too and they must stand together against it, however hard that might be. She moved over and leaned in against him to look out over the bustling palace yard and the roofs of Rouen beyond.

'We were promised England, Mathilda,' William whispered. 'We were promised the throne. People should stick to their promises. I stuck to my father's promise to give Edward safe shelter when England was against him, so surely now he should hold firm to his?'

'He should, William, truly, but not all men are as honourable as you.'

William growled low in his throat.

'Maybe not, but if so we must force them to it – for ourselves and for Robert.'

Mathilda nodded fiercely.

'And we will, Husband, I swear it.'

He tilted her chin towards him and looked hard into her eyes.

'We will have a fight on our hands.'

She looked hard back. He was right, there was no space for kindness here.

'Then it is a good job, William, that you fight so well.'

At last he smiled.

'It is. It truly is.' He turned and began pacing again, bouncing Robert up in the air as if he weighed little more than a fool's juggling ball. 'We will send to my cousin Edward asking for ratification of his promise.' He stopped in a window opening as if basking in the sunshine of his new purpose. 'And we will send to France too. King Henri will support us in this, I know he will.'

Mathilda looked back up the bower to the oaken casket Henri had sent her on their wedding day. It was stood next to the now re-set loom to hold all the wools for her weaving and on the pretty pearl lid she could see the golden words *Mathilda of Normandy* shining in the sun. She had long treasured it as a symbol of France's regard but now they needed more. It was time, it seemed, for her royal uncle to come to William's aid and she could only pray he would do so.

CHAPTER SIXTEEN

Bonneville, March 1053

'Invasion!'

The word ripped through the happy crowds in Bonneville's great hall, cutting off laughter and chopping conversations dead. This quiet seaside castle had swiftly become Mathilda's favourite of the ducal residences and she had made so many happy plans to celebrate Robert's first birthday here but now her dainty feast was halted by the all too familiar cry of war.

'By whom?' she demanded.

'By France.'

The word roared through Mathilda's mind – France? This was certainly not the response they had been hoping for when they had sent word of the forsaken promise last year. She looked nervously to William and found him already glaring at her over the great pyramid of spiced pastries that formed her carefully planned centrepiece.

'Your uncle turns on us, Wife,' he snarled.

'And *your* overlord, Husband.'

William's eyes turned black as new-mined coal.

'My overlord indeed, to whom I have ever sworn loyalty. Why is it only I who hold to such vows?!' He slammed his hand into the wall in fury, making the candles tumble from their holders and everyone scurry to be as far away from him as possible. 'Invasion? Why?'

He glared around, his eyes probing every last man and woman for the source of this betrayal. All cowered back and it was only Fitz who dared to answer: 'It will be England, my lord.'

William looked as if he would roar even louder at this but then something passed between him and his ever-faithful lord and instead he nodded grimly.

'It will, Fitz, it will. It seems Henri does not wish me, his sworn and ever-obedient vassal, to have a throne of my own.' He pushed the table aside, sending several pastries toppling to the floor where the hounds pounced delightedly on them. 'Can he not understand that if we stood side by side in this we could make France great? Is he so petty-minded that he cannot see past his own tiny borders?'

'It would seem not,' Fitz said. 'But he will not get the better of us Normans.'

He gestured around the men, already grabbing for their swords as if battle might be joined this very evening. Mathilda looked at Odo nudging a pretty girl off his knee to grab his shield from the wall, and La Barbe talking eagerly to Della, and Fitz now clowning around, flexing his muscles with little Adelisa hanging from his arm, her belly as rounded as an apple on the tree. For a glancing moment she despised these Normans, dressed as courtiers but still little more than soldiers beneath. Her carefully planned dinner was forgotten in the news of war and Robert forgotten with it. Irritated, she shifted her son forward on her lap where he was wriggling against her swollen belly.

'Surely we could parley?' she pleaded.

William barely even gave her a glance.

'Parley will count for nothing for he would not have turned on me lightly. There will be someone at the bottom of this, working treachery. There always is.'

'Always, William?'

'*Always*. Now, where are my captains?'

Fitz shot forward, Odo too. Fulk, however, was slower to rise as if, for once, his big body was too heavy for him and there was no sign of William's fourth man.

'Where's Hugh?' William demanded.

'He's ill, Lord Duke,' Fitz said.

'In what way?'

'I'm not sure. Ask Fulk. He was part of his hunting party when he sickened.'

William turned his sharp stare on Fulk, who shifted like a youngster caught scrumping apples.

'I don't know how it happened, Duke. He just caught a fever.'

William looked alarmed.

'Why has no one mentioned this before? What if it spreads? I cannot march on the French with a vomiting army.'

'It will not spread, Lord Duke. I think it was perhaps something he ate.'

William's eyes narrowed and he looked down the table to Mabel. She was also pregnant with her second child, having dutifully given Fulk a son barely nine months after their wedding, but was irritatingly elegant with it and was sitting serenely picking a piece of food out of one of her nail diamonds.

'You are caring for my captain of the cavalry, my lady of Belleme?'

Mabel gave a slow, thin smile.

'Of course, Lord Duke. It is sad that Hugh is ill but he is receiving the very best attention. I will have him slaying invaders for you within the week.'

William held her gaze for several heartbeats but then nodded.

'Do so. The rest of you – muster your troops. We will rout the French before Easter, I swear it!'

Fitz, Roger and Fulk bowed themselves out, plucking their men from the benches like ripe plums, and William turned back to Mathilda.

'I told you there was always treachery, and you can wager the Bellemes will have a hand in it. It is too damned wearisome. Perhaps I should let Henri have Normandy and the damned Godwinsons have England and take my sword to Italy where it is, at least, warm.'

'You would join the Guiscard, William?'

'Why not? Would he have me, do you think?'

He reached out a hand towards Robert, who seized at it delightedly and, relieved, Mathilda addressed their son: 'What think you, Robert? Would the famous robber baron take on a man who has defeated more rebels than there are Moors in Sicily? A man who can pull a longer bow than any other, who can fight for hours on end without tiring, and who can break a siege with ruthless efficiency?' She looked at Robert, who had cocked his little head on one side as if he might genuinely have the answer, and then supplied it for him: 'We think you might squeak into his lower ranks.'

William gave a grunt of amusement.

'And you, my Mora, how would you like Italy? You would have a "villa" with sun terraces and vines and, and . . .'

'And a husband who was ever out fighting. It would be little different, William.'

He sobered.

'That is true, Mathilda. We fight too much. Why must they oppose me? First Edward and his damned Godwinson pets and now Henri. Have I angered the Lord? Is it us, think you? Is it because our marriage was not sanctioned by the Pope?'

'Of course not. God believes in our marriage, William – see how he blesses us with children.'

William smiled and ran a gentle hand over the swell of their second child within her.

'You are right, of course you are. I will send more letters to Rome about our marriage and pray that God continues to favour us. I am just wary. When I was younger I worried that everything was a punishment for my mother's low status but I have grown out of that. Nobility, Mathilda, is in bearing, not in blood. Look at Mabel – she is of the finest pedigree and she is a poisonous witch.'

'I will find out what she plots, William.'

'You?'

'Why not? I will ask Emeline to . . . delve.'

Both their eyes slid to Emeline, chattering to Lord Bertrand. William looked her up and down.

'She is French, your attendant, is she not?'

'By birth, William, yes, but she has been with me since she was ten years old.'

'Almost a woman.'

'Hardly . . .'

'And definitely a spy.'

Mathilda's heart picked up a beat at the harsh insistence of his voice but she was determined to stand up for her attendant and dear friend.

'Not a spy, Husband,' she insisted, 'just a well-informed messenger.'

And, thank the Lord, he smiled.

The sun was barely over the horizon the next day before clangs of steel ripped through the air as men sought to sharpen up their fighting skills. William had been up late despatching messengers all across the duchy with a call to arms but he was still gone from their bed before she woke and when Mathilda looked out of the window she could see him at the centre of the sparring men. Odo was at his side, his bishop's tunic tucked up beneath a mail coat, happily wielding a huge spiked mace. As a cleric he was forbidden to spill blood but God did not, apparently, mind him crushing flesh and he clearly planned to ride to war with the rest.

Noting her precious pastry pyramid stood on a stool to one side, ravaged by hungry soldiers, Mathilda turned wearily away just in time to see Emeline creeping into the chamber, dark smudges beneath her pretty eyes.

'Long night?'

Emeline grimaced ruefully.

'Something about war makes men randy and Bertrand can be a bit . . . odd. But it was worth it. Mabel *did* poison Hugh.'

'I knew it,' Mathilda said, 'but why?'

'She didn't mean to. That is, she meant to poison someone, just not poor Hugh. She was after some cousin of his returned from fighting in Italy and trying to steal land from her borders.'

'Arnold de Giroie?'

'That's the one.'

Mathilda remembered inadvertently teasing the man about farming vines at the wedding. Clearly the Italian lands had not been kind to him and he had decided to try and claim some back home, though it would seem he'd made a poor choice.

'And Mabel thought it would be best if he was disposed of?' she asked incredulously.

'Yes. She made him a "special" cup of wine for his return from a hunt with Fulk the other day but he said he wasn't thirsty and all would have been fine, save that Hugh burst in and downed the damned drink in one. Apparently he fell to the floor within moments, frothing and flailing like a mangy cur. Bertrand was quite shocked.'

'Not as shocked as Hugh, I imagine,' Mathilda said dryly.

'No. He's coming round though, thank God. Of all the men to hurt, Hugh is surely the worst.'

'Why, Emeline?'

'He's so kind, that's all. Have you seen him with his horses? He treats them like men. Nay, like women – stroking them and soothing them and coaxing them to his will. It is magic to watch.'

'You sound almost jealous, Em.'

'I do, don't I? Who'd have thought it – jealous of a horse!' She laughed, then sobered just as swiftly. 'It seems Mabel moved quickly to purge the poison and now she is doing all she can to keep Hugh with us.'

'As she should.'

'Yes. By all accounts Fulk was furious and that seems to have upset Mabel in turn. Perhaps she likes her conquering husband more than she's letting on?'

'I hope so – for his sake. Poor Hugh. She cannot get away with this, Em. I'll speak to her.'

Emeline looked horrified.

'No! Oh, my lady, please don't or she will know where our information has come from.'

'I will not speak of Bertrand.'

'She'll know all the same.'

'Even so, I must speak. This is my household now and I will not have men poisoned within it. Fetch Mabel to the hall.'

'Now?'

'Yes, now. Cecelia will go. You rest, Em. You've done well and I'll see you rewarded.'

Emeline escaped to her antechamber as Cecelia ran to find Mabel and Mathilda headed to the hall and settled herself into her great chair. The babe rolled and turned inside her as if limbering up for the confrontation ahead and Mathilda put a hand to her belly to try and calm it. She was nervous enough already.

Mabel entered a little time later, a hassled Cecelia fretting behind her like a shepherd's dog.

'You wanted me, my lady?'

'I did. I wish to know a little more of Hugh's health.'

'It is improving.'

'It will need to. I hear he was laid very low.'

'You do?'

'Yes. Fulk believes it was something he ate. What could that be, do you think, when he dined with everyone else?'

Mabel thrust her chin up high, standing stiffly proud before her duchess, her hands hooked under her neatly bulging belly.

'Perhaps it was when he was hunting? Perhaps he picked a mushroom?'

'A mushroom? I wasn't aware Lord Hugh normally sustained himself with fungi.'

'Perhaps it was all there was available?'

'You did not arrange food for them, my lady?'

Mathilda's fingers twitched.

'Of course I did, but I do not know if it was eaten for I was not there.'

Mathilda stood up suddenly and approached Mabel.

'But you *were* there when they returned, yes? You *were* there when poor Hugh fell ill?'

'Well, yes, but these things can take time.'

'Or they can be very fast. He was thirsty, I hear?'

Mabel jumped.

'Who from? Who have you been talking to?' Mabel cast a wild-eyed look around the hall as if she might spot the miscreant hiding in the fresh floor rushes.

'Mabel,' Mathilda said quietly, forcing the other woman to look at her. 'I will not have it. Not here. You may choose to poison people down in the south amongst your own kind but I will not have such behaviour up here. It is not just.'

'Just? Is a man coming back from Italy and trying to steal lands from his neighbour just?'

'Hugh has been to Italy?'

Mabel ground her teeth.

'You know he has not. The drink was intended for his cousin Arnold. He is an unpleasant man, my lady, and would be no loss to anyone.'

'Is that not God's place to decide?'

'God is very busy. Sometimes it is better to relieve him of some responsibility.'

'How very Christian of you, Mabel.'

'You question my faith?'

Mabel stepped forward, so close their bumps almost touched and Mathilda was forced to look up at her haughty subject, but she refused to be cowed.

'I question your interpretation of it. You may have done as you wished here in Normandy whilst women were so sparse you could easily dazzle the men into turning a blind eye to your bitter potions, but that time is done. I am duchess now.'

'And don't we know it.'

'As you should, my lady of Belleme. William is on the alert for treachery and fears it in you.'

'No, I . . .'

'You were merely being selfish, I see that, but William may not for Hugh is very dear to him. Please tend our cavalry captain well, my lady. If he rides safely to join the army we will say no more of it, but that is by my mercy and not your power.'

'You are too gracious,' Mabel spat and then she was gone,

swishing out of the hall at pace, sending rushes flying and sentries leaping to open the doors.

Mathilda watched her go, frozen, and when finally the doors were shut again she sank into her chair and reached for her wine, taking a long draught to steady herself. She was shaking all over with rage and nerves and a rich, heady thrill. She'd done it – she'd confronted the serpent and, for now at least, she'd won. Taking another gulp of wine she reached for Cecelia's arm and headed gratefully back to her chamber. The screech of steel still tore up the air but now it seemed only to scratch at the back of her weary mind and she sank onto the little stool in the window embrasure to watch the men below, rubbing at her bulging belly as Cecelia fussed around her.

'My lady, do you feel unwell? You should eat.'

'No.'

'For the babe at least.'

'I can't.'

She leaned forward, looking for William down in the yard, but the movement cramped in her belly. It felt larger this time than the last. The babe was several weeks away yet but she could feel it straining at her skin already, pulling it so tight she feared it would not stretch any further. Her dress felt sticky and itchy and she was warm, so very warm.

'It's too hot in here,' she complained.

'It is not hot, my lady. Indeed, it is a rather cool day, though you do look a little flushed. Perhaps . . .'

But Mathilda, feeling restless and achy, stood up to ward off any fussing. Cecelia gasped and, turning back, Mathilda saw her pointing in silent horror at her skirts. She looked down and there, seeping through the beautiful fabric, was a thick red stain: blood.

*

It was an ugly fight and Mathilda was aware of every single moment. This babe was impatient, keen to come before its time, and Mathilda's little body picked up the rhythms of childbirth as quickly as it had with Robert, despite her best efforts to resist.

'You must not fight it, my lady,' Emeline told her, roused from her nap by Cecelia's cries for help.

'It's too soon,' Mathilda wailed.

'The babe does not think so,' Della said, ever practical.

'The babe does not think at all.'

'Perhaps not but it knows what it wants all the same and that is to see the light.'

None of them spoke the dread thought that though the light might fall on the babe it was unlikely to see it.

'You must push, my lady,' Cecelia told her and though Mathilda longed to disobey, her body was in control and she had no choice.

In the end, it barely hurt at all. The babe slid out and Della caught it. It made no sound. Cecelia and Emeline clutched Mathilda close as she raised herself to see and then, before all of their astonished eyes, Della held it high, dangling it by its tiny feet, and slapped it three times.

'Della, no . . . !' Mathilda choked but she was interrupted by a cry – a small, frail but determined cry.

'It lives!' Cecelia breathed.

'*She* lives,' Della corrected her. 'You have a princess, my lady.'

She placed the child gently in Mathilda's arms. She was tiny, barely bigger than her mother's hand, but perfect in every way.

'Will she survive?' Mathilda dared to ask.

'Only God can know. You should feed her.'

Mathilda looked down and sure enough the baby was rootling, her tiny lips pouting frantically. She pulled her shift aside and, like an arrow to the target, her tiny daughter latched on. She drank hungrily but after only a few moments she lolled back, exhausted.

'She can't do it,' Mathilda said, panicked.

'She can,' Della insisted. 'And she has. It will just take time. We must keep her very warm, feed her very often and massage her little limbs to be sure her blood is flowing.'

Mathilda felt a sob rise in her throat. This had all been so sudden, so unexpected, especially on top of the earlier sorrows. She had a sudden, stark picture of Mabel of Belleme stood so very close to her in the great hall earlier. Her wine had been nearby. Had she . . . ? Surely not? Surely even Mabel would not dare poison a duchess. She focused on the child.

'She's so little.'

'As are you, my lady,' Cecelia said gently, 'but it's never stopped you doing anything.'

Now Mathilda's tears flowed.

'William,' she gasped. 'William should see her.'

They sent a maid running and very soon footsteps rapped out along the stone floor and William swung into the room at a half-run.

'My dear, my Mora, what is this?'

Mathilda looked at the babe.

'This, William, is your daughter. It seems she feared you would go to war without seeing her.'

He crept closer, reaching out a tentative hand to the blanket in which the babe was swaddled.

'She is . . .' He hesitated. 'She is all there?'

Mathilda tipped her outward so he could see her tiny limbs, complete with minuscule fingers and toes.

'She is all there, Husband.' He sat slowly down, his eyes wide at this unexpected miracle. 'I thought perhaps we could call her Herleva?'

William flinched.

'No. That is, I think that for this, our first daughter, we should honour her royal grandmother. She will be Adela. You will like that, Mathilda, will you not.'

It was not a question.

'I will like that.'

'Good. It is fit. My mother is a wonderful woman but not a ruler. My father chose her for her sweetness, her simplicity, her empty-headed adoration.'

'William!'

'It's true, Mathilda.' Of course it was. 'And she has given me the same. I adore her, you know I do, but she is so much . . . so much smaller than you.'

'Not smaller, William.'

'Oh, I have not the words for it but you know what I mean. I can trust you to rule.

'But not to be your regent?'

'Not to be named as such but we both, surely, know the truth of it?'

Mathilda considered this. Perhaps she should step back as William's precious Normans expected. Perhaps she should stay in the bower and confine herself to being his wife rather than his fellow ruler. But she knew already that she would find that impossible.

'My mother raised me to sharpen my wits,' she said ruefully.

'Maybe, my Mora, but the wits are all your own. They scare me a little for I do not always know what you will do but I take pride in them too. I did not know before that women could be so fierce, or so intelligent. I have ruled this unruly duchy alone for so long and I cannot explain how much it means to me to share the burden with a like-minded partner.'

Mathilda swallowed.

'Are we so very alike, William?'

'In all the essentials, yes.'

She moved to protest but at that moment Adela gave a little cough and then a strange splutter and her tiny body spasmed. Mathilda panicked but William just took her and put her over his big shoulder, rubbing her back in circles until, with a funny little gurgle, she quietened.

'Where did you learn that?' Mathilda asked, astonished.

William shrugged self-consciously.

'Odo was a sickly baby.'

'You helped look after him?'

'Sometimes. At first. But then . . .'

He paused, almost as choked as the baby had just been.

'Then . . . ?' Mathilda dared to prompt.

'Then I had to go.'

'Go where, William?'

He looked out of the window, as if the answer might be in the clouds that were scudding across the moonlit sky.

'To my duty, of course. I went to become a duke.'

'You were seven?'

'Yes.'

'How . . . how did it feel?'

'Feel?' He thrust the baby back at her. 'It did not *feel*, Mathilda, it just was.'

'But you must have . . .'

'It did not feel. This sort of talk is why my men do not trust female regents. But no matter. You must sleep, my Mora, and I must return to my men for we have a war to fight and I will not let Henri get to my daughter's door.'

And with that, he planted a kiss upon her head, so hard that she felt it might dent her skull, and strode fiercely from the room.

CHAPTER SEVENTEEN

Rouen, July 1053

athilda kicked up one of last year's rotten apples as if it might somehow pierce the gloom of the day but it simply broke in an ugly mess against the nearest tree, making Emeline squeal crossly. For weeks the sun had refused to shine as it should at this time of year and little Robert had been going mad cooped up in the palace. They'd brought him out to the orchard at the rear of the Tour de Rouen in the hope of running some energy out of him but all they seemed to be doing was getting him muddy. Mathilda tugged impatiently on his tunic as he tried, yet again, to climb one of the lower trees, and looked to the low skies for patience. When would this non-summer ever end?

The French had invaded in force, piercing Eastern Normandy on two fronts with a clear aim of pincering in on Rouen as William's troops chased the attackers around the countryside beyond. La Barbe had suggested that Mathilda and her ladies withdrew to Caen in the west, out of the path of the invaders, but Caen was a stark, drear city and its people amongst the most rebellious even in Normandy and Mathilda had condemned a move there as madness.

As a result they were stuck, helpless, within the city and to make matters worse the unseasonable damp had turned the streets into rivers and filled the air with the perpetual sound of water dripping off sodden roofs in fat, angry splatters. Mathilda could not begin to imagine how it felt for the poor soldiers of Normandy out in this night and day as they struggled to defend their duchy and tried to be grateful for her pretty palace but it was hard. Adela, although thankfully still with them, was a sickly, troublesome child, Robert was a bundle of frustrated energy, and Emeline was worse than either of them.

'Why do they not just camp the army here?' she fretted now, climbing onto a tree-stump to peer uselessly over the wall that separated the Tour from the rest of the city. Ever since Hugh had mercifully recovered and ridden out on the tail of the army she had taken to searching the horizon as if the enemy might pop up at any moment. 'Why is William ducking around the duchy chasing the enemy's tail instead of meeting them head on?'

'He is weakening them,' Mathilda told her, dutifully repeating what William had told her before he left. 'He is picking off foraging parties and breaking up their units.'

'But why?'

'Why?' Della asked, pausing from chasing her own two boys around the trees, skirts rucked up around her ample hips to reveal boots that were far from elegant but enviably waterproof. 'Because they outnumber us three times over, that's why.'

'Lord help us!' Emeline wailed. 'We're doomed. Why did we even come to Normandy? I knew this war-addled duchy was trouble when I was dropped here as a child. Did I not get out as soon as I was able? And was I not right to do so? So why on earth am I back in this godforsaken city waiting to die?'

'Rouen is a beautiful city,' Mathilda said, pulling Emeline away from the wall.

'It's not as beautiful as Bruges though, is it? It hasn't her pretty canals, or her curving bridges or her safe encircling walls. Rouen sits on the big, fat Seine, just a boat ride from Paris, and we sit on her banks, waiting to be taken. We must do something, my lady.'

Mathilda put a comforting arm around her. She did not like seeing sunny Emeline this way.

'You are missing Lord Bertrand,' she suggested, trying to tease her out of her gloom.

'I am not.' Emeline stamped her foot then hung her head. 'Beg pardon, my lady. I am all out of sorts. I'm sorry. I am done with Lord Bertrand. I know he is useful to you but the Bel-lemes are as strange as a lily pad of three-legged frogs.'

Mathilda looked her up and down curiously.

'It matters not, Emeline. I am sorry I ever asked you to get close to him. You should find someone nicer to cheer you up.'

Emeline smiled wanly.

'Maybe. It's just all these wars and rebellions – they press on me like giant's feet. Sometimes it feels as if ever since we came back across the Narrow Sea in '51 things have been going wrong and now here we are with thousands of vengeful Frenchmen all but at our door. Even Raoul marches on us.'

'Raoul d'Amiens fights with the French?' Mathilda pictured him delivering her damned wedding casket and shivered. 'Why has he turned upon us?'

Della tutted.

'You are as suspicious as the duke your husband, my lady. Raoul has not "turned" on anyone; it is simply that he is Henri's man. He is not so much against us, as for the French.'

'Yet there is *some* treachery,' Emeline put in, 'for the French have taken Mortemer in the north of the duchy. It is held by Raoul's son-in-law, Lord Evelin, is it not? Convenient, hey, for an invading army to have relations with a key to the gates?'

Mathilda grimaced. It was convenient indeed and she dreaded William's response.

'Come,' she snapped, 'let's get inside.'

The others needed no second asking.

In the end, however, holding Mortemer did not aid the French victory as much as lead to their defeat, for a Norman battalion reached the city on the very night the French occupiers discovered Lord Evelin's wine cellars and drank them dry. The Norman soldiers were too well trained to miss such an opportunity and, firing the town, they massacred every last Frenchman as they came stumbling out of the flames. The news was enough to send the rest of Henri's troops scurrying back over the border and suddenly, as if God had sent a wind to blow the enemy away, Normandy was safe once more.

The women, even Emeline, danced with joy when the news came and then all was a fluster to prepare for the victors' return. But when William finally reached Rouen, it was at first light and everyone was abed. Mathilda started awake to find her husband standing over her as if dropped there by God.

'William!' she stuttered, fighting to shake sleep from her brain. 'Welcome.'

She reached for him, still only half-certain that he was truly there, but he put up his hands to stop her.

'I am dirty, Mathilda.'

'I care not.' But there was a strange, pale wildfire in his dark eyes and she hesitated. 'You are well?'

'I am well.'

Still he stood there as she awkwardly threw off the covers and rose to fetch him ale from the jug on the sideboard. There was no sign of Emeline or Cecelia but with William in this mood, she was glad they were alone. She nervously held it out to him.

'The French are defeated?'

'Yes, and fled for home – but you knew that, did you not?'

'Of course I knew that, William. Your messengers came with the news.'

William took a sudden step forward, his armour creaking alarmingly as if his very limbs were made of metal, and Mathilda started back, knocking the ale down her pale linen shift.

'They reported that you were not surprised to hear it.'

'Well, no. You told me that you always win, William, so why should I be surprised?' He faltered but still looked distrustful. He was searching for someone to blame, she saw, and she was first to hand. She placed the cup aside and rushed to him but he put up his hands to hold her off.

'I hear, Wife, that you have been writing to King Henri – our enemy.'

Mathilda swallowed. He looked so big standing over her in the dawn light, his eyes full of anger.

'I have, William.' He blinked, surprised, and she stepped closer. 'Of course I have. He is my uncle and I thought I might be able to appeal to him on your behalf. So yes, I have written to him wanting to know why he has turned against you – against *us*. I have written to my mother too but her answer was empty.'

'And Henri's?'

'Henri sent no answer at all.'

'How do I know that? How do I know you are not plotting with him? How do I know your slut of an attendant is not taking information into French beds?'

'William! Why are you talking like this? Of course I am not a spy. I am your wife, mother of your children.'

'But are you?'

'William?'

'Maybe it was not his allegiance to Emperor Heinrich that prevented the Pope from sanctioning this match, but some pact with King Henri. Maybe it has been there all along to offer you a way out of our marriage.'

Mathilda could only stare at him, amazed. Truly, he saw treachery everywhere.

'You think I would besmirch my honour and that of my children for *politics*? I am not a man, William; I do not think that way. Your interests are my interests for I am Duchess of Normandy and want only to serve her as you serve her. Who has been speaking to you, William? Who has been saying this of me?'

He looked to the window opening through which the skies were lightening in a soggy pink over Rouen's myriad roofs and spires.

'Lord Bertrand,' he admitted eventually. 'He said Emeline was liaising with some Frenchman. He said she was passing information – and he should know, Mathilda, for has she not been sporting in his bed these last few months?'

'Lord Bertrand? Oh, William, Emeline is not with any Frenchmen. She is forever drooling over Raoul d'Amiens but he has refused her.'

'Raoul?! Raoul is a serpent.'

'No. William, surely . . .'

'You would defend him, a Frenchman?'

Mathilda gulped.

'No, William. Of course not, not if he has done you wrong.'

'Wrong?! He fought against me, Mathilda. He was at Morte-mer.'

Mathilda tasted bile in the back of her throat.

'I heard. He is, then, dead?'

'No. He's a serpent, I tell you. He wormed his troops into the place via his treacherous son-in-law, Lord Evelin, and then when it all went wrong he got that damned man to sneak him out. They are both safely over the border with Henri and no doubt laughing at me as we speak.'

'They will hardly be laughing, William, for they are defeated. Routed. *They* are the ones who are laughable.'

'Maybe. We'll see. But are you sure Emeline has not had word from him? After all, she is French too.'

'And my devoted servant. Truly, the only person Emeline is spying on is Mabel and that is why Bertrand is sewing these doubts. He is hitting out because it was he who told us Mabel had poisoned Hugh and now he is afraid for his own skin.'

William sighed and seemed suddenly to deflate like a punctured bladder.

'You may be right. I apologise.' He took her hands in his, rubbing her fingers with his own dirty, calloused ones as if he could ease all the tension of war out into her care. 'I am tired, my Mora, that is all, and hurt by France turning upon me. But I should not have taken it out on you. You are my partner, are you not?'

'Of course. I am here for you in everything, William. Come to bed and let me soothe . . .'

But her words were cut off by a blood-chilling cry of pain from somewhere outside the main Tour. They both looked urgently round as it came again, cutting the dawn air like a blade with a run of terrified curses riding in its wake. William stared, frozen for a moment, then ran, Mathilda on his heels, though she soon fell behind. She could hear William barking out commands but still the cries continued, interspersed with hammering and shouting and when she finally ran into the yard she saw Cecelia pressed against the stable wall, crying into the wood.

'What's happening?' she gasped.

'Emeline,' she choked out and at the name Mathilda's heart seemed to climb out of her throat.

She looked to the barred stable door. Fitz was hacking at it with a rough axe he must have picked up from the woodpile but, like everything in William's palace, the door was built solidly and resisted even his strength. Still the cries came from within and now Mathilda could hear Emeline's dear tones in them and tried to run for the door as if she could do with her hands what Fitz could not with his axe. Cecelia pulled her back, jabbering manically.

'He said only that he wanted to see her. I told her not to go. I told her to wait until the court was risen but you know Emeline.' Her words were drowned in a new set of sobs. 'I went with her. I insisted, but what could I do? He just grabbed her, my lady, grabbed her by her hair and dragged her inside and, and . . .'

'Who, Cee?'

'Lord Bertrand.'

She paused as they all heard a scrabbling at the bolt. The screams had stopped enough for them to catch the sound of the lock rasping back and a new cry, lower and bubbling with blood. Then silence.

The courtiers who had all come running, most of them still in their nightwear, stood staring as William slowly stepped forward and pulled back the door. There, lying skewed across the hay-strewn threshold, his eyes staring sightlessly up at the lightening sky and blood running out from his throat, was Lord Bertrand. Mathilda's eyes flew past him and found Emeline, shaking and covered in blood and locked in the arms of Hugh de Grandmesnil.

'He attacked her,' Hugh cried. 'He dragged a poor, helpless woman into the stables and attacked her with a whip like a coward.'

The horses, tossing their heads in the stalls behind, whinnied agreement in an eerie chorus.

'How did you get in, Hugh?' Mathilda asked, looking at the paltry splinter marks Fitz's axe had made in the door.

'Trap at the back. In case of fire. Don't want the horses burning, do we?'

'Er, no. Thank you, Hugh, thank you so much.'

He shrugged.

'Anyone would have done it. That man had evil in his eyes. I saw it.'

'You did?' Mathilda asked curiously, looking from him to Emeline, supported by his strong hold.

'Yes. I woke early and, er, wanted to check on the horses. I saw Emeline go into the stables and thought the gentleman did not look, well, gentle. I . . . hovered. Just in case, you understand.'

Mathilda thought she did understand.

'Well, thank the Lord you did. We are all in your debt, are we not, Emeline?'

But the poor girl just broke into sobs.

'It was my fault. All my fault.'

'That's not true, Emeline,' Cecelia cried. 'How could it be your fault?'

She took a step forward to go to her friend but faltered at the body blocking her route. The blood from Bertrand's throat was congealing now but the red was reflected in the dew-damp cobbles like a hellish pool.

'He said I was a cruel little tart,' Emeline choked out, 'and I am – *I am*! He said I exploited him. He said I was a temptation sent to corrupt him from his duties. He said, he said . . .' More sobbing. 'He said if I was so free with my body he could be free with it too and he was right.'

'That's not true, Em,' Mathilda insisted, her heart breaking.

She steeled herself to step over the dead Bertrand but she was too slow. For now Hugh was taking Emeline's arms and moving her oh so gently away from him and all but lifting her so that she had to look into his eyes.

'That is not true, Emeline,' he said and his voice seemed ten times firmer and more determined than Mathilda's. 'And you must never, ever think it. Bertrand had no right to attack you. None. You are far, far too good for him as he proved this morning and he has paid the price.'

Emeline looked up at him.

'You saved me, Hugh.'

'Of course. I would, I hope, save any woman falling foul of such a man, but especially you.'

'Why?' It was more a breath than a word.

Mathilda crept up to William who was watching as fascinated as the rest of the court as Hugh pulled Emeline even closer, his eyes locked on hers.

'Because I love you. Have done so for ages.'

The women in the yard gave a collective sigh of joy. Mathilda felt it run across her flesh like a slippery silk, almost too soft to bear. She could find no words to speak and could only watch as William stepped firmly over Bertrand's corpse and patted his cavalry captain awkwardly on the back. Both Emeline and Hugh looked startled.

'You are looking, Hugh, to marry?' William asked, his voice strident and somehow overly purposeful after the hushed exchange of the couple still locked together.

'I am,' Hugh agreed, 'if the lady is willing?'

The 'lady', uncharacteristically shy, could only nod but it was enough for Hugh who claimed her lips with his own as the men yelled ribald encouragement. Mathilda felt herself sway and had to lean against the rough wood of the stable. Her legs, already weak with William's harsh accusations, felt as useless as a new-born foal's, and as men rushed to drag Bertrand's corpse from the stable door and close it delightedly on the newly betrothed pair, she made for her chamber.

She was glad for Emeline, of course she was, and so, so grateful to Hugh for saving her from who knows what dread attack, but the glow in the couple's eyes seemed to burn her shuddering heart. Why had William come home from war ready to suspect her of treachery and Hugh had not even for one moment believed loose-living Emeline had done anything wrong? The answer was clear – love.

She thought of how often she had seen the pair seek each other out in dances, of how Emeline had complained so fondly about Hugh's equine conversation and how worried she had been when he'd been poisoned. She remembered Hugh's doting eyes on Emeline when she was dancing with the young Saxon in Westminster that fateful Yule in 1051 when she and William had been talking crowns, not love, and realised the earnest cavalry captain had been looking for this opportunity for a long time.

Crowns are better than love, she reminded herself fiercely, but it did not feel so convincing today and she crawled gratefully back into her bed and prayed for the blissful oblivion of sleep.

CHAPTER EIGHTEEN

Falaise, August 1056

'England defies me!'

William's roar of anger shuddered through the soft willows above the heads of the court, making Mathilda want to jump up and apologise to their hostess. Herleva, however, was smiling as sweetly as if William were speaking poetry. She had invited the court for a few 'relaxing' days at her beautiful estate at Falaise and might justly be expected to feel aggrieved that her plans had been thwarted by the arrival of William's ever-vigilant messengers, but if so she gave no sign of it.

'The news is not good,' she agreed gently, rising from one of the lovely riverside benches on which she had been serving the noonday meal to her guests, 'but you will deal with it, William, as you always do.'

Such trust she had in him, Mathilda thought guiltily. Such absolute faith. Had she even truly heard what the messengers had said? The English were looking for some other royal – Edward, the grandson of a past king who had been exiled in the east his entire life. That could only mean one thing – they wished to give him the crown. Him and not William.

All the duke's worst fears were coming to pass, for his spies reported that the Godwinsons had a stranglehold on the king. Earl Godwin himself was dead but his sons were ruling most of England. The eldest, Harold, held powerful Wessex and ran the king's army so well that he was indispensable to him. And now it was he who had gone off across Europe to seek out a puppet prince of nominally royal blood.

Even Judith's husband Tostig was apparently an earl now, in control of the vast province of Northumbria in the north. In a quiet moment Mathilda had been glad that Judith would have a good home for herself and the single son she had apparently borne and hoped this Northumbria was a pleasant place. She'd recalled King Edward muttering something about it being 'a law unto itself' and prayed it was not dangerous and that it had enough pretty churches to suit her cousin. She had known better, however, than to discuss it with her husband.

Normandy's duke growled low in his throat and his courtiers cowered back, suddenly fiercely interested in the fish in the soft-flowing river behind them. Mathilda moved a little closer to Emeline who was lying luxuriously stretched out on a blanket with her pretty head in her husband's lap. Three years of marriage had done little to dampen the ardour between them and Emeline was forever extolling Hugh's virtues. Just the other day even quiet Cecelia had told her to 'go wrap your tongue around the wretched man if he's so delicious or I will cut it off.' Mathilda giggled at the memory but William's next words pulled her back to the harsher realities of her life.

'Not good news, Mother? It is dreadful. Why has King Edward sent his precious Earl Harold to find this lost prince? Why does he seek another heir when he already has one – when he already has *me*?'

'Because he is a fool, William.'

William looked up through the willows to the cornflower-blue sky above and gave a brief reluctant smile.

'Perhaps so,' he conceded, kissing his mother's cheek. 'Or perhaps he's just grown too old to know his true mind any more, or his true friends. The real question, however, is what do we do about it.'

For this, he looked to Mathilda.

'Earl Harold will not necessarily find this lost prince, William,' she said hastily but it was a poor response and she was not surprised when he glared at her.

'The very fact that he has gone looking is bad enough. Why has Edward turned his back on us? Why is he reneging on his promise? I would be his heir, he said, in recognition of our family connections and my strong reputation as a leader and my kindness to him when I was a youth. He said all that, did he not, Mathilda? Why, why, why did we not insist he wrote it down, swore to it?'

Mathilda bit back a reminder that she had suggested as much at the time.

'We were young, William, and on their soil. And Edward gave us his royal word.'

'Edward's word, royal or not, is apparently worth nothing. Nothing! He would choose some fool exile over me – his cousin and onetime protector, great-nephew of a Saxon queen and a proven ruler. We should have killed the Godwinsons when they were this side of the Narrow Sea in '51, Mathilda – when they were with your father.'

She knew better than to rise to that one and instead asked, 'What will you do now, William?'

'Do?! I will keep track of this "lost" prince.'

'And if they find him?'

'I will send someone for a look.' He cast his eyes around the assembled nobles fidgeting on their marble benches and crushing their dainty delicacies between their nervous fingers.

'Fulk perhaps? No doubt my high commander's lovely wife would like a trip to England.'

Fulk rose reluctantly, motioning for Mabel to join him, but before the lady of Belleme could do so Mathilda pulled William aside, leading him out of the shade of the willow trees and into Herleva's pretty garden beyond. The sun was glaring down and even the lavender seemed to be wilting beneath its relentless heat but, despite being pregnant again, Mathilda barely noticed.

'You would send Mabel de Belleme to, to . . .'

'To pass on our best wishes to the new heir, Mathilda, yes. It is time she did something to redeem herself.'

Mathilda stepped closer.

'Redeem herself for poisoning one by poisoning another?'

'Hush! Who said anything about poisoning?'

'William, you cannot,' she protested desperately. 'Mabel has only just birthed her third babe; she won't want to leave.' William raised a disbelieving eyebrow and Mathilda had to concede this was unlikely for Mabel, though every bit as fertile as Mathilda, did not share her interest in her offspring. That did not, however, mean she could be dispatched to England like a secret weapon. 'Well, then, you cannot, William, because what you are suggesting is wrong. It's too harsh.'

He reached for her, pulling her close despite the others just a leaf-screen away.

'I have had to do many things in my life, Mathilda, that have seemed too harsh but when you are a ruler you must think of the greater good above your own scruples. Already France has turned upon me and now we look sure to be losing England too. I cannot allow it!' She flinched back at his anger, hotter than any sun, and he visibly controlled himself, drawing a deep breath into his broad chest and unclenching his fists to take gentle hold of her arms. 'Fret not, my sweet one, I will take care of it. You are providing future rulers for us; let *me* ensure they have lands to rule.'

Mathilda folded her hands over her swollen belly and leaned gratefully against William. She had birthed him a second son, Richard, at the start of last year and this fourth child would soon be with them too. William had ordered the nursery at Rouen extended and Mathilda loved spending time with her little ones, though she sometimes wished there might be time between them for her body to recover for longer than it took William to plant his seed once more within it. Still, she could not complain. Look at the poor English queen – unable to produce even one heir for her country. If William were to be king, he already had sons enough to ensure the security of the throne and yet . . .

She glanced back to the court, gathered so gently here in Falaise enjoying the peace and prosperity of a year without war. Mathilda and Cecelia had worked with all the ladies of the duchy so that every residence had a warm, watertight ladies' bower and fine kitchens, and every hall a placecard order to prevent scrambles to table.

There had been grumbles at first but the system was settling and it was amazing how little people truly cared where they sat when the tables were bursting with rich harvests, gathered on time. And it seemed that the people in villages all across the duchy were similarly content. On their route to Falaise Mathilda had seen the crops ripening in the sun-kissed fields and, with the men still secure in their homes for once, it would be a bumper harvest in Normandy. Was a throne worth risking such prosperity?

'Could we not just let England go, William,' she suggested into his chest. 'If the Saxons are so keen to keep it for them-selves then let them. We have much to love on this side of the Narrow Sea.'

'Normandy is just a duchy.'

'But it's *your* duchy, William.'

'However hard it tries not to be. They have opposed me from the start, Mathilda – right from when I was seven years old.'

'But they do not oppose you now.'

'Which surely means that it is time to move on to more. I promised I would make you a queen, Mathilda, and I am not a man to renege on my promises.'

'It would not be reneging, simply making a new tactical decision.'

For a moment he looked almost as if he might believe her but then he just laughed.

'I owe you a throne, my Mora.'

'I do not ask it.'

'All the same, I wish to win it for you, for how else am I to prove my love?'

And with that he was gone, striding back through the willows leaving her stunned. Love? He did not truly mean love. He surely wanted England for himself and this was merely a knightly excuse. And yet, when had he ever said anything he did not truly mean? Confused, she snatched a linen square from her pocket to dab at her overheated face and headed reluctantly back to the court. Perhaps she could talk to Herleva about this; she, surely, would help her to understand why William was so desperate for a crown.

Her chance came later that day. The court were dressing for dinner in their various rooms on the new upper storey of Herleva's gracious manor house when Mathilda heard a soft voice commanding the servants below. She slipped down the stairs and found her mother-by-marriage overseeing the finishing touches to beautiful flower arrangements along the centre of the trestle tables.

'Mathilda. All is well? You are in need of something?'

'Not at all. Everything is perfect, thank you. I just wished to talk to you.'

'There is more trouble?'

'No. No, truly. I just felt we should get to know each other better. Whenever we are in the bower the children are always climbing all over you.'

'I am more than happy to be with them. Robert is such a lively child, is he not? And Adela so inquisitive. I wonder, sometimes, at the amount of questions she can fit in that tiny head.'

Mathilda smiled, though she often wondered the same herself. Adela, now a small but resilient three year old, was forever asking odd things and, to her shame, Mathilda found herself preferring the company of bumptious Robert and little Richard who was just learning to walk and very pleased with his newfound legs.

'You are right, Herleva, but it is nice, sometimes, to be able to at least finish a sentence to each other, is it not?'

'It is, my dear. Shall we take a seat?'

Herleva gestured to a wicker bench in the shade of the east wall and Mathilda nodded grateful assent, though when they reached the bench she realised it was not solely for her comfort that her hostess had suggested it. She noted Herleva steady herself with her hands as she sank onto the soft cushions and saw too that those hands shook a little.

'I'm sorry. You are tired. You've had much to do to entertain us these last days. I should not keep you.'

'Nonsense. There is always time for my duchess. Is all well?'

'At the moment, yes, but I worry that this matter of England is too much for William.'

'Too much? He is a strong man, Mathilda.'

'I know. But you told me once not to forget his finer emotions.'

Herleva smiled and took her hand.

'I did. And you do not. He seems very happy with you.'

'He does?' Mathilda flushed, unexpectedly flattered. 'But then surely I should advise him in this matter of England?'

Herleva looked surprised.

'I had not really thought of it that way. I am glad he has you to care for him, Mathilda, but I have always felt a man should make his decisions for himself. But then, my dear, I am not as intelligent as you.'

'That's not true. You . . .'

Herleva gripped her fingers and she quieted.

'It *is* true. Why deny it?'

Mathilda shook her head.

'You Normans and your obsession with truth – even you, Herleva.'

'Truth is best. It is dissembling that will lead you into trouble. Fret not, Mathilda. Whatever William decides, your future is an enticing one.'

She sounded wistful and Mathilda looked at her more closely.

'You are well?'

Herleva did not answer immediately and Mathilda felt her head start to buzz as much as the bees over the nearby lavender.

'I am content,' the older lady said eventually.

'But not well?'

Herleva placed a quiet hand over her own.

'Do not tell William, not yet.'

'How long . . . ?'

'Ask God. I have made my peace with life, Mathilda. And William has you to care for him now.'

'He does but, Herleva, he will want to talk to you. He will have things to say.'

'William? No. He is secure in my love and I in his. We do not need words – indeed they would be painful to us both. Now look, the others are coming down. Shall we go to dinner?'

And with that she rose, all her being concentrated on pushing herself up without outward show of discomfort as William strode towards them between a limping La Barbe and a red-faced Della, resplendent in a mauve gown.

'Della, my dear – you look beautiful,' Herleva said, clasping her hands and drawing her kindly into the shade.

Mathilda watched, humbled. This was love, she thought, hefting her own ungainly body up far less graciously than her hostess. This was selfless love and she feared she was learning from it far too late.

Herleva took to her bed some weeks later, just three days after Mathilda gave birth to her third son, named William at Mathilda's insistence, but instantly nicknamed Rufus for his flame of red hair, a more startling version of his mother's copper locks. When they took the baby to his grandmother on her sickbed, she was delighted and, Mathilda detected, relieved.

'She is ready,' Herluin confided sorrowfully as he watched his frail wife cradle the baby.

'But you are not?'

'No, but I never would be. Herleva has brought me such light and I will miss her every day that is left to me.'

'Which is many, I hope, for William looks to you still for guidance.'

Herluin laughed softly.

'Nonsense. William looks to no one for guidance save perhaps yourself, my lady, but it is kind of you to say so and I will not let go. There is much, I sense, of young William's life still to live and if Herleva cannot see it then I will see it for her.'

She died peacefully that night, with no one at her side save Herluin. She left no messages, asked no promises, just slipped away leaving even loquacious Odo shocked into subdued silence and William, her greatest legacy, devastated.

'Why her?' he asked Mathilda as they lay in bed that night, his arm tight around her shoulders and little Rufus curled up on his chest like a bird in a nest for he had insisted on keeping his new son close. 'Why leave the likes of Mabel in the world and take someone as sweet as my mother?'

'I know not, William. Maybe she loved so strongly that she wore her heart out?'

'Maybe.' He stroked a gentle finger down his new son's burnished hair. 'I was lucky in her. Men do not see that. They call me "bastard" as if it is the only point of note but I would have Herleva as mother over any countess or duchess or queen, for she taught me nobility is in your bearing, not your blood. Have I told you that?'

'It is a good lesson.'

'It is, Mathilda. I am the duke I am thanks to my father, but I am the man I am because of her. People think me hard and I *am* hard but without Herleva's care I would have been granite. She did not teach me how to fight, but she did teach me what to fight for – fairness and justice and loyalty and stability. She should have been a queen.'

Mathilda looked at his lean profile in the low light from the stars beyond the window, curtain drawn back to let a breeze into the warm chamber, and felt a fool. It was so simple. She should have seen this, should have understood that it was less the throne William sought than the affirmation of royalty – for himself, for her and, above all else, for their children.

'Maybe the lost prince will stay lost,' she said softly.

'Maybe he will.'

'And then England will see sense and acknowledge you as the most worthy man to rule.'

'Worthy,' he echoed. 'Throneworthy.'

He filled the word with a raw longing that cut at her heart and she was grateful when Rufus's tiny eyes suddenly shot open and his lips pursed hungrily so she could busy herself gathering him to her breast. William lay at her side and for a moment, in the warmth of their bed and the bittersweet threads of their shared grief, they felt like any family. But that was an illusion, she knew. Or perhaps the tiny kernel of truth beneath the illusion of the rest of their lives. For England was ever on their horizon, the only change being that where once she had glittered with promise, now she sparkled with danger.

CHAPTER NINETEEN

London, April 1057

'Are you proud, hey, Judith? Proud of your husband the earl?'

Torr puffed out his chest and sat high in his saddle, the movement unsettling his horse so that he had to grab at the reins to stay on. Judith did not bother to hide her smile. Torr had been Earl of Northumbria for two years but still he seemed to crave praise for the appointment.

'Very proud, Torr – you are a fine figure.'

He looked suspiciously at her but chose to believe her words.

'And you are a fine wife, Judith. I am proud of you, you know, and of little Karl too.' He looked back to their three-year-old boy, squirming with the nursemaids in the wagon, desperate to ride his pony. 'He is a good son.'

'And a legitimate one,' Judith sniped, unable to resist.

She had stuck to her side of their bargain, ignoring Torr's numerous indiscretions with as much dignity as she could muster, but it was still hard sometimes. She had taken petty revenge by refusing to name their son Tostig, insisting on a solid North Saxon name instead. He hadn't liked it but at least now Karl was all hers, even if Torr was not. To be fair though, he had also stuck to his promise and in Durham she could paint every day.

She had forged strong links with the monks at the White Church whose passion was manuscripts and whose bishop was proving a discreet and invaluable help with her gospel books. Already the first was finished and locked away for safe-keeping and she was working keenly on the second. It had been a wrench to have to make the journey south for King Edward's Easter court but Torr had been most insistent.

'Karl will enjoy being at court with us,' he was saying now, gesturing towards the horizon where the roofs of London were cutting haphazardly into the misty sky. 'He will have seen nothing so fine as Westminster.'

Judith prickled at the implied criticism of their new home-land. From the moment she had ridden into Northumbria she had known she'd found the place she was meant to be. She loved everything about it, especially along the coast. The light and colours were so strong, so assured. On a sunny day the sand often seemed to shine golden against the rich blue-green of the sea as if a half-crazed monk had slashed his inks boldly across a vast parchment and the vibrancy of the northern land-scape had touched the artist in Judith as no place ever had before. She only wished her husband would share her love of his earldom.

'Durham is a beautiful city,' she insisted.

'Beautiful, maybe, but quiet.'

'Only because you are never there.'

'Can you blame me? It is so far away from everything that is important.'

He waved imperiously up the road. They were drawing close to London and there were more and more people around them. Word had spread that the lost prince was due to sail in with Earl Harold at any moment and everyone was heading for the capital to see the much-talked-about new aetheling. Torr had been sniping about it for weeks so his sudden excitement jarred against Judith's tired bones.

'You're an ungrateful wretch, Torr Godwinson,' she told him. 'You were desperate to be an earl. You twisted King Edward's ear until he granted Northumbria to you and then poor Earl Alfgar lost his lands over it.'

Torr smirked.

'That was funny – Alfgar blustering and shaking and then drawing his sword on the king. I couldn't have forced a better reaction if I'd tried all year.'

'You *did* try all year,' Judith retorted. 'Did you see them leave, Torr? Alfgar's wife was beside herself and those children were too young to be cast out from all they know.'

'It was his fault, not mine.'

'It was both.'

He looked surprised at her boldness but she cared not. Taking this road into London recalled all too vividly the sight of Earl Alfgar's family riding in the other direction in '55, their heads low and their goods piled high in carts behind them. Lady Megan had been openly sobbing, the two younger boys skittish and confused, and the elder children – Brodie was it, and Edyth? – had sat rigid at the rear, the effort of maintaining their composure clear in the stiff lines of their young bodies. As Judith had watched, Edyth had looked back with such sorrow in her eyes it had torn at Judith's heart.

They had ridden into Wales from whence Earl Alfgar had returned in the autumn with Welsh troops at his back to secure his favour with the king. The girl, however, had been left behind to marry King Griffin, a man known universally as the 'Red Devil'. Judith thought of her often and prayed for her wellbeing but clearly her husband had no such compassion.

'You are honoured to be an earl at all, Torr,' she told him desperately.

There were travellers all around them now, on foot, in rough wagons and on tired-looking donkeys, and they would not like to hear him talk with such contempt of an office none of them could even dream of holding.

'Honoured? It was about time, Judi. Harold snatched Wessex the moment Father died and Garth was quick to grab East Anglia from Alfgar. I deserved this.'

'Why? Because you are a Godwinson?'

He looked puzzled.

'Well yes, I suppose so.'

'So you "deserve" an earldom because of your family name?'

'Why else?'

'Maybe because of your valour or your good works or your wise counsel?'

Torr laughed.

'This isn't a scald's tale, Judith. This is real life. My family is firmly back in power and I was a part of that.'

'Because of *my* family.'

'Well yes, but I was wise enough to marry you, wasn't I?'

She rolled her eyes, infuriated. They were close enough to the city now for many people to be pitching their tents on the open meadowlands either side of the road. Within a candle-notch they would be in the heart of Edward's court where such talk would be not just foolish but dangerous.

'Torr, please,' she begged. 'You are Earl of Northumbria. You must learn to love your land.'

He pouted.

'You're right. I know you are. It's just so empty, Judith. Not like here.' He waved eagerly around the bustling masses who were forcing them to slow to a walk. 'A man can ride for hours across Northumbria without seeing another soul.'

That was one of the things Judith loved the most.

'Durham is a fine city,' she insisted, 'and York too, and very ancient, you know – older, perhaps, than Winchester or London. Yours must be the most deeply rooted earldom in England.'

He ran a hand thoughtfully through his hair, washed especially for the Easter gathering and shining like new oak, then gave a little nod of pride.

'That's true. It must. That's good, Judith. It's still a bloody long way from the king though.'

'But you don't need the king now.' Judith fought to keep the exasperation from her voice. 'You have the earldom you wanted and you can rule it as you wish – as Earl Ward did.'

'Bloody Earl Ward. All I ever hear of my onetime foster-father is how wonderful he was.'

'So be *more* wonderful.'

Torr considered this but not for long.

'It's just such hard work, Judith. The men up there are not like these men of the south. They are so crude, so direct, and I can barely understand half of what they say. They may as well be Scots for all . . .'

'Torr, hush!' Judith looked round guiltily, grateful that they were on horseback where most others were on foot and, she prayed, out of earshot of his foolish conversation. 'You cannot speak that way. It is offensive and unworthy. You are privileged to rule and must do well by Northumbria.'

'Yes, yes, yes. I will, Judith, of course I will. I'm just saying – it's not Wessex. How come bloody Harold gets Wessex?' Judith did not even try to answer this. No logic would touch Torr's bitterness at being a younger son. 'Still,' he said suddenly, 'at least Harold is off fetching back Edward's damned imported heir now that my dear sister has failed to provide a homegrown one. Or, rather, the king to plant one in her.'

'Torr, please . . .'

'And who knows what dangers he has met on the road back from bloody Hungary. People are always dying out there.'

'Torr!'

At last he had the decency to look shamefaced, but not for long.

'It's a fool's errand anyway,' he said petulantly. 'This precious prince won't be safe until he's landed over there on Thorney Island. Or maybe even then. There are plenty of men not happy to see a royal heir in England, Judith, and even with his precious royal blood he will be no Saxon. I doubt he'll speak the language and he will know nothing of our ways. Why does Harold condone this madness?'

'Perhaps,' Judith dared to suggest, 'he thinks a foreign prince would be easier to control.'

Torr smiled slyly.

'Easier to control than whom, Judi?'

'Than any candidates closer to home.'

They did not ever speak of William, not openly. Now the Godwinsons were back in power in England they were working hard to prevent the much-whispered Christmas promise ever coming to fruition and Judith, God forgive her, was doing nothing to stop them. It was only fair, she told herself fiercely, for she had enough to worry about trying to keep Torr in the north without fretting over anyone else's concerns. The awareness of her mean complicity against her cousin and onetime friend was a dull, nagging pain in her conscience, but what could she do? She was Saxon now and Saxons did not wish to be ruled by Normans. This Hungarian import surely proved that and she hoped William and Mathilda would have the sense to listen to what it meant and stay away.

'Can I ride now, Mama?'

Judith turned gratefully back to see Karl leaping up and

down so hard that it looked as if he might fall out of the wagon. She laughed.

'Of course you can. Torr, stop a moment and let Karl mount.'

Torr clucked in impatience but called their already slow-moving train to a halt, clearly keen to see his son ride into the court in style. The groom brought Karl's pony round and within moments the boy was in the saddle and trotting up between his parents.

'Where's that?' he demanded, eyes wide and little finger pointed eagerly up the crammed road to where the houses built on either side of London Bridge rose tall against the sky.

'That's London, Karl,' Torr told him. 'You will love it.'

And Karl did, though he kept close to Judith when the crowds thickened still further as they finally crossed the bridge and made their way into the city proper. His little eyes were as wide as full moons as he took in the town houses, packed wall to wooden wall along the narrow streets, most with people hanging out of every window opening, shouting to friends or advertising their wares. Durham was not, whatever Torr said, a little place but never had Judith seen it as full as London was today and she kept a tight hand on Karl's lead rein as they crept slowly forward towards the royal palace.

Suddenly a hand caught at her ankle. She flinched away but then saw that her captor was but an old lady, holding up a piteously thinly woven basket with a bunch of wizened apples in the bottom.

'Apple, my lady?' she suggested with a gappy smile, looking as hopeful as if she were selling the finest fruit, though Judith saw the misery behind her eyes and noted that her skin was as thin as her basket.

'That would be lovely,' she agreed, reaching for her purse. They would do for the horses at least.

'Oh, thank you, kind lady. Thank you.'

Torr looked impatiently around but Judith took her time finding a silver penny. The woman's eyes widened as much as Karl's as she handed it over.

'For me?'

'With my blessing.'

'Then please, take them all – and news besides.'

'News?'

Torr was tutting impatiently but the lady was caught by a wracking cough and it would have been rude just to leave her. Judith put up a hand to keep him back and waited, praying she would use some of the money to buy herself a salve. Eventually she recovered and stood on wobbly tiptoe to get closer to Judith. Her breath reeked but her words, when they came, were worth the wait: 'The prince is ill.'

'The prince?' Suddenly Torr was at her side, all attention. 'What prince?' The old woman looked at him and, sensing his desperation, went slyly silent. Torr leaped down and pressed a second penny upon her. 'What prince, woman?'

'The Hungarian prince, Edward the Exile, who is to be the king's new heir.'

'He is here then?'

She grinned even more slyly and held out her hand. Karl was happily feeding his pony one of the apples that had, until now, been her only source of income but news, she was rapidly discovering, paid far better than fruit. Torr tossed his head, but gave her another coin.

'That's your last. I doubt it's a secret.'

'Oh, but it is, Lord. The king does not want it known, does he, but my sister works in the kitchens at the palace and she says the poor exile has taken to his chamber. Sick from the journey, they say, but who knows . . .'

Torr looked back to Judith.

'We must get to Thorney Island, Wife, and fast.'

The woman put a scrawny hand on his arm.

'Only the topmost nobles allowed in there, Lord, for there are so many visitors it is full to bursting with fancy folk. The king has guards on every bridge.'

Torr drew himself up tall and glared at her.

'I am the Earl of Northumbria,' he said haughtily.

'Northumbria?' she cackled. 'Good God – it's no wonder, then, that you do not know the news.'

Judith feared Torr would hit her and was glad when the woman, with new nimbleness, ducked away and was gone. Her husband's face had turned as dark as a storm and he began pushing his way fiercely through the indignant crowds, leaving her to follow as best she could, her mind whirring. It seemed, then, that Harold had found the aetheling and brought him home but that not everyone, as Torr had suggested, was glad to see him. Already she feared the slimy tentacles of the court and longed to be back in Durham.

CHAPTER TWENTY

Caen, April 1057

'We bring news, Lord Duke.'
The court looked up eagerly as the doors at the back of the rough hall burst open and Fulk de Montgomery strode in, his wife swishing behind him. Both held their heads high and were grinning like well-fed wolves. Mathilda, already uneasy out here in Caen, William's starkest and least welcoming of cities, felt a shiver of dread run right down into her belly where her fifth child was just starting to make itself felt.

'Fulk!' William leaped up from the big table where they had both been signing charters and rushed to shake hands with his commander. 'And your lovely lady wife, too. Mabel, welcome.'

Almost he kissed her and Mathilda blinked, astonished. William hated holding a quill rather than a sword and was always looking for distraction from paperwork but this was more than that. She looked enviously at the Lady of Belleme. Mabel looked more stunning than ever in a dress of purest scarlet belted with huge links of silver. Her eyes glittered as brightly as the diamonds in her long nails and Mathilda felt ridiculously small and dumpy with her ever-rounded belly straining at her tired gown.

The courtiers who had been ranged around the edges of the room chatting and niggling at each other as they waited for the business of the day to be concluded seemed to lean in, as if pulled towards the glittering pair, and Mathilda could see why. Fulk and Mabel were exchanging wickedly complicit glances, their quarrelsome ways clearly a thing of the past, and it was evident they had tidings worth the knowing.

'News, my Lord High Commander?' William prompted loudly, enjoying the theatre of the moment.

'Sad news.' Fulk de Montgomery's eyes were afire, though not with sadness. 'Sad news of the poor lost Saxon prince.'

'He is dead?'

'I am afraid so.'

William masked his intake of breath.

'That *is* very sad.'

'Yes. A great loss, for he looked a fine man. Forty-six years old but sprightly and alert. He spoke the Saxon tongue well and knew something of their customs and he had not forgotten his heritage. He was eager to rule, they say, and capable too, and he came with a fine wife, Lady Agatha – a bright-eyed, curly-haired beauty from Kiev – and three bonny children besides. A perfect choice he was, my lord duke, hailed as a true solution to the Saxon succession crisis, and there was much cheering in the streets of London. Much cheering. So sad.'

He glanced at Mabel, who put both hands dramatically to what passed as her heart.

'He was weakened, they think, by the sea voyage. Some men do not sail well and being raised in Russia he had never been on the open sea. It did not, it seems, agree with him.'

'Is that so?' William asked, a weird thrill in his voice.

Mathilda felt her blood curdle and looked down at her fingers, wrapped around each other in her lap. She wondered if Judith had been there with the Saxon court and if she was suspicious. Was she right to be? For Mathilda had not prevented this, had not insisted Mabel stay at home. She looked at the beautiful Lady of Belleme, unable to resist the biting memory of Adela's early birth, and felt nausea rise in her gullet.

'He sickened, my lord,' Mabel said, almost as if she could see Mathilda's struggle and was taunting her. 'He was frail to start with but he went downhill fast. Saxon food was, I fear, too rich for him.'

She was loving this, stroking her own sharp-boned cheek with one of her damned diamond nails as she looked around the funny little hall that made up the heart of the rough fortress of Caen. The royal residence here was just a clutch of simple buildings in one corner of a vast enclosure above the handful of shacks that passed as the town and was in desperate need of improvements but Mathilda felt little inclination to spend more time here than was necessary to keep the rebellious west at least partially tame. William said he liked its simplicity and the views out over the Narrow Sea, but for a sight of the waves Mathilda much preferred pretty little Bonneville and she resisted travelling to Caen whenever she could. Today's encounter was doing little to endear the city to her.

'You met him, Mabel?' William was asking, the poor charters gleefully abandoned for another day.

'Only once.'

'Once, it seems, was enough. And the king? Did you talk to King Edward?'

'We were introduced. He looked old, especially after the sad passing of his cousin, frail even . . .'

'She did not meet him again, my lord,' Fulk said firmly.

'Good. King Edward will go to God in his own time and amongst Saxons. But these exile children, one of them is a boy, is he not?'

'Prince Edgar, yes, but he is a babe really, just six years old and a puny thing.'

'Puny,' Mabel confirmed with a grey light in her eyes.

Goodness, Mathilda thought, did the woman look to wipe out all those in poor health? She should not meet little Adela; should not have a second chance at her. Mathilda's only daughter was four years old now but scarcely grown. Her limbs had stretched out, thin and gangling like one of Hugh's foals, but her body seemed shrunken, as if it struggled to hold on to the vital organs within. She was quiet, too, with none of her brothers' energy, and her one passion was the ancient texts – Greek and Latin. Her tutor adored her questioning nature and Mathilda knew she should be proud of her early scholarship but with Adela there was something forced and challenging about it. Maybe Mabel would be a mercy for her. She gave an involuntary gasp at her own evil thought and everyone looked her way.

'Sorry,' she said guiltily, holding her belly. 'A cramp.'

Mabel looked over the table at her.

'I have herbs that can help with that.'

'No! I mean, no thank you, Mabel.'

The other woman grinned.

'I can do good, you know, my lady, if you would only let me.'

She curtseyed low and again Mathilda felt nausea rise in her stomach but she could scarcely criticise. Deep inside she knew that although the deed may have been Mabel's, they were all complicit, all guilty. She thought of the lost prince's Russian wife, Lady Agatha, alone in a strange court with three young children. What a journey she must have been on, what hopes she must have had.

But we have hopes too, she thought. More than hopes – a promise. With the lost prince dead that promise was alive once more, though it was all too clear that Edward had little intention of honouring it.

And it soon became clear that Edward was not the only monarch opposed to Normandy. For as summer sighed itself out and the court returned to Rouen from the west, a new visitor was blown into court.

'Raoul d'Amiens!' William snarled. 'So, the serpent has crawled out of the heather.'

The men were in the orchard, practising their archery into old shields strapped to the poor fruit-laden trees, but all firing ceased as they clustered around the new arrival. Mathilda, who had been called from the kitchens where she'd been making plans with the chefs for bottling and drying – assuming the apples survived the morning – threaded her way breathlessly to her husband's side as the handsome Frenchman dared a flourishing bow.

'Not hiding, Lord Duke, for I did nothing wrong save serve my lord.'

'King Henri?'

'The very same. But I am sick of him.'

William leaned forward, his longbow dangling menacingly from his shoulder.

'You are?'

'I am. I seek a new lord. Indeed, Duke, I seek *you* as my new lord and as a token of such I bring you a gift.' William wrinkled his nose – he had little use for trinkets. 'A precious gift – information.'

'Ah. I see. What information? From France?'

'Yes, my lord. May I draw closer?'

William pretended to consider but not for long. He beckoned Raoul forward as his men formed a circle around them, arrows to hand. Raoul flushed but stood his ground and his voice remained firm.

'It is King Henri, Lord Duke. He is not happy that the Hungarian prince is dead and is mustering a new force. He means to attack again.'

Mathilda's heart shook. More war. She felt a fool for happily preoccupying herself with apples and plums as if they were all that mattered to Normandy's future and for an unseemly moment she longed to take Raoul and push him back through the trees as if she could stem the invasion that way. But it could not be done.

'From where?' William demanded.

'I'm not sure.'

'You *are* sure.'

Raoul inclined his handsome head.

'I might be, my lord, if you were to accept me into your service.'

'Why, Raoul? How do I know this is not some trick by King Henri?'

'I have reasons of my own for wanting Henri . . . disadvantaged.'

William's eyes widened.

'You have designs on the French throne, Raoul?'

'Oh no. Not the throne, my lord, though not so far away either. It is something of a more personal nature.'

He flushed and Mathilda stepped forward, her curiosity piqued at last.

'Your lady has not yet acceded to your love, Lord Raoul?'

Raoul bowed low.

'She is more than willing, my lady, but she is . . . shackled.'

Something shifted in Mathilda's mind, like pieces of a broken pot coming together.

'The queen,' she said.

Raoul bowed his head and William looked him up and down in astonishment.

'Queen Anne? Dear me, Raoul, you have set your fancy French cap high.' He reached up and wrenched an apple from a branch over his head, taking a loud bite of it as he looked to Mathilda. 'Shall we lend him Mabel, my dear?'

'William!' Mathilda took the apple from his hand and threw it to the ground. 'No Mabel.'

'No? Ah well, Henri may not survive his impudent invasion anyway, hey, Raoul?'

'His passing would not, I admit, cause me great distress but you will need to move fast, Lord Duke, for he is on his way.'

'Where?'

'My lord . . .'

William sighed.

'You are welcome at my court, Raoul, and in my army if you so choose.'

'I thank you. The king plans to attack up the Orne valley and has his sights set on Caen. It is not, I believe, your most loyal city?'

'No.'

'And there are, I am told, rebels rising to prepare the way for the French king.'

'Rebels?'

William groaned and Mathilda felt a rush of anger on his behalf – and her own. Had they not just spent the best part of a month in Caen? Had they not welcomed all the local lords and toured the villages and offered alms to the poor? What did they have to do to win the loyalty of the west? She looked accusingly to Mabel but the other woman threw up her hands.

'I have been in England, my lady – at your service.'

'At the duke's service,' Mathilda corrected primly. 'But then . . . ?'

'It is another close to her,' Raoul said, 'a man called Arnold de Giroie.'

'Arnold?' Hugh asked. 'My cousin?'

'The one Mabel tried to poison,' Mathilda added tartly but William had stridden away between the trees and did not seem to hear them.

'I have grown complacent,' he called back. 'The wolves never go away, you know, just sleep. Now they are prowling once more and I must sharpen my sword and polish my armour, for it seems Normandy needs me again.'

He drew an arrow into his bow and fired it at the furthest shield. It clanged against the very centre of the boss and Mathilda felt a shudder of desire at this sudden show of strength. William might not be the most romantic of husbands but he could still set her pulse racing, always had. She looked coyly towards him but he was too busy to notice.

'Caen,' he said grimly to Raoul. 'Caen would certainly turn with enough enticement. And a thousand French troops would prove enough, I am sure.'

'Two thousand, my lord,' Raoul supplied.

'Two thousand? Then we have work to do.'

And with that, William squared his shoulders and strode from the orchard, his men following eagerly in his wake as if they might march forth there and then. Left behind, un-noticed, Mathilda looked miserably down at the bitten apple at her feet and pitied her poor Normandy its lost peace. But she pitied the French more.

CHAPTER TWENTY-ONE

Rouen, October 1057

The army rode out barely a week later, high in their saddles and whooping with bloodlust. Then silence. Messengers reported that William was letting Henri come, luring his troops out like pieces in a tafel game. They reported also that French intelligence must be good for always they found them faster than expected. Mathilda, lying cold in her empty bed with her belly pushing painfully on her bladder, knew William would suspect treachery and feared it herself. Maybe they had been too ready to trust Raoul who could, after all, be feeding information on the Normans to the French rather than the other way around. That was the trouble with spies – duplicity was sewn into their very nature.

'What if they lose?' Cecelia asked one day when dark clouds had settled over a still-empty Rouen and it seemed as if God himself was seeking to crush them. They were in the schoolroom, supposedly supporting Adela in her studies, but the girl needed no encouragement and was poring over a Greek text with her tutor leaving them free to talk. 'What if William is defeated and King Henri rides into Rouen to claim it as his own?'

'Not possible,' Mathilda said stoutly, shifting her heavy body and straining to remember a time when her womb had been empty for more than a month. Sometimes she felt less a woman and more just a receptacle for ducal children.

'It *is* possible, my lady. Not likely perhaps, praise God, but possible.'

Mathilda supposed it was, for news had just come in that William was sick of playing cat and mouse with the French and, with winter fast approaching, was to engage them in open battle. He had marched to Varaville near traitorous Caen to meet Henri's troops at the point where they would have to cross the River Orne. Mathilda had called for maps the moment she'd heard, but a mark on a parchment was hardly a fit representation of the battle site, no doubt alive with men and horses and all the trappings of a war camp, and she had rarely felt so helpless. Roger was in control of matters of state and William matters of defence and she was left with nothing.

Part of her longed to ride forth to join her husband so she could at least be a part of whatever was happening to their people but she only needed to call up a memory of Alençon to send that foolish idea from her mind. War was best left to men but still she felt robbed of the title of regent and trapped in a world of threads and toys and babies, as if she had been in the bower so long she had been woven into one of her own woollens.

'What would we do if we did lose?' Cecelia fretted. 'Would we have to flee? Where would we go?'

Mathilda shushed her. Poor Cecelia had been very nervy recently and Mathilda suspected she missed Emeline, who was even heavier with child than her duchess and so vociferously miserable at her unaccustomed bulk that Mathilda sent her to rest whenever possible.

'If it came to it, I suppose we would go back to Flanders,'

she said to Cecelia, though the thought filled her with dread. She had pitied Judith her exile with her new husband back in '51 and had no intention of being so humiliated herself. 'But it is of no import, Cee. William will win. William always wins. His job is to secure our lands for our children, mine is to give birth to them. And this next one, I fear, is not far away.'

'Another boy, think you?'

'Perhaps. Whatever God wills.'

She looked guiltily to studious Adela, unwilling to admit even to Cecelia how much she would love another daughter. Mabel de Belleme had recently birthed her fourth child – a pretty little girl she'd called Sibyl. She'd been swiftly dispatched to the nursery with the other junior Bellemes but not before Mathilda had seen her and felt an ache of jealousy. Adela was a good child but she was undoubtedly fonder of her studies than her family and had little charm. Richard at two was a gentle, sweet-hearted boy and one-year-old William Rufus was a boisterous cuddler, at least for the length of time he could bear to keep still, but Mathilda longed for a girl she could dress up and cosset and dance with – perhaps above all dance with.

And God it seemed saw into her heart, for her fifth baby, born in less than a candle-notch one early dawn a few days later, was indeed a girl, pink as the new sun and kicking out healthily at life from the first moment. Mathilda burst into delighted tears the instant she saw her but had only a few days to enjoy the blessing before the birthing chamber was torn apart with new cries. The loudest yet.

'It hurts so much,' Emeline was wailing within barely a handful of cramps.

Mathilda grimaced apologetically at her.

'Grit your teeth, my sweet, it will be worth it when you hold your child in your arms.'

And it would have been, save that once Emeline was finally holding her tiny daughter the pains started up again.

''Tis the afterbirth,' Della said confidently but just minutes later she was chuckling and looking up from between Emeline's legs to announce that she was wrong. 'I've never seen an after-birth with a head of hair before,' she told them. 'Push down again, Emeline my dear – you have another on the way.'

'Trust Emeline,' Cecelia said but she gladly took the first baby as Emeline bore down to deliver the second.

'A boy!' Della cried gleefully. 'Goodness, woman, you've given your lord a full family in one go. What a clutch of babies for him to come home to.'

'Pray God he does come home,' Emeline said, gathering her twins tearfully into her arms. 'I must send word. This time at least, the poor messenger will have joyful tidings to carry back to Varaville.'

The messenger, however, had no time to even depart with the news for they were all awoken the next morning by the clatter of a hundred hooves on the cobbles of the ducal yard. Mathilda yelped for Cecelia to help her climb into a gown, scrabbling to force her hair beneath a headdress fit to receive the soldiers.

'Are they smiling?' she demanded, tugging Cecelia to the window even as she clipped the fabric into place. 'Do they look victorious?'

Cecelia squinted out of the opaque glass.

'They look tired,' she said dryly. 'And hungry.'

'Can you see William?'

'He is there in the centre. I'd know that big black horse anywhere.'

'And Hugh, can you see Hugh?'

'I don't know. I can scarce see anything through this glass

and with you twitching. You had better go down yourself and find out.'

'Quite right.'

Mathilda yanked away and made for the stairs, Cecelia running horrified in her wake, still trying to secure her clothing. And so it was that they tumbled into the yard to meet the full force of William's glare. Mathilda pulled herself up as tall as she could manage and looked up to him, still astride Caesar.

'Welcome home, Husband.'

'Thank you, Wife. I see you have scarce been able to sleep for worrying about me.'

She bristled.

'I have scarce been able to sleep for feeding your new baby, or, indeed, for helping Emeline birth hers.'

There was a gasp from behind William and Hugh leaped from his mount and came running forward.

'Emeline? How fares she? What has she had? Is it a son or a daughter? Not that I mind, as long as it is healthy, and she is healthy, and . . .'

'Hush, Hugh. Emeline is very well and has given you both a son and a daughter.'

'But how . . .'

'Twins. Just last night. You should probably go and see them.'

'No need.'

The whole company spun to see Emeline standing in the big doorway of the Tour de Rouen in a light gown, her hair loose and a babe on each arm. She smiled almost shyly at Hugh who rushed forward, ungainly in his armour, and swept them all into his arms.

'How lovely,' William rasped. 'God has been kind indeed.'

Mathilda edged nervously closer to Caesar. She should be

used by now to William riding home from campaign in a foul mood but the force of his bitterness surprised her all the same.

'What is it, my lord?' she asked. 'What's wrong? Have we lost?' He looked almost blankly down at her. 'The invasion,' she urged. 'Have the French overcome us?'

'Of course not. I've told you before, Mathilda, I never lose. The French are fled.'

'Fled? That is wonderful news. The battle then, went well?' 'Yes.'

No more seemed forthcoming and William made no move to dismount. Mathilda was left floundering in the centre of the yard and was grateful when Fitz stepped in.

'The duke had our army hidden, my lady, all save a tiny portion which he left in the open, like a goat on a stake to lure the enemy forward. The French could not resist. The water was low enough to ford and not one man amongst them, it seems, knew how fast the tide fills that valley once it turns. Our timing was perfect. Thousands died in the quicksands.'

Mathilda knew this should be cause for rejoicing but balked a little at the thought of all those Frenchwomen even now finding themselves widows.

'And the king?' she asked, focusing on the one rather than the many.

'King Henri was in the rear. He lives, much to Lord Raoul's chagrin, but he is broken and has run home to Paris to nurse his wounds.'

'He is injured?'

'His pride mainly, though word has it he took a sword in the shoulderblade.'

'As did I,' said William and all eyes turned his way as he at last swung himself down from the saddle.

'You are injured?' Mathilda asked, darting forward but he warded her off.

'Not in body, no, but in spirit I am, for someone has been working against me, Mathilda. Whatever we did and wherever we went the French found us.'

'I heard as much. Their spies must be very good.'

'I agree, Wife. So good as to make one suspect they might be Norman.'

'You have a rebel in your midst?'

'I believe so.'

'But who . . . ?'

William put up a hand.

'You have birthed me a child, Mathilda, that is good. A daughter, you said?'

She was thrown by the sudden turn of his conversation.

'That's right, my lord.'

'Good. I am glad to have another little princess. You have named her?'

'I have. She will be Cecily, if it pleases you?'

'It is a pretty name.'

It was but that was not why she had chosen it. She looked back at Cecelia, at her shoulder as ever.

'It is for Cecelia, who has ever been loyal to me.'

'An admirable quality.'

Steel cut along the edge of his voice and Mathilda felt nervousness shudder through the ranks of his soldiers. The horses had all been led away to the stables but the poor men were still standing awkwardly in the yard, though they must surely be fainting with tiredness.

'Shall we go within?' she suggested.

'In a moment.' William looked to Hugh, still fussing over Emeline and his surprise clutch of children. 'I am told, Mathilda, that many letters have issued forth from your chambers.'

'They have?'

'You did not write them?'

'No, my lord, of course I did not. Not after . . .' She stopped herself from reminding him how he had previously suspected her of treachery with her uncle, the defeated King Henri.

'I know you did not,' he said and it was all she could do not to snap at him, then, for asking.

Still he had not touched her, had not even kissed her hand. And she, the mother of his fifth child. Anger budded within her.

'Must we stand here, William? Your men must be cold and tired from their journey and ready for wine to toast your great victory. Come within.'

There was an eager shuffling amongst the men but their duke again put up a hand and it stopped instantly.

'Tell me who wrote those letters.'

Mathilda shrivelled back against solid Cecelia who held her firm, though she was quivering too.

'Cecelia?' she asked, looking over her shoulder. 'Do you know something of this?'

'It was not me, my lady, truly.'

'That is not what I asked. Do you know something of this?'

Cecelia seemed frozen but now Emeline was coming forward, her loose hair blowing in the low breeze and her hands crossed over her chest to hold her tiny babies on her shoulders like living brooches. For a moment she looked almost like some mystical warrior of old but then she spoke and the spell was broken.

'She knows that the letters were written by me.'

'You?' Mathilda gasped. 'But you cannot write, Emeline.'

'I can, for I made Cecelia teach me. But it was with no evil intent. I merely wished to send words of, of . . .' She faltered but then stuck her head up proudly. 'Of love to my husband, who was taken from me by war. Is that so wrong?'

'Of course not,' Mathilda assured her and turned keenly back to William. 'See, my lord. Love notes, no more. Nothing to suspect.'

'And yet, every time there has been trouble I have found your lady – your *French* lady – at the heart of it. First I hear that she is consorting with Raoul, then he betrays me at Mortemer. Next I hear that she is bedding a Belleme and they are found to be working against me.'

'Not against *you*, William,' Mathilda protested, driven to bravery by her fear for Emeline, standing fresh from her childbed before the whole court. 'But against Hugh.'

'Hugh whose cousin Arnold was at the heart of this latest rebellion. Hugh who she manipulated to wed.'

'*Manipulated?* He asked her himself. You are not being fair.'

The glare he gave her would have turned lesser women to stone and, indeed, Mathilda felt her little limbs lock as if his cruel suspicions had clamped around them, but she refused to give way. The soldiers were all looking uncomfortably at the ground but they could hear every word and Mathilda's anger grew at being subjected to this humiliation. 'You have evidence for Emeline's treachery, my lord?'

'I will have. People will soon speak out.'

'You think so? And what of me, your wife, Emeline's mistress. Am I – *again* – under the cloud of your suspicion as well?'

'Should you be?'

Mathilda wanted to scream.

'How could you even think it?'

'Because I would be a fool not to. Do not be so naive, Mathilda. In Flanders, where all is fashion and architecture, such pretty trust may serve but Normandy is a dog pit where anyone could bite you at any time. People turn, Mathilda; always they turn.'

'That's not true. Why must you always think the worst? Why must you always search for blame and search hardest in those closest to you? You think everyone is against you, even the Pope.'

'The Pope *is* against me.'

'He is *not*. He is simply playing games like everyone else. You accused me once of fostering the papal prohibition to give me a way out of our marriage but maybe, William, it is you who fosters it to pander to your damned need to have all against you.'

William sucked breath sharply in through his teeth and the reluctant crowd took a nervous step backwards.

'What I need,' he said, his voice like ice, 'is to have all *with* me, most especially my wife and her loose-tongued attendants.'

The court froze. Mathilda heard Cecelia whimper and saw Emeline shift her babies fretfully on her shoulders. She fought for words to answer her raging husband but then someone stepped in front of her and blocked him momentarily from her sight.

'How dare you, my lord?' It was Hugh, his usually quiet voice ripped through with ferocity. 'How dare you accuse my wife of treachery and me besides, for as her husband all that she is, I am too.'

'You would defy me, Hugh, after all I have done for you?'

'As you defy me, my lord. I am your loyal servant and gladly but you must be loyal in return. We are not all waiting for a chance to stab you and you do yourself a disservice to think so – and us too. Emeline is a good woman, my lord, and you have cast a slur upon her. I cannot let that stand.'

William stared at him, nonplussed.

'You are challenging me?'

Hugh paled.

'Is that what you want?'

'No, Hugh.'

'Nor I but it would be best I think, my lord duke, if I took my wife away. She is weary after birthing two babes and needs peace. We will leave. Now.'

'Now?' Mathilda gasped. 'But Emeline is newly from her childbed. She cannot travel.'

'I can,' Emeline insisted, 'if Hugh thinks it best.'

'No. The babies . . .'

'Will be well with us.'

'But where will you go?'

'We will head for Italy,' Hugh said. 'Where else is there for a lost Norman?'

'You are not "lost",' Mathilda cried. 'Tell him, William. Emeline is not a spy but a woman – a wife and a mother. She has no interest in war, save in its conclusion and the return of her husband.' He did not respond and she ran to him and grabbed at his arm. 'Tell Hugh not to leave, William, please. This is a madness. You are tired, that is all and no wonder. Tell him, I beg you!'

But William just shook her off.

'He will do as he chooses,' he said, breaking from them all and striding for the palace door.

As if released, the soldiers scattered and within moments Mathilda was left with Emeline. Behind them, Hugh ordered fresh horses and a carriage brought from the stables and sent his own servants running to pack clothes. Emeline looked shocked but resolute.

'Do not go,' Mathilda begged her. 'I will talk to William. I will explain. He has too often been cursed with treachery and sees it everywhere but I will make him understand his error. Stay, please.'

Emeline smiled sadly.

'I think it is best if we do not for he seems very certain.'

Mathilda felt her heart tear. She looked at Emeline, tousled in her loose gown, and remembered her on the night of her own wedding when she had clasped her tight and told her that she would never leave her – 'never, never, never'. How had it come to this?

'You cannot go. I cannot let you. It is not safe.'

Emeline, however, simply looked back at Hugh as he led the horses from the stable.

'It is totally safe, my lady, for Hugh will care for me.'

Her eyes shone. Even as she stood there in a hastily thrown-on cloak with her babies of just one day clutched to her milky chest, her eyes shone. She had not questioned his decision, not even for a moment. She was a better wife than Mathilda by far; or perhaps it was simply that Hugh was a better husband. Either way, there was little left to say bar God-speed before Hugh was there and she was handing the babies to him and climbing into the carriage as servants rushed up with blankets. And just like that, as if a whirlwind had spun through Rouen, they were gone.

Left alone, Mathilda turned miserably to the chapel to seek some comfort in God. Her prayers, though, were slow to come for all she could truly think was damn war for poisoning men's souls, and damn William for trusting no one, and damn her wretched uncle King Henri for proving him right to do so.

CHAPTER TWENTY-TWO

Rouen, May 1060

'King Henri is dead.'

The news rippled excitedly around the palace yard. The men had been preparing to ride out to hunt but all sport was forgotten with the arrival of the messengers. William came across to Mathilda who had been fussing over Robert, glad to spend some time with him after birthing a third daughter. Her eldest boy, now eight, had been preparing with great excitement to ride out with the hunt and would be the one member of the court disappointed to have his afternoon disturbed by news from France. His father's eyes, however, were shining.

'God has punished Henri for opposing us, Wife. We are blessed.'

Mathilda shifted uncomfortably. Was it Christian to crow at another's death, especially a member of one's own family? Many times in the long wait whilst the men had been at war she had sadly traced the patterns in the casket Henri had gifted her. She had considered burning it as a show of loyalty to her husband but it was so pretty and so useful that in the end she had simply covered the beautiful lid with a cloth.

And now it was Henri himself who would be so covered. She shivered.

'God is on the Norman side!' William was shouting delightedly to his supporters who were roaring approval, thankfully swallowing Mathilda's petty fears in their clamour.

'Who rules now?' he demanded of the messenger.

'His son, Phillipe, Lord Duke.'

'But he is a child.'

'Just six years old, my lord, yes. His mother stands as regent alongside Count Baldwin of Flanders.'

'Regent?' Mathilda asked sharply but William brushed her aside.

'This is better and better. Your father is in charge, Mathilda, and Queen Anne too, who is, of course, closely allied to Raoul, who is closely allied to *us*. This is fine news indeed. We must celebrate.'

The men needed no second asking. Handing their unhappy horses back to the grooms they poured into the Tour to toast their enemy's demise. Robert howled in frustration but was whisked up by Fitz who threw him on his back, promising to be his mount for the afternoon, and the lad was soon laughing with the rest. William held out an imperious arm to Mathilda.

'You will come and celebrate with the court, Wife?'

'Yes,' she agreed, though she heard her own reluctance.

So did William. He leaned in, sweeping an arm around her waist.

'Would you rather we celebrated alone?'

She jumped.

'It is afternoon, Husband!'

'Even better, for we grow old, my Mora, and sleep beckons us earlier these days. Come, it has been a long time – too long.'

'I am but newly churched, William.'

'It was three weeks hence.'

'It was?'

'Three weeks and four days.'

'You are counting?'

He looked sheepish.

'As I said, Wife, it has been too long.'

Mathilda buried her sigh. He was right, she supposed, and she did not object, not really. She might not have lost her heart to her husband but her body still leaped at his attentions and she was recovering well from her sixth birthing. It had taken longer than the others, though still, as the midwife had tactlessly pointed out, less time than for most women.

'Most women do not have a duchy to get back to,' Mathilda had snapped. It had been rude of her, and not really true either for there had been no war for three years and William was in full control, but she had been in pain and not thinking straight. All had felt better again once she'd held her third daughter in her arms, though she had cried like a fool. William had laughed and kissed her over and over and insisted on naming the child Mathilda.

'Why not?' he'd demanded when she'd protested. 'We have a William, do we not, in our fiery little Rufus, so why not a Mathilda too? I would like the world to have another you in it, for you make it so much better a place.'

That had set her weeping once more, out of gratitude and guilt and some slippery jumble of other emotions that had made her long for Emeline, now safely in Italy and, to Mathilda's great distress, enjoying it hugely.

The true spy had been flushed out within days of the Grandmesnils' departure and executed in front of the court. William, for once humbled, had sent letters begging Hugh to return but his jaunty reply had said that he was much in demand for his knowledge of horses and that he and his family should, in Norman interests, stay for a 'breeding season at least'. Mathilda had wept even more at that but she was, thank the Lord, finding her equilibrium at last. That did not, however, mean that she was ready to go through the stormy ride of childbearing again.

'Do you not desire me any more, my Mora?' William asked with a frown.

'Of course I do,' she said hastily. 'I just think that for now we should be with your men. There is much to consider.' She seized his arm as a new thought occurred to her. 'We should go to Paris, William.'

He looked at her for so long that she feared she had truly offended him, but then suddenly he swooped her into his arms.

'You are right, my Mora. You are so right. We will go to Paris and we will swear allegiance to the little king and restore good relations with France. And then if we should ever need their support . . .'

'You are thinking still of England?'

He took her hands.

'Always. Are you not?'

And God help her, she was. For now, though, France would be a blessed relief.

Mathilda stared in awe at the elegant spires on the horizon. They were approaching Paris down the dusty old Via Jules Cesar, built in the time of the great Roman emperor and, as far as Mathilda's jarred body could tell, repaired little in the thousand years since, but the French capital was a sight to ease all pains. The outer wall curved in a semi-circle towards their approach and the great Seine, silver in the half-sun creeping through the mist, cut into it to their right and then out again far over to their left, like an arrow through a heart.

'We are almost there, my lady,' Raoul said, riding up at her side. He had been delighted to arrange this visit and ridden out to the border between Normandy and France to personally secure their safe passage to the new king. 'Once within the walls all will be comfort, I assure you. The royal palace is newly refurbished and very fine. There are feathers in all the beds and glass in many of the windows and such fabrics and frescoes as you have never seen before.'

'I come from Bruges,' Mathilda reminded him haughtily.

'Of course, my lady. For a moment I forgot, for you are every inch Normandy's duchess. In that case, such fabrics and frescoes as you have not seen *for some time.*'

Mathilda smiled her thanks, though she felt a stab of guilt. She had brought little of Flemish culture to Normandy. Judith would have done more. She had an eye for beauty, Mathilda only one for order. Maybe, as William always said, she was more like him than she knew. Or maybe she had just been lazy. She looked to Raoul.

'You occupy a good place at court, my lord?'

'A very good place, thank you. I am, shall we say, at the heart of the French administration.'

'So you will marry the dowager queen?'

'Ah.' Raoul grimaced. 'That is trickier. The church is not so eager to see us together. But that matters little. Anne and I know the truth of our love and the French court is not troubled by it. The rest will come. But you understand, do you not? The church tried to block your love, but you did not let it stand in your way either.'

Mathilda nodded dumbly, happy to be equated to Raoul though she was troublingly aware that the circumstances of her own defiance had been rather less romantic than his. She and William had pushed their marriage for politics, not for love.

But love grows, she reminded herself; love *has* grown. Surely that was true? She admired William, respected him, and if those feelings were more like a warm milk than the spiced wine of her giddy dalliance with Brihtric, then so what? Milk was far more nourishing.

'I am glad you are happy,' she said hastily, 'and I look forward to meeting the queen.'

'She is a wonderful woman,' Raoul replied simply and led the way up to the gates of Paris.

The outer walls, close up, were rather derelict. Raoul explained that they were from Roman times but that he and the queen and of course the little king had great plans to restore them. Raoul and Queen Anne, it soon emerged, had great plans for restoring many things. As they traced their way through the streets towards the palace Raoul spoke of architects and builders and great projects and William was rapt.

'We can learn from this,' he told Mathilda eagerly. 'We can build too.'

'Rouen is beautiful already,' she objected.

'Rouen is, yes. It is not Rouen where we need work.'

'Where then, William?'

'Caen.'

'Caen?' Mathilda looked at him in horror. 'But Caen is in the west, William, where . . .'

'Where all rebellions take seed. Exactly.'

Mathilda's heart sank. She could see the sense of what he proposed but could not like it. She loved Rouen for it reminded her of Bruges with its tight, pretty buildings, but Caen was as stark and foreboding as Eu and she did not relish spending any more time there. Still, for now she was in Paris and must make the most of it.

They were approaching the French king's palace and it was a beautiful residence, made in stone as pale as a woman's skin with turrets and arches and elegant, soaring detailing. The floors were marble, smooth and easy to walk upon, the ceilings high, the windows tall and frequent so that the palace seemed flooded with light. In the main hall they even had rough-woven fabric in a wide band along the middle of the floor and Mathilda felt it bounce and give beneath her feet as they were shown along it towards two grand thrones at the top end.

In one sat a boy, the six-year-old King Phillipe, his feet dangling off the great chair but his little head held high beneath a heavy crown of state. In the other was Queen Anne, a handsome woman with sharp brown eyes and startling rich blonde hair that glowed beneath a slender diadem set all around with rubies. To her right sat an old man and it took Mathilda a moment more to recognise Count Baldwin.

'Father, what a surprise!'

'I am grown old, Mathilda. You did not recognise me.'

'Nonsense, Father. You are scarce changed.' She kissed him hastily on both cheeks. 'Where is Mother? Is she well?'

'Very well. She must look after Flanders.'

'Whilst you look after France?'

'No. Queen Anne looks after France; I merely offer a little support.'

'She is officially regent?' Mathilda asked.

She looked pointedly at William who had the grace to blush but before she could say more Baldwin was grabbing his hand and shaking it heartily.

'Duke William, good to see you again.'

William turned gratefully from her.

'And you, Count. And Lord Bruno too.'

Mathilda looked at him in surprise as he greeted her father's chamberlain.

'You know Lord Bruno, William?'

Her husband looked disconcerted again but swiftly recovered.

'I met him when I was courting you, Mathilda.'

That must have been true, she supposed, but the manner of their greeting had seemed more familiar and Bruno's thinning scalp had turned a very interesting shade of scarlet. Now, though, Queen Anne was with them and it was no time for dallying with a chamberlain.

'Welcome, Duchess Mathilda,' Anne said softly. 'We are honoured by your visit.'

'We are the ones honoured,' Mathilda replied, curtseying.

Anne laughed sweetly and raised her.

'We are both, then, honoured, so I trust we can be friends. Come and meet Phillipe.'

Phillipe stood and solemnly held out his tiny hand for Mathilda to kiss.

'God bless you, Sire,' she said and saw the boy colour.

'I pray that He will, my lady, for my father has left me a fine kingdom and I must rule it as he would have wished.'

Mathilda glanced to Anne who touched her son's soft head.

'He has grown old beyond his years. I suppose, as his regent, I must be glad of it.'

'The French accept your rule?'

She looked surprised.

'Of course. Why should they not?'

'I agree absolutely – but the Normans are not so liberal.'

'Then they are fools, my lady. A woman's mind is every bit as sharp as a man's, though I will admit that it makes my heart ache to see him so serious.'

Mathilda thought of her own boys racing around the yard with their toy swords and their pig's bladders and felt for the tiny king. Then suddenly she realised she was looking at the child William must have been when, like Phillipe, he lost his father and took on the heavy weight of rule, and all thoughts of her own status left her. William had had no Queen Anne to stand guard over him, only gentle Herleva who had offered so much love but so little protection against a harsh world. She prayed it would be different for Phillipe.

'You have our every support. I hope we can return to the happy days when France and Normandy stood as one.'

'I hope so too.'

Their eyes locked.

'We have no quarrel with France,' Mathilda said firmly.

'Only with England?' Mathilda jumped. 'My sister Agatha, you know, is in England. She travelled there three years ago with her husband, Prince Edward, though she was sadly widowed just days after her arrival.'

'That was sad,' Mathilda agreed nervously, adding, 'We have no quarrel with England either, my lady, as long as she has no quarrel with us.'

For a moment the air between them shimmered and then Anne smiled again.

'Such tedious things, quarrels,' she said lightly. 'Now, tell me, my lady, do you dance?'

'Oh yes,' Mathilda assured her, relieved the dread moment had passed. 'I *love* to dance.'

Those days in the French court were as giddy for Mathilda as the looping, floating reels that Raoul's band of highly talented minstrels played with tireless energy for the excitable court. Her only regret, as they feasted on rich foods and elaborate entertainment, was William's evident discomfort. He kept insisting he was pleased that his old alliance with France was back in place but it was hard to see it on his sombre face. If the court went hunting he excelled, leading the pack with confidence and grace, but as the boy king was not yet old enough for the rigours of the hunt, the court was often at lawn games which he found pointless. Usually he took refuge in a corner with Lord Bruno, the pair of them huddling over the tafel board William had brought with him, ignoring everyone else.

'How do you know Lord Bruno?' Mathilda quizzed him one day as they stood together half-watching a noisy skittles game on the rich lawns behind the palace. 'Was it before you met me?'

'I may have had dealings with him,' he said tightly.

'He's one of your spies?'

'Spy is a very crass word, Mathilda.'

'Well-informed messengers then. You never said.'

'You never asked.'

'How long has he been working for you, William? How long has he been spying on my family – on *me*?'

He did not answer, leaving her with painful questions – had it been before or after Lord Brihtric? Had Bruno told him how she'd danced in the arms of the handsome Saxon? Had he told him how she'd written asking him to marry her? Had William even seen the letter? Surely not; surely her father had destroyed it. Guilt itched at her, inflamed by an aching awareness that Lord Brihtric with his easy charm and light feet would have prospered far more in Raoul's elegant French court than William did.

'I hope,' she flung at him, 'that his information was good.'

'I married you, did I not?'

As usual with William it was truth, though perhaps not the whole truth.

'You are enjoying yourself here?' she needled.

'I am.'

'It does not look that way.'

'What does it matter how it looks?'

'It might matter to your hosts. Visiting people is meant to be fun.'

'Meant to be?'

She gritted her teeth but now a messenger was threading around the noisy game and bowing low before them. She recognised a young Norman, saw from his sweaty hair that he had hurried and her heart seemed for a moment to collapse in on itself. They had only been out of Normandy a few days – surely there had not been rebellion already. But the messenger, for once, was smiling as he pushed a parchment roll towards them.

'What is this?' William demanded.

'It comes from Italy, Lord Duke, from Emeline de Grandmesnil.'

'Emeline?' Mathilda asked eagerly, all quarrel with William forgotten. Della had kindly stepped in as her attendant but although she was solid and efficient she trod too regularly on Cecelia's delicate toes with her bluntness and had none of the teasing fun of the French girl. 'What says she?'

'I know not, my lady, only that the rider said it was of great importance and that I must guard the parchment with my life, so I hastened here.'

'You did right, thank you.'

He smiled shyly as Mathilda took the message and cracked the seal. There were two parchments, one within the other. She unrolled the first and read it slowly to William and as the words unfolded out loud they seemed to swell and grow between them:

Greetings from Italy to our dear Duke and Duchess. We pray that you and all your children are well and we hope the enclosed pleases you both. Hugh was invited to Rome, for the Pope is a fine judge of horses and a man very much in favour of the Normans. We had a convivial time with His Holiness and he assured us of his goodwill to the duchy.

He was kind enough to look at the verdict of the Council of Rheims on your marriage and was swift to see that it was poorly grounded. The objections were unsubstantiated and he, therefore, grants you this retrospective dispensation and asks only that you raise a church to God's great glory in penance for running ahead of the bishops. This dispensation matters little to you, I am sure, as you already know your marriage to be true and blessed in God's sight but earthly confirmation is still, I hope, welcome.

Mathilda looked at the second roll in wonder, then, trying to control a strange tremor in her hands, broke the seal. It fell apart to reveal, as promised, papal sanction of their nine-year marriage. She and William both stared at it, awed, as the court tapped balls unheedingly through hoops behind them.

Eventually William spoke: 'I turned Hugh away and he repays me with this great gift. He is a good man, Mathilda.'

'He is. And his wife is a good woman. You should not have doubted her.'

He shook his head.

'Still you do not see it, my sweet. I *should* have doubted her but I can still be glad to be proved wrong. She understands that even if you do not.'

'But . . .'

'But nothing, Mathilda. The past is gone and life is easier if you can accept that. Hugh and Emeline are content and our marriage is truly sanctified at last.'

'This is cause for celebration, Husband.'

'It is. All these years we have lived under a shadow. All these years we have feared someone might snatch this marriage from under us – have even, God forgive us, accused each other of doing so – and now it is lifted. We are in the light, Mathilda, and is it not glorious? The Pope asks for a church – we will give him two. One each to show how blessed we both are.'

'That would be wonderful, William.'

'It would. We will build them in Caen and if we leave space between we can fill it with fine houses such as we have seen here in Paris. We can encourage artisans and traders – develop the area and stamp our authority upon it at the same time. It is a fine idea, is it not?'

'It is,' she forced herself to agree, for she had neglected her duty to Caen for too long, and would be nice to do something more personal too. It had been so exciting to be in Paris and maybe now more was possible. 'We could, perhaps, make a pilgrimage to thank the Pope ourselves?'

'A pilgrimage?'

Mathilda's mind was racing now.

'Why not? Think of it, William – a pilgrimage to Rome. We could pray at St Peter's own altar. We could thank the Pope for his intervention and we could visit Hugh's horses on the way back.'

'And bring him home with them – his wife too?'

'Perhaps.'

He pulled her close, crushing her against his chest.

'It is a nice idea, Mathilda.'

'It is a *good* idea,' she corrected him but already she'd heard the steel in his voice and remembered, too late, that his father had died on pilgrimage. 'And it is safer now, William. I hear there are well-trod routes with inns and monasteries and many willing to ease the way for a traveller, especially a duke.'

'Mathilda . . .'

'And many rulers are doing it. Did not King Cnut himself ride to Rome? And Macbeth, King of the Scots. If they can journey so far, surely we can?'

'I do not doubt it, but . . .'

'And I hear tell that Judith's husband proposes a pilgrimage, perhaps as early as next year. We could maybe travel in her party?'

'With *Godwinsons*?!' he asked, stepping back.

'It could be useful.'

'It could be suicide. We cannot do it, Mathilda.'

'They cannot be that dangerous . . .'

'No, no. I mean simply that we cannot go that far. The journey would take months. Normandy will turn.'

'No, William. Why must you always think that?'

'Because it is true.'

She hung her head. Norman truth seemed always to be so hard. On the lawns the game had finished and someone had called for wine and minstrels. A pipe suddenly picked out a pretty tune, a lute following its lead, and giggling courtiers fell over themselves to form an impromptu set. Mathilda closed her eyes against their joy and prayed for patience. She felt William take her hands softly, almost apologetically, but could not force her eyes open for him.

'Maybe, my dear, this Tostig would appreciate somewhere convivial to rest on his way home, and your dear sister too.'

'Cousin.'

'Sorry?'

She forced her eyes open.

'Judith is my cousin.'

'Of course. And mine too for that matter. Either way, it would be a chance to see her, would it not?'

'And for you to pick their brains on England.'

He did not deny it.

'Invite them for a visit, Mathilda.'

'A visit?'

'Yes, a visit. They are meant to be fun, are they not?' He had turned her own words upon her, as he had always done so well. She sighed and he tugged her closer. 'It is not the same as travelling to the Holy City, I realise that, but it is surely

245

something? I'm sorry, Mathilda, that I cannot be as, as impetuous as you would like me. I know it makes me dull.'

She strove to deny it but the words stuck in her throat and still the notes of the pipe and lute swirled around them.

'Dance with me, William,' she said instead.

'Why?'

'Why? Because I want to hold you, to hold on to you. Our marriage is blessed at last and we have done so much together, do you not think?'

'And can do so much more yet, yes – but why need it include shuffling around like fools?'

Mathilda felt her blood rise.

'This dance is very simple.'

'For you perhaps.'

'I could show you.'

'I doubt it. Can you draw a bow, Mathilda?'

'You know I cannot.'

'But it looks easy, does it not?'

'It looks elegant, certainly, when you do it, William.'

He looked a little surprised.

'Thank you, Mathilda. But believe me, if *you* tried, it would not.'

'Thank *you*, William,' she said dryly.

'It would be no fault of your own, my dear. It is simply that it needs much practice to do it well.'

'I am sure that is so, but dancing is not nearly so skilled. It is a matter of feel, that is all.'

'Feel?'

'Feel for the music, in your body.'

He tipped his head to one side, considering, but then shook it furiously.

'All that the music makes me feel, Mathilda, is irritation. Dance with someone else.'

'But I want to dance with *you*.'

His eyes narrowed.

'That will not happen. I go to seek the chapel, my lady, to give thanks for the Pope's blessing on our marriage at last. You need not accompany me.'

'I do not mind. I am your wife.'

'I release you.'

'As your wife?'

'No, Mathilda. Now you are being foolish. Today. I release you today. You may go and trade pretty steps with someone else for I am no use to you. Good day.'

And with that he was gone and Mathilda was left to be pulled into the dance by six-year-old King Phillipe, standing stiffly in his solemn little hold and wishing someone had done the same with William when he was first duke, instead of forever leading him to war.

CHAPTER TWENTY-THREE

Caen, May 1062

Judith pulled back the flap at the side of the covered carriage and peered out – Caen. It looked stark and forbidding after the glories of Rome and she felt a rush of something deliciously like pity for Mathilda, stuck here whilst she had been in Italy adventuring. She'd heard tell her cousin had been to Paris but, really, that was nothing to Rome and for once she considered herself lucky in her husband.

Their recent pilgrimage had perhaps just been another way of escaping Northumbria, which Torr still found stark and dull, but she had not complained. All her life she had yearned to see the Holy City and it had not disappointed. Finally she felt that she had seen such glories as would make life worth living, for Rome had opened her eyes to the possible scale of art and made her own ambitions to illuminate her gospel books – now half completed – seem modest.

Sadly, though, they were heading home and Judith felt as if the sun were fading on her back with every mile they'd ridden north. This stopover in Normandy was only making things worse. Torr had seized on the unexpected invitation from Mathilda, picking at the sparse words for meaning and making plans straight away. He had been edgy recently. Everyone was edgy, for King Edward was ill and with no heir named, save the tenuous and never-mentioned promise to Duke William, the future was a frightening place. Some people were talking of Torr's brother Harold as the Saxons' future king and Torr did not like it; he did not like it at all.

'You would like to see your sister, would you not?' he'd urged, shaking Duke William's wretched invitation in her face.

'She's not my sister.'

'Words, Judi, no more. She is clearly keen to see you and it will be excellent to see her too, will it not? And Duke William. And perhaps you could visit your mother too.'

The latter had only made her dread Normandy more but, fresh from a visit to the holiest of cities, she had felt duty-bound to call. The visit had not been a success. Eleanor had been thin and frail and interested only in her prayers. Even Karl, now a quiet and courteous lad of eight, had not been able to incite in her any interest in God's physical world and Judith had left as soon as she was able without any sense of peace or blessing or even anger. Her overriding emotion had been a fierce determination to be a good mother to Karl and, if she were not much mistaken, to the new babe finally growing in her womb.

There had been a man in Rome, a kind, quiet man, called Lord Wulf of Bavaria who had taken a great interest in her gospel books. She had been touched and had talked to him as much as she could but Torr, to her great surprise, had been jealous. Wulf's simple attention – just artistic interest, she was sure – had inflamed his passion in a way she'd not known since the first days of their marriage and this baby must be the result. She was longing to get home to Durham to keep it safe but first there was this visit to endure.

She nudged her pretty carriage companion awake as they clattered down the sparsely built but surprisingly busy streets of Caen and onto the slope towards the gates of the formidable ducal fortress. Once within the gates, Judith kept behind the carriage's door-flap so she could sneak a look, unnoticed, at the ducal fortress. It was enjoyably unimpressive with much of the huge space on the hilltop just bare grass and Judith thought fondly of pretty Durham with its winding streets and well-established houses and her own elegant enclosure. But her dear home was far off yet and now they were drawing to a halt and two guards were leaping to pull back the flap and she only just sat back in time not to be caught peeping. She looked again to her companion.

'Ready?'

'Absolutely. I cannot wait to see her face.'

Judith smiled stiffly and led the way out into the open, her legs weak from the journey so that she staggered stupidly as she stepped out to meet Mathilda. She waved away all help and righted herself to look at her cousin. She had forgotten how small she was, and how little that mattered for Normandy's duchess held herself even more regally than she had in their youth. The ten years since they'd last been together had at least drawn a few lines across her face but they only served to emphasise her natural beauty.

'Judith, my dear, how lovely.' Mathilda offered her a formal hand but then stopped, her eyes fixed over her shoulder. 'Oh and, and . . .' Judith watched amazement turn into a joy that had been notably absent from the initial greeting. 'Emeline? Emeline, is that really you?!'

And then she was pushing past Judith to take Emeline in her arms and their bellies, both swollen, were bumping against each other and they were laughing and crying and calling for Cecelia and all was a confusion of tears and laughter. Judith stood awkwardly to one side until at last Mathilda looked to her again.

'You brought Emeline back.'

'It seemed churlish not to.'

'I'm so glad. And Hugh? Is Hugh back too? William will be delighted.'

That, Judith knew, was the plan. Torr had fallen over himself to offer the Grandmesnils transport home, as if they were his personal gift to William, and that made Judith uneasy. She looked around the yard but the men had dismounted and gone inside for ale.

'Hugh is back,' Emeline confirmed. 'And our children too. Meet Amaury, Claudine and Beatrice.'

'Gosh, how the twins are grown!' Mathilda exclaimed as the three children who'd bounced off the linen walls of the carriage most of the journey finally sprang free.

Karl followed more sedately but went unnoticed as Mathilda's six children came rushing forward to line up before Emeline's three.

'Why are you that funny brown colour?' asked a bullish boy with bright red hair that Judith could only assume was the one they called 'Rufus'.

'*You're* the funny one with that crazy hair,' little Beatrice shot back and the two mothers hastened over to the standoff.

'She reminds me of you, Emeline,' Judith heard Mathilda laugh as they dived in together to keep the peace and she had to put a hand to her belly to curb the instantly flaring jealously that she had all but forgotten her lively cousin always inspired in her. She stepped determinedly forward.

'This is Karl.'

Mathilda turned as the rest of the children scrambled off together and smiled politely at the boy.

'Welcome to Normandy, Karl.'

'Thank you,' he mumbled.

Judith longed for him to dazzle Mathilda but he had not his

father's ready charm – nor, she hoped, the foibles that went with it.

'Why don't you check the horses?' she suggested and watched him break thankfully away and escape to the long run of stables against the palisade fencing that marked the perimeter of the royal lands. She wished she could go too but Mathilda was taking her arm.

'And how is life over the Narrow Sea, Cousin?'

'It suits me well, thank you.'

Neither of them mentioned the events of '51 when they had moved in and out of England as if God was somehow choosing between them. Maybe He still was.

'You live in the north, I believe?' Mathilda pushed.

'I do. What of it?'

'Nothing *of* it, Judith. I was simply asking.'

'Of course. Sorry. Torr – Tostig – is a little sensitive about his office. We live in Durham which is a fine city with a wonderful cathedral and beautiful countryside all around but it is, you see, quite a long way from Westminster. Sometimes Torr feels . . . isolated.'

'I see. And you, Cousin – how does this Durham suit you?'

'Oh, I love it there and have much to do with the people and the cathedral chapter. I am more than content to manage our estates whilst Torr travels with the king. Edward values him highly.'

'How nice. Shall we go inside?'

Judith nodded thankfully, praying she could get somewhere to rest a while for she was so tired with the new babe. Already, though, she could hear Tostig throwing his weight around in the hall and knew she dared not leave him to talk to these cunning Normans alone. How she dreaded the evening ahead.

*

'And how does my cousin, King Edward?' Duke William asked Torr, sleekly casual.

Judith felt the words spike across her skin like nettle rash. The feasting had gone every bit as badly as she'd feared. All evening Duke William had been feeding her husband both flattery and wine and Torr was edgier than ever. She put out a warning hand to her husband but he did not even notice.

'He is old,' he told their host recklessly, 'and dull. He can scarcely keep his seat in the hunt.'

'Really?' William half-smiled. 'I remember him as such an accomplished rider as a young man. How sad for him.'

'He is well enough yet,' Judith said quickly.

William looked at her curiously but Torr was leaping in again.

'We should perhaps, Lord Duke, speak of England alone?'

Judith felt every part of her clench with nervous fear.

'Alone?' William said, drawing out the word so it seemed to take on even more import. 'Of course, Earl Torr. It would be a pleasure. Perhaps you would like to see my wife's new abbey of La Trinité? It progresses fast.'

Torr blinked at his host, then looked to Judith. They both glanced to the window opening where the dying sun was turning the sky a dull orange.

'Now, Duke William?'

'Why not? It looks beautiful by moonlight. Not as fine as Roman monuments, perhaps, but a modest achievement all the same.'

'Of course,' Torr stuttered, putting his well-used wine goblet down with a clatter. 'I would be honoured.'

'And your wife?'

'If you wish.' He was sweating, Judith noticed, caught out by William's speed. He wasn't ready for whatever he had planned. 'Perhaps Hugh and Emeline would like to come too?'

'Oh, they are tired,' William said easily, 'and wish to settle their children back into their new home, do you not?'

'We do,' Hugh agreed hastily, nudging Emeline to her feet.

Judith felt a sudden crazy urge to hold onto her tenuous journey-friends. William looked alive, focused, dangerous. They had been mad to come but there was no going back for the duke was already leading the way out of the hall, guards falling in behind them. The sun had gone but the moon was near full and as they trod towards the half-built abbey, Judith felt like a ghost of herself. The city of Caen lay, as far as she could tell, to the south of the enormous compound in which William's castle nestled, but Mathilda's abbey was in the east and William's, so he told her, was just being started in the west.

'So we can spread the city out,' he said companionably as they walked, and looking at the new houses that were being built all along their route in a mixture of wood and stone Judith saw how they were helping to create a new city, more modern and elegant than the huddle of buildings directly beneath the fortress.

It was a clever plan, a vision even, and she looked for Torr to plead with him not to underestimate this man but he was sauntering along with Mathilda, chattering about shoe designs, seemingly oblivious to any possible trouble ahead. And now, here they were at the new abbey. The guards held torches but William waved them back as he led them under the open arch-way and into the cavernous space of the developing nave. Judith looked up at the half-grown church and it seemed to her that it was reaching cravenly towards the sky, as if it were Normandy itself, ever grasping for more.

'What do you think?' William asked Torr, gesturing expansively.

'It will be very beautiful. It reminds me a little of the new Westminster Abbey.'

'Does it?' William's voice was sharp. 'It is finished, this Saxon abbey?'

'No, no. It is not so far progressed as this, though it is bigger of course.'

'Of course?'

Judith longed to step in and stopper Torr's mouth but she dared not.

'It is the king's own project.'

'I see. And kings need bigger abbeys than everyone else, do they?'

At last Torr stiffened, sensing danger.

'The abbeys, surely, are for God, Lord Duke?'

'Of course. It is good that King Edward is building. The abbey church was in poor repair when I was last in London in '51. You remember? Oh no – you were in exile at the time.'

'I was in Flanders with Count Baldwin, your wife's father.'

'And *your* wife's brother. We are virtually related, Earl Tostig.' Torr looked uneasily at William who clapped him on the back and strolled forward, as if admiring the stonework. 'I enjoyed my time in Westminster,' he said into the night sky. 'I got on very well with the king, my cousin. He and I are related too.'

'Distantly.'

'His mother was my great-aunt.'

'A maternal line,' Torr replied but his voice was thin and Judith saw him wrap his fingers nervously into his hazel hair.

She moved towards him but just as she gained his side William spun back.

'Why are you here, Earl Torr?'

'A family visit, Duke. And I brought Hugh back.'

'For which I am grateful, but that was not, Torr, out of the kindness of your paltry heart. So I ask again – why are you here?'

His bluntness was ruthless; it left Torr nowhere to go.

'I wondered, William, if you would consider backing me as King of England.'

'You?' William looked at Torr with contemptuous disbelief. 'You as King of England?' He laughed, a dark, harsh sound that scraped off the ragged columns around them. Then suddenly he stepped so close to Torr that the moon behind them seemed to pull their faces into one. 'King Edward promised *me* the throne of England on his death.'

'I have not heard of that promise, Duke William.'

'Rubbish. Of course you have. It is whispered everywhere.'

Torr gripped Judith's arm.

'But not declared aloud,' he said stoutly and Judith thought she had rarely seen him so brave.

'Not yet. King Edward is a cunning man and does not want disruptions in his own reign. He promised me England in recognition of our family connections and my strong reputation as a leader and my kindness to him as a youth. He said the crown would be mine if there was no other heir and there is none.'

'Edgar.'

'The Hungarian child; the lost prince's son? He is just a boy. No one will have him as king. You are right to think of an alternative candidate, Torr, but it is not you. You are right, too, to think of your own gain but you aim too high. Do you like Northumbria, Torr? Does it mean much to you, or would you rather, perhaps, rule Wessex?'

The last word came out as a hiss and Judith flinched. How did the Duke of Normandy know of Torr's avoidance of his own lands? She glanced nervously towards the guards but they were the other side of the archway keeping dutiful watch outward.

'Come, Torr.' William's voice was all softness now. 'I am not threatening you, far from it. I am offering you a deal.' Torr's green eyes widened, big as the moon above their heads. 'My wife has taught me to sharpen my wits, Torr, as yours has perhaps taught you – so now is the time to use them. You are a younger son, yes? Never first in line. Never rewarded . . . as Harold is rewarded.' Judith closed her eyes against this nightmare – William knew Torr so well. 'You are worried, Torr, that your brother will be king.'

'No, I . . .'

'Yes you are. And you should be. Will he give you Wessex, think you, if he rules? I doubt it.'

Judith felt Torr shudder and knew that he doubted it too. He had come to Normandy, it seemed, on some fool's errand to win support for his own bid to the Saxon throne but he needed to think again.

'A deal, my lord duke?' she asked.

Torr looked annoyed but the time was past for his foolhardy approach. William straightened.

'Swear allegiance to me, Earl Torr. Swear to uphold me as King of England when the time comes and I will give you Wessex.'

Torr sucked in his breath. Wessex! Judith knew that, bar the throne, ruling Wessex was the one thing that could tempt him. But he could not swear, not to Normandy. No Saxons liked the Normans, no one would back William's claim and Torr would have no power to sway any opinion – though he may not realise that. She watched her husband fearfully.

'I will gladly swear allegiance to you when the time comes, Duke William,' Torr said but William just gave a dark chuckle.

'Very good, Torr, but no, that will not do. You must swear now.'

'Now?' Torr looked hopefully around the empty half-church.

'Here,' William corrected smoothly. 'In Normandy. In my hall, before witnesses and on holy relics.'

Judith felt herself shaking and Torr must have done so too for he pulled her close and shook his head.

'You know I cannot do that, Duke. I am an earl of England, sworn to King Edward.'

'Sworn to King Edward who has promised me the throne. I ask only for your matching promise of support once you are free of that allegiance.'

'And if I do not?'

William shrugged and picked up a stone, running a hand over it as if testing for weaknesses.

'That is your own free choice, Earl Torr. I will not force you. But know this . . .' He slammed the stone suddenly across the floor where it splintered, tiny fragments spinning out across the hardened earth. 'I demand loyalty of my men and I demand it up front. If you swear to me now, I will give you Wessex when I am king. If you do not, I will give you nothing save the sharp side of my sword. You are with me or you are against me. Choose.'

'You may not become king.'

'True. I may lose.'

William smiled as if this were ridiculous.

'Or you may choose not to challenge.'

'Without your support, you mean? I would not rate yourself so highly, Earl Tostig.'

Neither would Judith but now was not the moment to say so. Torr looked to the heavens for a long time as the rest of them stood, suspended, then finally he extended his hands to William.

'I am your friend, Duke, truly. As you say we are nearly related and this is, surely, enough? How can I know where England's throne will be promised? It will be my duty to serve whomever King Edward nominates but trust me, if it comes to you, I will honour you with all my being and gladly.'

'You do not think it will be me?'

'Only God can know.'

'And you will not choose now, Torr? You consider your loyalty too great a bargaining piece to give away so soon? You will not pin your colours to my mast?'

Torr looked straight at William, his eyes as sharp now as his host's.

'It seems to me, Lord Duke, that you have no masts to pin them to.'

He looked pleased with himself but William did not even flinch.

'No,' he agreed. 'No, Earl Torr, but if the need arises I will have and you, it seems, will not sail beneath them. A shame but it is your decision. I will not ask again and neither, believe me, should you.'

They were up at dawn. Judith had been awake half the night and even Torr, usually hard to pull from slumber, jolted up at the first bright streaks of sun over Caen. Rousing a sleepy Karl, they made for the stables, keen to be gone, but they were not the only ones.

'You will ride?' Mathilda asked, stepping inside just as Judith was preparing to mount.

She turned reluctantly.

'It is quicker.'

'You will not be harmed here.'

'Not yet.'

Mathilda grabbed her hands and Judith looked round for Torr but he had already gone out into the yard with Karl and she was alone with her cousin.

'Could Torr not think again, Judi? If war comes, we will be on opposing sides.'

'As we were in '51?'

Mathilda sighed.

'That was not war. Our fates were counterbalanced, yes, but not set with battle-lines drawn against each other.'

'I have no sword, Mathilda.'

'Come, Judith, there are more ways to fight than with raw steel, as well you know. You could persuade your husband.'

'Persuade him to swear to Duke William? To Normandy rather than to the land of his birth? Why would I do that?'

Mathilda bit at her lip.

'Because Normandy will win. William will win.'

'How do you know?'

'William always wins.'

'So far but these are cruel times, my sweet one.'

Mathilda looked distressed.

'Must they be so between us? You want to fight me?'

'Of course not.'

'You do. You want to fight me and you want to win.'

Judith's cheeks flared. She had not wanted to come here. She had warned Torr how it would be and he had laughed at her but she had been right. Mathilda might look sweet and friendly but she was out for herself, as she always had been.

'Can you blame me, Mathilda?' she demanded, feeling words battering to get out. 'Always you have come first. Always you had the best gowns and the highest place and the greatest titles but not any more. You are a duchess, I am an earl's lady. You do not outrank me now, Mathilda, and neither will you do so by becoming queen. The Saxons will not have it.'

Mathilda stared up at her, stunned.

'You have always felt this way?' she asked when she could find words.

Judith turned for her horse, flustered by her own unaccustomed anger, but then forced herself to turn back. This was important. In London when the poor lost prince had died so strangely she had prayed Mathilda would have the sense to stay away from England's proud shores, but now she had a chance to tell her to do so herself and she could not duck that responsibility.

'I do not want us to be set against each other, Maud, but it seems it is always to be that way. You made it to Westminster before me back in '51 but I am there now. Why can you and William not leave it alone? Why can you not be content with what you have here?'

Mathilda shook visibly.

'It is William who wants England,' she muttered but Judith had heard enough.

'No, Mathilda, it is you both. You are alike, you and William.'

'No!'

'It is the truth. William is clever, ambitious and determined and you are the same, always have been, whether you see it or not. Thank the Lord poor gentle Lord Brihtric turned you down, for you were made for the bastard duke. But do not forget, Mathilda, you are a Lady of Flanders and he a Duke of Normandy and though they are both fine lands, they are not England. Do not reach too high, Mathilda, I beg you. Now, farewell.'

And with that, she leaped into the saddle, for once grateful to follow Torr, and rode away from Caen with her heart pounding. She felt a sharp sadness for she had never been one for arguments, but she had said her piece and felt the better for it. Let Mathilda battle for England if she must, but let her do it alone.

CHAPTER TWENTY-FOUR

'Tell me of Sicily, my lord.'

Hugh and Emeline were newly arrived in the busy hall to break their fast but already William was upon them.

'Let them get some food, Husband,' Mathilda begged weakly.

She was still shaken from last night's encounter in her half-built abbey, not to mention from Judith's harsh words in the stable. She was scarily aware that after five years of relative calm, everything was suddenly picking up pace again and she looked nervously around the men and women of Normandy who were chatting and eating and making noisy arrangements for the rest of their day.

'Get some food?' William queried, as if she'd suggested they lay down in the mud.

'Yes, Husband. Our dear friends travelled a long way yesterday and you do not want them to regret returning, do you?'

It was a mean blow but she could not help herself. William sniffed but flung himself onto the nearest bench as servants hastily served the Grandmesnils pottage from the bubbling pot over the central hearth and they came to join him. There were still men curled up on pallets around the edges of the hall but, as if sensing action, they all began leaping up and turning their blankets back into cloaks, as if ashamed to be caught doing anything as indulgent as sleeping.

'So, Sicily?' Hugh said the moment he landed on the bench across the table from his duke. 'What would you know?'

William leaned eagerly forward, his chagrin forgotten.

'It is an island, yes?'

'Yes, though a big one – nigh on the size of Wales. It has been seized over the years by the Moors. They build their infidel mosques in the cities and bring in their own people to fill them. The good Christians there look to the Pope for liberation but the Pope doesn't have the army for the job.'

'But the Guiscard does?'

'Yes, though it is more his younger brother, Roger, who leads the way in Sicily.'

'You met him?'

'Oh yes. We met them both.'

'What is he like, the Guiscard?' William demanded, moving over a little as Roger and Della slid curiously in at his side.

'Forbidding,' Hugh said carefully. 'And mercurial. You are never sure from one minute to the next what mood he will be in.'

'That must be bad for his men,' William said smugly.

'It is, and for his brother. They are forever falling out. It is foolish – they could achieve far more stood together.'

'Loyalty,' William said firmly.

There was an awkward pause until finally Hugh said, 'Last spring, for example, working together they took Messina, the capital of Sicily. It is a great prize.'

'They fight on foot?'

'No, no.' Hugh had taken a spoonful of his pottage and spluttered in an effort to swallow it. 'They are Normans, William – they fight as cavalry.'

'So where do they find the mounts?'

'In Italy. You have seen the horses I've brought back with me, Lord Duke. You would not, I'm sure, choose from anywhere else.'

'No.'

William leaped up suddenly and leaned across the table, banging his hands keenly down in front of Hugh. Mathilda looked at her husband – his eyes were glowing silver with a fierce interest that was surely more than politeness towards his returned lord and she feared his intent. Fitz, who had been showing a couple of lads the best way to sharpen their swords, detached himself and came over. And now Fulk, too, was drawing close, pulled by William's energy.

'But how do they get these fine Italian cavalry onto the island of Sicily?' the duke was asking.

'Ah!' Hugh smiled and rose to meet his lord's eyes. 'They do it by boat.'

'Boat? All of them?'

'Yes. Last May the Norman forces transported more than five hundred warhorses over the Strait of Messina to take the city.'

William's eyes were like arrowheads now – sharp and dangerous and hooking into his men in a way they seemed to welcome. Mathilda felt her stomach curdle as much as Hugh's neglected pottage and crept closer to Emeline.

'How, Hugh?' William demanded.

'They have special carriers, wide and strong with stabling divides to keep the horses calm.'

'And this strait is how big?'

'I believe the sail was several hours and the currents are tough.'

'I see.' He dropped his voice so that the group were forced to lean close to hear. 'So such a boat could, then, cross the Narrow Sea?'

No one spoke. Mathilda gaped at her husband, her brain smoking as much as the hunks of bacon the men were cooking over the fire behind. Boats full of warhorses – it was madness, wasn't it? It couldn't be done.

'You don't like boats, William,' she said huskily.

'There are many things, my dear, that I don't like but sometimes it is necessary to get on with them anyway.'

'But why?'

He looked slowly around his men. They were grinning. Every one of them was grinning.

'You know why, my Mora,' he said calmly. 'I might wish one day to take a trip across the sea.'

'A trip?'

He shrugged.

'An invasion then.'

The word shuddered around his closest advisors. Glancing behind, Mathilda could see others in the hall had stopped what they were doing and were looking their way, sensing their future being shaped in the hands of their silver-eyed duke.

'You think it will come to that?' she whispered.

He detached himself from the men and came round the table to her, catching her waist and pulling her close.

'I hope not, Wife. Truly I hope not for you know that I have never sought war. But I *do* seek the crown I promised you on our wedding night, the crown King Edward promised us in good faith on Christ's own mass in '51, and if war is what it takes then we must be ready. It is good, indeed, that Hugh has come home for it seems we may need him.'

The men, always eager to fight, cheered raucously but Mathilda could not share their enthusiasm and could only hope King Edward would remember the promise he had made in '51 as vividly as did the man to whom he had made it. Then, to her surprise, Fitz put up a hand to quieten them, before dropping it onto William's broad shoulder.

'None of us seeks war, however it may seem.' He gave a brief nod to Mathilda, who coloured. 'But you should know, Lord Duke, that we all of us believe that you are the best choice to be the next King of England. That you are, indeed, the *rightful* choice. I pray justice will be done but if it takes swords to ensure it, you have ours.'

His fellows nodded, solemn now, and chorused: 'You have ours. Always, you have ours.'

William looked almost overcome at this quiet show of loyalty.

'I know it,' he said, looking round them all, his eyes lingering on Hugh. 'And I thank you for it, for it means the world to me.'

His emotion touched Mathilda but the men's tight shared intent also scared her. She tried to recall the thrill the prospect of being a queen had set alight inside her on her wedding night eleven years ago but it was hard. If it took an invasion to seize the English throne, all these men happily singeing their breakfast and fighting in the latrine queue and smoothing their bedtime hair as their favoured women entered the hall would be drawn into it.

Hers would be the crown, but theirs would be the lives on the line to win it. Could she ask that of them? Could William? Should she have stopped his grand plans right back at the start? All she had really wanted was a man to offer her a dance or two, maybe a poem, a few petals in her bed – how had she ended up with one who thought romance was a flotilla of warships?

CHAPTER TWENTY-FIVE

Rouen, March 1064

'Shipwreck!'

'Shipwreck?' Mathilda asked the messenger, astounded. Despite her worst fears after Tostig Godwinson's visit, Normandy had remained quiet, as had France and indeed England. There had thankfully been no need for any shipbuilding but now, it seemed, ships had somehow come to them. She looked the man up and down. William was training in the yard, trying out cavalry drills with Hugh's Italian horses, so the messenger had been shown to the bower. He wasn't one of William's usual riders though, for he was bedraggled and torn and spoke in a thick, awkward accent.

'Where was this shipwreck?' she asked him.

'At Ponthieu, my lady. The count there, Guy, has claimed wrecking rights and taken the men prisoner. I was amongst them but I escaped and am come to you begging aid.'

'Aid for whom?'

The man bowed low.

'For Earl Harold Godwinson, my lady.'

William was delighted.

''Tis a gift!' he cried, boyish in his joy. ''Tis a gift from God,

Mathilda – a second Godwinson and the greater one this time. Prepare a feast, my sweet, the finest ever seen. Let's show this grand Saxon the riches of his future king.'

He went riding off to Ponthieu to rescue his 'noble guest' from the clutches of Count Guy and Mathilda dutifully slaved to ensure all was ready. She sent messengers out across Normandy and nobles came pouring into Rouen, panting with curiosity after several unprecedentedly quiet years. With the rebels, it seemed, finally reconciled to William's rule, the single event of any real note since Tostig's unsettling visit had been yet another ducal child – a daughter whom they'd named Constance, William's choice for the constancy of Mathilda's support, though to Mathilda it seemed more because she was constantly pregnant.

The only other tidings worth the hearing had come from France. Raoul had, so it was said, 'chanced upon' the queen at a small chapel in the Forêt de Montmorency whilst conveniently riding with the Bishop of Mantes and they had seized the God-given opportunity to marry. Mathilda had sent messages of congratulations and tried to ignore Emeline's contented raptures over the 'romance' of the event. It had hardly been news, after all, but now there was finally something of real excitement happening and the court was agog.

Mathilda could only be grateful for the last year of peace and fruitfulness for, despite the long winter, the barns were still part full and the cattle fat. She sent orders out to grocers, bakers, brewers and slaughterhouses. La Barbe and his sons organised great hunts, offering rich prizes for venison and boar, and word went out that the palace was paying well for coney so that a constant stream of local lads arrived with beasts caught in the woods. The kitchens were soon so strung with meat that the chefs could hardly move and Mathilda had to order a store built behind to keep it all. Anticipation mounted and it was a relief when, at last, word came that the duke and his guest were on the way.

'What will he be like, this Harold?' Emeline pondered as she chased her children around trying to get them into smart clothing. 'I hope he is nicer than his brother was.'

'We will find out soon enough,' Mathilda said crisply, and indeed barely had they dressed her than horses clattered into the yard to a great rush of noise from the myriad pavilions pitched in the gaps between the houses around the grand Tour de Rouen.

Mathilda smoothed her gown. It was her original wedding dress, the one she'd brought from Flanders and not, in the end, worn. William's gift was too grand, for she did not want to give this Harold illusions of his own importance, but this gown felt right. Pushing her head up high, she went forth to greet her guest but no fine gown would ever have been enough to protect her from the sight of him.

'Duchess Mathilda, an honour.'

Harold of Wessex swept a low bow before her, dropping a kiss on her hand and glancing up as he did so through thick blonde lashes. Mathilda stood frozen, fighting the giddy sensation of falling through time, for the damned man looked just like Lord Brihtric.

'You are welcome, Earl Harold,' she managed eventually, pulling her hand away before his touch could suck her any further into the past.

She supposed she should have expected some similarity to her early suitor but Earl Torr had been thinner and more brown than blonde. This brother, however, had eyes like a summer pond, a shock of corn-ripe hair and a rich, full beard. The lower reaches of Mathilda's heart pulsed treacherously within her breast and for a moment she fought to breathe.

'I trust you are well after your harsh experience at Ponthieu?' she choked out.

'Very well, thank you,' Harold agreed in a butter-soft voice, his Norman near perfect. 'Your husband has been a most gracious rescuer and I am greatly indebted to him for my freedom.'

'You are,' William agreed cheerily, 'but I trust you will repay that with friendship? You will stay a while.'

It was an instruction and Mathilda winced at the lack of subtlety but Harold just smiled.

'Nothing would please me more, William. I have heard much of Normandy's beauty and it seems it was all correct.' He was looking at Mathilda. She shifted as a strange heat rushed over her, but then he went on: 'I have been lucky enough to rest at several of your abbeys on our journey – such beautiful architecture. We have little like it in England.'

'What about your new abbey at Westminster?'

'Yes, that is very fine – modelled on Jumièges, I believe?'

'Indeed,' William agreed loudly. 'King Edward was very inspired by Norman art in the many years he spent here as a young man.'

Harold smiled again.

'I'm sure he was. Oh, are these your sons, Duchess? What fine young men.'

He bent over to solemnly shake hands with Robert, Richard and Rufus, asking them their names and admiring their swords. Even Rufus, now seven, had his own blade and the boys were soon proudly showing them to their guest as if they had known him for years.

'I have three sons, too,' Harold told them. 'They are a little older than you but I'll wager you'd give them a run for their money in the yard.'

'Are they with you?' Rufus asked eagerly, as if he might give it a go there and then.

William placed a steadying hand on his red head.

'Sadly not, Rufus, but maybe you will meet them one day.'

'Here?'

'Or in England. Shall we dine?'

Mathilda waved hastily for the gong to be sounded.

'Where's Adela?' she hissed to Cecelia as everyone flocked to table.

Cecily, Maud and baby Constance had been confined to the nursery, much to the disgust of Cecily who, at six, thought herself every bit grown-up enough to join the adults. Mathilda was inclined to agree for Cecily was as sharp as a needle-tip and as pretty as a tapestry – certainly far more so than her eldest daughter who, having just turned eleven years old, had been instructed to present herself for dinner.

'She is inside some manuscript, no doubt,' Cecelia replied and hurried off to find her.

Mathilda took her seat at William's right side with Harold on her other. She glanced nervously between them. They seemed to have made friends on the journey from Ponthieu but there were big issues at stake here and she did not want a moonlit standoff with this Godwinson. Why was Harold here? What did he want? As duchess it was down to her to find out, so, despite his discomfiting appearance, she angled herself determinedly towards the Saxon.

'Are your ships ruined, my lord?'

'Not ruined, just damaged. Duke William has kindly offered me the use of his shipyards at Bonneville to have them repaired. My men are patching them up to move along the coast.'

'That will take some time?'

'I fear so. You are stuck with me, my lady.'

'It's our pleasure. We are neighbours, after all. Where were you headed?'

He leaned in a little.

'Here.'

'Oh.'

He offered no more and she somehow dared not ask. He had an open, generous face, this Saxon, but his big beard made his ready smile hard to read.

'I do not think,' she said in the end, 'that you came just to admire our architecture?'

'No. In truth, the finer points of design are lost on me. I am a crass man, Duchess Mathilda, a mere soldier.'

Mathilda looked the big man up and down, taking in his rich tunic, patterned with hunting hounds around the hem, his intricately worked gold cloak clasps and the artistic bands around his muscled forearms – this was no 'mere soldier'.

'You do yourself a disservice, my lord.'

'Call me Harold, please. And you may be right. A Saxon does not like to sing his own praises.'

'Surely that is foolish, for who else will do so?'

'Poets.'

'Who praise only for coin.'

'Or for their own praise.'

'Too true. You like poetry?'

'If it is well written and the subject interests me.'

'And what subjects interest you, Earl Harold?'

'Hawking, horses, fair women . . .'

'Legends?'

'I prefer to make my own tales. But you, my lady, what interests *you*?'

Mathilda stared at him, her mind suddenly blank. She could hear the chatter of the court as the first dishes were served, see the steam rise from the capons and smell their rich, earthy juices. She could hear the glug of wine into goblets and see the tapestries, newly beaten into brightness, above the faces of the great and the good of Normandy, but she could not *think*.

'What interests me?' she repeated stupidly.

'Yes. Is it so strange a question?'

'Of course not. Many things interest me. Normandy interests me.'

'Normandy?'

'The fate of Normandy. I am her duchess, after all.'

'You are and a fine one, I am sure, but I am talking of *you* –
what interests you?'

Mathilda flinched.

'What interests *your* wife, Earl Harold?'

'Svana?' His voice softened instantly. 'Svana likes nature.
She loves all creatures, though the smaller ones most of all.
There is forever an injured mouse or hedgehog in her kitchens
at Nazeing. She likes walking and riding – usually too far for
her own safety, I am always telling her off for it – and she likes
flowers, especially the sweet-scented ones. She likes the children . . .'

'I like my children,' Mathilda interrupted, seizing on this.

'Of course. And is this your daughter now?'

Mathilda looked over as Cecelia brought a pouting Adela to
the table.

'This is Adela, my eldest girl, yes. Adela, come greet our
guest.'

Adela looked at Harold.

'Does that scratch?' she demanded.

Harold looked taken aback.

'Does what scratch?'

'That hair on your face. It looks scratchy.'

'Adela!' Mathilda admonished, horrified, but Harold
laughed.

'It is quite soft, I assure you. Would you like to feel?'

'No!' Adela squealed, though her fingers twitched. 'I don't

like men,' she added rudely and then whirled away to fling herself, glowering, into her seat.

'My lord, I do apologise,' Mathilda said, mortified.

'No matter. I have daughters too, my lady. They are mercurial creatures at times.'

'As are women.'

He put up his hands with a charming smile.

'You said that, not I. But come, what interests you?'

Damn – he had not given up on that.

'Music,' she blurted, catching sight of the minstrels tuning up in the far corner.

'You play?'

'I dance.'

It was out before she could stop it. Why had she said that? Fool.

'Dance? Excellent. I love to dance. Perhaps you will partner me later?'

Memories skidded across her skin like flames. She had danced with Brihtric. Danced too often and too close.

'I . . . I'm not sure. I do not dance much these days. Now look, your capon grows cold.'

She took her eating knife from Cecelia and set on her own little bird with determined focus. Who was this Saxon to ask her, Duchess of Normandy, to dance? It was hardly fitting, hardly right. Let him kick his feet up with others; she would keep to her chair – however much her treacherous feet itched.

'What do you think of him?' William demanded later, much later, when finally they had retired.

Mathilda had hoped he would wish to withdraw early, for the minstrels had been in fine tune and every note had seemed to tug her out of her chair until she was worn down with the effort of keeping to it. William, however, had lingered, eschewing the tafel board for once and even taking a rare glass of wine after dinner, though whether from genuine enjoyment or a desire to keep a close eye on his guest, she was not sure. If the latter, Harold had not seemed aware of it, dancing with all who chose to, and many did. He'd even led Cecelia out though Adela, clamped even more fiercely into her chair than Mathilda, had refused his advances.

'He is very lively,' Mathilda managed as William untied her laces.

Ever since their first night together he had preferred to do this task himself when he could, dismissing her ladies before they even retired.

'He is. He quite liked you, I think.'

'He is all politeness.'

'Yes. You must encourage him, Mathilda.'

'What?'

'Gain his confidence. You are better at this conversation business than I and if he is relaxed he might say something of use.'

'Oh. I see. Yes.'

'That will not be too arduous for you?'

For a moment she thought he was teasing but then she remembered this was William – he said only what he meant.

'I will manage, William.'

'He is entertaining enough, is he not, and a handsome man, surely?'

Mathilda, halfway through removing her shift, yanked it off and dived, confused, for the bed.

'He is very . . . Saxon.'

She closed her eyes against the treacherous image of Lord Brihtric so many years ago – the same cheery blondness, the same lively eyes, the same teasing manner. No one teased her these days, save maybe Fitz. She had forgotten how to deal with it but she would learn. If William wished her to be his conversational spy she would do so.

'You like him?'

Still the questions. Mathilda's head ached and she longed for him to stop.

'He seems nice enough.'

'You would like to be close to him?'

'William, what are you saying?'

He slid into bed beside her.

'He might, do you not think, my Mora, make a fine son-in-law?'

Mathilda gasped.

'He is married, William, to a lady called Svana. He talked of her with great warmth.'

She remembered the way Harold's blue eyes had lit up as he talked of his wife nursing woodland creatures in their kitchens and felt a prickle of some rough, dangerous emotion. Not jealousy, nothing so foolish, but an awareness, perhaps, of some other way of being.

'Lady Svana is his handfast wife only – his mistress. He is still free to wed.'

'I do not think he would wish to.'

'Nonetheless . . . Adela is eleven. Have her courses started?'

'William!'

'It is just information, Mathilda. Have they?'

Mathilda shifted awkwardly.

'I know not.' He stared at her. 'She's very secretive, William, and always at her books. She is not like the others – she avoids me.'

'Well, seek her out then. Ask. Such an alliance would bind Harold to us nicely.'

'But William, Adela hates men. She told Harold so to his face. She will not do it.'

William's face darkened.

'She will, Wife, if I tell her so.'

'Harold does not seem a man to take an unwilling bride.'

'Harold is a politician, my dear. Do not let his geniality fool you; he is as sharp as a spear.'

'Do you like him, William?'

'I believe I do. He is a little brash for my taste but despite that I warm to him. He is a man of honour, I think, and that is all to the good. I might take him fighting. But not yet, Wife. You may work your charms on him first and maybe we can coax him to the altar.'

So Mathilda set herself to try, though her time with the Englishman always left her feeling strangely fragile. Harold was so charming and so good at turning the conversation away, moving it forever onto her concerns and interests – newly rediscovered interests. She found herself discussing astronomy with him, a subject she had not touched on since the schoolroom, though she had loved it then. She discussed the benefits of educating women and exchanged thoughts on music.

She even, just once, found herself talking of Westminster but she stopped the conversation instantly, scuttling to bed before she could be drawn further. William had entrusted her with extracting information from Harold but too often it seemed to be the other way round. And always the Saxon resisted any talk of marriage, though Mathilda had not found a way to admit as much to William before he broached the subject with his daughter. Not that, in the end, it mattered.

'I will not marry him!' Adela shouted when the match was put to her, stamping her foot and glowering at her father who glowered back.

'You will do as you are told, Adela.'

'Not in this.'

William gaped and looked crossly to the door of the ante-chamber beyond which his court could be heard buzzing excitedly around the Saxon guests. He was not used to such defiance from anyone, least of all his slip of a daughter.

'It is your duty,' he said. 'And it is for the good of Normandy.'

Adela looked him straight in the eye.

'I care little for Normandy. Why should a political entity control my personal happiness?'

William went puce with rage and spluttered so hard Mathilda feared he might choke. She stepped forward, uncomfortably aware of her own confrontation with her father over William back in '49. She had been determined, yes, but Adela was something else. She was as stubborn as a devil and her wits were so damned sharp they cut in an instant.

'You are a princess, Adela,' she told her. 'Your happiness is not a priority.'

'You do not want me to be happy?'

'Of course I do, we do. But we want you to be happy in a suitable role.'

'Wife to a Saxon earl more than twenty years my senior – that is suitable, is it?'

'Eminently,' William roared, finding his voice at last.

'And Harold wishes this match?'

Mathilda shifted, avoided William's eye.

'Harold sees the wisdom in it, yes – as should you.'

'For what, Mother? What am I to do in this marriage? Be your vanguard? Forge ahead into England to prepare the way for you?'

William moved as fast as an arrow from his own longbow. He seized Adela's chin, lifting her almost off the ground.

'That is *exactly* what you should do, yes, and the fact that you realise it proves you are perfect for the role. Do you not wish to further your family?'

Tears sprang to Adela's eyes.

'I wish to give myself to God,' she choked out.

'God?' William let go of her so suddenly that she flopped to the ground, her dress like a pool around her. He stared down. 'You wish to be a nun?'

Adela nodded miserably.

'I suppose we could give her to God as a sacrifice?' Mathilda said hesitantly.

William snorted.

'It would be little sacrifice, Wife.' He leaned over Adela. 'Very well,' he snarled. 'You will not marry Harold.'

'Truly?'

'No. I will find you someone else, someone less important and a lot further away where you cannot embarrass us with your churlishness.'

'No. Oh please, Father, I . . .'

'Get out of my sight, Adela. Now!'

She ran for the door and yanked it open. For a moment the hubbub of the court rushed in on them, then she slammed it shut and they were alone again. Mathilda longed to pity her daughter but felt only relief that she had gone.

'Will you really, William?' she whispered.

'Of course. Why would I say it if I did not mean it? There is an ambassador from Spain out there looking for wives for the noble men defeating the Moors in the south. The "reconquista", they are calling it – a holy war, a crusade to God's glory. Maybe that will appeal to our choosy daughter? And I trust, Madam, that the others will grow up more pliable?'

'They will. I will see to it. And Harold?'

'I will take Harold to Brittany. Lord Riwallon is threatened by Duke Conan in his stronghold at Dol and needs my aid. Harold can serve as my right-hand man. It will be useful for him – for us both.'

'Will he go with you?'

William smiled.

'His ships, sadly, are not yet ready. The weather has been too poor for fast work.'

Mathilda glanced towards the small window where a bright spring sky was punctuated by only the lightest of clouds.

'I see.'

'Fret not, Mathilda. We will not be long and when we return we will get to the meat of Harold's visit, I promise you. He is a good man and a valued friend.'

'You think he is a friend?'

'I pray so, Mathilda, for with him behind us we cannot fail in England. We will go to fight and soon. Nothing binds a man like standing side by side on a battlefield and after this he will see I am a worthy ruler.'

Mathilda looked at William, duke of a thriving Normandy, and saw a seven-year-old boy twitching to prove himself to the world. Her heart quaked for him.

'He will, William,' she said, taking his hand in hers. 'I am sure that he will.'

CHAPTER TWENTY-SIX

Rouen, May 1064

*T*he men rode into Rouen to even louder trumpets than those they had ridden out to, crying victory on the bright air. Conan had been sent scuttling back up his precious peninsula and Dol was free and loyal to Normandy. Bishop Odo, always ready to carry God's word into battle, had excelled and been left in full control of the borderlands and several Breton treasures would now be adorning the already bulging altar at Bayeux. The men were in high spirits, including the Saxons.

William and Harold leaped from their horses as one and landed before Mathilda laughing and outdoing each other in the depth of their bows. Mathilda played along before William suddenly seized her around the waist and, lifting her almost off her feet, kissed her hard. Harold stepped back and she struggled free.

'Welcome, lords, you are victorious?'

'Of course,' William said. 'Am I not always?'

'You are.' She looked to Harold. 'He is.'

Her senses were quivering. She'd had word from Bonneville that the Saxon ships were finally repaired and now the men were back it was time, it seemed, to test the mettle of this osten-tatious new friendship. William seemed very certain of it.

'Harold excelled,' he told her, leading them both into the great hall as servers ran to prepare food and those ladies who had lingered in Rouen hastened to greet their men. 'He res-cued two of my soldiers from the quicksands at Mont-St-Michel, when everyone else had given them up for lost. He is a worthy general.'

'As are you, William,' Harold countered. 'Your husband is a horseman like no other, my lady.'

'He is a Norman,' Mathilda said. 'They are bred on horse-back.'

'So it seems. We Saxons rarely fight with cavalry. It has been most interesting.'

'Took to it like a pig to mud,' William said proudly. 'And he's even a half-decent tafel player. Pushed me right to the edge one time and not many do that. A fine right-hand man.'

Harold looked away and Mathilda moved hastily forward.

'Your ships are ready, Harold.'

'They are?'

Both men squared their shoulders.

'Then it seems our time together is almost done,' William said, 'for now.'

'It does.' Harold looked around the hall. 'A shame but come, let us not overshadow our victory with partings. We must cele-brate. William, let me toast you!'

And he did, repeatedly, though Mathilda saw her husband tip half his wine into the rushes and did not know whether to be proud or ashamed of his caution. Harold seemed to throw all his back but lost none of his reason. Were all Saxons like this, she found herself wondering, so assured, so calm in their authority? Were their roots, like England's own, so firm in the soil that they were able to grow straight and unwavering? And if so, how would William, so unsure of his own worth, stand over them?

He was a warrior, her brave husband, not a politician. He had no guile and though that was a great strength in him, it could also, in a more subtle land, be a great weakness. He would need Harold and others like him if he were to succeed as King of England and she could only hope the great earl saw it that way too.

'So, you must leave us,' she said softly to him as the sweetmeats were passed around.

'It seems so.'

'And yet you have not told us your original business here.'

'Must there be business, Mathilda?' She raised an eyebrow. 'A visit of friendship, no more. King Edward wished me to assure you of his goodwill.'

'He did?' William was upon them, leaning across Mathilda to eyeball Harold.

'He did. And to ask me to promise you as a token of such, Lord Duke, lands in Dover.'

'Lands? In Dover? In England?'

'As a token of goodwill in recognition of your family connections and your strong reputation as a leader and your kindness to him as a youth.'

William beamed at the familiar words but Mathilda was not satisfied.

'You mean as a token of his promise?'

'Promise?' Harold said lightly, giving William a slow wink.

'Yes,' Mathilda tried to insist but William was shushing her, calling for order. 'William,' she hissed, 'you cannot leave it like that, not this time.'

'Don't go too fast, Mathilda. Patience.'

'Patience?! He has been here several months.'

'King Edward said he could not declare an heir until death

was close, remember? These Saxons are curiously subtle beasts. They are like horses, Mathilda – better coaxed than coerced.' He turned to the ragtag crowd. 'A toast!' he roared. 'To friendship, to alliance, to the future!'

The men and women of Rouen took this up gladly, then William was, to Mathilda's great surprise, calling for minstrels.

'Will you dance, Harold?' he asked and for a moment Mathilda thought the two of them, dark and fair, would step out together, but instead William lifted her own hand and placed it in Harold's.

'Will you, my lady?' the blonde Saxon asked.

His fingers tightened slightly and, the past swirling dizzily around her, she rose.

'I will.'

They took to the floor, all eyes upon them, and immediately Mathilda could feel the pulse of the dance – the insistent thud of heart against heart, the light turn of the reel lifting her high onto her richly slippered toes, the sweeping assurance of strong arms.

'Normandy has been good to me, my lady,' Harold said, his words whispering across her cheek like butterflies, trailing blushes.

'She has,' she agreed, clinging desperately to the present, 'so I hope you will be good to her in return?'

He smiled at that and his fingers tightened just a touch around her own. He lifted her closer to his broad chest and then, with a low laugh that laced dangerously through the feast-smoked air, spun her until her royal blood pulsed against her skin as if trying to escape and Normandy was, for a moment, forgotten.

The rush of the reel was a potion stronger than any wine and she felt suddenly as if she could dance forever, dance out of Normandy and out of England and out of all the crazy mangle of promises and duties. The music thrilled through them – the merry melody of the fiddle, the trill of a tiny flute and the pulse of the drum beneath. She could smell the low scents of war upon him, horse and metal and warm musk, now mixing with the meaty smoke of the fire. And she could see his eyes, Saxon blue, like summertime skies as they bore into her own, all laughter gone and in its place a rich, deep intent.

'I fear, my lady, that I cannot repay you well enough for your kindness this spring but I suspect that it always came with too high a price.'

Other dancers had joined them now, laughing, circling, creating a safe swirl of bodies. But then he moved her to the edge, beneath the shadow of a pillar, and she felt sixteen once more, small and giddy and breathless. He leaned over and asked suddenly: 'Why, my lady? Why England?'

She did not want the question; it felt wrong. She looked up at him.

'Your eyes – they are encircled with gold.'

'Bronze more like. Why England, Mathilda?'

'It was promised,' she stuttered.

'Are you sure?'

She frowned. With every year that passed that mysterious, shifting Yule in Westminster seemed less and less real and now, here, in this intimate dance, nothing was certain.

'I am sure,' she forced out, knowing she did not sound it. 'You know what William wants of you?'

'My oath to him as King of England.'

'Will you give it?'

'Should I?'

'Why would you not? Would you be king yourself?'

'Should I?'

His voice was so calm, so warm, so strong.

'You would be a good king, Harold.'

There was a rustle behind them, a low rumble, almost a growl. She turned, scared, and in that moment Harold stepped away.

'But not as good as William,' she panted but Harold was gone, melted into the crowd leaving a single blonde hair on her shoulder. She snatched it away and suddenly he was back, looming over her, only when she looked up it was not Harold but Fitz. And his eyes, his dancing, ever-friendly eyes, were black with fury.

'Where is your loyalty, Mathilda?'

Her words to Harold screeched through her guts like a butcher's knife. Her head spun and she scrabbled at the wall to drag herself out of the mist Harold's Saxon arms had weaved around her.

'You misheard, Fitz.'

'I heard very clearly. After all William has done for you, Duchess? After all he has given you, all he has trusted you with – you would do this? Has he turned your head, the golden Saxon? Or have you been working for him all the time?'

'No! I told him – I told him William would be better.'

'Too late,' Fitz snarled, the dear hound showing his teeth at last and all the more fearful for the change.

'Perhaps,' Mathilda cried, putting up her hands to ward him off, 'but I meant it no less. William is my husband, Fitz.'

'But not the first man you loved.'

'What? No . . .'

Fitz advanced on her.

'Brihtric, wasn't it? A pretty Saxon, my lady, yes, like this pretty Saxon? Is that why Adela is not to marry Harold, Mathilda? Do you want him, perhaps, for yourself?'

'No!' Mathilda grabbed at William's steward's tunic, clawing at him. 'Does William know?'

'That you support Harold as King of England?'

286

'No! I do not. I mean Brihtric. Does he know of Brihtric?'
Fitz just laughed.

'Of course he knows. Your father's precious chamberlain, Lord Bruno, told him years ago.' Mathilda sucked in an angry breath but she was hardly in a position to judge. 'William knows everything, save perhaps that his wife is a traitor.'

Mathilda felt faint. She longed to run to her chamber and hide beneath her covers but they were William's covers too. She was not a child any more but a woman – a mother, a wife. She must stand strong.

'Fitz, please, you know me.'

He looked briefly lost.

'I thought I did but now I am not so sure. To speak so to the Saxon . . .'

'Was foolish perhaps, but no more.'

'It *was* more, Mathilda, much more – it was disloyal.'

That word again, that dread word. William's speech at Alençon ricocheted through her memory and she flexed her wrists as if the axe were already upon them.

'I swear, Fitz, it was not that way. I sought only to gain information. Do not tell William of this. It is nothing, a woman's error. I am behind my husband in everything, you know I am.'

'With all your heart?'

'Yes,' Mathilda cried but she heard the wobble in her voice and knew Fitz must have heard it too.

He looked to the rafters.

'I will not tell him,' he said eventually.

'Thank you. Oh, thank you, Fitz.'

'I do not do this for you, Mathilda, but for him for it would break his heart. But know that I am watching. Now go – he waits for you.'

She needed no second urging but turned and ran to her

husband, ducking frantically between the dancers, disgusted suddenly by their carefree turns and twirls.

'Let us retire,' she begged William. 'Let us slip away, as we always do. We must be fresh for the morrow. We must pin Harold down. We must make him swear – swear out loud, before witnesses. We have lived too long on secret promises, William. Harold *must* declare for you.'

'Steady, my Mora.' William kissed her. 'Why such passion all of a sudden?'

'Because time is slipping away, William. Harold is slipping away and with it England – do not let him fail you.'

As you have failed him, a voice rasped in her ear and she welcomed it.

'God forgive me,' she whispered but God, it seemed, was not in a forgiving mood.

CHAPTER TWENTY-SEVEN

Bonneville, May 1064

They prepared to make Harold swear. They dispatched him to Bonneville to inspect his ships under an 'escort' led by Hugh, then sent for every holy relic in Normandy – the bones of St Rémy, St Philibert, St Barbara, St Eternus and St Maximus. Mathilda amassed them, carefully folded in finest silk, inside a carved casket and they set out to bid Harold farewell.

She and William approached Bonneville from the west, reaching the port before the castle. Several long jetties stretched out into the shallow sea and many boats bobbed along their edges as men ran back and forth from the long wooden sheds lining the shore, carrying goods to and from trade vessels or tools to do repairs. Mathilda looked for Harold's ships but it was high-masted Spanish ones that she saw first.

'Adela!' she breathed.

William, true to his word, had arranged for their troublesome older daughter to be married to Alfonso, son of the King of Leon and Castile, a fiercely ambitious youth who had earned himself the byname El Bravo for his fighting against the Moors. It had been Mathilda's hard duty to see her furious daughter kitted out with bridal finery and dispatched under poor Roger de Beaumont's care to the ships the young prince had sent for her – the very ships in front of them now.

'Why is she still here?' William snapped.

'She definitely sailed,' Fitz said from behind them. 'La Barbe saw her himself. He told me that just before she went on board she kicked him so hard in his bad leg that it's not stopped aching ever since. He was glad to see her sail away.'

'Then it seems,' William said grimly, 'that she has sailed back.'

He kicked his horse into a canter and Mathilda exchanged glances with Fitz before, just a step behind, they both did the same. They had made a tentative truce since the terrible night of her dance with Harold.

'Adelisa says I was wrong,' Fitz had told her the next day, seeking her out in private. 'At least, she says I was hasty. I can, you know, be a little hasty. I may possibly have read too much into your conversation with the Saxon.'

'You did, Fitz, truly. I was just trying to draw him out.'

'That's what Adelisa said. It seems a funny way to go about it to me, though.'

He was right. Mathilda had been doing nothing so sane for she had been lost in her past but admitting as much would help no one.

'To me too now, Fitz. It was a strange night.'

'These are strange times. Do you want to be Queen of England, Mathilda?'

'That's a strange question too.'

'Just an honest one.'

Had it been a test? She hadn't been sure but she was taking no chances now and, as ever, she needed exact truth less than these black and white Normans she called her own people.

'If William wants to be king, I want to be his queen,' she had told the faithful steward stoutly.

'He'll be a good king,' he'd replied, 'for it means so very much to him.'

That she had agreed with wholeheartedly, though occasionally she wished they had thought to direct their royal ambitions south to France. Had William only pursued Henri when he'd had the cheek to invade, he could have claimed that crown, but William's loyalty to his overlord, despite his betrayal, had prevented it and she should respect him for that. Even so, France would have been so much simpler a country than England, wrapped in its own precious customs and antiquities. But they must go forward, not back, and if forward was over the Narrow Sea, so be it. Fitz, William's guard-dog, was watching her still, she knew – though not as sharply as she was watching herself. She was determined to secure Harold's oath for her husband, but first, Adela.

She reached the ships just as William was striding up the first jetty and leaping aboard.

'William,' she cried, 'should we not first check . . .'

But her warning was cut off by a shriek as loud as a mating owl's, and suddenly a loose-robed figure flew at William, hair streaming and nails out. William, warrior-swift to react, planted his feet wide and caught his daughter's wrists so that she flailed uselessly before him. He looked back to Fitz and Mathilda.

'Stay there. Do not come aboard. She is hot as the sun.'

'Hot as hell,' Adela screamed at him, kicking out with bare feet. 'This is God's punishment on you for sending me away.'

'On *me*?' William asked mildly. She screamed again. 'Perhaps, Adela, it is God's punishment on you for being disobedient to your father and to Normandy.'

'A curse on Normandy!'

'Adela!' William looked back to Mathilda. 'Was there ever such ingratitude?'

Several servants had come running, scrambling aboard, babbling in a mix of French and Spanish. There had been a fever on board, Mathilda gathered, straining to understand. Spanish had not been one of the languages her mother's tutors had taught her but it was like enough to southern French to seize some meaning. Several sailors were ill, no, they were *muertos* – dead. They'd been killed by a terrible pain in their stomachs she gathered, more from the elaborate gestures than the words, and been thrown overboard.

The sailors had brought the princess back, terrified of losing her, but as Mathilda looked from them to her daughter, now babbling more than the men, she feared they were too late. She should run to Adela, she knew. If it were Cecily, she would run to her, or Maud or Constance, but any of them would welcome her. Adela, however, was spitting poison and raging as if the devil did, indeed, have her in his clutches. And then, before Mathilda could make herself move, the girl gave a sudden piercing cry, shook like a sapling in a winter storm and went limp.

Mathilda ran to the boat but William shouted her back.

'Is she . . . ?'

His eyes when they found hers said it all – Adela, poor awkward, struggling, bitter little Adela, was dead and suddenly, painfully, Mathilda knew she'd been waiting for this moment all her daughter's troubled young life. Always she had feared that Mabel had poisoned her in the womb, forcing her out too early. Possibly the poor child had been carrying that poison ever since. She forced herself to breathe as William laid Adela gently on the deck. He took off his rich scarlet cloak and wrapped it softly around her, smoothing her matted hair from her face before, finally, covering it over.

'Order a coffin,' he said to Fitz, 'a fine one. We will see her buried in honour.' He turned to the cowering sailors. 'I thank you for your care; you will be rewarded.'

Mathilda saw them glance, stunned but delighted, at one another and felt a rush of new warmth for William. He rewarded loyalty as generously as he punished treachery. She shivered at the thought of how close she'd come to such a charge and crossed herself. She looked at her daughter's motionless form beneath William's cloak, still so slight as if she had never quite found the strength for this world. Mathilda could scarce blame her for that; some days she could hardly find the strength herself. This day, though, this bitter day, she must, for it was far from over yet.

Harold had heard of Adela's death by the time they rode through the decorated gates of Mathilda's favourite fortress. Clearly he had spies too, or maybe the garrison was just reverberating with the delicious gossip of it. Mathilda and William accepted his condolences gravely but declined his oh-so-generous offer to forgo the farewell feast.

'We must swear on our friendship,' Mathilda insisted, fired with a flaming determination that her daughter's hideous passing had only fuelled more strongly.

'Our friendship? Of course, my lady.'

He looked at her askance and shifted his big feet nervously.

'And our intent,' she pressed.

'Intent?'

'Fret not,' William said, stepping in. 'I have had the words written; you need only say them. You can read?'

'Of course.'

'Good. I cannot. I have never seen much need for it. I am more eloquent with a sword than with words – as are my men.' The said men moved forward a little. Harold glanced around him. 'Shall we get on with it? Here, maybe?'

He gestured to a little table set up on the dais at the top end of the stone hall. It was covered in a soft linen cloth of sumptuous purple and beneath it, Mathilda knew, sat the casket of relics.

'Shouldn't we tell him?' William had asked when she'd suggested this.

'Afterwards.'

'Very well.'

Harold, Mathilda noticed, had lost his customary ease. His laughing eyes were shadowed and no smile cut across his beard. He was no longer the teasing dancer and she was glad to see it for she had been teased enough. She watched coldly as he looked to his men but they were flanked by William's and he was trapped – a tafel defender surrounded by attacking pieces and forced to surrender.

Mathilda would have felt cruel but it was not their fault if he ducked and twisted and dissembled. Harold had tried to play her, tried, even, to seduce her in some subtle Saxon way, as Brihtric had seduced her too many years ago to remember. He deserved all he got. Besides, William was right – a man should say what he meant and now, at last, Harold of Wessex would have to mean what he said. She watched intently as William took Harold's great hand and placed it on the cloth.

'Read it, Harold,' he instructed as a man unfurled the parchment and held it up before the earl. Still Harold hesitated. 'Read it! It says nothing more nor less than you have been promising these last months of "friendship", and nothing more nor less than King Edward vowed to in 1051. It does not ask you to deny your king but simply to acknowledge his successor. In return, I acknowledge you as Earl of Wessex and my senior councillor. It is, Harold, to the benefit of us both. Now, read it!'

And read it Earl Harold did:

I, Harold, Earl of Wessex, do acknowledge thee, William, Duke of Normandy, as the rightful heir to the throne of England on the death of King Edward, whenever that might be. I swear to uphold that claim and to support you with my voice, my person and all the forces at my disposal should they be necessary. God grant us King William.

He did not falter, though his hand shook. He spoke bravely, regally almost, and finally it was done, done fully, before witnesses and on holy relics. Harold paled when the casket was unveiled.

'You tricked me,' he hissed at William.

'Only as you have tricked me, Harold. But come, this is the start of our friendship, not the end. And who else, really, could be king?'

'Ask your wife,' Harold said and strode away, clattering from the hall with his men at his back and making straight for his ships.

William looked at Mathilda, puzzled. For a dread moment she saw Harold dancing her around the hall, saw her own lips telling him he would make a good king, saw Fitz's blood-red rage as he stepped between them. She lifted a hand to her husband and he reached out to take it, but then, without warning, his face twisted and he clutched at his gut and, with a strange groaning noise, fell at her feet, dark eyes rolling back in his head and his breath twisting from him as if it meant to leave forever.

CHAPTER TWENTY-EIGHT

*A*ll was panic and confusion. For a moment everyone stood stock still, as if waiting for their duke to leap up and tease them for falling for his jest, but this was William – he did not jest. Fitz recovered first. He ran to his lord and friend, dropping down before him and feeling in his neck for the pulse of his lifeblood.

'He lives,' he shouted. 'Fetch a pallet and fast. We must get him to his chamber.'

Roger de Beaumont leaped forward, summoning a pallet bed from the back of the hall with an imperious wave of the walking stick he now used. Mathilda stood helplessly to one side as Fitz and Fulk eased William onto the pallet as carefully as if he were made of precious glass and lifted him themselves. Hugh and Odo rushed to help and they bore him from the hall on their shoulders as if he were dead already.

'William . . .' His name escaped her lips as she went after them, a whisper at first and then louder: 'William!'

He could not die, must not die, not now they were so close to their goal. They'd endured all these battles and rebellions and she had never once had to face the possibility that he might die, so why now? She pictured Adela shuddering out of life this very afternoon and tears raked at the back of her throat. She had not grieved, not enough. She was Adela's mother. She should have been struck down by her loss, but instead she had let her go and turned to the business of Harold's oath. Perhaps God was punishing her by taking William too; or perhaps he was testing if she was as callous about her husband as her daughter.

Mathilda felt the lurching, painful sensation that this was a fair test. That foolish dance with Harold had proved it. Tears ran down her cheeks as William's loyal men laid him, at last, on his bed, easing the pallet from beneath him so he could sink into the softness of the mattress Mathilda had ordered brought from Paris when she had refurbished this apartment two years ago – a treat to herself after all the work in Caen. She looked around the soft blues and greens she had so carefully chosen to match the colours of the shifting sea beyond and wondered if she had made it beautiful simply to lose him within its elegant walls. Adela had been born in this room, she remembered – born too early, only to be lost too early too. And now William.

He did not move, not a sigh of relief, nor a wince of pain, nor any sign at all that he still breathed save the faint rise and fall of his broad chest. Mathilda pushed past the men and scrambled up beside him, clasping his hand in hers.

'He's hot! He's so hot; we must cool him.'

She fumbled at his tunic clasps.

'Are you sure, my lady? Is that not dangerous?'

'Less dangerous than letting his blood boil inside him.'

'She's right,' Fulk said unexpectedly. 'At least, that's what Mabel always does. Shall I fetch Mabel, Mathilda?'

'And her poisons? No, thank you. I will care for William. Cloths please, and water, cool water, and, and . . .' She had no more knowledge. 'And prayers! Send messages to all the abbeys and all the churches. Normandy's duke has given himself for her all his life and now she must give a little back. All must pray.'

'Yes, my lady.'

Fulk bowed out, Hugh and Roger following, but Fitz lingered at William's feet, head low. Mathilda took up the cloth the servers had brought and bathed William's burning temples and strong wrists. She ran it over his muscled chest, dipping it tenderly into the scars and grooves of his life as a warrior. So many battles and this, the worst of them all. She looked back to Fitz.

'Did you tell him?'

'What?'

'What I said about, about . . .'

Words failed her and she fumbled again for William's hand, clutching it and willing his fingers to at least twitch against her own.

'No, Mathilda. I said I would not.'

'So you *did* not. Of course. You are very like him, Fitz.'

'I am nothing like. He is ten times the man I am.'

'That's not true. He is a duke, yes, but . . .'

'It's more than that. William isn't just a duke by title or even by his actions, but all the way through to his core. He is a tough man but an honourable one. He sees so very, very clearly how the world should be and his vision is right. He wants only justice and fairness and people rewarded according to their actions.'

'Bad as well as good?'

'Of course, but he is not harsh, my lady. So many lords have been pardoned these last years, so many rebels returned from exile or released from prison. He does not want opposition – he wants loyalty, craves it almost, and why not? If all stand behind their leader none can break them and William is a leader all should stand behind.'

'All,' Mathilda repeated faintly – all including his own wife. She remembered how she had refused to marry him at first, refused as Adela had refused Harold. She had been as guilty as the rest of thinking his bastardy lessened him, when all the time her own haughty blood had been the weaker. 'Nobility is not in blood but in bearing,' he had told her at Herleva's death and he had always borne himself as a noble indeed.

'He cannot die, Fitz,' she cried, 'he cannot.'

'But what can we do?'

'I know not. Just be here, talk to him, show him we care.'

So they did. They pulled two high-backed, softly cushioned chairs away from the window and up to the bed and they talked to the prostrate figure upon it. Fitz spoke of victories they had shared, of camps on strange hillsides and in deep woods and around many a town and city and Mathilda had a glimpse into the rough road of a soldier. He spoke of their childhood, before their fathers had died, when all had been apple-scrumping and wall-climbing and river-jumping, and Mathilda wished William had told her more of this himself – and that she had asked.

She spoke to him of Caen, of how grand they would make it once he recovered. She talked of their wedding, of their children and later, when Fitz dozed, of their bed. There, as in all aspects of their life, he had ever worked for her joy and she, like a fool, had thought the heat between them to be more about skill than passion. She had even wondered if others, like Emeline, found lovemaking somehow headier, less workman-like – more like dancing. Always she had been obsessed with dancing.

'Please, William,' she begged, twisting the soft green bed-hangings around and around in her hot fingers, 'please don't die. I don't care about the dancing. I gave up on such stupid-ities when I married you and it has only been my weakness if

I have at times forgotten that. We are rulers together, remember – *together*.'

He did not move. He did not even twitch until much, much later as darkness enfolded them and his face flickered in the candlelight and the plainsong of the monks singing for his life filled the still air. And then, suddenly, he was speaking – nay, rambling. He thrashed out in his bed, knocking Mathilda so she had to scramble away. He shouted and babbled and clawed at his stomach as if trying to rip it out. Mathilda and Fitz tried to hold him down but he was too strong.

'He'll break himself!' Fitz gasped.

'The bed is soft,' Mathilda said, 'let him fight.'

So they stood back but William was weakening already, his hands flapping uselessly now and his head crashing from one side to the other on his pillows, sweat pouring from his forehead.

'He's fading.'

'No!'

Mathilda leaped forward again, dodging William's still-jerking arms to wipe at his face with the cloths but he was moving so much that it splashed and splattered ridiculously.

'William, please rest. You must rest.'

'He never rests,' Fitz said. 'Except maybe with you. It was the same with his mother, God bless her soul.'

'He is not going to her,' Mathilda said fiercely.

Herleva had asked her to look after William; perhaps she had not done it well enough.

'I will,' she said to the ceiling. 'I will care. I *do* care.'

'William knows that.'

'Not enough. He doesn't know enough.'

'He does, Mathilda, for he loves you.'

The word punched all the air out of her. She stared at Fitz over William's prone form and as she fought to regain her breath she saw the simple truth of it. William loved her, loved her because he had been open to doing so, as she had not. He had called her his 'Mora' from their very first night together. He had told her that he wished to gain a throne to prove his love for her. He had told her that clearly but she had not listened. She had chosen to believe that he was too hard a man to truly love, when the truth was that *she* had been the hard one. Hard and foolish too, confusing poetry-and-petals wooing with true feeling.

She thought guiltily back over the last years in which she'd mooned around comparing her own marriage to Hugh whisking Emeline off to Italy, or to Fulk and Mabel with their sparky complicity, or even Raoul marrying his royal love in a deserted chapel. She'd thought them all so romantic but such things were not romance. Emeline said Italy had been hell at first, whilst William had always kept her in comfort and security. Fulk had only won Mabel over by exerting a control bordering on cruelty where William had ever been gentle with her. And what was so wonderful about a deserted chapel? William had defied the entire Roman church to wed her and then fought unceasingly for the sanction of what he had always told her was a true marriage. True because he loved her; he had always loved her.

'I thought him hard, Fitz,' she whispered.

'He is but there are two sides, surely, to everyone?'

Mathilda looked again to the bed where William now lay unmoving, though his hands gripped madly at the air and his lips moved as if fighting to speak. She leaned closer but he took a sudden shuddering breath and was still again. Fitz scrambled for his life-pulse as she watched, horrified.

'He's not dead but it's weak, Mathilda. We need help.'

He was right. She could not lose him, not now – there was too much to say. Mathilda drew in a deep breath of her own.

There are two sides to everyone, Fitz had said and pray God he spoke true.

'Fetch Mabel, Fitz.'

'Truly?'

Mathilda swallowed. Mabel might be a poisoner but she was the only chance they had.

'Truly, Fitz. Please.'

He ran, slamming out of the door calling Fulk's name, and Mathilda was alone with William. She crawled onto the bed again and lay herself against him, curling into the crook of his powerful arm as she had done so many times, though this night it did not curve around her as it always had before. His fingers did not run across her skin and he did not speak to her so that his voice echoed out of his hard chest into her ear. He just lay there and Mathilda felt a huge emptiness looming over her and clutched madly at him.

'Don't go, William. Don't leave me.'

She knelt up, taking his chiselled face in her hands and bending in to kiss his lips as if she could breathe her own life into him.

'Heavens, Mathilda, it's hardly the time for that!'

Mathilda whirled furiously around.

'I'm just . . .'

But Mabel put out a hand.

'I know. I'm sorry. I cannot help myself. There is so much darkness in the world, it is sometimes easier to make light.'

'Much of the darkness is your own creation, Mabel.'

'Perhaps, but what can kill can also cure.'

'You won't kill him?'

Mabel stepped closer to the bed.

'Something else is killing him, I'm afraid.'

'A demon?'

'No! Or if so, one made in nature to eat at him from inside.'

Mathilda looked at William, seeing dark, scurrying bugs within him, teeth scraping at his flesh, and could not bear it.

'It is in his stomach, I think, like the Spanish sailors.'

'Good.'

'Good?'

'Good information, Mathilda. I can work with that.'

Mabel set down a basket on the carved sideboard and began removing little vials and caskets, busily mixing several liquids into a stone bowl.

'Mint,' she said, seeing Mathilda staring, 'and chamomile, to ease the cramps. And yarrow for the fever. Now, help me get it into him.' Still Mathilda stared and Mabel tutted impatiently. 'It is not poison, Mathilda. Now, please, can we help William before it is too late?'

'Of course. How?'

'Hold his nose.'

'But . . .'

'Now, Mathilda. If he cannot breathe through his nose, he must open his mouth.'

'Or not breathe at all.'

'As will happen if we do not hurry. Now!'

Mathilda held William's nose and watched as her poor husband opened his mouth and Mabel, slick as a grass snake, slid her potion between his lips and clamped them shut.

'Let go.'

Mathilda did so. William struggled and then swallowed. His eyes shot open and he looked wildly around, then he closed them again and groaned.

'What have you done?' Mathilda demanded. 'He sounds awful.'

'Oh, and he was the picture of health before, was he? It probably just tastes unpleasant. I hadn't time to sweeten it with honey as I usually do.'

'You do?'

'Oh, Mathilda, grow up. I may know how to poison but I take no joy in it. Bad things are always reported – and credited – more than good. Look at the lost English prince.'

'Who you killed,' Mathilda snapped but Mabel just smiled. 'You *did* kill him, Mabel?'

'Believe what you wish.'

'But why would you want people to think that of you if it is not true?'

Mabel just shrugged.

'It might be true. It certainly *could* be true. Let people think what they wish, Mathilda, for they will anyway, especially of us women, and you might as well make use of it.'

'By making them all terrified of you?'

'Exactly!' She gave a low laugh, then, glancing at William again she sobered. 'In truth, Mathilda, I care little for poisons and far more for their antidotes. Medicine is the future, I am sure of it. Imagine if we could learn how to break fevers and stop wounds being infected and make childbirth safer.'

Mathilda jolted.

'Childbirth?'

'Of course. We women surely owe it to each other to ease it all we can.'

'And that is what you did for me?'

'When?'

'When Adela was born early – just hours after we talked of you poisoning poor Hugh.'

Mabel stared.

'You think I did that to you? To another pregnant woman? To my duchess?'

Mathilda shifted awkwardly.

'I feared so, yes.'

Mabel looked for a moment as if she would erupt in fury but then she released it in a low sigh.

'As I said, people will think what they wish. We have been too long enemies, Mathilda. It is foolish of us both.'

She was right.

'I'm sorry. It's just William. I'm . . . worried.'

'As you should be.' Mathilda blinked. Would she ever get used to this Norman predilection for such ruthless honesty? But then Mabel placed a hand on her arm – a surprisingly gentle hand. 'But we have done what we can. It is in God's hands now. I will be next door. Call me if you need me.'

'I . . . Yes. And Mabel, thank you.'

'I don't do it for you; I do it for William. He has been the making of Normandy and he can be the making of England too.'

'If he lives.'

'Yes.'

CHAPTER TWENTY-NINE

*T*he night uncurled, candle-notch by candle-notch. William did not struggle so violently but he continued to twitch and gasp until Mathilda began to wish he were deathly still again. She prayed. She prayed as she had never prayed before, begging God's forgiveness for not being a good mother to poor Adela, for sneaking around after her husband at Alençon, and above all for thinking him no more than a partner in rule.

'Love is not something that can simply be allowed to sweep over you,' Baldwin had told her all those years ago when she'd rejected even the idea of William as a husband. 'Love must be earned with years of partnership, with mutual goals and considered plans.' She had thought him mean back then but she saw now that he had spoken true and that only foolish stubbornness had stopped her from realising it in these last years. She had clung onto the idea of damned Brihtric, but he had not been romancing her with his fancy wooing, merely exercising his power, propositioning her to test if his damned Saxon curls would tempt her.

William in stark contrast was solid and caring and so, so generous to her and she could not bear to lose him. She watched as he muttered strange, stray words and waited, agonised, for her own name but it did not come. Then, suddenly, with the first licks of dawn light, he started up on his pillows, staring as if he had spotted the answer to some great mystery.

'Dance,' he blurted. 'Must. Dance. Mathilda must dance.'

'No, William,' she said urgently. 'I do not need to dance. I just need *you*. I will sit out every dance forever more if I can do so at your side.'

He seemed to freeze, looking for a terrifying moment like his own effigy, and then, in a miracle, his eyes opened and he stared straight at her.

'But I would like to dance,' he said, as lucid as ever.

'William? Oh God, William – is that you?'

'Of course it is, Wife. Who else would it be?'

'William!' She fell against him, laughing and crying, and felt him pat her back as if she'd simply got herself in a fret about one of the children, or an ill-fitting gown, or a poor menu choice. 'I am so glad to see you well – truly this dawn is coloured with promise.'

She gestured to the gloriously rosy sky beyond the window opening.

'Coloured with promise?' he repeated, half in disdain, half in hope. Then suddenly he remembered something. 'The oath! Harold swore the oath?'

'He did, William.'

'And then . . . ? I don't remember. Why don't I remember? Was I drunk?'

He looked at her incredulously and she shook her head.

'Would that you had been. You've been ill, William, so very ill. It was like Adela. We thought we'd lost you. I had to call Mabel.'

'Mabel?' William pushed her gently back to look down at her. 'You *must* have been worried.'

'I was. Oh God, William, I was, though maybe she is not as

bad as I feared. Not that Mabel is important right now.' She clutched at his arms. 'I love you. You do know that?'

'I love you more.'

'You do not.'

'It's the truth, Mathilda.'

'No. It isn't. You're wrong. And I'm sorry if you thought that and I admit – if we must be truthful – that at times I maybe thought so too, but I was wrong as well.'

'It doesn't matter, Mathilda. You are worth more than me anyway.'

'No!' Mathilda hit at his chest and he flinched. 'Oh Lord, I'm sorry. Did I hurt you? Are you well?'

'Quite well. I'm not such a wreck yet that a titch like you can hurt me. Though I might lie back a little.'

She helped him settle on his pillows, tucking the pretty blue-green blanket over him and hovering until she was sure he was not relapsing.

'You must listen now. You are worth more than most, William, and certainly more than me, for I am vain and selfish and frivolous.'

'Frivolous maybe, but you are a woman – you are meant to be so. Life would be altogether too dull without.'

'William, be serious.'

She could not believe she was talking to him like this. He had been so still and then so delirious. Was it really possible he was on the mend, or was she dreaming? She reached out to prod him.

'Ow!'

Not dreaming then.

'The point is, William, that there is not a person in the world who would not benefit from knowing you, nor a title you do not deserve.'

'Including King of England?'

'Definitely,' she asserted then winced at the memory of her treacherous dance with the Saxon.

'Mathilda? What is it?'

'Truthfully?'

'Of course.'

'It is bad.' He just waited. She gulped. 'I told Harold that . . . that he would make a good king.'

He looked at her from his pillows, puzzled.

'He probably would.'

'But is that not disloyal of me?'

'I know not. Did you say you would back him?'

'No, of course not.'

'Then it is not disloyal.'

'Oh, William! Will I ever understand you?'

'I am very simple. And Harold, you know, *could* be king even if he has no royal blood but I'm not sure if he would last. He wins hearts easily, far more easily than I for he is all charm, but has he the steel to rule? He is too impetuous, I fear – he sees the fight before him, not the bigger picture. He is the same at tafel. He could beat me if only he would hold his nerve.'

'Tafel, William? This is not a game.'

'You think not? Nay, you are right, but it must still be played with skill. Harold is all heart, Mathilda, but is his mind sharp enough? He is best at someone's right hand and I pray to God that he will be at mine for I like the man, truly I do. Oh, God, I am tired.'

'I'm not surprised. Shall I leave you?'

'Please don't. I'm sorry you did not feel you could tell me. I tell you everything.'

'You don't.'

'What?' She clamped her lips shut. 'Mathilda, what have I not told you?'

'You did not tell me that you knew of my . . . my entanglement with Lord Brihtric.'

'Brihtric? But you were a girl, Mathilda, and it was before I met you. It did not concern me. All girls have such weaknesses – look at Emeline.'

'It was *not* like Emeline. A dance or two, no more.'

In truth, it had been far more, she could see that now, for the pretty ease of her time with the loose-limbed Saxon had hooked into her heart and kept her from giving it fully to her dear husband.

'I must learn to dance,' he said, as if seeing into her mind.

She grabbed at his hands.

'No, you must not. It is not important.'

'It is to you, so it is to me. I have been lax. It is not like me but I will learn.'

He half rose, as if he might take a turn immediately, and Mathilda put a firm hand on his chest.

'Not right now you will not. You must get better.'

'In bed?'

'Yes.'

'With you?'

'I will stay of course, but not like that.'

'Shame.'

She looked at him, astonished; he truly was strong.

'You will improve very soon I'm sure,' she said.

'I will if you are my lure.'

'Oh, William.' She curled against him and this time, praise God, his arm tightened around her shoulders. 'Why are you never unfaithful to me?'

'What a question, Mathilda! It is very simple. It takes no great control or denial – I simply do not want anyone else.'

'I am very lucky. I would have you always with me, you know; this dread night has shown me that.'

'You did not know before?'

'I was not sure enough. Goodness, William, how do you speak truth all the time? It is most uncomfortable.'

'It is best.'

'It is. Your dear mother told me once that it is dissembling that will lead to trouble and perhaps she was right.'

Mathilda shifted unhappily and glanced longingly towards the window through which she could see the early sun glinting promisingly across the pale sea.

'There is more, Mathilda?'

She swallowed and forced herself to look back at him.

'One thing more, though you may of course know it already.'

'Know what? Come, my Mora, no more secrets, please. Know what?'

She ran a hand down his chest and sent the words after it.

'That I was at Alençon.'

'Alençon? No, I did not know that.' She felt a flurry of pride that she had at least kept this from him but now he was shifting over, turning with a wince to look at her and all felt difficult again. 'Where, Mathilda? And when?'

She drew in a shaky breath. She did not want to speak of it but she must. It was time. No more secrets.

'I was in the trees, William. I'd come to tell you I was with child. It was foolish I suppose but you'd been at siege for so long and I thought the news might cheer you.' She looked at him but he did not speak, just nodded her on. 'We arrived just as your men were storming the city, so Roger said we had to stay back.'

'Roger de Beaumont?'

'Don't be angry with him, William. I made him take me and he got me away as soon as he could but not before . . . before . . .'

'You saw the men, the townsfolk?' She nodded dumbly and

saw his eyes fill with sorrow. 'I am sorry for it. So many times I have thought over that, Mathilda. I was a madman that day.'

'You did not look mad.'

'Madness takes many forms. Mine was cold and hard like an ice-ball in my heart.'

'Because they disrespected you?'

'Because they disrespected my mother; because they thought her circumstances in life worth turning into ugly, thoughtless taunts; because they thought that doing so would crush me.'

'Did it, William?' she whispered.

He looked at her and she saw a tear in the edge of his dark eye, glinting like an Indian diamond against the silver lights in his pupil.

'A little,' he whispered back, then cleared his throat. 'And I could not have that. I am Duke of Normandy, Mathilda – I cannot be crushed. It is good for no one.'

'Is that, then, why you cannot trust? Why, as Hugh once said, you always expect to be stabbed in the back?' He paled and she felt instantly terrible. 'It matters not,' she said hastily but he reached out and touched her lips into silence.

'It matters a great deal and I am sorry I have not told you before. I thought it was my own cross to bear.' He paused looking into the bed-hangings as if they might leap up and twist around him, then he took her hand and grasped it hard.

'I was fourteen, old enough to sleep alone, save that I was a duke and needed protection, so Lord Osbern, Fitz's father, was always at my side. Not that he protected me that night, nor I him. Our enemies came in the darkest hour, Mathilda. Came all the way into the bedchamber but I did not wake. Can you believe it? I was old enough to have a sword beneath my pillow but not to draw it in time, though I have not made that mistake since.'

'You sleep little, Husband.'

'Some nights I barely sleep at all but at least I have you now. Watching you sleep is rest enough.'

'Oh, William, I'm sorry. What happened?'

He gathered himself.

'What do you think? They stabbed him. They stabbed him in the darkness, so I know not to this day if they intended to take him or me. The first I knew of it was my own name on his lips, the warning drowning in his dear blood. And then the light came, Mathilda – a jumble of panicked torches and candles. And that's when I saw the true nature of treachery. I looked at my Lord Osbern's body, ripped apart in the centre so violently that I could see his still heart nestling uselessly within his cracked ribcage, and I found out – a man's enemies do not just want him gone, but hollowed out, emptied, made void. It has been hard, I fear, to trust anyone since.'

There was nothing to say. Mathilda felt lost in the pity of him carrying this weight around all this time. No wonder he and Fitz were close if they were bonded by this terrible grief.

'Thank you,' she said eventually. 'I think, perhaps, I understand you a little better now.'

He laughed softly.

'Oh, Mathilda, it does not take a shared past to know each other but a shared future. You have always understood me, for you are like me.'

That again. She looked at her husband, strangely vulnerable on his pillows, and forced herself to think about it. William was ambitious, as was she. He was quick to make decisions and strong in acting upon them, as was she. He was curious about the world and keen to take a part in shaping it, as was she. She *was* like him and she'd been a fool to deny it all these years, to be ashamed to be the same as him. Judith had seen it. Fitz knew it and William of course, William had seen it from the start. Only *she* had been blind, chasing notions of sweet-tuned romance.

'We are partners, William.'

He smiled.

'We are, though I did not know before I found you that I needed such a thing. I thought I could do it alone but I was wrong. I could hold Normandy's enemies at bay but I could not grow her as we have grown her together. And without you I definitely could not . . .'

'Rule England? Well, you do not have to, for I am here. I will always be here, and we will rule England together.'

'And rule her well.'

'As well as we are able.'

'And as they will let us.'

She stared at him. It was a chilling thought but not one for now. He was pale and there were still high spots of colour on his cheeks.

'You must rest,' she said firmly, 'and I must go and tell all of Normandy that her prayers are answered and you are well again.'

'All of Normandy?'

'Of course. She loves you, William, as I love you. Now, rest. I will go and pray.'

She kissed him and slid out to find Fitz and Fulk and Mabel and all the others but at the door she looked back and saw William, her dear William, staring at the ceiling, his eyes darting about as if watching his own thoughts and she remembered what Fitz had said – 'he never rests'. Maybe that, like so much else today, was true. Or maybe once he was king it would be different. She prayed so, for he was a good man. Theirs was not a romance, perhaps, not a soft, giddy, giggling love, but a hard, real, truthful one, solid as a rock. And that, she knew at last, was worth so much more.

CHAPTER THIRTY

Caen, December 1065

'I prostrate myself humbly before you, Duke William.'
'Humbly?!' Judith flinched as William looked down at Torr, no longer an earl but an exile. 'I do not believe, Torr, that you have ever done anything humbly in your life.'

'I have seen the error of my ways, Lord Duke.'

'You have been *shown* the error of your ways, Torr. It is not the same thing.'

Torr shifted uncomfortably and Judith watched, wishing she could feel sorry for him but not finding it within herself after the last months of horror. She had told her husband not to come to Normandy, had told him William would not welcome them, but he had not listened. He never listened any more, not since the rebels had cast him – and her – out of Northumbria. She shivered and tried to keep her mind in the present.

The fortress at Caen was sumptuously decorated, she noted. Mathilda had obviously been busy, for the drapes and tapestries were new and there was even fabric upon the floor. It must be cushioning Torr's knees, but only a little. Still William kept him there and still Judith watched, one arm around Karl, now a strong eleven year old, and the other holding three-year-old Skylar on her hip. Tostig had tried hard to have this second boy named for himself, then suggested Baldwin and even Godwin but Judith had insisted on another solid Northumbrian name. She had never truly been a part of any family but this, her own, and she'd wanted to start it anew. She wanted that still.

'I told you, Torr, when you were last here – what did I tell you?' William was talking to Torr as simply as to a child, which was probably fair.

'You told me, Duke William, that if I swore allegiance to you as England's next king before King Edward's death, you would promise me Wessex – so here I am, ready to swear.'

William held up a single finger.

'Very kind of you, Torr, and good attempt but, no, I did not say "before King Edward's death". I asked for your oath there and then and you chose not to give it. That was your right, as I also said, but I insisted – *insisted*, Torr – that you were not to ask again. Did you not think I meant it?'

'Circumstances change, Lord Duke.'

'But allegiance should not.'

'I can help you, truly. I have much to offer.'

William strolled casually around Torr.

'Like what?'

Judith glanced to Mathilda, sat neatly on her grand seat behind William, and felt guilty. Here she was scorning Torr for trying to change sides but had she not done the same? Had she not turned her back on her cousin and friend, been rude to her, wished her ill, and all out of what – petty jealousy? She deserved this humiliation as much as Torr.

'Like what?' William pressed.

'Like ships, Lord Duke.'

'From where?'

'I have money.'

'Gained, I gather, from the lords of the north – the ones who threw you out of your own earldom for bleeding them dry.'

'Money all the same,' Torr said boldly.

'I have money enough, Torr. What else?'

'My family's influence.'

'Your family who presided over the trial that saw you driven from England?'

'That was just Harold,' Torr spat.

'Harold, the Earl of Wessex and King Edward's most trusted advisor?'

'Harold who will be king.' William sucked in his breath and Judith saw Torr's shoulders straighten as he sensed William's interest. 'They are calling him "sub regulus" in England, you know. It means . . .'

'I know what it means, but who are calling him "under-king"?'

'It is on charters. I have seen them.'

Judith watched as Mathilda went to William's side, clasping his arm as tenderly as if they were newlyweds. William looked to her and they whispered something close together, then he turned back to Torr.

'This is good news, Torr, for Harold is sworn to me and I will have need of a sub regulus when the time comes.'

Torr laughed, a hard, sharp bark of derision that made William's guards go for their swords. The rasp of blades leaving scabbards echoed around the hall and Judith flinched and drew her sons closer. Her husband, however, stood slowly, deliberately, and looked straight at William.

'You know less than you think of England, Duke William, or maybe choose to avoid your own knowledge. Harold is saying his oath to you was false – made under duress. All Saxons talk of him as the next king and even now he will be marrying.'

'Marrying?'

'You have not heard? Oh dear, William, your spies grow lax.'

'Marrying whom?'

'I want Wessex.'

'I know you do. You will not get it from me.'

'Because you promised it to Harold? How sweet. You say what you mean, William, and that's very honourable but sadly it blinds you to the reality that other men do not. Not everyone plays the game straight, you know. Harold is not your friend; indeed Harold is your greatest enemy.'

'Marrying whom, Torr?'

Torr looked round as William's men drew closer and thankfully chose not to defy him further.

'Edyth of Mercia, widow of King Griffin of Wales and sister to Edwin, Earl of Mercia, and Morcar, newly Earl of Northumbria.'

'Your replacement?'

'My replacement, maybe, but a danger to you too.'

William seemed to consider this and Judith felt a shudder of dread. She had told Torr that this mission to William would be a waste of time but she hadn't realised until this moment how much she had relied on that being so. She was fed up of power-games. Mathilda used to tease her when they were younger about wanting a quiet life but was that really such a poor goal?

Her father had granted Torr the castellany of St Omer. It was more than he deserved and it had delighted Judith. St Omer was peaceful and quiet and the light was good. Not as good, perhaps, as Northumbria but Northumbria was gone. Judith had known that the moment she'd seen the twisted faces of the rebels.

Don't think of it, she told herself, but it was impossible. The faces leered in on her again, friends turned to foes, smiles to threats.

'It is not you, my lady,' one man had told her amidst the chaos. 'You have done your best for Northumbria and it is appreciated but your lord has treated us with contempt. He has ripped much-needed money from his loyal servants to feed his fun in the south and it cannot be tolerated any longer. He must go and you with him.'

It had felt so unfair. Why should she be condemned for her husband's failings? Why should her good work be drowned in his poor dealings as if it were of no account? But they had leered still, their daggers sharp and determined, and then news had come of men dead at York and she had known their compassion would only last so long, so she'd taken the boys and fled.

She'd gone to the only place she'd ever felt truly safe, the priory at Durham Cathedral, and the monks, God bless them, had taken her and her sons into their guesthouse. She had spent a strange, almost blissful fortnight there, the boys mainly in the herb gardens and she mainly in the scriptorium. As news had trickled in that rebels had seized the treasury at York, that they had taken young Morcar as earl, and that they were marching south gathering support everywhere they went, she'd poured herself into the last of her gospel books, looking to its vibrant colours to paint over the dark shades of real life. But however hard she'd worked, real life had persisted and in the end an escort had been sent to accompany her to Torr at Dover and from thence to Flanders – her only use, it seemed, in her birthright.

She'd longed to refuse, to insist on staying behind the doors of the priory but she was a woman and could not outstay her welcome as a guest or endanger the monks with her presence. Even so, it had felt as if she were being ripped from the womb and she'd cried much of the journey south, grateful for the autumn winds to blow her tears from her face before they upset the boys.

She'd pulled herself together on the sea journey, so reminiscent of that other dread trip back in '51. This time, too, Torr had raged at Edward and sworn revenge, but this time he'd been alone, his rage as much at his brother as at the king. The best they could do now was to settle gratefully into the castle at St Omer and live quietly. But living quietly was not something Torr had ever done well.

'You need me more than you think, Duke William,' he insisted now, jabbing a reckless finger at his host.

William, however, just looked him up and down and finally said, 'No, Torr, I do not,' before adding, 'I trust your horses are fresh?'

'But . . .'

Judith ran forward, letting go of Karl to tug on Torr's arm.

'We should leave, Husband.'

He looked scornfully at her.

'Already? I thought you wished to spend time with your sister?'

'She's not . . .' Judith started but caught herself. Mathilda was all the sister she had and she would deny it no more. She looked to Mathilda. 'I do. Have you time, Mathilda, for a walk whilst Torr sees our horses readied?'

Mathilda rose slowly and for a terrible moment Judith thought her cousin would refuse her, but then she came forward and held out her arm.

'I would like that.'

Judith smiled. She passed Skylar to a startled Torr and urged Karl towards him too.

'Help your father, boys,' she said and then took Mathilda's arm and moved with her towards the door.

The last thing she heard as they left was William saying to Torr, 'Don't hold him like that, man', and then she was out.

'We don't have long,' she said to Mathilda.

'No and I'm sorry for it. I do not wish to part as we did last time, Judi.'

'Nor I. I was hasty, rude even. You have done better in life than I, Mathilda – though that is little surprise.'

'Nay, Judi, you could not help your husband's poor character.'

'You warned me against him.'

'Not firmly enough and what could you have done anyway? All his family were in Flanders for the wedding. Cancelling it would have been a disaster and I think I knew that. Maybe you were right and I was just gloating. Have you been very unhappy with him?'

Judith smiled.

'No. Truly. He is a fool at times and far too lustful and greedy but he has been kind to me in the main and we have had some happy times. He can be fun, Mathilda.'

'I am glad of it.'

'Though he is fun no more. I wish he would settle to a lesser life but I know he will not.'

Mathilda squeezed her arm.

'I can understand that.'

'William wants England?'

'Does everyone know?'

'Is it a secret?'

'No. No, I suppose not. He was promised it, Judi, in '51.'

'A long time ago.'

'True, but Harold confirmed it last year and really, who else is there?'

'Harold.'

'You say that too? I thought it was just Torr bluffing. The Saxons would choose a mere earl over a proven ruler? Are they fools?'

'They are . . . inward-looking and very protective of their own. They have not the flexibility of the continental peoples.'

Mathilda looked around her nervously and pulled Judith close.

'Is it a good country, Judi?'

'Oh, yes. I have been very happy there – as will you be.'

'You mean that?'

Did she? Judith thought about it closely. She pictured Mathilda when she'd first heard she was to marry William, sixteen years ago. 'I have been bred to be a queen,' she'd told her furious parents, and it was true.

'I mean it. You will be a good queen, Mathilda.'

'Thank you. I pray that when the time comes Edward sees it that way too for William does not want to fight. Indeed, he has fought far too much already. You were right, Judith, you know, about how similar William and I are. I did not wish to see it. I did not wish to be so hard as he, but I am.'

'Oh, Mathilda, you are not hard at all.'

'And neither is he.'

Judith blinked, considering, but now the horses were coming out of the stables.

'I have to go.'

'Will you be well, Judi?'

'I will. I have my boys and I have my art.'

'You paint still?'

'Every day if I can. Count Baldwin will be horrified.'

'Count Baldwin,' Mathilda countered fiercely, 'married you to an oaf so he cannot complain if you find solace where you are able. Anyway, a civilised man should appreciate art.'

With a sharp pang, Judith thought of Lord Wulf of Bavaria her kind friend in Rome. He had loved her third gospel book every bit as much as she, begging leave to read it and praising the illuminations in a most earnest way. His company had been hugely welcome to Judith, a comforting contrast to the drunken sycophants around Torr, and she had been saddened more than her uneasy conscience felt she should be when he'd had to return home before them.

She looked anxiously around but Torr was not yet here. She had time. Swiftly she drew her gospel book from her bag. It was the fourth and last one of the set and only partly completed but she thrust it at Mathilda, who opened it and gasped.

'You did this, Judith?' She turned the pages with care. 'All of it?'

'All of it and three other books besides. Are you shocked?'

Mathilda looked up at her, then reached out a hand to touch her cheek.

'Not shocked, Judi, of course not. Impressed, astonished. They are beautiful. Whatever else may have happened to you, if you leave these in the world you will have made a glorious mark upon it.'

Lord Wulf had said something similar and Judith felt tears well in her eyes again but not, this time, of sorrow.

'Thank you, Mathilda.'

She took the book back and tenderly replaced it in its leather covering, then suddenly Mathilda was hugging her, her arms wrapping fiercely up around Judith's back, and Judith found herself hugging her in return as if, by clasping each other close enough, they could travel back to their girlhood when all had been so simple.

'Be safe, little sister,' Mathilda said into her ear.

'And you, big sister,' Judith whispered back and, with Mathilda barely as tall as Judith's shoulder, they both laughed.

Now, though, Torr had emerged with the boys and shouted impatiently for Judith. Mathilda walked with her towards him, taking her time as only Mathilda could.

'Good luck in St Omer,' she called up to Torr but he just

snorted and Judith knew that they would scarce be back before he'd be off again, perhaps this time to his Danish relatives in his endless quest for Wessex.

She looked to the skies, heavy with the threat of snow. 1065 was almost at an end and who knew what 1066 would bring for them all.

'Pray God, Mathilda,' she said as the carriage was brought forward, Karl and Skylar hanging out of the window looking for her, 'that we are not set against each other in the year ahead.'

Mathilda shook her head, as determined as she had ever been.

'We will not be. Remember Father telling us, way back when Tostig first came asking for you, that "women are more subtle than men". He told us we could "surely manage any minor conflicts", and though it pains me to say it, he was right. We should not have forgotten ourselves. Our husbands may fight and there is little we can do to prevent that, but *we* will not. Never again.'

Judith drew strength from her assurance. This trip to Normandy had not, after all, been a waste of time. Torr might be angry but these days Torr was always angry so that made little odds, and for herself seeing her cousin had brought new peace. She leaned out of the window, despite the first flakes of snow, and waved madly at William and Mathilda, stood together in the yard of their brave city of Caen, until they were just dots in the corners of her eyes.

PART THREE

CHAPTER THIRTY-ONE

Forest of Quevilly, January 1066

athilda lifted her cup high, sending steam curling eagerly up into the thatch of the hunting lodge as if heading for an illicit encounter with the clouds.

'A toast,' she proposed, 'to our fine princes who rode so well today.'

The gathered men and women roared their approval and Mathilda felt more warmed by their cheers than by the fur lining of her cloak, or the roaring fire in the central hearth, or the heady spices in her mulled wine. It was the end of the festive period. Twelfth Night had been four days back and they should all have been dispersing to their own castles, but a heavy snowfall had kept them confined in Rouen and now that it had settled William had seized the chance for one last big hunt in the game-rich Forest of Quevilly before the ducal family were left in the usual end-of-winter quiet.

The boys had been delighted and begged to be included and William had agreed. Robert, now nearly fourteen, was a strong young man, taller than Mathilda and well able to keep pace with the older riders. Richard was finer-boned and more studious. He was the only person in the court close to matching William at his beloved tafel but he was very fond of Hugh and, having spent a lot of time with him in his stables, was an excellent horseman. Rufus was only nine and should not really have been allowed along in such weather but what he lacked in years he made up for in fire and determination and his father indulged him.

It was never openly spoken of but Mathilda could see that, much as she could not help a certain preference for clever little Cecily, William's red-haired namesake was his favourite. The boy was similar to William in his determination and straight-talking single-mindedness but Mathilda also wondered if it went back to those first days of his life when William, grieving for Herleva, had carried him close to his chest. Certainly today Rufus had repaid his father's belief in him for it was he who had successfully shot a small boar and he was making the most of it, swaggering about the lodge like a hero whilst the other two glowered. She chose not to mention this in her toast but sat again, leaning against William as he put an arm around her shoulders and kissed her.

'I am glad it snowed,' he said, 'or we would have missed this.'

'It has been a happy day,' she agreed.

'And will be a happy night, my Mora.'

His eyes blazed and she giggled self-consciously.

'William! You know that out here there is nothing but curtain separating us from the others.'

'So? Who will complain? I am their ruler.'

'Maybe, but are you *mine*?'

He rolled his eyes.

'I fear not. You are the one person, my dear wife, who can command me.'

'Then,' she said as Fitz lifted a little pipe and struck up a jaunty jig, 'I command you . . .'

But her words were cut off by a banging at the outer door.

All eyes turned and Fitz's tune dribbled into nothing. At a second bang, William rose.

'Open the door,' he bellowed at the guards.

They jumped to do his bidding and a heavily cloaked figure stepped in on a swirl of cold dusk air. Behind him stood a horse, a fine creature, steaming in the snow.

'Roger?!' William cried out as the man threw back the hood of his cloak.

La Barbe's famous beard was icy and his moustache lacked its usual curl. William's chamberlain had, as usual, stayed with Della in Rouen to oversee any chance business and as his leg ached badly in the cold these days, it must be sore news to bring him out – or great news. Mathilda's heart pounded so loud it was as if it were knocking on the wooden floor of the lodge. Surely only one event would bring La Barbe deep into the forest at nightfall. She stood up at William's side.

'Speak,' he urged as the lords and ladies pulled back to let Roger approach.

The laughter had leached out of the gathering and everyone watched in silence as Roger crunched forward, ice shaking from his boots with every step.

'Is it news from England?' Mathilda asked, unable to bear it.

'It is, my lady, my lord duke. King Edward is dead.'

The packed room held its breath, the only noise the crackle of the fire. William grasped for Mathilda's hand and she clutched it tight as Roger bowed low. He did not drop to one knee, as was the due of a king, but maybe his sore leg did not allow it.

'King Edward is dead,' he repeated, 'and Harold of Wessex is declared king. He was crowned the same day, Duke, that your royal cousin was sent into God's care.' William's fist slammed so hard into the table that plates and cups were sent clattering and bouncing across the floor. Sauce splattered over

Roger's boots like blood and he looked down at them. 'I beg pardon, my lord, to be the bearer of such news, but I knew you would wish to be informed as soon as possible.'

William fought to control himself.

'You are right, Lord Chamberlain, and I thank you for it but these are poor tidings.' He looked round the room. 'You all rode with Harold, knew him for a good man, an honourable man, but where is his honour now? He is an oathbreaker and a cheat. He has stolen my crown and your rights. Which of us, I ask you, is the bastard here?'

His voice was rising, his eyes growing silver-pale as he stared around what had been, before Roger's arrival, a joyous crowd but that now felt foolishly detached from reality.

'Rouen,' William blurted. 'I must go back to Rouen.'

'Now?' Mathilda asked, horrified.

He rounded on her.

'Yes, now, Wife. Informants may be arriving from all over and there are plans to be made.'

'What plans, William?'

'Plans,' he repeated bleakly. 'I know not what. I have not prepared. God in heaven, I have not prepared for this, despite all the warnings. I trusted Edward would name me as he said he would. And I trusted Harold would back him. Why?' He yanked on Mathilda's hand. 'Why did I do that, Wife? Why did you let me? In 1051 we were promised the throne and every year that has passed has taken us further and further from it. We have been stupid, arrogant, ill-prepared. Even Torr, snivelling, wretched little man that he is, said this would happen and I did not listen. And now see how we are repaid!'

'But William . . .'

He jerked away.

'Rouen,' he said again and then he was gone, pushing past

Roger and heading for the door, throwing himself onto the poor heated horse and wheeling it round.

Mathilda ran after him, begging him to stop but he was deaf to her – to everyone. She spun back.

'He's not safe alone,' she said, a sob catching at her words. 'I'll go.'

Fitz leaped up and made for the stables. The next minute he emerged, bareback on his horse, and shot after William.

'He'll catch him,' Roger said. 'William's mount will be tired. Fitz will catch him; he'll see him back safe.'

'Safe?' Mathilda laughed, a bitter sound like the crackling of the fire. 'How can he be safe now that England has been denied him? I must go too.'

'But, my lady, it is near dark and it is an hour's ride to Rouen in the snow. You are better here.'

'No.' Mathilda drew herself up. 'I am better with my husband. Take me to him, Roger, please. Take me to him now.'

It was a hard, terrifying ride. Roger went first with Mathilda behind him and Fulk and Hugh behind her, all with swords drawn against any creatures of the night, animal or human. Mathilda focused hard on Roger's hunched back, recalling another ride, years ago, to Alençon where she had first seen what William was truly capable of. That had been just a border town, though, a handful of peasants driven to action by a jealous lord. Now that they faced a whole country, what would William do?

She rode into the Tour de Rouen, barely hearing the men's sighs of relief as she leaped down and made for the hall. No William. She looked in the antechamber but he was not there either so she made for the curved stairs up to their chamber. The door was shut fast and Fitz was leaning wearily against the wall. Their eyes met and he nodded to the door. Mathilda strode forward and pushed on it but it was latched shut. She banged her hand hard on the wood.

'I've told you, Fitz – leave me be.'

'It's not Fitz, it's Mathilda, your wife. Let me in, William.'

'Mathilda?!'

'Yes, Mathilda. I can ride too, my love – and I can rule. Let me in.'

She heard the latch slide back and nipped quickly in before William could change his mind. Fitz did not even try to follow and she felt for the devoted steward, left outside like the faithful hound he had ever been.

'Why shut Fitz out?'

'I had to think. Fitz talks too much.'

'Fitz loves you.'

'It's hardly the time for love, Mathilda.'

'On the contrary, it is exactly the time for love – love and loyalty. That is what will get us through this.'

He looked at her, then up at the ceiling, staring at it as if memorising every swirl of the carved wood.

'Through it how, Mathilda?' he said eventually.

She moved closer.

'How do you wish it?'

'Right now, I wish to take my sword in my hand, ride my horse over the waves, and cut the crown from Harold's treacherous head.'

Mathilda drew in a deep breath.

'Then that is what you should do, only not right now. First we need information.'

He almost smiled, then sank suddenly down onto the edge of the bed.

'But is it wise, Mathilda? If we have to invade to claim the crown we will risk everything and we could therefore lose everything.'

'You never lose, William.'

Now he did smile, if thinly.

'Your faith in me is touching, Wife, but I have forged my victories on sieges and ambushes, on wars of attrition and stealth. It could not be that way in England.'

Mathilda knelt before him, placing her hands on his knees.

'You have forged your victories, William, on courage and belief and heart and you have all those still if you choose to use them.'

He placed his hands over hers and looked deep into her eyes and Mathilda felt the world close in around them – Flanders, Normandy, England, all sucked into the space between their faces.

'Should I do it, my Mora? Should *we* do it – should we challenge for England?'

She tried to think, tried to conjure up lines of argument for and against but they didn't fall into place, wouldn't stay straight. All she could see was a golden glow – not a crown but a dream, a dream founded on a promise when they had been young and newly duke and duchess and starting on the path of their lives together. This moment of King Edward's death had been on the horizon for them ever since, their two thrones waiting. How could they turn aside?

She met William's gaze steadily.

'We should do it,' she said, clear and sure, 'we should challenge for England.'

They faced the court together – William, Mathilda and Fitz. The faces that stared up at them were white with anticipation, the excitement as intense as the air before a lightning storm. No one had left Rouen, all were poised for William to speak. He cleared his throat.

'Men of Normandy, we have been wronged.' A murmur of

agreement shot around the room – a good start. 'We were promised England, promised her by King Edward, my cousin, in an official visit to Westminster in 1051. Many of you were with Mathilda and me at that time. You were a part of that promise as much as we were and you have been betrayed every bit as much as us by the breaking of it.'

Mathilda saw William's lords look at each other indignantly. They felt the loss, that much was clear, but how keenly?

'Harold of Wessex,' William went on, his voice calm and clear, 'has taken England from us. I have had word from Westminster telling me that Edward roused himself near death to charge Harold to "take care of England according to your oath". That can only be his oath, lords, to me, William, Duke of Normandy, sworn in Bonneville on the holy saints of our great land and before you all.

'Harold is an oathbreaker and a cheat. He has snatched the crown out of his own greed for power, despite having no royal blood and no right to rule. He has cowed the council with his military might and forced them to crown him – forced them, note, on the very day my blessed cousin Edward was commended to God's care. Is this the action of a man confident of his place? No! This is the action of a guilty man, snatching a throne like a thief in the night, and it cannot go unpunished.'

The men roared approval but Mathilda heard only 'thief' and over the pulsing crowd saw William as tarman and blonde, smiling Harold with his great limbs severed and torn, hot tar pushing the lifeblood back into the charring stumps. She felt momentarily giddy but a glance at William steadied her. This was not revenge, but right. There was no room for foolish wavering.

'England is ours!' William cried. 'I have dispatched messengers to demand it is given up to us in peace but I fear they may not succeed.'

Cries of derision told Mathilda that William's men felt the same.

'I therefore consider us in a state of war. I have ordered all our ports blockaded to Saxon ships to keep spies away – though of course our own sail freely.'

The men laughed, cheered again.

'And I have dispatched clerics to Rome to put this case before the Pope. Harold swore on holy relics, this is therefore a holy war and I am confident the papacy will see the justice of our cause. We must, therefore, prepare to force that justice. Who is with me?!'

More roars, though cut through with an undertone of concern.

'You mean, Lord Duke, to invade?' someone called from deep within the crowd.

'I do.'

Men looked at each other.

'But how?'

'By ship,' William said simply. He beckoned Hugh forward. 'My cavalry commander has studied warships in Italy and knows the perfect vessels to transport both men and horses. We will fight as cavalry, I assure you – we will fight as Normans.'

This was met by murmurs of approval but Mathilda could sense the concern growing too. This was not the usual call to arms. William's men could not just pick up their shields and ride to the fray and, perhaps more vitally, neither could they ride away. Once they landed on Saxon shores it would be victory or death. Their greatest enemy right now was the Narrow Sea.

'We don't have ships,' another voice called, though it was impossible to see whose. These fears were carefully anonymous but fierce all the same.

'We can build ships. We have forests and we have craftsmen and we have Norman spirit.'

'And money?'

The crowd of nobles stilled. This was what it came down to – their own lives, yes, but also their own purses and that was maybe the greater concern, for Normans had ever been careless of their lives.

'We will need money,' William conceded. 'We will need investment. I want ships and men from every one of you.' A rumble rippled round the crowd. 'And,' William pushed on, 'the more you give, the greater the rewards on the other side.' The rumble shifted, wobbled. 'England is a great land, rich with resources and the systems to garner them. It has officials aplenty, I am told, but it seems to me that it lacks leaders – lords of fire and purpose who can take this ancient land forward into the future. *We* are those lords.

'Normandy was only created one hundred and fifty years ago and look how far we have come. But lords, we are not just brave and strong and forward-looking, we are also fertile.' He paused for the cheer. 'Our wives are the prettiest in the world and the most fruitful and we are bursting at the seams. Our youngsters head to Italy and look what greatness they are achieving there, so how much more glory is to be found in England – for you and for your sons? And but a short hop home to those lovely wives to make more.'

Mathilda watched closely. Men were assessing each other, nervous of what might go wrong in England but nervous too of missing out if it went right. William had been clever but they were not there yet. It needed one man to start the charge rolling and all would surely join. She nudged at Fitz.

'Say what you will give, Fitz – say it now.'

Fitz looked from her to the men and back to her, then

nodded. He pushed his wild hair out of his eyes and stood tall and proud before the gathered Normans.

'As your loyal steward, I pledge sixty ships to the cause, Lord Duke, and I know my fellow men in the east will be behind me, for we are tough out there and know a wise adventure when we see it – do we not?'

He eyeballed several of his lesser neighbours who scrambled to agree, looking bewildered but increasingly certain as they promised ships from their forests.

'We in the south are no fools either,' Fulk weighed in quickly, puffing out his broad chest. 'Have we not kept the border safe for years? Just because we are furthest from the Narrow Sea does not mean we fear her. As high commander, I also pledge sixty ships and my men will pledge more, will you not, and be there to lead them in person besides?'

The men of the south, stung at the implication of cowardice, fell over each other to offer ships, outbidding their fellows in an ostentatious display of loyalty. William glanced at Mathilda and she saw hope in his eyes. She looked in turn to Hugh who, ever William's quietest lord, gulped visibly but set his shoulders back.

'We may not be subject to border quarrels in central Normandy, but that does not make us weak. Indeed, I challenge any man to best us, Lord Duke. As cavalry captain, I pledge to bring you the finest horse ships – all we need – and my men will offer as befits their bravery.'

And so they did but still they looked nervously to each other and Mathilda sensed these were promises that might yet falter. And then, with a quiet cough, Roger de Beaumont laid his stick aside and stepped forward.

'And I, Duke William, your chamberlain, promise sixty ships.' He hesitated then added, 'And myself to command them.'

'Yourself?' William burst out, for once too stunned to control himself. 'But Roger, you've never ridden to war.'

Roger stroked his moustache, smoothing the ends as if their tidiness was a matter of the utmost importance, then said simply, 'It has never mattered so much before.' All eyes locked onto him and, with another small cough, he faced the crowds. 'All our other fights have been small – rebellions and spiteful invasions, fought mainly to stay still. But this, this will move Normandy forward as nothing else ever could. This will put us on the European map forever. This will make our names and our sons' names and it is the duty of every man here, I believe, to embrace that opportunity. That is why I will fight and I hope you will all be at my side.'

The meeting went wild. Mathilda stared at La Barbe, ever her companion behind the battle-lines, and saw him flush with a mix of embarrassment and pride and slide back behind William as others clamoured forward. Odo, in a flourish of a mace from his clerical robes, promised one hundred vessels and then the floodgates were open. Normandy, at last, was joined against a common enemy across the sea and every lord pressed forward to be a part of the new force.

Mathilda summoned a clerk to her side and had every last promise noted in full and signed. And when it was done, William called for wine to toast the mission and, perhaps, to fuzz the edges of the bemused-looking men who now found themselves part of an invasion force – part, indeed, of a navy, a new venture for any Norman this far north since their founder Rollo had sailed in and claimed the land they now called their own. But they had done it in Italy and they could do it here.

Mathilda looked around the room feeling, for the first time, not antipathy at these war-hungry subjects, but pride. These men would follow their duke to the ends of the earth if he commanded it and Mathilda felt strangely jealous and longed to be a part of this, their greatest mission. She would commission a flagship for William, she decided – a great vessel worthy of his command. And she would include a cabin for herself. If William was going to England, she was going with him. Let the boat building begin.

CHAPTER THIRTY-TWO

Caen, April 1066

'She's in here. Are you prepared? She's beautiful, you know. You'll love her. She . . .'

'Mathilda!' Emeline put a hand on Mathilda's arm. 'Stop babbling and let us in, then we can see this wonder-ship for ourselves.'

Mathilda grimaced but nodded to the guards who stepped forward to open the huge doors. She took a last, nervous glance around, but could see no one; her plans were still safe.

She'd promised William after his terrible illness that there would be no more secrets but this was different. This was less a secret than a surprise and every time she saw the ship it thrilled her to imagine William's face when she presented it to him.

Normandy had gone boat mad. The forests rang with the sound of trees being felled and the dockyards and beaches were lined with wooden skeletons slowly but surely being turned into Normandy's first ever fleet. William had frugally bought an old boat off Count Baldwin for himself, saying it 'would do' but Mathilda had other plans. She had sourced a boatbuilder deep in the woods a little way up the River Orne and commissioned this ship. It was to be a gift for her husband, as he had gifted her a wedding dress fifteen years ago, and it was to be every bit as magnificent.

Mathilda could not stop herself jigging on the spot, much as little Constance might, as the doors of the great boatshed creaked open and her ship was revealed to her friends. The vessel truly was beautiful. Built in the classic style of a Viking warship, such as had first carried William's ducal ancestor Rollo into Norman ports, she was as long as ten men laid end to end, with clinker-built sides growing elegantly up and out from the exposed hull like the curve of a woman's hips. She was made of glowing new wood, painted around the gunwales in glorious colours and capped at either end by magnificent figures of Mathilda's own choosing. Mathilda dragged Emeline and Cecelia forward.

'Come and see how the oar-holes are trimmed with silver. And look at the detailing in the gunwale patterns and see the figurehead – it's almost complete.'

Emeline squinted up through the shafts of light pouring in through the long run of windows either side of the boatshed.

'What is it?'

'It's a child,' Mathilda explained impatiently, 'pointing forward to England.'

'Why a child?'

Mathilda looked up at it and smiled.

'It is William,' she said, 'because he was born to this – not to a poor girl in an illegitimate bed but to this, to greatness. It is his trueborn destiny.'

'You believe that?'

Mathilda looked squarely at Emeline.

'I do.'

'And you are not afraid?'

Mathilda turned her eyes back to the wooden child.

'Of course I am afraid but I cannot let that stop me. I was

afraid at Eu, was I not? And yet we have been on a wonderful journey since then.'

'We have,' Cecelia agreed, running a hand along the smooth, high side of Mathilda's ship, 'but we are happy. Why take such a risk now?'

'Because, Cecelia, the journey is not over yet and this is where we have always been heading.'

'England?'

'Yes.'

'And you will go with William?'

'Yes. If I cannot rule Normandy as regent, why should I not go with him to be queen?'

'Must we, then, go too?'

Mathilda looked at her two ladies, standing in the curved shadow of her warship and saw terror writ across their dear faces.

'Of course not,' she said, though her heart quailed at the thought of facing the Narrow Sea without them. 'It is simply that I must go for William.'

Cecelia looked at Emeline, then they both looked at Mathilda.

'Then we must go for you. We will not, though, fight?'

'No! We will not fight, of course not. I intend to stay in this beautiful ship with my captain at guard so that when the victory is won I can stand at William's side.'

'And if it is not . . . ?'

But Mathilda put up a hand.

'It will be. It must be. Now come and see the cabin. It is so neat and pretty. You will love it.'

She was babbling again, she knew. She must sound mad; maybe she *was* mad. Maybe they were all mad but if so it was a glorious madness. Normandy was filling up with boats so fast it was as if the forests were turning themselves out onto the shores. In addition to the new ships every fisherman and trader had been commissioned to sail when the time came and already they were taking nervous soldiers on short trips to get them used to the swell and turn of the waves.

And it wasn't just ships. Men were arriving every day too, troops from little Phillipe's France, and from Flanders, Maine, Brittany and Anjou, as well as mercenaries from all over who had heard of William's 'holy war' and wanted a part of it. And with every eager hired-sword who flocked to William's banner, the confidence of his own men swelled a little more.

News had come, though, of boats gathering in Norway – a Viking invasion fleet led by Harald Hardrada, the fearsome warrior who had stormed across the Rus and Byzantine lands as a youth winning honour and treasure everywhere he went before he'd taken a wife – or indeed two – and settled as King of Norway. Clearly he was settled no longer. Reports of a second enemy were daunting but were also proof that it was not just the Normans who thought Harold had no right to the Saxon throne.

'Hardrada claims England was promised by Harthacnut to his nephew Magnus, King of Norway before him,' William told his council when the reports arrived.

'They are very free with their promises, these Saxon kings,' Fitz said scornfully.

'And very poor at keeping them,' Fulk snarled.

'No sense of loyalty, it seems,' William said lightly. 'Well, we will show them.'

'Yes, and the Viking too.'

They were all returned to battle rhetoric, the concern gone in the anticipation of glory ahead, but for Mathilda the thought of Hardrada was a daunting one. Raoul knew a little of the Viking, for he was married to Elizaveta of Kiev, sister to Anne, and Anne had known him as a child. He was a giant of a man, he'd told her, with white-blonde hair and a sword-arm as wide as a tree trunk. But at fifty-one he was old, and he did not know England.

'*We* do not know England,' Mathilda had replied.

'Maybe not, but William has plenty of men who do – they have lived there for years.'

'Since '51?'

'And before. They know every curve of the land, every turn of the roads and every plan of every soldier. If we are lucky, the Harolds will fight each other first and the victor will come to us already battle-weary.'

'And if they do not?'

'Then we will defeat one and meet the second buoyed by our victory.'

Mathilda did not point out the clear flaw in his masculine logic – how would the enemy be wearied by a first battle, but their own men buoyed by it? Rhetoric again, but they needed it. Belief and heart were almost as valuable weapons as axes and must be sharpened with just as much care.

Mathilda rode back into Caen, full of the joy of her secret ship, to find William waiting for her.

'Where have you been, Mathilda?'

She flushed.

'Women's business, William. Cloth you know for, erm, clothing.'

'Oh, right. Well, I'm glad you're back. You must come into the hall – now. Messengers are here with news from over the Narrow Sea and the clerics are returned from Rome.'

'From the Pope?' Mathilda's stomach clenched. 'What says he?'

'You'd best come within,' William said but Mathilda saw a smile twitch at the edges of his mouth and felt a surge of hope.

Sure enough, as she walked into the new hall, the greatest now of all their halls, she saw it – a papal banner, held aloft by a barrel-chested young soldier. Her hands flew to her mouth.

'His Holiness approves our cause?'

It was only now that she realised how much she had feared that he might not.

'He does, Wife. He sends us his holy banner to fight beneath and an edict besides that condemns Harold as an oathbreaker and declares our cause just. All men who fight for William fight for God!'

He raised his voice to the people gathered in the hall and the cheer that greeted his words seemed loud enough to reach the Lord himself. Mathilda felt joy suffuse her body and longed to let it out in a roar with the rest, but she was a duchess so she must be decorous – on the outside at least. Inside, though, she was whooping. They were right. Their cause was just – the Pope said so. The throne of England was theirs to take with honour and fairness and decency and now all men would see that. They would see that William was an instrument of God's justice and they would back him. Maybe, indeed, if word of this reached Harold he would stand down, bow the knee to William and beg pardon and there would be no war, save per-haps with the Viking who would surely be easy to see off with the might of Saxons and Normans and God combined.

'Praise the Lord,' she said, looking round the room as men and women cheered and clapped and cried praise with her. 'We must order masses all across Normandy, Husband. We must send word to all our monasteries to pray for us, and coin too to furnish their altars to God's honour. We must . . .' She dried up for he was looking at her strangely. 'Must we not?'

'Yes, Mathilda, absolutely we must and more, I think, besides.'

'More?' He took her hands. She glanced around awkwardly

and tried to pull away but his grip was too tight. 'What is it, William? What do you plan?'

'We must do something, Mathilda, to show our personal commitment to this holy war.'

'Personal?'

'I wish, my sweet, to give Cecily to God in sacrifice.'

Mathilda felt faint. She saw William the tarman, lifting a dagger to her precious daughter's heart.

'No, William, not Cecily. She cannot die. She . . .'

'Die? Mathilda – what do you think I am, a barbarian? I thought we had talked of this?'

'Yes. Yes, I'm sorry. I was just confused.'

'I mean, Mathilda, that Cecily should be sworn to the nuns as a novice. At La Trinité, I thought? It is your own foundation, so fitting, and of course you will often have reason to visit . . .'

Mathilda stared at her husband. He was right but Cecily was her brightest, most affectionate, sweetest daughter.

'Sacrifice?' she repeated, recalling William dismissing her suggestion of sending Adela into the church. '*It would be little sacrifice, Wife,*' he had said then and he'd been right, but this would. 'Why not Rufus?' she demanded. 'He could be a monk.'

William just looked at her and she saw the foolishness of the suggestion in a moment. Rufus would be driven insane by the quiet of monastic life but clever Cecily loved learning. She might enjoy the cloister, even flourish there and, after all, Mathilda would have Maud and Constance still at home with her.

'I would visit often?' she whispered, fighting tears.

'Very often, my Mora.'

She swallowed. It was a sacrifice indeed, yet every man in Normandy was preparing to invade a foreign country to fight for her. Cecelia and Emeline were bracing themselves to sail at her side. The Pope had put his name to this, and the mercenaries had signed their swords to it and the nobles had provided untold ships and men and horses and all for her. She may have been bred to be a queen but thousands would have to risk all to make her so. She owed something in return.

'So be it,' she said, though her heart tore at the words.

William drew her close.

'God will care for her, Mathilda, as He will care for us all.'

She prayed he was right but surely, in England, in Norway, even in Flanders, others were looking to God for protection and, in the end, He could only bless one of them. Who could say which it would be?

CHAPTER THIRTY-THREE

Bruges, May 1066

Judith balled her hands into fists, scrunching them furiously into the soft fabric of her best gown. It would make nasty damp creases in the wool but she didn't care. Count Baldwin was calling this 'her day' but he had taken that from her at Easter when he'd snatched her last gospel book away.

She looked at it now, set upon the altar of St Donatian's church with the other three, a supposedly perfect set. Only she, in this whole octagonal nave full of her half-brother's sycophants, knew how imperfect it was. Three and a half books had been worked with care and love by Judith and the last half had been completed by a paid artist with little concern save for his fee.

That's not kind, Judith berated herself. She had met the artist, a neat monk of about her own age who had praised the project and told her the book would be an honour to complete. He'd even praised the artist who had gone before him, believing it to be a Saxon monk left behind when Judith had fled. Little did he know that the artist had not been left in England; only her dreams.

'Such fine work, Lady Judith,' an elderly woman said now,

fluttering up at her side. 'You must be very proud of your commission. It honours God greatly.'

Judith smiled tightly. The books did honour God and surely that was more important than the trifling matter of who had daubed the ink onto the pages. She should stop being so self-seeking.

'I am glad you like them, Lady Agnes,' she said smoothly.

'Oh, they're beautiful. Is England full of such talent?'

Less full than it was, Judith longed to say but she dared not. She was here by her brother's kindness and she could not betray that, not even with truth.

'They have many excellent scriptoriums,' she said instead.

'And many rich churches and lords to make use of them, I believe?'

'Some,' Judith confirmed tightly.

People were always trying to talk to her of England. At first she'd thought it was kind of them to be so interested but then she'd learned where the conversation always led – 'And William prepares to invade, does he not, to claim his right to the throne? And Mathilda with him – your sister?'

'Cousin,' she'd correct them, not out of spite to Mathilda – she was done with that now – but simply to confuse them and offer a chance of escape.

'You must be sorry to have left,' Lady Agnes probed unsubtly. 'You hope to return?'

'I know not. We must see what God sends for me.'

'Or what your husband wins?'

Judith's smile strained at the edges and with a nod that might have been agreement, she moved away. She doubted Torr would win her anything, though he had thrown his lot in with the infamous Harald Hardrada, so who knew? He had no connection whatsoever to the King of Norway and she'd heard the man was a mighty warrior and a fine ruler, so what he wanted with Torr she had no idea.

'He needs me to show him around England,' he'd told her defensively when he'd returned to Flanders, prancing around in his Viking furs and boasting about his fearsome new ally.

'You told him you could do that?' Judith had asked, unable to hide her scorn, for Torr had regularly got lost in Durham, a peninsula city of few streets in which their residence, alongside the soaring spires of the White Church, could be seen from every one.

'I have men to do that, Judith. A leader leads.'

'Right. Did you tell him that you know the northern lords too?'

'I do.'

'And that you'd bring them to his cause?'

'Some were loyal to me – the older ones. It was the upstarts looking for a way into power who broke me.'

'And these "upstarts", having found their power, will welcome you back with your Viking friend, will they?'

'The men of the north are very close to their Norse neighbours, Judith, as well you know.'

He'd had her there. The people of Northumbria *were* very close to their Norse heritage. There was much trade across the Northern Seas and many men had Scandinavian wives and bore Scandinavian names. They might welcome Harald Hardrada as they had once welcomed King Cnut and if he won with Torr at his side then Judith might be summoned back to a court ruled by a Norwegian king and a Rus queen. She didn't want that but neither did she want to stay in St Omer – not since the dread day that Count Baldwin had paid her a surprise visit and found her at her painting frame.

Oh, he had been angry. He'd kicked the frame away, sending her scrabbling after it like a peasant after coins.

'Is this what you've been doing in England, Sister?' he'd spat, as if she'd been whoring herself in the streets.

'It is to God's glory,' she'd defended herself, clutching the parchment to her chest.

'It is to your own vanity, Judith.'

That had hurt.

'How can it be vanity in me and not in a monk?'

'Because you are a woman.' There'd been no sense to it, no logic, but also no way of making Baldwin see that. 'Give it to me,' he'd demanded.

'No.'

'Give it to me, Judith, or I will rip it from you.'

He would have done, she'd seen it in his eyes. He would have ripped it from her and quite possibly ripped it to pieces besides. She'd had to give it up, for its own safety, but if doing so had saved her precious pages, it had ripped out her heart and she'd wept like a child for days.

'See,' Baldwin had yelled, jabbing the book at her. 'See how it has possessed you? It's not natural, Judith, not right. Thank the Lord I caught this in time to save you.'

Then he'd marched off, thrusting her precious manuscript at a soldier – a mere soldier – and sending more to hunt the castle for the rest. He had been gone before nightfall, all four books in his saddlebags, and she had been left more alone than she'd felt since first arriving in England.

The only blessing had been that Baldwin had seen the value of the gospel books once back in Bruges, possibly under the influence of the ageing but still formidable Adela, and had them safely stored. He had commissioned the artist to complete the last one and even invited Judith to meet him. She had gone, because she couldn't bear not to, but it had been painful and when Torr had come back to beg ships from Count Baldwin she'd pleaded with him to demand her book back as well.

'Book?' he'd said, squinting at her.

'My gospel book, Torr – the last one in the set.'

'Oh. Why has Baldwin got it?'

'He's given it to an artist – a man.'

'Why?'

For a moment this had given her hope but Torr's tolerance of her art had always been more out of lack of interest than support and so it had proved this time. She'd explained Baldwin's unreasonable opposition to her work and he'd patted her hand but only said, 'I can't afford to anger your brother, Judith, not when I need his ships so badly. It can wait, surely? And when Hardrada and I have the victory we will return to England and you can paint all the pictures you wish.'

It had been a kindness of sorts, she supposed, but he hadn't understood. For ten years she'd worked on this set and she'd so wanted to complete it. She moved towards the altar now, gazing on the books and trying to love them as she once had.

'They are exquisite,' a voice said at her shoulder, soft and low and rich with an echo of happiness she couldn't quite place.

She looked back and a pair of warm brown eyes met hers.

'Lord Wulf!'

Judith felt herself colour in delight to see the quiet pilgrim from Rome again.

'You remember me? I'm so pleased, for you made a great impression upon me.' She looked bashfully down and he hurried on. 'I remember your book too. It was the third one, was it not? I remember the picture of the resurrection especially – such a fine piece, glowing with light as if Christ Himself was within it.'

Judith felt tears well dangerously; he truly did remember.

'You are too kind,' she managed.

'No, you are too modest.'

'But it is not me who . . .'

'Must we pretend, Judith?'

She'd wondered if he had guessed when he had quizzed her closely on the designs in Rome but they had not spoken of it openly. Now, looking around the church full of empty-headed courtiers, a flare of anger cut through her distress, making her bold.

'Apparently we must, Lord Wulf.'

'Count Baldwin is not, perhaps, as forward-looking as he would like to think?' Judith spluttered, fighting to hold back not tears this time but laughter – glorious, delirious, dangerous laughter. She looked to Wulf and saw amusement in his lovely eyes too, but something else – concern? 'We have fine artists in Germany, you know, my lady,' he said, his voice low. 'Some are women.'

'Truly?'

'I would love to show you sometime if you were ever . . . free.' He was looking at her intently now. She knew she should avert her gaze but could not pull away. 'Your husband goes to war, I believe?' She nodded dumbly. 'That can be . . . hazardous. I don't wish him ill but if anything were to happen to him might you, perhaps, look to me for protection?'

'I . . . I have sons,' Judith stuttered.

'Fine boys. I have met them. Your youngest challenged me to swordplay this morning in the yard. They would, I am sure, be happy in Bavaria if their mother was. Do you think, Judith, that you could be happy in Bavaria?'

Now Judith didn't know whether to laugh or cry.

'I cannot, Lord Wulf, hope for my husband's . . .' She stopped, flustered. 'But were I ever to be widowed . . .' She looked around again. This felt so risky but she had taken precious few risks in her life, save for her books, and maybe this warm, kind, generous man deserved one. 'Were I ever to be widowed,' she said more firmly, 'I would be honoured to come to Bavaria.'

'And happy?'

'Oh, yes,' she said, throwing caution to the sharp Flanders winds, 'I think I would definitely be happy.'

'Good. Very good.' He smiled at her. 'Shall we go and talk with your brother? I would like to praise the fine art on display, though the latter pages, I fear, are not quite as skilled as the rest. I would like to recommend that he sticks with the former artist for any future work – much more delicate and careful, do you not think?'

'As a woman I could not presume to say,' she said but felt laughter well inside her again and saw it mirrored in Wulf as she took his arm, as warm and steady as his gaze, and moved quietly forward at his side. Let Torr and Harold and Mathilda scrap for England; it mattered little to her now.

CHAPTER THIRTY-FOUR

Caen, June 1066

'Mathilda? Mathilda, whatever is it? Whatever's wrong?' William rushed forward into their chamber and Mathilda scrubbed, too late, at her tears. 'My dear one, my Mora, what's happened?'

The pet name set her going again. Mora: it was the name she had given her ship. Only last week she had seen the letters carved, tall and bold, onto the side of the beautiful craft and painted with gold for all to see. It would mean little to most but William would see it and know that this ship was *them*, carrying them both forward to England. Only not now.

'It's all spoiled,' she said, tugging at the bedcovers beneath her. 'All my plans are all spoiled.'

'Why? Mathilda, please, you're frightening me.'

'I am?' She looked up at him and saw he was, indeed, pale with concern. She sighed. 'I'm with child, William.'

'But that's wonderful. That's . . . oh.' He understood suddenly. 'You cannot sail?'

'I could. Why should I not? A ship is surely no less safe than a carriage?'

'Unless there is a storm.'

'We won't sail in a storm.'

'No. Absolutely right but, Mathilda, at sea storms can come up out of nowhere.'

'And you'd know that, would you? How often have you been to sea, William?'

'Once, as you well know – once to England in 1051.'

The memory silenced them both. Mathilda pleated her skirts forlornly. She didn't need William to tell her the risks or to remind her of the import of this mission. She knew it all but it made it no easier to accept. Over three years she had gone without a child and she'd thought that perhaps her time was done but now, when it mattered most, God had tied her firmly to Normandy by her womb.

'It's not fair.'

His arms went around her.

'We have our roles, my sweet.'

'But must we be constrained by them? I wanted to sail with you, William. I wanted to be there for your victory.'

'And I wanted you there too. I want you crowned at my side, Mathilda, but I can wait. Your safety is the most important thing.'

'Mine?! What of yours, William – you are the one riding to battle.'

'Beneath God's holy banner and with half the mercenaries of Christendom at my back. I will not die, I promise you.'

'*I* might.' It came out small, squeaky.

'Mathilda?' William was puzzled, as well he might be. 'What's this? It's not like you, my love, to worry so. You give birth as easily as I defeat rebels.'

'But I am old, William.'

'Nonsense. You are every bit as trim and pretty as you were the first day I saw you.'

'The day you swept me onto your horse?'

'And nearly dropped you in the process. What was I think-ing?'

'You were, I believe, trying to impress me.'

'And have been trying ever since.'

'And succeeding. I'm so proud of you, William, and I so wanted to be there.' Her voice rose, petulant again. 'I even had a cabin and . . .'

She caught herself, horrified.

'A cabin? Where, Mathilda? What do you mean?'

She put her head in her hands. Months of secrecy blown in one slip of the tongue. It was the babe; it fuzzed her brain and made her foolish.

'You had better come with me,' she said wearily.

They rode out together, Mathilda side-saddle for the babe and grumbling about it all the way up the riverside to the boat-builder's shed. But there, at last, excitement swallowed up her bad temper and she glanced to William who was staring wide-eyed at the great doors before them.

'What have you been up to, Wife?'

'Come and see,' she said coyly and rapped three times at the door.

There was a scuffle within, a rattle of locks, and the head boatman's weather-beaten face peered anxiously out of a tiny crack in the doors.

'My lady?! And, and my lord duke. What an honour. But you shouldn't . . . That's to say, I wasn't expecting you.'

'No,' Mathilda agreed. 'This wasn't planned but we are here now. May we see her?'

'Her?' William asked.

'No more questions,' Mathilda told him. 'You will see soon enough.' William subsided obediently and the boatman stared, astonished. 'May we see her?' Mathilda prompted and he jumped.

'Of course, my lady, of course. Would you wait a little and I can have all the window-drapes drawn back to let in more light. We are just working at the stern today.'

'Stern?' William said as Mathilda nodded at the man and he scuttled away. She smiled at him.

'I have not ordered you a horse, William.'

'A sea horse perhaps?'

'Perhaps.' A great clatter arose from within as the drapes were pulled and the workshop, no doubt, hastily tided. 'Ah, here we go.'

Two young lads came out and grabbed at the doors, thrusting all their weight behind them to fling them back with as much drama as they could muster. It was not quite the public unveiling Mathilda had imagined, all trumpets and cheer, but suddenly it felt so much better.

The morning sun was still low and cut into the shed from the east side in shafts of light that caught on the silver trims and lit up the reds and blues of the child figurehead and the bold gold of the name – Mora – on the prow before them. The Viking-style ship looked almost mystical, like a modern-day dragon ready to be released, and when Mathilda slid her gaze to her husband she saw he was indeed staring up at his gift with all the wonder of a man facing a legend.

'I thought,' she said, suddenly shy, 'that you should have a craft worthy of you.'

He looked at her, tears shining in his eyes.

'Worthy of me?'

'Absolutely. Now, come and see.'

She took his hand and tugged him forward, taking him round every detail: the silver oar-holes set into the top strake; the fine oars, made to the latest design to cut the waves most efficiently; the solid rowing benches, their lids sealed with wax so the men could stow their weapons with no fear of the salt water eating into their edges. She showed him the figurehead with no need to explain its significance for he saw it right away. She showed him the name and he showered her in kisses as the boatmen nudged and chortled from the shadows and finally she showed him the cabin – a fine structure towards one end of the open boat, containing little more than a bed, not grand but elegantly carved and just big enough for two.

'Oh, Mathilda,' William said as she ushered him inside. 'It's perfect.'

'And look,' she said, pointing to the floor, painted with squares.

'Our very own tafel board!'

'With a king at the centre, William.'

'And a queen.'

'Not now.' She pouted. 'Now you will be in it alone – or with Fitz.'

William chuckled.

'I pray not. Fitz snores far worse than you.'

'I do not snore at all.'

'You do a little, my Mora, especially when you are . . .' He looked to her belly and stopped himself.

'When I am fat as a barncat in spring?'

'Gorgeously rounded with little princes and princesses,' he corrected, grabbing her. 'But come, it would be a shame to let this cabin go to waste, would it not, now that we are here?'

'William!'

'We must christen the *Mora*, my Mora – we must play our tafel game.'

'The babe . . .'

'Is in there now. Come,' he kissed her neck, 'I want to show you my appreciation . . .' He untied her laces and loosened them, moving his lips lower . . . 'for this magnificent gift.'

Mathilda squirmed but more in pleasure than embarrassment.

'This,' she protested weakly as her gown fell to the floor of the tiny cabin, 'is why I am forever with child.'

'And why I am the happiest, luckiest man in the world. Now hush . . .'

They emerged a little later, flushed and, despite Mathilda's best efforts in the tiny copper mirror on the wall, dishevelled. The boatmen grinned knowingly and William tossed them a bag of coins, making them grin even wider.

'Outstanding workmanship,' he said. 'She is stunning and will lead us to England in true style.'

They bowed so low that their noses almost touched the sawdust at their feet as William led Mathilda back out into the sunshine.

'Ever, Wife, you surprise me,' he said as he helped her into the saddle.

'I'm glad.'

'And I wish you could be in the cabin with me when we sail but you would, you know, rather distract me.'

'Nothing distracts you if you do not wish it to, William.'

'Ah, but with you I *would* wish it. But seriously, my love, although this may be my loss, it could be Normandy's gain.'

'In what way?'

'I need you to keep the reins of government tight here.'

'As I always do, with La Barbe at my side.'

'La Barbe is sailing with us.'

'Of course. Well, with Della then.'

'And perhaps Robert?'

'Robert? William, what are you thinking?'

But at that he just smiled and kicked his horse into a canter.

'You will see, my Mora,' he called back over his shoulder as he went. 'You will see soon. You are not the only one who can do surprises.'

A month later, they gathered at Bonneville, as they had done two years ago to hear Harold of Wessex swear the oath he had never meant to keep. Mathilda was tired, for she and William had been on progress all around the duchy, urging all men to valour. Everywhere they'd gone, even in the once-rebellious west, they had been cheered. Normandy was united at last in her support of William and in her excitement at the venture ahead.

The talk was all of England and men flocked to the papal banner wherever they went. Copies of the edict blessing those who took part in this holy war against the oathbreaker had been distributed to all the major churches throughout northern France and William's vast army was growing every day. The men were mustering on the rich open plains either side of the mouth of the Dives river, north of Caen. William had ordered the *Mora* to be sailed in splendour up the river and it was now moored prominently in sight of the Narrow Sea, a glowing call to arms for the excited soldiers who arrived there daily.

La Barbe had been a busy man too. With Della as his self-proclaimed right-hand woman and his two boys as his runners, he controlled a vast team of officials stationed at Troarn to coordinate supplies into the growing camp and the removal of waste to keep bodies strong and spirits high. William had sworn not one farm would be ransacked to fund this mission and the chamberlain and his family were making good that promise with wagons travelling incessantly in and out of Dives. Decent prices were being paid for grain and game and every man not fit to fight, and many women besides, were keeping food supplies topped up. In return, in addition to their pay, they received mountains of manure from the fields of war-horses Hugh was gathering further up the coast at Fécamp.

There had been concern about how to load the new horse ships. The horses could hardly leap into the boats from the shallows as the men did. It might have been possible for one or two but far too risky for the three thousand horses needed for all the knights of Normandy and beyond. In Italy, Hugh had told William and Mathilda, they used the deepwater ports created from stone by the Romans as the horses could be led aboard directly from the walls at the waterline. For some time his engineers had puzzled over how to mimic this until Fulk had recalled a port seen when riding with William to rescue the oathbreaker from Ponthieu. St Valery, it emerged, still retained its neat Roman structure and was perfect for loading the horses.

A deal had been struck with William's avaricious neighbour, Count Guy, and the problem was solved. The deal, Mathilda knew, revolved around land in England, as did many such deals William had brokered as 1066 had unfolded and she prayed there was land enough in England to honour them. For now, though, all was set fair and the lords and ladies of Normandy were in high spirits as William stepped up to address them from a dais, built in the open air before the palace of Bonneville so that the Narrow Sea might sparkle invitingly behind him as he spoke.

Mathilda looked around the company, letting William's familiar words wash over her. She was sat on her seat of state with her children all around her and her eighth swelling lightly within her belly and she wished Count Baldwin could be here. He had sent messages of support as well as ships and men but personally he was keeping his distance. It was perhaps because of his brother-in-law, Torr, now lurking somewhere in the Northern Seas where he had reportedly sold himself into the service of Hardrada, but more likely because Count Baldwin had always excelled on the sidelines of political crises. He was not a man to plunge into anything and Mathilda felt a renewed swell of pride that William, although not as smooth-tongued or cultured as her father, was at least prepared to stand up for what he believed in and face opposition head on.

She smiled over at him as he spread his hands wide to a roar of appreciation from the crowd. He was getting good at speeches, she reflected, remembering his almost cut-throat use of pure fact when she had first known him. Suddenly, though, she realised he was speaking words she had not heard him speak before.

'And that is why,' he was saying, 'it is my very great pleasure to formally designate my son Robert as heir to this great duke- dom of Normandy.'

So this was William's surprise. She looked to her son who did not seem as startled as her, but was stepping calmly for- ward, his hand on his sword and his head obediently bowed to his father and his people, already every inch the duke. He was up to William's shoulders, she noticed as if through a mist, and his own were broadening nicely. He had more swagger than his father – a result of a youth spent in contentment, not fear – but he stood well and the appointment was met with eager cheers.

Had William's been so greeted, she wondered, when, aged seven, his own father had presented his bastard to his nobles before he went off on pilgrimage? She doubted it and felt a swell of joy that William could do this for their son. It was a mark of how very far he had come and she prayed he was enjoying it. He seemed to be, for he was smiling widely.

'Robert will rule Normandy in my stead whilst I am away securing England.' Another roar. William put up a hand for silence. 'But as he is yet young he needs guidance and as La

Barbe sails with us . . .' more cheers ' . . . I leave him ruled in his turn by the one person who holds Normandy as dear as I and who can keep her steady and strong until we return. I name as Normandy's regent my wife, Duchess Mathilda.'

'What?' Mathilda stuttered indecorously but William was still speaking.

'It has not been the usual custom in Normandy to name a woman but there are not many women in Normandy like my duchess – *our* duchess. I trust her absolutely to hold our homeland firm whilst we sail forth to claim more and ask that you do so too.'

There wasn't even a moment's hesitation. The roars of approval were deafening, the faces a blur of open mouths. Gradually the sound coalesced into a steady chant: 'Mathilda, Mathilda, Mathilda!' Mathilda felt Emeline prod her and rose, moving forward as if in a dream. She looked up at William and saw his grin, wide and delighted with himself, and all came back into focus.

'This is your surprise, Husband?'

'It is a good one, is it not? And well deserved, Mathilda, as the people clearly acknowledge. We have done this together, you and I, and we will keep doing it together and if England fails . . . If England fails, Wife, we will have Normandy still. She is our heartland and you, my Mora, are her heart. Take good care of her.'

'I will,' she promised, putting an arm around Robert, though she had to reach up to do so, and feeling William's bigger, stronger arm enfold them both. 'I will, William, and she will be here, secure, when you return.'

She looked out across the cheering crowd and then back to where the Narrow Sea, as intended, sparkled its promise. Praise God that the sun was shining, she thought, for the effect would not have been as dramatic in the rain. She remembered

Fitz, way back at the start of their marriage, solemnly telling her that William had 'the devil's own share of luck'. It had proved true so far and now she could only pray that it would hold.

CHAPTER THIRTY-FIVE

St Valery, September 1066

The rain lashed across the camp, riding high on fierce onshore winds which tugged viciously at tents, blew out feeble fires, and pulled mercilessly at men's spirits. William strode from one group to another, his beaver-fur cloak thrown back so he could suffer with his men and endless words of encouragement on his lips. Half-running behind him, though, Mathilda could see him glance endlessly to the fishermen's weathercock atop the church of St Valery and knew how much this storm pained him.

All had been well at Dives. The weather had been fair, still warm though the days were shortening, and the mood had been high. Many had been eager to sail there and then but William had held them off, waiting for the end of the forty days of service that he knew the Saxon king could legally demand of his subjects. The decision hadn't been popular.

'Why wait?' Fitz had demanded, impatient as ever, but William had just put a calming hand on his arm and hushed him.

'It is sensible, Fitz. Why throw our men into the jaws of a fully armed battle camp if we do not need to? Why waste lives and weapons and even our chance of victory just because we're a bit bored? Come, this is how we have always succeeded, with information, cunning and patience. Think of this, my dear Fitz, as a siege. Just because we cannot see the enemy does not mean it is any less effective. Their corn will be rotting in their fields, their men fretting to be home, and the fighting season is almost done. They will believe we do not mean to attack this year.'

'Why would they believe that?'

'Because some of their spies are actually my spies,' William had told him with a wink.

He'd been enjoying the game then, using the chosen delay to train up his disparate groups of soldiers into a combined force, confident in the knowledge that the moment Harold disbanded his troops he was ready to strike. And it had been a good plan – until the storm.

It had blown up as they were sailing out of the shelter of the Dives and into the open sea, flinging rain and spray against the sides of the boats as they struggled east, as close to the shore as they dared, towards their meeting point at St Valery. Boats had been lost, more than anyone dared admit to, and although most of the fleet had finally battled their way into the relative calm of the Somme's mouth, Mathilda was sure that low tide all along that stretch of Normandy must reveal the skeletons of lost craft to the locals – hardly an inspiring omen for invasion.

She shivered and slunk lower into her own cloak, feeling no need for any show of defiance. Her boots were more mud than leather, her hair, rust-red, hung like rat's tails beneath her limp headdress, and every one of her gowns was sodden. The smell of wet wool hung permanently in the air, fusty and foul, and those lucky enough to have beds found them nearly as soggy as the earth. It was almost impossible to keep the grain dry so it was rotting before it could be ground and La Barbe's troop of waste-removers could hardly tell dung from mud in the swampy fields. Nothing, it seemed, was clear or dry or wholesome and the men were muttering louder and louder with each drear day.

She saw William look again to the weathercock but the bird's head was still set to the north, facing bravely into the teeth of the wind blowing from England. Even if any man would dare the waves that threw themselves in a perpetual tantrum onto the shore there would be no way of getting to England with the wind so determinedly in their faces. Even the spy boats were stranded so that William's stream of inform-ation – his campaign lifeblood – had dried up. Harold was gone from his camp on the southern shores, they knew that much, but no one knew where. The Viking could have attacked anywhere down the east coast and they would be none the wiser. Had the gamble of waiting turned against them? The pos-sibility was making everyone irritable and William most of all.

'I thought God was on our side,' he'd moaned to Mathilda as they'd huddled in bed together last night, their bodies finally warm, though the covers steamed.

'He is, William. This weather must have some purpose.'

'This weather is keeping us from England.'

'Then the time must not be right to go. Have faith.'

He'd kissed her.

'You are right, my Mora – you are always right. Do we not have the Pope's blessing?'

'We do.'

'And did we not dedicate our dear Cecily to God's service?'

'We did, William, and many others followed our example.'

It had been a fine day and Mathilda had thought she might burst with pride as Cecily, still only eight, had walked up to the altar of La Trinité in a pure white dress, flowers woven through her hair. She and William had been waiting there for her and William had taken her up in his arms before everyone and declared loudly that he was dedicating her to the Lord and

Cecily had smiled around, as composed as a child twice her age, as other young ladies had been ushered forward to join her.

Mathilda had been at great pains beforehand to explain to Cecily that she would come to La Trinité often to see her and that she would have lots of friends and learn wonderful things and Cecily had accepted all this easily. She was used, Mathilda had realised, to not seeing her mother for long periods when she travelled with William and her little room at La Trinité was a charm for her – a constant place that she could call her own.

She would share it with Mabel's daughter, Sibyl, and although that made Mathilda a little nervous she could only hope that if Sibyl shared her mother's interest in the natural world, she did not share her ruthless use of it. She'd glanced to Mabel that day and, for the briefest of moments, had been locked in maternal feeling with her. It had been a peculiar experience but life, it seemed, was more complicated than it looked when you were young.

The only issue had come when Cecily had asked, 'What happens, Mama, when it is time for me to marry?'

Mathilda had been forced to explain that if she went on to take full orders she would never marry.

'But how then,' Cecily had demanded, 'will I run my own household?'

Mathilda had kissed her.

'Maybe you can run the household at La Trinité, Cecily. Maybe you can be her abbess.'

'Abbess?' The little girl had rolled the word around her tongue, trying it out and, it seemed, liking it. 'Yes, I shall be that.'

Mathilda prayed she was right. There was no reason why she should not be, as long as Normandy stayed in William's hands, as long as he did not lose it on a fool's venture to another land. She shook herself. She must not think that way. Just because there were mutterings around the damp camp-fires did not mean she had to succumb too.

'Overreaching themselves, if you ask me,' she'd overheard one man saying to his fellows this morning as they fought to swallow soggy bread. 'What's wrong with being Duke of Normandy anyway?'

'You tell me, Luc. You signed up to this mission.'

'For all the joy I've had of it.'

'So far. Come, man, don't you want to bash the Saxons?'

Mathilda had crept away, grateful for the second man's positivity, but horrified by his attitude. Is that all this was about to them – a glorified tavern brawl? But then she'd reminded herself that it didn't matter how they felt as long as they helped William to win. Why should they care for promises and oaths and laws of succession? They cared only for food in their bellies, coin for their families and, it seemed, bashing the Saxons – if they ever got the chance.

The camp was strung out across the vast plains around the Somme estuary at St Valery and having reached the eastern edge, Mathilda turned to look back across the whole port, trying to picture it as it would have been when it was first built six hundred years ago, full of Roman trading vessels and yachts. It was perhaps not as far distant as she imagined for today St Valery was crammed with boats, albeit ones rough-hewn for war. Hugh's horse ships were moored in tight lines all along the stone walls at the river mouth, jostling each other in the winds as if as eager to be away as the men. There were one hundred and forty of them, newly built and designed to carry twenty knights and their mounts – nearly three thousand fine cavalry and all ready to go, if only the wind would turn.

The myriad other boats were a less regular lot. The richer craft were drawn up on the banks of the river around the *Mora*, still shining in the angrily iridescent rain. The rest were on the far bank, or held at anchor in the middle of the River Somme, fishing vessels alongside trading craft, alongside the new transport boats every man in Normandy seemed to have been crafting since their lords pledged to provide them back in January. They were simple boats, their only job to get soldiers over the Narrow Sea and hopefully, once victory was secured, back home again in triumph. That moment, though, seemed horribly far off.

'Will this wind never cease?' someone asked and she turned to see William coming towards her with Fitz, Fulk and Hugh in tow.

They ranged out at her side, peering at the mist-shrouded water as if they might somehow see all the way to the other shore, and Mathilda looked fondly at them. These were William's core men, the companions who had been with him all his reign – his bodyguard, his elite officers, his loyal supporters. They drew closer, a tight circle, every one of them a head taller than Mathilda who felt giddily enclosed within their damp, masculine formation.

She remembered the night she'd first met them all at Eu – Fitz bounding over like a puppy, great big Fulk being teased about Mabel, Hugh already caught in Emeline's spell, though they had not realised it at the time. They'd been boys then, eager and impetuous, convinced of their invincibility, and over the years they had proved themselves justified in that conviction. They had grown together into the men that now stood with their backs to the first Norman navy as the Narrow Sea lashed mercilessly at their dreams. They were more grizzled, perhaps, and more sober, but still invincible and desperate to prove it. All, perhaps, bar one.

La Barbe was joining them now, moving painfully slowly and leaning heavily on his stick, his son Robbie hovering solicitously at his side. Mathilda looked anxiously at her old friend. The chamberlain's back was stooped so he seemed nearly as short as her, and the lines in his gentle face were pronounced, as if some cruel force was etching them deeper in with every dark day.

'Roger – you are not well.'

'I am not *ill*, my lady, but no, I am not well. I will be little use in battle, I fear, save perhaps to organise the supply carts.'

No one spoke. The truth of this statement was too plain and they had never been men to duck the truth.

'I release you, Roger,' William said.

'No.'

'Please. You have served Normandy loyally and well and will continue to do so but you are right – the frontline is no place for you and to put you there would endanger others.'

Mathilda flinched but Roger just bowed his head.

'I meant it about the supply carts,' he said quietly.

'It is an important role.'

Roger looked up at William and the two men's eyes met.

'Not that important,' Roger said sadly, 'but I will do it all the same.'

But now Robbie was stepping up at his father's side, standing taller than him and far straighter. Mathilda remembered his father pointing him out as a toddler in the rushes on her very first day in Normandy and now he was a man. Time had gone too fast; what if it was running out? She fought down the foolish thought. This is why women did not go to war. Men were far more focused on the fighting than the outcome, as Robbie was now proving.

'Let me go in your stead, Father,' he was begging. 'Please. I can fight, you know I can, and I am strong. I will carry your standard against the oathbreaker and your men will follow it.'

There was a long pause. The wind whipped across the

flatlands and between the men who stood watching La Barbe as he looked at his son, at his future. Finally he nodded, clasped Robbie's hand.

'You are a good boy – a good *man*. I will be proud for you to carry my standard. Though your mother,' he added wryly, 'may kill me for it far quicker than any Saxon.'

The men laughed, the tension broken, but William held up a hand.

'No Saxons will be killing any of us, or being killed by us either if this wind does not change. So, my lords, what do we do?'

His men looked back, unflinching.

'What *can* we do?' Fulk asked. 'We have to wait until the winds turn.'

'We could disband?'

'No!' Not a moment's hesitation.

'We've come this far,' Fitz said, 'so we must see it through.'

'The men are ready,' Roger agreed.

'The horses too.' Hugh.

'If we let them go now,' Fulk said, 'only half will return again in the spring. We must wait.'

'And pray,' William added. 'Let's call a service. It will draw the men together and we can speak to them – if I can make myself heard over this damned wind!'

They all nodded, clasped shoulders a moment, and then went off to organise their troops. There were some eight thousand men ranged down the estuary and clearly not all would be able to get into the church further up the river, or even in front of it, but at least inland it was slightly more sheltered so they might be able to hear the speakers better. Mathilda just prayed William could find the words to rouse the troops for they had been here for fourteen long, soggy days and by the looks of the skies they were not in for a break yet.

She traced her way wearily back to her pavilion where she found Emeline flapping her gowns in a desperate attempt to shake some of the moisture from them.

'Ruined,' she wailed when she saw Mathilda.

'It's just water, Em. Where's Cecelia?'

Emeline wrinkled her nose.

'She went for a walk. Something about seaweed and fishermen. I don't know what. I swear she's going dotty these days. Perhaps we should find her a husband?'

Mathilda laughed.

'A man is the answer to everything, is it, Em?'

'Of course not. They are fun though, are they not?'

'Not so much at the moment.'

'No. All Hugh does is fret over his precious horses. I swear he'd sleep in those stables of his if I let him, even though the roof leaks and it smells to high heaven.'

'They're beautiful horses.'

'They are that. Shame they have to go to war.'

'Em?'

Emeline turned away.

'I just worry, Mathilda. This isn't like a rebellion or a siege. This isn't even like defending against the French. We're the invaders this time and that's not something our men are used to. It's all new. Horses across the sea, foreign soil, pitched battles – Normans don't do that, so what if they *can't* do that?' She rubbed a hand across her forehead, as Mathilda watched, helpless. 'Oh, never mind me. I know the cause is just. It's this waiting, that's all – too much time to think.'

That was it exactly. All the heat and the passion and the drive had been taken out of the mission to England, sucked down into the mud of St Valery, and in its place doubt and fear had room to creep in.

'We are to have a service,' Mathilda said but just got a dull 'oh, good' in return and she turned thankfully as the flap lifted and Cecelia stepped inside, shaking water from her hem.

Seeing Mathilda she smiled a surprisingly broad smile and ran forward.

'I've been talking to fishermen, my lady.'

'You have?'

Mathilda raised an eyebrow; maybe Emeline was right and Cecelia did need a husband.

'Not like that! They are well versed, as you might imagine, in the matter of tides and winds . . .'

'Fascinating,' Emeline said.

'And *weather.*'

'Weather?' Mathilda looked at Cecelia more closely and even Emeline put down her gown and came over. 'And what do they say?'

'The seaweed pops, my lady.'

Emeline groaned.

'See, Mathilda – she's going dotty.'

'I'm not,' Cecelia said, putting impatient hands on her broad hips. 'They hang seaweed in a sheltered place. If it is moist it will rain . . .'

'No?!'

'Emeline, listen! It's to do with the moisture in the air. If it is dry, there will be no rain or *the rain is going to stop.*'

'And it is dry now?'

'Exactly. That's why the pods will pop. And there are sheep in the sky and the flies are gone.' Emeline spluttered. 'Sheep, Emeline. If you look to the west, you will see that not all the clouds are leaden any longer. Some are softer, woollier – empty of water.'

'And the flies?' Mathilda questioned, intrigued.

'Flies come lower when there are rainclouds so if they disappear it means they are happy back up in the sky again, or so they tell me. It may not be entirely accurate but all the signs are there – the weather is turning. The rain is stopping and the winds will shift round.'

'When, Cee?'

'Soon. Tonight, most likely. Dusk, they tell me, is when most changes occur.'

'They have told you a lot,' Emeline said, grudgingly impressed. 'How peculiar.'

'How wonderful,' Mathilda corrected her. 'I must find William – now. Come along, quick. We can use this, don't you see? We can use this to draw the men out of the mud.'

'Are you gone dotty too, Mathilda?' Emeline gasped as Mathilda pulled them both outside where she could swear the rain was already dissolving into a half-hearted drizzle.

'No,' Mathilda said cheerfully. 'On the contrary, I feel sane for the first time in days. To the church!'

She found William as swiftly as she was able in the crowds but he thought her mad too when she made her suggestion.

'A procession, Mathilda?'

'Of St Valery's bones, William, yes, to ask God's blessing on us and his assistance with the weather.'

'Yes, yes, I see that but Mathilda . . .' He pulled her aside, his voice lowered to a harsh whisper. 'What if it doesn't work?'

'It will work.'

'How do you know?'

'Seaweed,' she said with a grin.

'Seaweed?' he echoed faintly, but he did as she asked.

Slowly the men gathered along the open river bank, shuffling reluctantly into two lines running out from the stone church.

'What'll that old saint do?'

'God's given up on us anyway.'

'We'd be better off at home.'

Mathilda ran around supervising the lifting of the casket holding St Valery's holy remains and Odo, ever one for drama, mustered all his clerics into their best robes to create a decent show. In all the fuss few noticed that the rain had more or less stopped and that far out at sea the water was, for the first time in ages, an optimistic green. William, however, was one of the few.

'Seaweed?' he whispered again to Mathilda as they prepared to walk solemnly behind the casket, the papal banner before them, a little worn but flapping proudly in the lighter wind.

'Local lore,' she whispered back. 'Signs of change.'

'Not God's hand?'

'God's hand is in all things, Husband. All we are doing here is showing that to those who find it harder to understand.'

William shook his head.

'You've always been the clever one, Mathilda.'

'And you the brave. You will be able to sail now. Are you ready?'

He took her hand, tucking it into his arm as the procession began to move forward, the men cheering despite themselves at Odo's grand show.

'I am ready, Mathilda. I have been ready, I think, all my life – now I just need to make it happen.'

It was hailed as a miracle. The procession was barely halfway down the river bank when the clouds parted and a shaft of sunlight fell, not on the saint himself – that would, perhaps, have been too much to ask – but upon the boats moored mid-river, as if lighting their way forward at last.

''Tis a sign – a sign!'

'God blesses us!'

'The time has come.'

The men snatched at the good omen like starving creatures

at bread. They would need no dragging from the mud, Mathilda realised, for they were keen to scramble from it and needed only the slightest encouragement to do so. St Valery was hailed all the way up the river and back and no sooner was he safely returned to his rest in the church than men were running to sharpen their weapons and polish what armour they had. And then, as dusk settled in a thin line of pink across the camp, the weathercock on the church creaked, sighed almost, and swung slowly and deliberately round to the south.

'We sail tomorrow,' William declared and then the frenzy really began.

William ordered the cooks to make a feast with all they had left and stews bubbled in vast pots over fires that flared at last, as if keen to finally show their true colours. He ordered barrels broached and the men, bellies full and heads swimming, swung as easily as the weathercock from grumbling to anticipation. There was far less talk of God's displeasure around the huddled groups and far, far more of bashing the Saxons, and the Norman camp finally settled to sleep a happier, more positive place than it had been since it had limped into St Valery over two weeks ago.

For Mathilda relief quickly gave way to fear. The men were going into action at last but for her and her ladies it would mean more waiting and she dreaded it.

'I could still come,' she said to William when he finally crept into bed in the early hours of the morning.

'And wait on a hostile shore instead of your own? You are not coming into battle, Mathilda.'

'No. This fat belly would hinder my sword stroke!'

William kissed her.

'You will be busy, my love. Life does not stop for battles and Normandy needs you. Robert needs you. He could be a good duke but he is, I fear, a little spoiled. He thinks too much of his own pleasure so you must help him harden to his duties.'

'He asked me the other day if he would get to be King of England.'

'If he does,' William growled, 'it will be by my hard work.'

'I told him as much. But William, would you prefer him to have to fight as you have? As you will?'

There was a pause as William considered. Mathilda lay, feeling his body warm and strong against hers and listening to the collective snorting breaths of eight thousand soldiers on the brink of war.

'I would not prefer it,' William said eventually. 'Of course I would not. Why would I wish a reign of endless challenge and uncertainty on my sons? Have I not battled for the security we have now?'

'Always. And yet . . . ?'

'And yet I fear that not having to do so will make him soft and his brothers besides.'

'Is soft so bad?'

'I'm not sure.'

His voice snagged and she held him, crawling tight against him and pushing her arms as far around his big body as she could reach. There was a seven year old in him still, lost and unsure.

'You are not alone, William,' she told him urgently. 'You have good men at your back and you have me. We are loyal to the cause because we know it to be just and we are loyal to you because we know you are worth that loyalty.'

'Truly?'

'And because we love you. Now sleep. Tomorrow is a big day.'

'Sleep, Mathilda . . . ?'

'William!'

'One last time?'

'No!'

'But . . .'

'I mean, William, that it will not be the last time – just the last time until you are king.'

CHAPTER THIRTY-SIX

Hastings, 14 October 1066

It's dawn. Mathilda likes the dawn. She says the sky is painted with promise at dawn. She says things like that, my wife; things that sound as if they mean so much but actually tell you nothing. How can the sky be painted with promise? And yet today, as I stand here in the pink mist rising up off Saxon soil, I hope it is true. Today I am aware more than ever before of tomorrow's dawn and what it will bring. For the sun will surely rise over me, be that as king or corpse, and I do not want to be a corpse. There's so much still to do.

I glance along the lines – thousands of men stood to arms and all awaiting my command. It is a moment of almost beautiful calm. The preparations are done and we are ready. Normandy's new navy sailed and landed safely in the Roman harbour of Pevensey where Hugh's horse ships could unload unmolested by even local resistance. We set up camp as easily as if it were a hunting trip and not an invasion, but then, Harold was in the north fighting the Viking, just as we'd hoped.

He won. I'll admit that surprised me. At some place called Stamford Bridge he killed the great Hardrada and his treacherous brother Tostig too – not that he was any loss to the world. I imagine even his poor wife did not weep at his passing. Mathilda would weep at mine these days, I think – not that I intend to give her the chance.

Harold's swift return to the south surprised me but his haste, heroic as it was, may be his undoing. I can just about see his ranks above us on the ridge and I'd say we're evenly matched. That's more than we could have hoped for. There may be reinforcements coming of course but for now it is a good sign, a promise in the sky perhaps – though it is very much on land that we will fight today.

Next to me Fitz draws his sword, impatient as ever, and the sound focuses my mind. Now is not the time to dawdle in the past or dream into the future. Now is about now. Battles are won by calm and logic and sense. These men, these thousands of men who have sailed to England out of duty, excitement, greed, revenge and all manner of motivations of their own, are my tafel pieces today and I must arrange them as best I can to win the advantage. For now I cannot see them as men, not even loyal Fitz at my side, or big Fulk leading the left flank with Roger's brave young son, or my brother Odo on the right, but as pieces in the game. If one falls it must be replaced. There will be time to mourn afterwards.

I look up. The sun is over the horizon to our right and the field is lit up before us, green and innocent. The Saxons are on foot, not a cavalryman amongst them, despite what Harold saw of their efficiency when he campaigned with us in Brittany. More fool him to still fight on foot with his peasants. They are too sentimental, these Saxons. I can use that.

I can see Harold's 'fighting man' banner in the centre, his brothers' either side. The southerners, I am told, the Kentish men, are on the left beneath Harold's younger brother. They are not used to fighting and may be a weakness; they can perhaps be drawn from the precious shield wall that lines the ridge from end to end. They plan to defend, which is wearisome of them, but it makes this a besieging and besieging I know well. What difference is a shield wall to a castle wall, save that it will crumble more easily?

I look along my lines again, see my bold commanders on their fine horses, all fresh from their sea trip thanks to Hugh's Italian ships. What chance do the Saxons have against such superiority? And yet every one of these men knows, as I know, that we have never fought a battle like this. Even at Varaville we won more by trickery than outright skill and in truth, this is the first full battle I have properly commanded. I must do it well – I owe my men that much.

It is speech time. I do not like it, do not see the need to remind men why we are here and what there is to win, for they surely know it themselves, but it seems it helps so I fling out the usual phrases about honour and pride and glory and winning land for their sons and by the end they are all roaring with bloodlust. The sound is loud enough to cover the heart-drum 'Ut, Ut, Ut!' of the barbarian Saxons. Out, out, out – never! I am here now and I intend to stay. Let battle commence.

It is hot work. The sun, though autumn-low, is large and warm. The horses pant and I fear for their stamina but Hugh has a great run of the lower ranks bringing water from a pond behind us and the beasts are well refreshed between charges. They work hard but, I must admit, with little gain.

'We cannot break them,' Fitz gasps as the sun climbs to the top of Mathilda's precious sky.

'Patience,' I tell him. 'Come, muster – let's go again.'

I lead the charge myself this time, feel the pulse of the very earth beneath me as a thousand hooves pound up the slope towards the huddled Saxons in their paltry human castle. Blood rushes in my veins but I hold my lance steady and

Caesar on an even course until suddenly, as we reach top speed, another animal, more skittish than mine, rears away from a Saxon arrow and crashes sidelong into my flank.

Caesar's back legs are knocked and he staggers, collides with another horse and bolts, flinging me from his back so I land in the mud and can only cover my head and pray to God that I am not crushed by my own cavalry. A gasp of horror – not mine – runs across my ranks, whispering over my head like a pain but I cannot stand, not yet. It is not safe.

'The duke,' I hear. 'The duke is dead.'

It is spoken in Norman at first and then, louder, in Saxon. The words grow in volume and when finally I look up, I see the shield wall straining, especially at the end where the less experienced Kentish men are bursting for an easy victory and starting to break ranks. Perfect. I get slowly to my feet, my head low. I can hear Fitz and Fulk calling order and the horses pulling back into formation and am delighted to see discipline is holding in my Norman ranks. Unlike the Saxons'.

I smile and then, just as their left end breaks and the undisciplined infantry begin to charge, I whip off my helmet and stand tall, as tall as I can, and I am seen. I am seen by Hugh, who charges forward and leaps from his horse to proffer it to me. It is nobly done by my cavalry captain and I have a moment to clap him on the back before I leap high into the saddle to cries of '*Le Duc, le Duc, le Duc!*' With renewed energy our ranks surge in on the fool Saxons who have run into the open field and cut them down.

I control my new mount and look out across the Saxon ranks as all eyes are drawn to their falling comrades – or not quite all. For there he is, Harold, looking straight at me, as well he might. We lock eyes. *It didn't need to be like this,* I try and tell him. *You should be at my side, not against me. We could have done so much that way. We still could. Surrender,* I will him.

Surrender now and I will be merciful. But he will not read my message and will not compromise. He rips his eyes from mine and turns to his men.

'Hold the wall!' I hear him cry and I know that the moment for surrender, if ever it was there, is gone.

I retreat with Hugh to regroup the cavalry and reset the archers, who are doing a fine job. Those days at Pevensey and then at Hastings were well spent for we have arrows aplenty. Sadly most of the Saxon wall has obeyed Harold and stayed put but we have had the first real blood of the day and it lifts our hearts. And there is more, for the gap on the left end is not filled. Harold has no reinforcements it seems and that information is more vital to me than the mini-victory. All we need now is patience. All we must do is maintain discipline and keep up the cavalry attacks and they will falter. And so we do.

It is long and hard and wearying. Men fall. The green field fills up with bodies, ugly heaps of flesh that make the horses stumble. Blood runs between the crushed blades of grass, making each charge slippier and more dangerous than the last. Hugh's ranks bring more water and men and horses drink desperately from the same buckets. There is food but few want it for the very air is putrid as men claw it into their straining lungs. The banners, even the holy papal one, are spattered and torn. Men lean upon each other nursing wounds. Spirits are dipping as fast as the sun and for the first time I feel fear. The Saxons are not giving up and we must win. We must win today for who knows what further Saxon ranks are even now marching upon the field and we have nothing at our backs save the merciless sea.

I pull my commanders together.

'We must draw them out, split them as we did when I fell. We must smash their damned wall; it's the only way.'

'But how?' Fitz asks.

He has taken a cut to the head and the right side of his face is scarlet with caked blood. For one terrible moment I see in him his father, red in my bed and screaming for his soul, but I force it away. I have no time for memories. I must think. The Saxons hover still on the ridge, jeering at us, trying to draw us on again, but they will not attack so I have time. I need calm, logic, sense, for that is how battles are won. I force myself to breathe slowly. What does Mathilda tell the children – 'You must sharpen your wits.' Now I must sharpen mine.

'They broke ranks before when they believed I was dead, when they thought they had the upper hand. If they think that again, they will come.'

Fulk's eyes shine.

'A feigned retreat?'

'It would be hard. Controlling the horses is not easy. I would need skilled men.'

A Breton steps forward, a stout little man known as Count Alan Ironglove, and clearly someone with an eye for a chance of advancement.

'My men have the skill, Duke.'

It is true. I saw it for myself at Dol. The Breton horses are smaller and stouter than ours, like Count Alan himself, but they are nimble and the Saxons may believe the Breton loyalty could waver. Harold, who fought against them at my side, may well believe that. I glance at the skyline to the left where the sun is flinging itself towards the earth. There is no time to dispute further.

'It is decided then. We charge, you break, and if they come after you we encircle them.'

'And if they do not?'

'They will.' There is no room for doubt now. For this to work it must be done with total conviction. 'They will come.'

*

And they do. In the end it is easy, so easy that I wonder we did not manage it before, though no doubt the fading light and fading strength of the men has something to do with it. I lead the charge, the men fanning out behind me like one of our own deadly arrowheads, Fulk's on the right and Count Alan leading the Bretons on the left. We hold the fight as long as the horses will bear and then I catch Alan's eye over the flailing swords and spears between us and he gives the slightest of nods and screams a command.

Suddenly his men are peeling away and pounding off down the slope and our other ranks pause and watch as if dismayed, though in truth we are merely straining to see how, at such speed, the Bretons will pull their sturdy little mounts around if it is needed. And it is. The Saxons pour after them like grains of corn from a ripped sack. I hear Harold's voice, hoarse and desperate – 'hold the wall' – but they are not listening. He has lost command. In that moment he has lost command and lost England and I know, with still certainty, that the day will be mine.

The rest is but a training exercise, only with blood – so much blood that after a while we cease to notice it. Is that callous? No, it is honest. Truth is a habit of mine, though some do not appreciate it. My senses shut down as I watch the Bretons encircle their pursuers even as Harold's housecarls encircle him, ready for their last stand. My nostrils close themselves to the stench of death, my ears shut out the sounds of unending pain, my tongue refuses to taste the Saxons' fear. My fingers feel only the reins of my borrowed horse as I hold her in check so I can monitor my gaming pieces. My eyes see only the patterns of victory in the gory mass of limbs all around.

Calm logic, sense – they are what win battles, but I confess I cannot stop a thrill running through me as an arrow arcs across Mathilda's sky of promise and I hear Harold roar in pain at the centre of his ever-dwindling band of men and I know I have him. I turn from his death. I wish it hadn't been this way. I wish he'd acknowledged my right as he'd sworn to do. I wish that he'd surrendered earlier in the battle before this senseless waste of life on both sides. I wish it for two reasons – the first because I liked the man; the second because England is going to be so, so much harder to rule without him.

But rule it seems I will. They are bringing me the crown. It is tarnished with blood but I can hardly wipe it away when all around men are suffering so much worse, so I take it and place it as it is on my head, ignoring the stickiness of death at its edges. I did not choose this fight; it was forced upon me. But God was at my back and the day is won and I am, somehow, King of England.

I look at Fitz and he grins the infectious grin he's been giving me all my life and then he throws himself flamboyantly down on one knee before me.

'God bless the King!'

The men take up the chant and all around they drop to the bloody ground in prostrated lines blurred at the edges by the darkness as the mist blurred them this morning at first light. Tomorrow's dawn will come now, I think, and it will be mine, and a giddy, skipping, ridiculously glorious happiness rushes through me. I grab Fitz, raising him.

'Send to Normandy,' I command. 'Send to Normandy and to Mathilda. Tell her I have made her the queen she was bred to be. Tell her that England is ours.'

CHAPTER THIRTY-SEVEN

Bonneville, March 1067

William bounced onto the jetty and came running towards Mathilda, so light on his feet he was almost dancing. He swooped in and picked her up, lifting her high in the air in front of everyone, then clasping her tight to him and kissing her long and hard to whoops of joy from the vast crowd fanning out across the open port.

'William!' Mathilda giggled as he finally let her go and turned, arm still firmly around her waist, to wave to the crowd, beaming and giving funny little bobbing bows to people who caught his eye. 'What have you done with my husband?'

William kissed her again.

'I have made him King of England, my Mora.'

'It suits him.'

It did. Mathilda had never seen William so relaxed, so happy in himself, so at ease with the crowds crushing forward to welcome him. She watched him shaking endless hands, nodding and smiling and chatting – yes, chatting – to all his well-wishers and hurried after him, marvelling at this new man who had finally come back to Normandy from over the Narrow

Sea. He was being proclaimed as a conquering hero and here he was, every inch the part. She felt her loins stir.

'I have never been bedded by a king,' she whispered in his ear.

She saw his body react first and then he glanced over his shoulder, a wicked silver gleam in his dark eyes.

'Oh, you will be,' he promised. 'For I long to be bedded by a queen.'

'Not yet crowned.'

'No,' he allowed with a grimace. They had both wanted her to make it to Westminster for his coronation at Christ's mass fifteen years to the day after they had been promised the throne, but the seas had been rough and with Mathilda newly out of her childbed it had not been possible. 'But you will be.'

'When, William? When can I come to England with you?'

For a moment he looked strangely unsure, then he smiled so swiftly and widely that she thought she'd imagined it.

'Very soon, my love.'

'This summer?'

'That would be perfect, wouldn't it?'

It wasn't really an answer.

'Is all well in England?'

'Becoming so, yes. Fitz and Odo have it all in hand, I'm sure.' He didn't sound sure. 'But come, I am back. I am here in Normandy and everyone is so glad to see me.'

He looked around almost incredulously and Mathilda slid closer.

'You are glad to be home, Husband?'

For a moment Mathilda thought she saw a tear in his eye.

'I think I have never been gladder.'

'Your mother would have been so proud.'

'She would. I hope she is looking down from heaven to see her bastard son acclaimed a king. Oh yes, Mathilda, it is good to be home.' He looked all around again and Mathilda saw him draw in deep, gulping breaths of Norman air, almost as if he might drown for its lack. 'Oh, and I have news for you – your cousin, Judith, who was sadly widowed by the oath-breaker . . .'

'Yes,' Mathilda prompted eagerly, for she had thought often of Judith and wondered how she fared alone in bleak St Omer.

'She is to wed again, to a Lord Wulf of Bavaria in the German empire. He is, I hear tell, a quiet, kindly man with a great interest in art. He met Judith in Rome and when she became free he moved swiftly to claim her hand. She goes gladly, I am told.'

Mathilda's heart swelled.

'That is joyous news indeed, William, thank you. But who has told you this – your spies?'

'My well-informed messengers, Wife,' he corrected with a wink and now her bouncing husband was turning and exclaiming, 'And look, here are my children, my wonderful princes and princesses,' and to Mathilda's great surprise, he dropped to his knees, his arms wide.

There was a breathtaking moment of hesitation and then Cecily, freed from La Trinité for this great occasion, stepped into his embrace and suddenly he was saying her name and holding her close as Maud and Constance squirmed in too. Eventually he stood, one smaller girl on each hip and Cecily close and now Rufus and Richard bundled into him as Robert stood more self-consciously to one side.

'Robert!' William said, somehow releasing a hand to shake his eldest son's. 'You have cared for Normandy well in my absence – she looks glorious.' Mathilda heard a small catch in his voice and thought again that he might cry but he composed himself and looked around once more, his eyes roaming over the cheering crowds and up to the ducal palace on the hill above, before returning to his family. 'And I hear I have a new daughter too?'

'You do.'

Mathilda reached back to the wet-nurse, an older lady who had not approved of taking the baby out into the cold spring air and the rough crowds. Mathilda had defied her, insisting the girl must be there for her royal father's homecoming, and she was glad now that she had. William put the other two down and took the baby tenderly in his arms where she looked so small and soft, cradled against his chainmail. He dropped a kiss on her pink forehead.

'What have you called her, Wife?'

'Adela.' He raised an eyebrow. 'To honour my mother and her lost sister.'

'Quite right – we should not forget our past.' Mathilda raised an eyebrow at him but he just smiled again. 'She came easily?'

'Easily enough and in good time. She is healthy and well, William. We are blessed.'

He kissed her and she could not help but remember the harsh night right here, in Bonneville, after they had lost their first little Adela to Spanish fever and so nearly lost William too. Thank heavens he was home with her.

Hugh had come back briefly in January, bringing news of William's glorious coronation, but had sailed again after less than two weeks, pleading anxiety for stabling of the warhorses he was busily rehousing in rich new pastures at somewhere called Leicester. He had taken Emeline with him and Mathilda had longed to go too but she'd still been recovering from the birth and, besides, Hugh had told her that William was planning this trip home and she had wanted to make everything ready for him.

'I hope you have ordered a great feast, Mathilda,' William said now, 'and food and wine for all.'

'Wine, William? It is Lent.'

He waved a careless hand as Raoul or Fitz might.

'Not tonight. Tonight God forgives us our fast for he has granted us glory and we must honour that with joy.'

Mathilda nearly fell over. William had ever been rigorous about Lenten fasting, embracing its privations gladly as, in truth, they suited his own strict discipline better than the looser ease of the rest of the year. Until now.

'I shall see to it, William,' she stuttered, gesturing gratefully to Cecelia, who nodded and slipped off towards the fortress to issue orders to the kitchens and the cellars.

There would be a scramble but a welcome one for no one would be sorry to drop their fast, especially on their duke's orders. The cheering grew even wilder.

'It is a joy to celebrate with my own people,' William roared, leaping onto a crate to address the crowd.

His eyes strayed briefly down the jetty where Mathilda saw a group of stiff-backed Saxons huddled with Fulk standing over them like a colossus. William's messengers had told her he was bringing some key lords with him 'to share the celebrations of our union' but the surly faces on the men – more prisoners, she saw now, than guests – did not suggest that they saw this as anything worth celebrating. She stepped back a little from the rocking crowd to see them more clearly.

The one in archbishop's robes must be Stigand, apparently the first cleric to submit to William at the end of last year. He, at least, looked relaxed and interested in the scenes before him. At his side, however, a lanky youth, all limbs, was glaring out from beneath greasy, overlong hair and Mathilda assumed he must be Edgar, the 'aetheling', the one whose father Mabel may or may not have poisoned. She'd felt sorry for him back then but he was not now being at all gracious in defeat.

Beyond were two tall men, still young but fierce-looking.

They were both watching William intently, their bodies rigid as if poised to spring and their faces dark with the knowledge that to do so would be death. These must be the northern earls Edwin and Morcar, brothers to the upstart girl who had been briefly queen and was now fled somewhere leaving her throne for Mathilda. They did not look happy about it and as Mathilda turned back to William, bouncing on the crate as merrily as if he'd drunk half a jug of Bordeaux, she saw suddenly how hard it must have been – must, indeed, still be – in England.

The news at this end had been largely positive, reports of victory after victory. True, the first information that London had not submitted after the great battle had been a blow but after that it had been a run of submissions – Romney, Dover, Canterbury. Then places she had not heard of – Wallingford, Berkhamsted. William, finding his way into London barred, had circled the capital, putting up a ring of castles so that the towns all submitted as he went. It was only a matter of time, the messengers had assured her, before London itself gave way and at last, in December, as ice blew across Normandy, it had. Edgar had bowed the knee to William, the northern earls shortly after, and her husband had ridden into Westminster in triumph.

Triumph, yes, that's definitely what they had told her and Mathilda, fresh from her eighth childbed, had pictured West-minster as she'd seen it back in '51, trying to add in Edward's new abbey and palace, apparently so like Jumièges that it was a natural home for William. She'd imagined her husband rid-ing in full regalia and people lining the streets as they'd done when they had visited together.

She wasn't stupid. She hadn't imagined wild joy, but defin-itely curiosity, respect, acknowledgment. Had it not been that way? Had the coronation not, after all, been glorious? Now she came to think of it, there had been some mention of a fire, of disorder. She felt a sudden protective rush of sadness for her solemn husband, desperate to do his best for the new country of which he was so proud. Was William giddy here at Bonneville as much with relief as joy?

She pushed back through the crowd and stood beneath William, suddenly desperate to be with him. She tapped on his foot and he looked down from the crate, smiled, and then bent and took both her hands in his, hoisting her up at his side as easily as if she were little Constance.

'It has been hard, William?' she whispered.

He dipped his head to press his face into the softness of her neck.

'Hard,' he confirmed, so quietly she only just heard it. 'But it is done. England is ours and I am home.'

'Surely England is home now too?' she asked, but he was distracted by a question from the crowd and she got no answer.

It was a grand feast that night and the next and the next as William and Mathilda moved through Normandy in a victory parade that culminated in an Easter feast at Fécamp, the like of which no man had ever seen in Normandy. People flooded in from all over the duchy – lords and ladies in pavilions packed so tight against each other they looked almost like one vast, rainbow tent; visiting dignitaries keen to bend the knee to the rising powerforce in Europe; common people, sleeping in the streets to gain a position closest to the new king and queen; and traders and artisans from all over Europe, looking to profit from the ebullience of a nation.

Raoul d'Amiens came riding in with Queen Anne herself at his side, full of praise for William's endeavour and assurances of France's support. Mathilda saw William near burst with pride as he addressed Anne, one royal to another, assuring her that he had promised friendship to France as a new duke of just seven years old and that he would always stand by that.

'Loyalty is steadfast,' she heard him say from out of the darker reaches of their shared past. 'It chooses its allegiance and holds to it. It does not sway on the lightest of breezes.' It was so very true, however tainted it had seemed when she'd first heard him roar it at the rebellious townsfolk of Alençon. But they were out of those shadows now and need surely fear no more rebellion. Normandy was happy, everyone cried fealty to William, Fécamp was a whirl of colour and noise, and William lapped it all up.

On Easter morning Mathilda woke to find him at the window opening, still naked, looking out into the yard where already the noise of a thousand people breakfasting was rippling across the soft air.

'A fine sight,' she said, admiring the muscles in his back, the neat triangle down to his still trim waist, and the taut buttocks below.

He looked over and smiled gently.

'I was made my father's heir here,' he said, 'on Easter day 1035 – thirty-two years ago, Mathilda. I was seven years old and I thought it all a fine game. I saw only the fancy clothes and the feast I was to stay up late for and the new sword. Above all, the new sword. Little did I know, Mathilda, how often in the years ahead I would have to wield it.'

'Or how successfully you would do so.'

He came back across to the bed, sitting down on the edge.

'I may have to wield it more yet, my love.'

She looked into his eyes, all darkness.

'You are afraid?'

'The best things come from fear.'

She shook her head.

'No, William. The best things may be won by overcoming

fear, but they are best once the fear is gone. The best things come from joy and having you back with me is joy indeed.'

'Being back is joy.'

'Then let's make the most of it.'

'Oh, we will.' William smiled suddenly, a dangerously mischievous smile, and his eyes became pure silver.

'William?'

'What?'

'You are plotting. What are you plotting?'

'Plotting? Nothing, Wife.'

'You are. You look wicked.'

'Do I?' He rose and grabbed his tunic. 'Good. Now, come along, it is time to dress, my sweet one. We have church shortly and, though I would not mind it one bit, the people might be a little surprised if you processed to the altar in God's own finery.'

And with that he bounced to the door, leaving Mathilda to stare incredulously after her newly mercurial husband. She called quickly for Cecelia. She would need help dressing this morning for she intended to wear her wedding dress, the one he had surprised her with on her first ever night in Normandy. Wearing the indulgently rich fabric had made her feel like a duchess from the first moment she'd stepped out in it and now she wanted it to make her feel like a queen. Fitting into the gown, fifteen years and eight children after that first time, proved something of a challenge but luckily Cecelia's hasty stitches on her wedding day were there to unpick and William's broad smile when he saw her was all the reward she needed for the breath-squeezing grip of the laces.

'Very appropriate,' he said approvingly. 'Very appropriate indeed.'

'Appropriate?'

She'd been hoping for beautiful or even, maybe, slim, but he just grinned at her and offered his hand to escort her out to greet the court. All through the service he kept looking knowingly her way. All through the procession around Fécamp, for the people gathered in their thousands, and all through course after endless course of the Easter feast, he hugged his secret teasingly until she was almost helpless with curiosity.

And then, as the last of the wild boar was sucked from peoples' fingers with contented sighs, a fanfare sounded and two chefs came in from the far doors, proudly carrying a huge platter between them. They moved up the hall to 'ooh's of appreciation. Mathilda strained forward but not until they drew close to the top table could she see the beautiful pastry – an intertwined WM, dripping with nuts and honey and crowned top and bottom with gold leaf.

'You can scarce tell which is which!' she exclaimed.

'Exactly,' William agreed, rising at her side. 'I am not king because I won the battle or subdued the lords or built a tower in the middle of London, Mathilda, not in my heart. I am king because you are queen, and you are queen because I am king. We owe it to each other.'

Her eyes filled with tears.

'And we will enjoy it with each other,' she told him, 'and do it justice with each other.'

'We will.'

He reached down to wipe away her tears and for a moment the hall faded away and it was just the two of them, on the crest of a wave they had been riding for so long, looking out into a new future.

'This was your surprise, William?' she asked.

'This?' His eyes sparkled once more. 'No. No, not this.'

'Then . . . ?'

'Roger!'

La Barbe bobbed up, limping still but in a rather stylish way and with his moustache curled up at one side and down at the other in a wicked parody of himself. Mathilda laughed to see it but then he gestured to the back of the hall and with a flash, a great curtain was pulled back to reveal a troupe of minstrels maybe twenty strong. Mathilda gaped and looked to Raoul, sat along the table with Queen Anne, but he was just as surprised as her.

'I brought them with me from England,' William told her, his grin now almost splitting his face apart. 'They like dancing there, Mathilda, like it very much.'

'I remember,' she whispered, seeing again the riotous entertainments of '51, glimpsed out of the corner of her envious eyes as she was forced to retire with William to pray for the promise that Edward had finally given them and that now, at last, had come good. Her feet twitched.

'You would like to dance?'

She hesitated. The entwined WM was still before her, the honey-coating sparkling in the rush lights.

'No. No, I will stay with you and . . .'

'You would like to dance?'

She caught his tone and looking up saw he was holding out his hand and moving towards the edge of the dais. Her heart filled up as if someone had poured a bucketful of love straight into it.

'With you?'

He shrugged, suddenly, beautifully self-conscious.

'I have been practising, Mathilda.'

Of course he had.

'Then I would love to.'

She put her hand in his and he led her forward as the chefs scrambled out of their way, and the minstrels struck a chord, and the whole Norman court rose around the edges of the great hall and watched them step out together.

Mathilda saw Cecelia, hands clasped delightedly; Roger, his arm around Della as they looked on like benevolent parents; and Fulk, his big hand holding Mabel's slim one, ready to join them. She thought of Hugh and Emeline, setting their Norman horses to grass in England, rich with a strain of Italian blood from their previous travels together. She thought of Odo, the world's most unlikely bishop and now lord of all Kent; and of Fitz, loyal, good-hearted Fitz who had skidded up to greet her for the first ever time and was now holding the regency of the most ancient land in Christendom on their behalf. She looked to her children, a beautiful clutch of seven whose future she and William had surely just secured forever, and the love in her heart tipped over, unsettling her balance so that she fell gratefully into the strong, steady, constant hold of her husband, William – king to her queen.

She closed her eyes and felt the insistent thud of his heart against her heart, the light turn of the reel lifting her high onto her richly slippered toes, the sweeping assurance of the strongest of arms. He had practised and now he excelled, as he always excelled.

'You are too good for me, my lady.'

The words whispered across her cheek like butterflies, trailing blushes.

'I am not,' she insisted, for it was true.

Yes, she was Lady Mathilda, eldest daughter of the great Count Baldwin and aunt of King Phillipe of France, but he was Duke William, son of the founding line of Normandy and of a woman of true nobility. Yes, she was Lady Mathilda, once destined for a great match, linking Flanders with an advantageous land, but he was the man who had offered her that match and she could never thank God enough for her hard-soft husband, now King of England.

'You dance well, William.'

He smiled at that and his fingers tightened certainly around her own. He lifted her closer to his broad chest and then, with a low laugh that laced deliciously through the feast-smoked air, spun her until her royal blood pulsed against her skin as if trying to escape and her own laughter burst from her lips in heady joy. This was better even than being queen and she knew she could dance forever with this man.

The rush of the reel, like the rush of their life together, was a potion stronger than any wine. He leaned down and kissed her, not in the way kisses were giggled over in the bower, all frenzy and moisture, but more as if his words ran along the curve of her mouth and disappeared again into the press of other dancers.

'My Mathilda, my Mora, my queen.'

EPILOGUE

Jumièges Abbey, Spring 1067

'And is it just like that?'

Mathilda raised a hand to the magnificent abbey, glowing in the spring sunshine in the valley below them, and tried to imagine a similar building in place of the rickety old London church in which she had celebrated a tense Christ's mass fifteen long years ago. She could still picture the old buildings on Thorney Island, rough and worn but so very, very sure of themselves. She could still see the great hall, rich with festive greenery and full of the bobbing blonde heads of their Saxon cousins, now her subjects. She could still see Emeline dancing and that young guard rescuing the girl from the horse and King Edward leaning over a brazier like an everyday neighbour and promising them the throne. It had been a long road from that day and one that had felt, at times, impossible, but at last they had reached their destination.

'Like that only grander,' William assured her. 'The new Westminster Abbey is a beautiful building, Mathilda. It honours God greatly and I cannot think of a richer place to see you crowned Queen of England.'

Queen of England!

She remembered her father talking of such a possibility

when she, fool girl, had been trying to refuse William's suit. She had thought Baldwin mad but in fact he had seen clearer than most. He had been to visit recently, old now but propped up with pride. He was not long for this world, she feared, but he would leave it content and she was glad to have been a part of that.

'See, Maud,' he'd said, 'I told you Duke William would make a good husband for you.'

'You did, Father.' She'd kissed him. 'And you were right.'

A tiny, still youthful part of her had baulked at the words but she'd chased it away. Count Baldwin *had* been right. William had matched her all the way for determination and ambition and drive and any day now she would step onto the *Mora* at last to sail to her new kingdom.

She turned to the north but the Narrow Sea was too far away to see. No matter. The boats were almost ready to carry William and his still-surly Saxon 'guests' home and she was to go too. She would be crowned at Whitsun and could begin to get to know her new people and their ways. It would be a challenge but she was ready. She and William had brought Normandy a long way in their years here, despite their subjects forever petulantly rebelling. England would, pray God, be far more stable and Mathilda would finally be able to focus less on holding power and more on developing it with art and culture. Judith, safe in her new Bavarian home, would be proud of her.

She looked back to the abbey.

'It has been a hard path to travel, William.'

'Not really, for I have had you at my side and that has made everything easy.'

More tears. She batted at them.

'William – you old romantic!'

He grinned and opened his arms and she stepped gladly into them, turning her face up to his for a kiss, but as she did so a cry echoed up the hillside. They turned reluctantly to see La Barbe riding towards them.

'Goodness,' William grumbled, 'can we have no time alone?'

But his chamberlain was closer now and they could both see his horse frothing with the hard pace he was driving and the stiff determination in the line of his usually loose shoulders. William's hands tightened around Mathilda's back and her own, against his chest, thrummed with the drum-beat of his heart.

Roger reined his horse in and leaped down before them.

'What is it?' William asked. 'What's wrong?'

Roger looked from William to Mathilda and back to William again, his eyes black.

'I have had word from Fitz,' he said hoarsely. 'It is rebellion, Lord King. Rebellion in England.'

HISTORICAL NOTES

Many readers ask me why I write historical fiction and I will admit that there are times in both the research and planning stages of my writing that I ask myself the same question. The answer, of course, is that I am fascinated by past lives and by the shape our ancestors' decisions and actions have imposed upon our own, but writing from 'real life' does carry a huge responsibility. I live in almost constant terror of getting something wrong and am very well aware that I will have done so somewhere in this and other novels.

I research as exhaustively as I am able but there will always be more to know and at some point I have to stop looking up history and start writing my story. I hope readers will forgive me any minor errors and am always happy to hear from anyone with greater knowledge than my own. For now, however, here are a few notes on areas I found especially interesting or wished to explain further than is possible within the story.

*C*haracter *D*etails

Lord Brihtric

The novel opens with Mathilda's 'dalliance' with Lord Brihtric and this liaison is a documented fact – or, at least, a documented rumour. Brihtric Mau (Snow – for his blondeness) was, as portrayed here, a wealthy English landowner with big estates around Tewkesbury. He travelled to the Flemish court in the mid-1040s and, according to the Chronicle of Tewkesbury, got himself involved in a minor scandal in which he and Mathilda, who was about sixteen years old, grew so close that when he had to return to England she sent an envoy after him, offering herself in marriage.

Brihtric did not take her up on this generous offer. Clearly understanding that ambitious Count Baldwin would not look favourably upon such a lowly match for his eldest daughter, he stayed well out of the way. Accounts suggest that Mathilda was madly in love with Brihtric and whilst such tales are almost certainly exaggerated it is more than possible that her concerned father decided to marry her off before she did anything else foolish. William was an ambitious young man on the lookout for a bride and the match seemed perfect to all, bar pining Mathilda. And so our story began . . .

Herleva, the 'tanner's daughter'

Herleva (or Herleve, or Arlette, depending on sources) has gone down in history as the daughter of 'Fulbert the Tanner'. Tanners were the tradesmen who cured the hides of beasts to turn them into workable leather and as this was done largely by soaking them in urine they were considered the lowest of the low and kept to their own rather smelly areas of town.

There is little record of Fulbert, but what we do have notes him as a ducal chamberlain. This was not necessarily a high office but it does indicate that he was a man of some import in Falaise and not just a lowly tradesman. It is likely, therefore, that he was more of a fur-trader than an actual workman and that although he may have had dealings with tanners he was not one himself. 'Furrier', however, does not make such an effective insult and so was conveniently forgotten by history. Certainly it seems a well-known story that the men of Alençon received the harsh treatment they did after hanging hides over the walls and abusing William's mother as a 'tanner's daughter'.

Whatever her father's actual profession, Herleva was certainly not a noble and was a royal mistress solely on account of her beauty. Duke Robert probably had other mistresses but he seems to have favoured Herleva, especially after she'd borne him William. Certainly he cared enough to ensure her a comfortable future by marrying her off to Herluin de Conteville, a well-born Norman nobleman. There is some suggestion that Robert was in negotiations to marry Estrith, sister to King Cnut, and this may have motivated him to see Herleva securely settled. It may also have prompted the pilgrimage which ultimately killed him, leaving William as his only son.

William seems to have genuinely loved his mother and to have promoted both her and her family at court, offering various maternal relations high office and great lands. He shows no signs of having been ashamed of her or of giving in to any criticism of her – as the men of Alençon found out to their cost!

William, 'the bastard'

William is often spoken of as William 'the bastard', a derogatory term gleefully embraced by the Saxons in preference to the more glorious epithet of William 'the conqueror'. That said, William was called 'the bastard' before the conquest, more a point of fact than an insult, though he does seem to have been rather sensitive to it, reacting violently to slights. He also, perhaps more tellingly, remained notoriously – and unusually – faithful to his wife.

His sensitivity is interesting, for in the pre-1066 period it was far from unusual to be born to a mistress or handfast wife – indeed both Harold of Wessex and Harald Hardrada had such sons – and it is one of the intriguing features of poor William's life that he seems to have been so vilified for his birth.

It is probable that he was simply born in the wrong place and at the wrong time. From the mid-eleventh century there was a huge movement of church reform from the papacy. Indeed, the Council of Rheims at which William and Mathilda's match was banned (for very political reasons, as described in the novel) was largely concerned with stamping out simony (buying offices), pushing for church marriages, and persuading the clergy into celibacy.

William was born at the start of a zealous move towards a far more moral and monogamous way of life and Normandy was at the heart of that reform. Ironically William giving his duchy the prosperity to embark upon a huge, pious programme of abbey building – very much encouraged by himself and Mathilda – may have fostered an atmosphere in which the circumstances of his own birth were held against him far more than they would ever have been before.

Mabel de Belleme, the poisoner

Readers could be forgiven for assuming Mabel de Belleme is a creation of my own but she was in fact a real noblewoman and genuinely seems to have been a proper fairytale witch. There is even a recorded story of her killing someone with a poisoned apple!

Mabel was the sole heiress to the massive Talvas estate, so was a powerful, financially independent woman and made the most of that fact. Orderic Vitalis describes her as 'extremely cruel and daring', characteristics she seems to have inherited from her father, William Talvas, who stands out in recorded history for his brutality at a time when brutality was pretty much the norm. This is a man who grew so bored of his wife berating him for his lack of morals that he had her strangled on the way to church. He then went on to invite a rival to his second wedding to 'make peace' but proceeded to have him seized, blinded and mutilated! Mabel must have learned her vicious ways from the cradle.

Poison is known to have been favoured by Normans as a conveniently untraceable way of disposing of rivals and has also long been held as a female weapon. Mabel de Belleme, along with the more famous Lucretia Borgia later on, seems to have been one of the women who helped to create that image.

In the novel I show her poisoning Hugh de Grandmesnil with a cup of doctored wine, which is something she is genuinely known to have done, though not to Hugh. As shown here, Arnold d'Echauffour, the son of her father's mutilated rival, tried to claim some of her lands and Mabel clearly couldn't be bothered with legal dispute when good old murder would be so much simpler. In reality it was Fulk's brother Gilbert who drank the poisoned chalice but I hope readers will forgive me transmuting the incident to avoid introducing yet more characters. Poor Gilbert did, in fact, die, as, some time later, did Arnold.

Mabel herself died as she lived, having her head cut off in either her bed or her bath (depending on the imagination of the chronicler) by a man called Hugh Bunel whose lands she had taken by force. I suspect she was little loss, although I have indulged myself in the novel by showing a more positive side to her herbal crafts.

Judith's gospel books

Judith of Flanders seems to have been, as I have hopefully shown, a quietly strong woman with a dedicated interest in religious art. She had very little independent income but still managed to secure funds for considerable patronage of the White Church at Durham and, later, St Martin's Monastery in Weingarten. She was unusual in this time in that she did not endow or refurbish any abbeys or churches and her interest seems to have been primarily in movable goods, perhaps reflecting the rather unsettled life the poor woman was forced to lead.

Primary among her commissions was a set of four gospel books which are still in existence and, indeed, are unique in being the largest group of extant Anglo-Saxon manuscripts any-where in the world from a single patron. Two of the books are kept at the Pierpont Morgan Library in New York, one is in Italy and one in Germany. All four are sumptuous, distinctive and costly works, using extensive gold in the illustrations and the lettering. Two of the covers are sadly lost but those we still have are magnificent, made of metal and encrusted with jewels.

A study of the gospel books by Jane Rosenthal and Patrick McGurk demonstrated that the same scribe worked on them all and that the first three were completed in England and taken to Bruges with Judith when she had to flee into exile in 1065. The fourth seems to have been started in England but completed by a Flemish artist soon after Judith's sad return to Bruges.

There is no evidence that Judith herself was the artist and it is probably unlikely as such work was normally done by monks, but the possibility is there and I enjoyed playing with it. What is clear is that Judith took great pride in these gospel books and that they meant a lot to her and so I felt that extending her involvement in them was warranted for the story.

Missing Characters

Students of the Norman era will no doubt have noted the absence of several key figures from this story. There are more Norman records than there are for their Saxon or Viking cousins so I was able to locate a wide number of people in William's court. Trying to include them all in the story, however, would have resulted in an overcrowded narrative so I had to be selective. In particular I was forced, reluctantly, not to include the following:

Lanfranc: Lanfranc was a famous and very influential scholar and monk who brought Italian learning to Normandy and was part of the reason why the church flourished in William's reign and afterwards. He was also, it seems, William's personal chaplain and one of his advisors. He later became his Archbishop of Canterbury and was a key prop in the post-conquest government of England. I studied his life in some detail and found it fascinating but in the end I chose to hone in on William's four military companions – Fitz, Hugh, Fulk and Roger – instead of this more spiritual one.

Robert Champart: Champart is mentioned in the novel but does not feature as a character. He was the Abbot of Jumièges Abbey near Rouen and travelled to England with Edward when he went to join his half-brother Harthacnut in the court. He was with him, therefore, when Harthacnut died at a wedding feast in 1042 and Edward was suddenly made king and he was his key advisor in the early years of his reign.

Champart was also responsible for the promotion of Norman interests in the English court and it was his appointment as Archbishop of Canterbury in 1051 that led indirectly to the Godwinsons' exile and opened up the way for William to be invited to England and offered the crown. When the Godwinsons fought their way back into favour in 1052 Champart fled and died, a few years later back in Jumièges, a bitter man. He was in the novel up until the final edit but had little narrative arc of his own and cluttered the path of the story as a whole so sadly he had to go.

Robert, Count of Mortain: In the novel I feature Odo of Bayeux, William's half-brother, son of Herluin de Conteville, but he actually had another brother, Robert. As there were already a number of young men around William, however, I decided not to include him. It is probable that William also had several sisters and half-sisters but they barely feature in records so I chose not to include them either.

Sweyn Godwinson: In Chapter Nine Tostig tells Judith that his brother Harold is likely to get Wessex for he 'gets everything'. In fact, in 1051, their elder brother Sweyn was still alive and was the one in the running for the main God-winson inheritance. Sweyn was a wild child, noted in history for capturing and running away with the abbess of Leominster who may well have been the mother of his son, Hakon. He was exiled for this conduct in 1047 and then, after persuading his cousin Beorn to help him get back into the king's good books, fell out with him and stuck a sword in his back – resulting in further exile. By 1050 he was tentatively returned to favour and after the family's exile in 1051–2 he seems to have repented of his sins (or just decided to stay out of the way) and gone on pilgrimage to Jerusalem. Like so many others in this period – William's father included – he caught a fever on the way back and died. Harold became the eldest Godwinson and was a far more worthy heir. I decided, although a year early, to have Tostig refer to Harold as the oldest to avoid confusion with Sweyn who was so nearly gone from the story anyway.

*N*ame *C*hanges

The Normans, like most nations at the time, were not given to originality in the naming of their children. In researching this period, therefore, I came up against a seemingly endless parade of Williams, Roberts, Richards and Rogers. I can only assume that this would have been as confusing for them as it is for us and that, although official records would always be in their formal name, they must have had a way of shortening those to differentiate in day-to-day speech. Rarely do we know what these informal monikers were ('La Barbe' for Roger de Beaumont is one that is recorded), so for the purposes of this story I have had to choose a couple of my own.

Fitz: William FitzOsbern was known to be William's closest companion and they cannot have always called each other William. Fitz is almost certainly not a shortening they would have used as it simply means 'son of' (the same as Mac in Scottish surnames or indeed 'son' in English and Norse) but for me it retained a feel of the original and also felt like an appropriately jaunty-sounding name for William's lively friend.

Fulk: The man I call Fulk de Montgomery was actually named Roger. He became very well known as the first Earl of Shrewsbury after the conquest, but in this story he was all too easily confused with Roger de Beaumont. Montgomery was a little too formal for continual use and I did not feel I could shorten it to Monty because of the far more famous General Montgomery. In the end, I decided to rechristen him as Fulk – a core Norman name that I liked and that did not feature elsewhere in the story. I hope he will forgive me this imposition and enjoy his more unique name.

Historical Events

Harold's visit to Normandy

It is documented in the Anglo-Saxon Chronicle that Harold's ship was wrecked at Ponthieu and that he was rescued from Count Guy by William himself and thereafter spent some time in the ducal court, fighting with William in a successful Brittany campaign and making some sort of oath before he left. What is not documented is exactly when or, indeed, why he went. Theories range from him being blown off-course on a fishing trip, to him trying to rescue his hostage brother and nephew, to a diplomatic mission from King Edward. We will never know but this was clearly a vital period as the men who would meet on Hastings Field two years later spent a considerable time together. I touched upon the effect of his visit on Harold in *The Chosen Queen* but it was fun in this novel to explore the Norman side of the story.

It is documented that Harold and Mathilda sat up together at times during his visit and there are even vague hints of a possible scandal. This is highly unlikely but it is nice to indulge in the possibility that Harold was tempting for Mathilda, if only because he was so very different to William.

There certainly seems to have been an attempt to make a marriage alliance with Harold. Some historians believe that one of the few women in the Bayeux Tapestry, shown in the scene where William takes Harold to his court, is meant to be William's daughter being offered to Harold as a wife. There are others, however, who believe that it could be one of William's possible sisters, or even one of Harold's sisters, offered as a wife for young Robert in exchange for hostages. Any such marriage plans, however, were clearly abandoned once Harold and William were set against each other as enemies.

William's near death

There is documented evidence that at some point between 1063 and 1066 William fell gravely ill and was laid on the ground as if at point of death. The story goes that he vowed to establish canons in the cathedral church of St Mary in Coutances if God would let him live and Mathilda went to that church and put one hundred shillings on the altar praying 'that God and St Mary would give her back her husband'.

It's recorded that her hair was loose and dishevelled, suggesting she was distressed and perhaps that she had been up all night with William. Contemporary chroniclers took this as proof of her devotion to him and in the novel I chose to use it as a crisis point for the couple.

In reality William's illness seems to have happened in Cherbourg and we have no evidence that it was linked to Harold's departure but narratorially it seemed to me a satisfactory moment for it to happen. Similarly, we have no evidence that it was linked to his daughter Adela's death of what may have been Spanish flu but Adela was sent to marry Prince Alfonso at around the same time and does seem to have died on the journey, so the possibility is there.

Mathilda's coronation

In the end, Mathilda was not crowned as Queen of England until Easter 1068, although when she was, it was with newly drawn-up rights as a Queen Consort that saw her more clearly acknowledged than ever before in English history. We do not know that she intended to sail to England with William in 1066 (although it was possible – Elizaveta of Kiev sailed with Harald Hardrada) but she was certainly pregnant with Adela and was also named as regent, so it is probable she was always intended to stay and hold Normandy firm. What is curious, however, is why it took so long for her to travel to England.

The answer, of course, is the start of the rebellions, which made it too dangerous for her to sail into the country and foolish to attempt anything as potentially incendiary as a coronation. In the epilogue I have William intending to take her back with him in Spring 1067. We do not know if this was actually his plan but he was keen to establish her as queen and it seems likely to me that it was the rebellions in Kent and Mercia that stopped her travelling that first year. By Easter

1068 William had put down both of these rebellions, plus another centred on Harold's mother in Exeter, and the way was tentatively clear for the new queen to visit her subjects. The coronation seems to have been a success, although there were to be further rebellions in Northumbria, the south-west, and again in Mercia later in 1068.

Whilst in England, probably in Yorkshire, accompanying her husband against rebels, Mathilda gave birth to her last child, Henry. This English-born child was later to become Henry I, arguably the most successful of the Norman kings.

The history of Normandy

In the opening chapter Mathilda calls Normandy a 'province barely one hundred years old' and at several other points characters refer disparagingly to the duchy's relative youth, especially in comparison to England. This is a valid point as William was only the seventh ruler of Normandy, a province that had been created in the tenth century when Viking invaders were carving up Europe.

France at that point was not so much a single country as a set of duchies and counties that owed nominal allegiance to the French King Charles II, known as 'the Simple'. When a Danish invasion fleet under the command of Rollo (or Hrolf) sailed into the Seine Valley in 911 Charles seems to have been unable to repulse his attacks. Instead, he took the common route of attempting to buy him off, not with money but with land – namely the land around Rouen, already effectively in Viking control. This was ratified in the Treaty of St-Clair-sur-Epte and a year later in 912 Rollo converted to Christianity and named his lands Normandy – quite simply 'land of the northmen'. His foot was well and truly in the door.

Being a fierce Viking leader, however, he was not content to settle for such a small territory and kept pushing to expand his borders. In 924 King Ralph granted him the concession of Bayeux and Maine – now central Normandy – and in 933 his son William Longsword was granted 'the lands of the Bretons situated on the sea-coast', i.e. Avranchin and Cotentin – lower Normandy.

William Longsword, born and bred around Rouen, stepped away from old-style Viking raiding and instead made treaties and marriages to ally himself to other leaders in western France. He was then succeeded by Richard I who ruled for fifty years, consolidating and stabilising the duchy and, in the process, turning the Normans more and more French in terms of language, government and architecture. His successor, Richard II, also started to reach out of northern France when, in 1002, he married his daughter Emma to Ethelred of England – inadvertently setting in motion events leading to the fateful Battle of Hastings.

Richard was succeeded in 1027 by his eldest son Richard III who died mysteriously (or perhaps not so) a year later to make way for his ambitious younger brother Robert I – William's father. Robert led a fairly loose-living and vicious life in his early years, including claiming the beautiful Herleva as his mistress, but he seems to have sobered considerably after William's birth and in 1035 he undertook a pilgrimage to Rome to atone for his sins. Before he went he made his bastard son William his heir and forced all his nobles to swear allegiance to the child. It was presumably not a promise he thought they would have to fulfil but he died of a fever on the journey back and William, aged just seven, became Normandy's seventh duke.

The death of the Norman legacy

The Normans were achieving amazing things in this early period of their history. I was astonished when I began researching them in detail to discover that way before they conquered England they had already triumphed in southern Italy. They were clearly an ambitious and effective nation but for various reasons they were soon assimilated into France and became simply a subsidiary province, little heard of until the tragic Norman landings in the twentieth century.

Despite William being succeeded on the English throne by two sons – William II (Rufus) and then Henry I – his line died out when Henry's son William was killed in the White Ship disaster of 1120. Henry named his eldest daughter, the dowager Empress Matilda, as his heir but he'd also been negotiating with his nephew, Stephen of Blois, and on his death Stephen invaded to successfully assert his claim. Matilda did not take this lying down and for years the parties of Stephen and Matilda fought each other. Matilda was never actually crowned queen though she did rule for some months in 1141 (the first female monarch in England) but the dispute created a form of anarchy in England that was only eventually broken by a truce in which Stephen took the throne in return for naming Matilda's son, Henry, as his heir.

That son became King Henry II in 1154, so technically speaking he was still of William's bloodline but he was known as an Angevin king because of his father Geoffrey of Anjou and his Norman roots were all but forgotten. King John then lost Normandy for good in 1204 and although English kings continued to fight for possession of parts of France way into Tudor times, Normandy was not among them.

Sicily and southern Italy, both firmly in Norman hands in

1066, went much the same way. Sicily, which was so gloriously recovered from the Saracens by the Norman Roger de Haute-ville, was ruled by a German king by 1194. And Italy soon splintered into city states, ruled by lords who considered themselves very much locals even if they had Norman heritage.

What is interesting in all this, however, is that William was not the only Norman conqueror. I love the way he was not so much a stand-out ruler as one sitting within a set of driven, ambitious and successful men. But it was not to last. The Nor-mans were essentially Vikings and Vikings all over the world (for example, in England, Russia and Ireland) showed an amazing skill at absorbing the culture of the places they con-quered, marrying local girls and taking on local customs rather than trying to impose their own identity. This may have been why the 'Norman' adventurers disappeared from history as a defined set of people.

Historical Features

Guardrobe

In Bruges Mathilda and Judith select their dresses from a guardrobe, a room I show as an innovation introduced by Mathilda's French mother, which is perfectly possible. The word is French in origin (garde, meaning 'watch' or indeed 'guard', and robe, meaning 'dress') and was originally used to denote a room such as I describe in Chapter Three. Even today in European public places, the word garderobe denotes a cloakroom or wardrobe used to temporarily store visitors' coats at functions.

Readers could be forgiven, however, for thinking I had made an error in using the word as at some point in the development

of castles in medieval England, it seems to have shifted meaning to denote a toilet-chamber. The reason for our word for a
wardrobe being used for this very different room is lost in the
mists of time, but it may simply be to do with its comparably
small size.

Bedchamber

In the novel, William and Mathilda share a bedchamber everywhere except when they go to Westminster and this may strike
some readers of later historical novels as odd. Certainly by
Tudor times highborn lords and ladies had their own chambers, indeed suites of rooms, but pre-conquest this was an
alien idea. Indeed, it would not be unusual for a lord and his
lady to sleep in a bed in their great hall, surrounded by their
retainers with the curtains around their four-poster bedframes
as all the privacy they would expect.

William and Mathilda, as Normans, were living in stone-
built castles and palaces with several storeys (rather than the
Saxon and Viking residences that tended to be separate wood-
built chambers) so it is possible they had separate chambers
but very unlikely. Privacy was not a concept that had yet been
fully developed, as life was lived, even at a high level, in a very
communal way, so having a chamber just for the two of them
would be luxury enough. Similarly, in the daytime a queen or
duchess like Mathilda would not keep to her own rooms as in
later periods, but would go to the ladies bower, often above the
hall, to join the rest of the women of the court for weaving and
needlework and, presumably, gossip. It was not really until the
1400s that family/court life began to be segregated into independent rooms in any significant way.

Tafel

Tafel was a strategy game played on a chequered board – a precursor to our chess, which evolved in the twelfth century. There seem to have been a variety of different ways to play but the general rule was a two-to-one ratio of 'attackers' to 'defenders'. Attacking pieces were set out around the edges with the goal of capturing the lesser defending ones around the king in the centre whose own goal was to escape to the edge of the board. Clearly it mimics battle strategies and as such was favoured by war leaders. We do not know if William enjoyed it but the more I learned of it, the more it seemed the perfect game for this stern, careful ruler.

The Ship List

This is an extant record of the contribution of ships and men made by William's magnates in 1066. The copy we have actually dates from c. 1070 and was almost certainly drawn up at Fécamp Abbey but can be presumed to be a good copy of the original. It details them thus:

When William, Duke of the Normans, came to England to acquire the throne, which by right was owed to him, he received from William FitzOsbern the steward sixty ships; from Hugh, who later became Earl of Chester, the same; from Hugh of Montfort fifty ships and sixty soldiers; from Romo (Remigius), almoner of Fécamp, who later became Bishop of Lincoln, one ship and twenty soldiers; from Nicholas, Abbot of St-Ouen, fifteen ships and one hundred soldiers; from Robert, count of Eu, sixty ships; from

Fulk of Aunou forty ships; from Gerald the Steward the same numbers; from William Count of Evreux, eighty ships; from Roger of Montgomery sixty ships; from Odo Bishop of Bayeux one hundred ships; from Robert of Mortain one hundred and twenty ships; from Walter Giffard thirty ships and one hundred soldiers. Apart from these ships which altogether totalled one thousand, the duke had many other ships from his other men according to their means.

Note that the tally given does not 'total one thousand' but seven hundred and sixteen, so either the clerk could not add up or he did not list all provisions (notably Hugh de Grandmesnil is missing, though two other Hughs are listed). Nonetheless, this remains a vital source for establishing who was working with William to make the invasion the success that it ultimately was and shows how vitally important the ships were. It is also an astounding primary source in a period seriously lacking in such sources.

The *Mora*

The same 'ship list' also details William's flagship:

The duke's wife, Mathilda, who later became queen, in honour of her husband had a ship prepared called 'Mora' in which the duke went across. On its prow Mathilda had fitted a child who with his right hand pointed to England and with his left hand held an ivory horn against his mouth. For this reason the duke granted Mathilda the earldom of Kent.

There are a number of theories about why Matilda called the ship the *Mora*, including suggestions that it was an anagram of 'amor', or an allusion to her Flemish ancestors who were known as the Morini. I chose to stick with the idea of 'amor' but to make it something more personal to the couple – an 'in joke' to keep her in his mind as he sailed with his men.

Horse ships

No self-respecting Norman noble would ever have fought as anything but cavalry, so the key to a successful Norman invasion in 1066 was undoubtedly the ability to transport horses across the sea. This was not something the Normans had done before – except in Italy. Researching this led me to a fascinating article published in 1985 by Bernard S. Bachrach suggesting that Norman experiences in Italy were vital to the fleet that crossed to England and also suggesting reasons for them to have sailed from St Valery to Pevensey – locations that have often been presumed to be a random result of storms and tides.

Bachrach cites a Danish experiment in 1967 in which historians proved a horse could jump out of a shallow boat if it was beached, tilted and secured by lines, as shown on the Bayeux Tapestry, but that a boat like this would not survive the channel loaded. To do that it needed gunwales at least five feet high – too high for a horse to jump. What William needed, therefore, were experts in equine transport and they were to be found in the Mediterranean where the Greeks, Byzantines, Arabs and Romans had long since been taking their mounts across the sea. It is documented fact that Hugh de Grandmesnil was exiled to Italy for a period (although not over Emeline, who I made up) and as he was my cavalry captain he seemed the perfect conduit for this knowledge in the novel.

Bachrach suggested that William used Byzantine-style horse-ships – hippagogoi – to carry the horses and their riders to England in 1066 and that these special ships needed proper, Roman-style ports to load them. Records show that St Valery had a recognised Roman port as did Pevensey. I suggest in the novel, therefore, that William did not end up in St Valery because he was forced to flee there after storms prevented a first attack as is often thought to be the case, but that he planned to go there all along (though he almost certainly did lose some ships in storms on the way). Similarly his fleet did not end up at Pevensey because they missed Hastings first time round, or just because the tide took them there, but went there with the specific aim of safely unloading their precious cavalry horses. After all, William was a planner – why would he not plan this as well as the rest of the conquest?

Offices

The Norman court was a very male and martial one. There were a huge number of families fighting for supremacy below the duke and, indeed, looking to supplant him with a claimant of their own. William's early years as duke were fraught with danger and it is down to the courage of both him and his protectors that he made it to adulthood. Gradually over the first ten years of his rule, however, as William put down rebellion after rebellion by branches of his own family, he replaced them as his closest companions with the men with whom he had been raised – his chosen companions and ones he knew he could trust.

By the time he married Mathilda, William FitzOsbern, Roger de Beaumont, Roger (Fulk) de Montgomery and Hugh de Grandmesnil were his key supporters. Their offices are not formally recorded but it felt likely to me that William would see them publically acknowledged as important men and rewarded with titles and land. Fitz does seem to have been steward, like his father before him. There is some hint of Hugh being captain of the horse and Roger as chamberlain and certainly he seems to have been the man who, alongside Mathilda, kept government on track whilst William fought his endless wars. There is no high commander reported as such but Montgomery was very much one of William's key right-hand men so it seemed the correct position for him to have been awarded.

William was undoubtedly a man who prized loyalty above all things, almost certainly because of his early – and indeed ongoing – experiences of treachery. He had to spend his entire life looking over his shoulder and that is why it is so sad that in England, a land he was so very keen to rule, he met only further opposition. It has been interesting writing the 1066 story from the Norman side for he was very much my 'baddie' in the previous two novels, but looking at it from his point of view has softened my feelings towards him.

William was probably the most disciplined, earnest and well-intentioned ruler of the three men fighting for the throne of England in 1066. Had the English accepted him as king (easier said than done, I know) I am confident he would have ruled them sternly but well. He was known to generously reward those who served him and had a record of exiling rather than executing rebels and, indeed, of pardoning them later. Initially he kept many Englishmen, including both of the northern earls, in his service and I honestly believe that he was a man who wanted to rule magnanimously. The constant opposition over the first years of his reign, however, left him with little choice but to take harsh reprisals to prevent further problems.

The terrible 'harrowing of the north' in 1069–70 was the

final and most horrific example of this and is, sadly for William, what he is most remembered for in English history. The epilogue in this novel is not meant to hint at a sequel to come but rather to take the reader, with William, back to earlier times when he faced constant rebellion to try and show why, perhaps, he reacted so violently to it in England. The rest, as they say, is history . . .

ACKNOWLEDGEMENTS

Firstly, I have to thank my husband, Stuart, for his endless patience and his uncanny ability to know when to listen and when just to tease me out of melodramatic sulks. And secondly my family in general for appreciating – or perhaps just not noticing – that a tidy house is far less important than a well-crafted battle scene!

Special thanks for this novel must go to Brenda, my great friend and now fellow Norman enthusiast, for accompanying me on a brilliant research trip. I must thank her in particular for her knowledge of deciduous woodland, for finding me an oyster that I actually enjoyed (after years of fruitlessly seeking such sophistication), and for driving fast enough for us not to miss the ferry after getting rather too immersed in the amazing Falaise castle!

As acknowledged in the dedication of this novel, I thank my parents from the bottom of my heart for always being so encouraging of my love of writing. Despite both being of a scientific turn of mind, they swiftly recognised that test tubes and I were never going to get on well and did everything they could to support my interest in literature and history. I firmly believe that one of the most important things a parent can do is to support their child in choosing their own path in life and I only hope I can do that as well for my own children as Mum and Dad did for me and my siblings. That thanks extends to my step-parents, Polly and Arthur, for their unending care and to all four of them for the babysitting!

Perhaps my writing gene skipped a generation and I would like to give a mention to my dear grandmothers on both sides. My father's mother, Courtney Gibb, gave me my middle name and ultimately my pen name and was the daughter of Howard Swiggett who wrote wonderful American crime novels in the fifties. I wrote my first novel aged ten (a rather derivative boarding school book) at her house. My mother's mother, Sandie Shaw, was president of the Scottish writer's association for years and is still fondly remembered by those members old enough to have shared her time there. If both passed me a little of their writerly talents, then I am unendingly grateful to them for saving me from life as a chemist!

Another pair who deserve a mention are my history teachers at Loughborough High School who enthused me with their love of their subject. Both Penny Armstrong and Julia Morris (now Burns) showed me that the real interest in studying the past is in the people who inhabited it and I hope I have carried that with me into these novels. It was wonderful to meet Penny again at one of my talks last year and I hope they both know what fantastic teachers they were and how much that can mean to students.

I want to thank the team at Pan Macmillan, particularly my new editor, Victoria, for taking me on and showing such care for my novels and Jess, my lovely publicist, for her unfailing enthusiasm and hard work on my behalf. Heartfelt gratitude goes to the wonderful Susan for her insightful and hugely helpful comments on the MS and to my agent Kate for backing me with this third novel which wasn't always easy to write. Thanks, too, to ILA for selling my novel to Hungary and Germany which has been very exciting, and to all the lovely bloggers who have posted such supportive and insightful reviews of my novels. It means the world to me.

Lastly, I want to thank my readers. This is not something I have really been able to do before and it gives me a huge thrill to be accruing what might tentatively be called 'fans'. The greatest joy of attending the wonderful 950th Battle of Hastings celebrations at Battle Abbey in October 2016 was having people coming up to me saying how much they'd loved my first book and how keen they were to buy the second. I sincerely hope that this third novel lives up to expectations and that readers enjoy discovering the 'baddies'' side of the 1066 story as much I enjoyed creating it.